A Collision of Secrets

A Mystery Novel

William Coleman

RoseBrooke
PUBLISHING

A Collision of Secrets

Copyright © 2025 by William Coleman
All rights reserved
First Printing, 2025
ISBN 978-1-969330-01-8

Dedicated to my lovely wife, Vicki, who has supported me every step of the way through each of my novels by allowing me the time to write, being my first beta reader and my primary editor. By being my biggest fan and my sharpest critic, she has helped me produce final manuscripts for you to enjoy.

1

R ichard. We're going to be late," Sonia called down the hall. Her tone wasn't whiney, almost playful in fact. Richard knew they were running late, and she knew he was taking his time for a reason. He did not want to go. He had not wanted to go from the very beginning. In truth, Sonia didn't want to go either. But sometimes you have to do things you don't want to. Not necessarily on time, though.

"Five more minutes," Richard called back to her.

"Five minutes?" she said. "You haven't even started getting ready yet."

"In five minutes, I'll start getting ready," he explained. He was already walking toward their room, his tall frame stooping as he neared the door. He waited in the hall for a moment longer.

"Are you serious?" Sonia stepped through the doorway to where he stood, her hands nestled on her hips as if she were scolding a child. Late was one thing; very late was something else.

Richard reached out and grabbed her around her slender waist, pulling her to him and off her feet. She screamed in surprise and protest, though she did not fight him. He spun and she laughed as she wrapped her arms around his neck for support. Their faces came together and when their lips met, they kissed firmly. The warmth of their mouths melted one another and all else was forgotten for the moment. When Richard finally pulled away, the smell of her lilac perfume filled his nostrils. He looked into her bright green eyes and said, "Very serious."

"You're lucky I love you." She kicked her feet as they dangled inches above the ground. "Now let me down and get ready."

"Okay." He exaggerated defeat as he lowered her to the floor. "That was the best I had, and it didn't even phase you. You are a cold woman indeed."

"It phased me," she smiled, smoothing out her slip. "But I know that isn't the best you have to offer."

"Oooh, I think I'm breaking through," he smiled, his eyebrows bouncing.

"Just get ready," Sonia laughed. "Before I break something."

"You wound me so." He placed a hand over his heart as stepped into their bedroom. "Blue suit okay?"

"Why don't you wear the gray pinstripe?" She followed close behind. "I think you look your best in it."

"Are we trying to impress?" he smirked. "I thought we were trying to avoid."

"Hilarious. Now get ready."

Sonia gave him a gentle shove, and he crossed to the closet, disappearing inside. Searching through his clothing, he found the suit in question and pulled it out. He examined the garment for dirt and wrinkles, his mind drawn to the day they bought it a couple of years ago. Sonia had insisted he try it on, then insisted no other suit would do. She was right, of course, as she always was with fashion. Her eye for such things was exceptional. She used that vision to decorate their home, selecting each piece of furniture, every accent piece and, of course, all the wall art. She always asked for his opinion, but her mind was made up by then. If he selected wrong, she would nudge him in the right direction, as she had just nudged him in the closet.

Besides the suit, Richard brought two shirts and three ties out of the closet and lay them on the bed. Then, with a quick glance at her in the mirror where she was carefully applying her makeup, he walked to the bathroom so he could shave and comb his hair. He returned moments later to discover she had selected the proper shirt and tie combination, the remaining items waiting to be returned to their place.

He examined her choice, nodded his approval and dressed. A few minutes later, he took position in front of the full-length mirror to work his tie. Mid-knot, he saw her reflection as she emerged from her closet tightening a belt around the waist of her dress.

He turned slowly, looking her over from head to toe. She noticed his gaze spinning for him, the skirt of her dress flaring as she did. The black material hugged her bodice. Strapless and cut low in the back, Richard could only wonder what kept it from sliding off her body. Sonia tilted her head and winked at him playfully, her dark brown hair brushing her shoulders. "You like?"

"Like?" he grinned. "You are the most beautiful creature I have ever seen. I could look at you forever."

"You're just saying that so you won't have to go."

"Not true." Richard put a hand to his chest. "I was also hoping to get lucky."

"Come willingly," she crossed the room to him, "and chances are you'll get lucky when we get home."

"Promise?"

"Promise."

She slipped her arms around him and raised up onto her toes to kiss him. He bent to receive her lips. In the eight years they had been married he never tired of kissing her, longed for it when he wasn't with her. She pulled away and he had to resist pulling her back to him. He reached instead for his jacket, still on its hanger so he could hang it from the hook in the car's backseat where it would not wrinkle while he drove.

Spreading his arms wide with the jacket dangling from two fingers he said, "All ready."

She grinned at him. Traffic willing, they would only be about fifteen minutes behind schedule, still early enough to call it 'fashionably late'. Draping her purse over one shoulder, she took his free hand and curled her dainty fingers into his. "Thank you."

Tonight was the Halstead's annual party. Richard did not know why they called it an annual party when it occurred every six months. Very outgoing and normally the life of any party, he hated the Halstead's annual parties. He referred to the events as 'the gathering of the bores' and always insisted he would never return. A hollow threat given that Mr. Halstead owned the firm where Sonia worked. With her being up for a promotion, the Jensen's attendance was expected, if not mandatory. The evening promised to be a 'kiss ass and laugh at bad jokes' kind of night.

"They aren't that bad," Sonia insisted. "And they find you absolutely charming."

"Of course they find me charming," Richard glanced her direction. "They would find anyone that can tell a story without putting half the room to sleep charming."

"You're impossible," she laughed.

"Impossible is sitting through one more telling of the time Mr. Halstead started his firm from scratch with only five clients and no more than two-hundred grand in the bank," Richard rolled his eyes. "Are we supposed to feel awed by his ability to succeed from such meager beginnings?"

"And he always leaves out the fact that the five clients he stole from his former employer were all high rollers," Sonia agreed. "But you know it's bound to come up again tonight."

"And I will express my amazement at all the appropriate places, as painful as it may be."

"You are a sweetheart."

The night was warm and breezy, reminding them of their last vacation, traveling to the Bahamas. It had been one of their best trips. The weather was perfect, the landscape beautiful, and the water crystal clear. They had spent nearly two weeks in paradise and only left their room a few times. Richard sometimes said they could have gotten a room downtown and saved a fortune, but Sonia knew he was joking. Something about being on the islands that was just sexy. Anywhere else would have just been another vacation.

Richard held Sonia's hand while he drove, always did. Always would as far as he was concerned. She would sometimes lean into him and rest her head on his shoulder and that was even better. Tonight she did just that and he couldn't help feeling proud. She was beautiful, smart and successful. And she loved him. He was successful, but men were expected to be the breadwinners. She worked hard, harder than he did he was pretty sure, and he was proud of her for it. She was up for this promotion and he was proud of that. Mostly he was proud that she still loved him the way she did when they first started. With all the passion and romance they could have. He hoped they would never lose that.

He squeezed her hand and released so he could use both hands to make a turn. They were only a couple blocks from the Halstead's house and the roads in the neighborhood were narrow and curvy, an engineer's technique to reduce traffic and speed in the wealthy neighborhood. Richard had a strong feeling the engineer did not live in such a neighborhood. The turns were too sharp at times and there were several blind corners. During the day it wasn't a terrible problem, but at night the streetlamps were more decorative than functional, another failure of the engineers, like children's nightlights in a warehouse.

"If they are going to continue with these parties," Richard muttered, "they should move."

"It's not that bad," Sonia said. She smiled up at him and he relaxed.

She had that power over him. Whenever he felt stressed, anxious or angry, just the sound of her voice grounded him, relaxed him.

He hit the brights on his headlights, illuminating the street before them. Richard gave his wife a half smile and refocused on the road ahead. A few moments later, the Halstead's home came into view, a two-story colonial-style house with large white pillars guarding the porch, like a plantation estate.

An ornate chandelier hung above the front door, similar to what might be expected in a dining hall, looking very out of place. Every light in the house was on and exterior lights lit the yard like daylight. Richard wondered if the house was always lit up like a small city or just on party nights.

Luxury cars lined the circular drive and the street, making the road even narrower. Richard found a spot and rolled to a stop. Exiting the vehicle, he walked around to Sonia's side and opened the door for her. Offering a hand, he helped her out of the car and the two of them walked hand in hand to the house. The music from inside flowed down the steps to them. Richard pulled her to his side and slipped his arm around her waist.

"Last chance to play hooky," he whispered.

"Just ring the bell," she laughed.

2

Richard shrugged, pushing the button to activate the chime that would announce their arrival. The resulting tune was one he had heard but could not identify. He was still trying to remember where he knew it from when the door swung open, revealing the foyer beyond. The doorman, a gray-haired man attired in a tuxedo, bowed at the waist inviting them in with a wave of his hand. They stepped inside and moved toward the main room of the house, arm in arm. With a quick glance at one another, they walked into the light and noise of the party.

A dozen people stood around the entrance with drinks in hand, talking in small groups that grew louder as they struggled to be heard over the next conversation over as well as the stringed quartet playing in the background. The combined odors of women's' perfumes, men's colognes and alcohol assaulted Richard's nose. Like everything else at Halstead parties, it was over the top and he had to work at not coughing.

Some guests greeted the new arrivals briefly before returning their attention to engrossing conversations. Sonia met each of them with a smile and pleasant responses. Richard didn't recognize many of them.

A man about Sonia's age appeared in the same doorway the Jensens were walking toward. The man was looking back as he walked straight into the couple, his muscular shoulder colliding with Richard's chest.

"So, sorry," the man turned to his victim. "Oh, Sonia. Are you just getting here?"

"You know me." Sonia gave him a genuine smile. "Fashionably late. I want you to meet my husband, Richard. Richard, this is Jeremy Griffon."

The men exchanged nods.

"Jeremy works in my department," Sonia continued. "He's quite the hot shot."

"You're embarrassing me," Jeremy said. "But it's true. Although I don't compare with you."

"Where are you going?" Sonia asked. "It looks like you're running away from someone."

"You know how Halstead feels about me." Jeremy shrugged. "I made my appearance. I'm getting out of here before things take a turn."

Sonia gave him a loose hug and watched as the man made his way out of the house.

"Have you introduced him to me before?" Richard said to the man's back.

"I don't think so." Sonia smiled up at her husband. "He's been with us just over a year but this is the first Halstead party he's been invited to. He really has been doing well.

"Perhaps he reminds me of someone," Richard thought aloud. "He seemed familiar, but also not."

"Maybe he looks like one of your clients?" Sonia offered.

"Could be," Richard agreed. "What was with the Halstead comment?"

Sonia chuckled. "He decided it would be a good idea to date the boss's daughter."

"Enough said," Richard grinned. He placed a hand on the small of Sonia's back. "Shall we?"

They continued to the next room, a small library where the quartet played in one corner. Straight-back chairs lined the walls, filled with men and women in groups large and small. High school dances in gymnasiums came to mind, where more talking took place than dancing. Some whispered the latest gossip, while others roared with laughter at jokes old and new. Both the conversations and laughter of these guests came across as fake to Richard, making him wonder how his remarkable and dynamic wife fit in with them.

A short, balding man in his sixties stood in the center of attention, dressed in an expensive Italian suit and alligator-skin shoes. His thin wire-rimmed glasses rested low on his nose, and he looked over them at the men gathered around him as he spoke. Clinging to his every word, the men laughed when appropriate, remaining silent otherwise. The Jensens entered his line of sight and the man excused himself mid-sentence to approach the couple.

"Sonia." The man clasped onto one of Sonia's hands with both of his. "So glad you could come." He paused for only an instant before releasing his capture. "Richard. Nice to see you again. I can't tell you how happy we are that you allow us to borrow your lovely wife every day."

"Hello Mr. Halstead." Richard accepted the hand offered him. "Thank you for the invitation."

"Please call me Charles."

"Alright, then. Charles."

It had become a ritual between the men to have this same conversation at the start of every party. Richard refused to call him Charles before the ritual was completed. He claimed it would take the fun out of the evening. Sonia allowed him this one game as long as he limited himself to it. Richard agreed to the rule with reluctance, although he did not always resist when an easy opportunity presented itself.

"The place looks lovely, Charles," Sonia said in a flattering tone that made Richard cringe as if hearing car gears grind. "Where is Diana? I really should say hello."

"I think she's in the kitchen yelling at the caterers." Charles leaned forward as if to whisper, though the volume of his voice did not change. "You know how much of a perfectionist she can be. They probably put the rumaki next to the crab cakes again. She really hates that."

Richard stifled a laugh because the look in the older man's eyes suggested no joke was intended. The thought of Mrs. Halstead reprimanding a group of tuxedo clad young men and women on the proper presentation of hors d'oeuvres was a tough image to suppress.

Sensing her husband's tension, Sonia excused them and directed Richard toward the kitchen. Charles returned to his conversation with the men, who remained in a semi-circle awaiting him, picking up his story from the point he had left off. Sonia gave Richard's arm a sharp pull, steering him into a small hallway. Once they were out of sight, Richard began to chuckle.

"That was close," he managed to say.

"Richard, you promised," Sonia scolded.

"I know. I know. But . . ."

"I know," Sonia sighed. "The world is your playground and you want to play."

"I'm sorry" Richard regained his composure. "I promise to control all natural instincts until the party is over. But then watch out."

"Fair enough." She grinned, raising up on her toes to kiss him softly on the lips. "Behave and be rewarded."

"I can do that." Richard took a deep breath to control himself further. "Lead the way, my dear."

Diana Halstead was not in the kitchen as promised, but rather in the main dining room. She wore a long, blue silk dress with a diamond broach that glistened when she moved. She was not yelling at the help but advising them how she wished to have dinner served. The Jensens waited patiently while the woman spoke, in slow and articulate sentences, to the two men she had captured in her web. The men nodded in response to each of the woman's directions while trying to divert their eyes from the light reflected by the broach.

Diana took the action of turning their eyes away to be a sign of inattentiveness. Impatiently she began questioning them on the points she had just discussed. Impatient themselves, they repeated, again, that they understood what was wanted without going into the details. In turn, she took this to mean they understood nothing and was on the verge of using some choice phrases she had learned from her husband over the years when she caught sight of the Jensens in the corner of her eye.

"Sonia." Diana gestured to her to approach even while she was crossing the room, leaving the caterers unsure if they could leave or not. Making their own decision on the question, they scattered like flies trying to escape a shadow. "Richard. So good of you to come."

"Thank you for the invitation." Sonia smiled. They met near the edge of the large dining table, sharing a brief hug.

"Always glad to attend one of your parties." Richard stayed a couple of steps behind his wife, hoping to avoid a hug, but Mrs. Halstead stepped around Sonia and wrapped an arm around his chest with a quick squeeze. It was part of Diana's nature to touch, never too much but enough to bother Richard who preferred a handshake at most.

"You two are so cute together," Diana admired, moving back to look them over more thoroughly. Without warning, realizing the caterers had left the room, she spun on her heels and started for the kitchen calling one of their names as she went.

"Always glad?" Sonia looked up at Richard. "Have you no shame?"

"Would you rather I told her how I would sooner have a root canal than come to the next party?"

"Point taken." Sonia leaned into her husband. "But they really are nice people."

"I didn't say they weren't," Richard defended. "I just can't tolerate the large amounts of hot air being blown around these events. One on one I enjoy the Halsteads. At their parties, they bore me."

"I understand." Sonia slipped her arm around his waist and squeezed for a much longer time than Mrs. Halstead had. "That's why I hate to say this."

"Say what?"

"We need to get back in there and mingle."

"You wound me so." Richard grinned. He put his arm around her and steered them toward the music and crowds.

3

The Jensens moved about the different rooms making an appearance at each of the segmented groups. Conversations varied, though the central theme was always the workplace. Richard swore he had heard three or four different men tell the same story of saving the day at the office. In each story, the storyteller came to the rescue of all involved. Not once did someone else rush to their aid. Richard wondered if the men knew they were all telling the same story, with the only change being the champion. Since they did not seem concerned the actual hero might challenge them for credit, Richard assumed one of their secretaries who saved the day.

"Richard?"

A female voice brought Richard and Sonia around to face a woman wearing a navy pantsuit in a sea of dresses. She looked at Richard with cautious curiosity. Deep auburn hair framed her face, bright blue eyes holding his gaze. Richard's own face took on a look similar to the one he would have whenever Sonia requested he repeat something she had just said, knowing full well he had been distracted and not listening. Sonia looked the woman over and slipped an arm through Richard's, pulling him closer to her.

"You don't remember." The woman phrased it as a statement, not a question. Anyone looking at Richard at that moment could tell he did not recognize the woman standing before him, having made the trek across the room.

"I'm afraid not," Richard admitted, glancing at Sonia as he said it. He hoped his wife might know who the stranger was. Sonia gave him a shrug with her eyebrows; a skill Richard had never mastered.

"Carolyn Winters." The woman spread her arms just enough to suggest a 'ta-da' was in order. Her arms dropped when she realized Richard was still staring with the same look of confusion he had when she first called his name. It did not prevent her from searching his face for some sign of recognition.

"Oh, silly me." The woman tapped her forehead and grinned a mischievous 'I know something you don't' grin. "How about Carolyn Brechenstanch?"

A light went on behind Richard's eyes, and a broad smile took over his face. He released Sonia and took Carolyn in a bear hug that made his wife a little nervous. He let the woman go and stepped back next to Sonia, putting an arm around her shoulders. The smile never left his face, never faded for a second. Carolyn made eye contact with Sonia for a second, then returned her attention to Richard.

"Where are my manners?" Richard said, as if he had missed his cue. "This is my wife, Sonia. Sonia. This is Carolyn Brechenst . . ."

"Winters," the woman corrected.

"Right," Richard said. "So, you married. Is he here?"

"I did." Carolyn's tone changed. "But it was short-lived. He passed less than a year after the wedding."

"Oh my." Sonia put a hand to her chest. "How sad. You poor thing."

"Don't worry." The woman turned to Sonia. "That was six years ago."

"Still," Sonia said. "So, how do you two know each other?"

"Carolyn and I used to work together," Richard answered. "Before I ever met you."

Sonia had met no one from Richard's past that wasn't family. He never spoke of that time in his life. Looking at Carolyn, she could see why he may not have mentioned her.

"Oh," Sonia said. "Are you a programmer, too?"

"A programmer?" Carolyn's brow scrunched ever so slightly. "No. I . . ."

"Carolyn was in operations," Richard interrupted. "We both were. That was before I switched to programming."

"You're in programming now?" Carolyn looked her former colleague over.

"I am." Richard put his arm around Sonia's shoulders again. "I have my own internet security company."

"My goodness," Carolyn smiled. "How things have changed."

"They have," Richard confirmed. "How long has it been, anyway? Ten years?"

"Twelve," Carolyn corrected. "Mexico City."

"That's right." Richard became somber.

"Mexico City?" Sonia inquired.

"It was a job we did together," Richard explained. He looked at Carolyn. "Didn't quite go as planned."

"Not quite," Carolyn agreed. She sighed. "Then you left."

"It was time," Richard dismissed the topic. "I can't believe you recognized me after all these years."

"You haven't changed a bit." She looked him up and down.

"I've changed some," Richard disagreed. "But you. You've changed."

"A little," Carolyn blushed, though Sonia did not think it genuine.

"A little?" Richard was incredulous. "A hair cut is a little. You look nothing like the plain, unassuming girl I knew back then."

"Richard," Sonia scolded. Relief flooded her with the sudden assurance that Carolyn was no old flame to be rekindled.

"Don't worry, Mrs. Jensen," Carolyn grinned. "He's not exaggerating. I was very plain, almost boyish. Ugly in fact."

"Who said ugly?" Richard protested.

"Call me Sonia," Sonia offered her hand to the woman. Hearing Carolyn call her Mrs. Jensen made her feel old somehow. "And I'm sorry for Richard's insensitivity. He is usually much better in public than this."

"I never said she was ugly."

"I know." Carolyn's eyebrow raised slightly. "But you never asked me out either."

"We were friends," Richard defended. "And we worked together. Two major no-noes' in the dating world. Don't date friends or you'll lose them. And don't date colleagues because you just can't. Besides you were with…"

The sentence ended without the lingering word of someone trying to remember, but a full stop.

Sonia looked at her husband. "Are you okay?"

"Lance," Carolyn said. "His name was Lance."

"I know his name," Richard sighed.

"But before I was with him," Carolyn said, "you never gave me a second thought."

"Colleagues." Richard seemed to drift. "Why does it matter anyway?"

"Typical male." Sonia smiled up at her husband. "Why did I ever marry you?"

"Because of my irresistible charm, my dear," he said in his best Bogart.

The simultaneous laughter of the two women increased as they fed off one another and could not stop. When they gained control, Sonia managed between breaths to say, "Lucky for you that wasn't it."

4

As the evening went on, the two women grew more comfortable with one another, especially when talking about Richard. Carolyn told stories about how he had been fifteen years ago, and Sonia reported how he was different or, in many cases, not. The women often laughed at Richard's expense, and he laughed right along with them. And why not? Everything they said was close to true. Even those things he insisted weren't. So he laughed. It was the best time they had ever had at a Halstead party.

The music stopped, and the guests were herded toward the dining room while the quartet packed their instruments, being dismissed for the evening. Everyone gathered around the large table and located their name tags for their assigned seating. Richard and Sonia found themselves near the head of the table where their hosts sat. Carolyn was quick to switch her tag from halfway down the table to the seat next to her old friend.

"I've been meaning to ask." Richard leaned toward her and whispered. "How do you know the Halsteads?"

"The Halsteads?" A quizzical expression covered Carolyn's face. "Oh, you mean the hosts. No, I don't know them."

Richard glanced at the woman's name tag on the table. "But you were invited?"

"Not really," Carolyn sipped from the glass of water the server had just filled. "I'm a plus one."

"You're here with someone?" Richard could not hide the surprise in his voice. "Where are they? You've been with us all evening."

"Don't worry," Carolyn patted his arm.

"Who are you here with?" Richard asked.

"Stanley?" She seemed to search her memory. "Stanley Webber."

"Really?" Sonia leaned across Richard. "How do you know Stan?"

"He and I collaborated on a security matter," Carolyn explained.

"Security?" Richard looked at her.

"Didn't I tell you?" the woman said. "I'm in security now."

"Like Richard," Sonia said.

"Oh, no." Carolyn chuckled. "I'm in physical security. Not digital."

"Unusual for a woman," Sonia observed.

"Not really," Carolyn countered. "A lot of women are in my field."

"I didn't mean to offend you," Sonia said.

"No offense taken."

Sonia looked around the room. "Where is Stan anyway?"

"Funny thing," Carolyn chuckled again. She focused on Richard when she continued. "Right after we arrived, he took ill and had to leave. I stayed for the free food. Luckily, I brought my own car."

The high-pitched clinking of silver spoon to crystal goblet brought silence to the room as all eyes turned to their short, balding host.

"I want to thank you all for coming," Charles began. "I know we have these dinners often. Some may even say too often. But we at Halstead Enterprises are family, and we do enjoy your company each and every time. Tonight, though, we have a special occasion to celebrate. One that has been a long time coming. I would like to announce that Sonia Jensen, whom you all know well, will become V.P. of Customer Accounts effective Monday morning."

The room came alive with applause and words of congratulations. Charles remained standing and waited for everything to settle down. Richard squeezed his wife's hand in support. She gave him a smile that showed how happy she was.

"Okay. Okay." Charles raised a hand and silenced the room. "Sonia. You've worked hard and deserve this. Welcome to the executive wing."

"Thank you," Sonia acknowledged. "I look forward to the challenge and won't let you down."

"I know you won't," Charles nodded. "Now, I understand my lovely wife has arranged for us to have some hard to pronounce and often hard to identify dishes from across the globe. Please enjoy."

The man sat and two rows of servers entered from opposite sides of the dining room, each carrying two dishes. They moved down the table, placing bowls in front of the first two guests they came to, moving on so the next server could attend to the next two guests. With practiced efficiency, the staff completed the entire ordeal in no time at all.

Richard leaned over what he guessed to be some type of salad, as he saw signs of green leaves beneath whatever was nested in the center. With a quick glance at Sonia and then Carolyn, who were both studying their own dishes, Richard picked up what he guessed to be the salad fork and gave the gelatinous outer portion a tentative poke. It collapsed to reveal a mixture of finely chopped vegetables inside. He balanced a small amount on the prongs and brought it to his mouth. Surprisingly, it wasn't that bad.

Bowls were removed as they were emptied or pushed away. The staff did not give second chances. If someone appeared to be finished, a server moved in to take the dish. When the last bowl was cleared, the next course arrived in the same fashion as the first.

The second, a creamy soup, was so packed with flavor that Sonia commented about requesting the recipe. Richard agreed and promised to remind her.

They cycled through each course of the meal in the same way, a high-class assembly line of tuxedoed men and women who remained stoic throughout the process, as if they had been warned not to smile. Four young women circulated, keeping water and wine filled. No one was ever without a beverage.

As the dessert plates were finally removed to the kitchen, Charles stood and told everyone to enjoy coffee or drinks, depending on their preference. He took his own glass of amber liquid on ice and moved back to the library. It only took a few seconds for others to follow his lead. Moments later only Mrs. Halstead, Sonia, Richard and Carolyn remained.

"That was wonderful, Diana," Sonia said to their host.

"Thank you," Diana smiled. "It went well, didn't it?"

"It did," Richard confirmed. "Very smooth."

"I know it was a little more over the top than normal," Diana said. "I just wanted to try something new."

"Well, you've outdone yourself," Sonia beamed.

"So kind of you to say," Diana's smile faded. "Well, I guess I should get out there and mingle."

The woman rose to her feet and brushed at her dress to minimize the wrinkles from sitting. Satisfied, she excused herself and moved away.

"That was quite an experience," Carolyn said once their hostess was out of the room. "Is it always like this?"

"Like she said," Richard sat back, "this was more over the top than usual. But essentially, yes. It's like this all the time."

"I could get used to it," the woman said. It seemed to the couple she was talking more to herself than them.

"You said you're here to collaborate," Richard said. "Are you local?"

"Collaborate is probably the wrong word," Carolyn shifted. "More like consult. And no, I am not local. I live on the coast."

Charles Halstead appeared in the doorway. He hesitated for just a moment before approaching. "Sonia, could you join us? You're an executive now. You need to mingle with the staff. You don't mind do you, Richard?"

"Not at all." He and the women stood as if on cue.

"Do I know you?" Charles turned to Carolyn.

"No, sir." She held out a hand. "Carolyn Winters."

"Nice to meet you, Ms. Winters," Charles shook her hand.

"Likewise," she said. "But I should really be going."

"Don't leave on my account," Charles said.

"That's not it," she assured the man. "I have a flight to catch early in the morning."

"I can show you out," Charles offered.

"That's okay." She released his hand. "I want to say my good-byes here. I can find my own way."

"Very well," Charles hesitated. He turned to Sonia. "Don't be too long."

Abruptly, he turned and rejoined the party.

"That was odd." Richard watched him go. "I don't think he's ever been at a loss for words."

"Not too often anyway," Sonia agreed.

"Well," Carolyn sighed. "I actually do need to go. I have a couple things to take care of before going back to my hotel."

"It was so good to meet you." Sonia stepped forward and gave the woman a brief hug. "Richard doesn't talk much about his past. I was beginning to think he didn't have one."

"Nice to meet you, too." Carolyn returned the gesture. To Richard, she said, "Good to see you again, after all these years. Let's not wait another twelve years."

"Of course." Richard hugged her as well. "Let's keep in touch."

"I know how to get ahold of you." The woman patted his back. "I'll reach out. Now, if you'll excuse me."

She gave them a nod before turning on her heels and headed toward the kitchen. Richard was about to correct her, then decided she was just trying to avoid the rest of the guests. He slipped his arm into Sonia's and clasped her hand. His wife looked up at him and grinned, tilting her head into his shoulder.

"Let's go charm the socks off these people," Richard suggested.

"You lead," Sonia said. A few minutes later, they were making the rounds.

5

It was well past midnight when the party finally began winding down, although Richard believed Halstead parties started off wound down. He had been hinting to Sonia for a couple of hours that he would like to go. She was immersed in her new role, circulating through the party for one-on-one conversations with other executives and those who would report directly to her. Each time her husband whispered in her ear; she would give him a gentle pat on his arm with a promise of soon.

Couples with children at home were the first to break formation, claiming they needed to let their babysitters go home. Soon after, the older men and women who had been with the firm long enough they were beyond winning brownie points excused themselves. The Halsteads walked each guest to the door, thanking them for coming and offering an open invitation for another visit.

Once the party started to thin, others took advantage and began making their way to the door to say their goodnights and thank-yous. The Jensens saw their moment and joined the line to escape. Stationed at the door, the Halsteads spoke to each guest at length before releasing them. When Sonia and Richard reached the couple, they were the end of the line, though others still milled about.

"Sonia, congratulations." Charles clasped her hand. "So glad to have you on the team."

"Thank you." She clasped his hands in return. "Say, did Stan get a chance to tell you about what we talked about?"

"He did," Charles said. "It's late. Take the weekend. Write it up and we'll meet in my office on Monday. Okay?"

"That sounds good," Sonia nodded.

Another couple stepped up behind them.

"Richard, always a pleasure." Charles shook the man's hand. "Drive safe."

"I will," Richard assured.

Diana said her goodbyes, and the Jensens were released into the night. They walked down the steps hand in hand, following the drive to the street and ultimately their car. Richard held the door for his wife as she climbed in. He moved to circle the back of the car but found his path blocked by the SUV that had parked just inches from his rear bumper. The large metal frame wrapped around the front made it look like a police car, but the racing stripe across the hood suggested otherwise. He grumbled at the inconvenience and circled back around the front of the car to slip into the driver's seat.

He sat silent for a moment before allowing a huge smile. "You did it."

"I did it," Sonia nodded. With more enthusiasm, she repeated, "I did it!"

"Congratulations." Richard leaned toward her and gave her an all-consuming hug. "You deserve it."

"I do, don't I?" She looked up at him and smiled.

"Well, aren't you modest?" he laughed. Sitting back, he adjusted his frame. "Let's get you home."

He started the car, glanced into the rearview mirror at the SUV, and pulled away from the curb. Using the Halstead's circle drive to turn around, he headed out of the neighborhood the way they came.

"Carolyn is nice," Sonia said.

"Always was," Richard agreed. He knew she was fishing for more information. Not willing to share any details, he said, "She was a good friend."

"Why did you lose touch?"

"Mexico City," he said. "I won't bore you with specifics. The job went bad, so I resigned and moved on."

"And you didn't maintain any contact?"

"We were friends because of the job." Richard knew exactly why they had not maintained the friendship, another detail he wasn't ready to share. "Once the job was gone, I didn't see the point."

"Is that why you never talk about that period of your life?" Sonia asked. "Because of whatever happened in Mexico City?"

"Part of it," Richard confirmed. "And I don't see that changing anytime soon."

"Okay." Sonia settled back in her seat wondering about the past her husband shared with the woman she had only just met. She wasn't sure how she felt about them having a secret connection.

Richard steered them down the winding road that would take them out of the neighborhood. The night was overcast now, even darker than before as Richard leaned forward to peer through the windshield at the street just in front of the car. He smiled at Sonia, assuring her everything was fine. She was tense but relaxed a little as he made his way to better lit streets. They would be home soon.

6

Morning came and Richard felt a déjà vu moment as the two of them rushed to get ready. He passed by his wife, slowing just enough to kiss her forehead before moving on.

"Did you call Gavin?"

"Getting ready to." Richard held up his cellphone to offer proof.

Years ago, Richard went back to college to finish his degree in programming and met Gavin Barr in one of his classes. Gavin was about five years younger, having not taken time away from his education, but the two became fast friends and often worked together on projects and helped one another with studies. When they finally graduated, it only seemed inevitable they would go into business together. Years of struggling and hard work paid off as they established themselves as a premier firm.

Richard and Gavin, despite being friends and working well together, were nothing alike. Richard was low key yet charming. A natural born speaker, he was the face of the company, the one who convinced clients to put their faith in them.

Gavin was eccentric and loud. He loved a good joke, adventure and risk. He liked to push the limit any chance he got. They complimented each other, which Richard credited for their success.

"What's up?" his friend answered on the first ring.

"Hey, Gavin," Richard said. "Listen, last night Sonia received a promotion."

"That's great," Gavin responded. "Tell her congratulations."

"I will," Richard promised. "Anyway, we decided to celebrate by running up to the lake house for the weekend. So, I'm going to miss our game today."

The two of them had a standing tee-time at the club where they were members, every other weekend for the past five years. The friendly competition allowed them to relax while also making time for shop talk outside the office. To keep things cordial, the two men kept their own score cards and did not discuss the final results.

"Are you already there?"

"No." Richard laughed. "We don't move that fast. Should leave in about half an hour, give or take."

"I understand," Gavin assured his friend. "You go enjoy yourselves. You can lose next week just as easily."

"Oh, that's how it is?" Gavin's humor about his shortcomings always amazed Richard. They both knew what the outcome of every game would be. Richard was the better player, but his partner was never deterred. He was always eager to play.

"You know it," Gavin said. "While you're lounging on your boat, I'll get some practice rounds in. Prepare to lose big."

"I'll be ready." Richard watched Sonia walk into the room carrying two suitcases, one large and one small. She set them on the floor next to his small duffle bag and computer case. "I'm getting the evil eye. So, I better get going. I'll see you Monday morning, Gav."

Richard disconnected the call, dropping the phone into his pocket.

"Evil eye?" Sonia tilted her head. "Exactly how bad do I look?"

Richard wrapped his arms around her shoulders. "You couldn't look bad if you tried. Are you sure you have enough? We are going to be gone almost two whole days."

"Sarcasm is not a good look on you," Sonia returned the hug and squeezed, pressing her cheek into his chest. She always felt safest in his arms, his strength telling her she was protected. "If you'll pack the car, I'll make some sandwiches for the road."

"Mrs. Jensen are you offering me a bribe?" he feigned shock. "I don't know how I feel about that."

"That's no bribe." She raised up on her toes. Just before kissing him, she said, "This is a bribe."

A half hour later they backed out of the driveway, their fingers entwined on the console between them. With light conversation and laughter, they drove out of the neighborhood and steered east. It was a two-hour drive on a two-lane highway, and Richard wanted to get there early enough to enjoy their sandwiches on the back deck for lunch.

Purchasing the lake house three years ago had been an opportunity to get away for the weekends, to unwind and relax. What had started as a weekly excursion soon became monthly, then quarterly until eventually they only made the long drive for special occasions. They had even discussed selling the place a few times but decided against it.

Driving over the posted speed limit was not unusual on this route, and most traveled faster than Richard was willing to go over hills on a curvy road. He always gave a wide berth to those trying to pass him and was always happy to see the periodic passing lanes. One vehicle in particular came up behind them at an unusually fast pace. The SUV reminded Richard of the way television and movies depicted federal vehicles, with dark tinted glass all around. The image grew in his rearview mirror, making him feel like they were going to rear end him. A large metal grate mounted on the front resembled a police vehicle, giving it a threatening appearance. It looked familiar to Richard, but he couldn't remember why.

The SUV continued to approach at a high speed, prompting Richard to tighten his grip on the steering wheel. At the last second, the driver steered into the oncoming lane and sped past them.

"Someone's in a hurry," Sonia commented.

"If they get there without killing themselves," Richard added. "Or someone else."

The next half hour was uneventful as they alternated between small talk and listening to the radio. They searched the stations for local news while they watched a wall of clouds float in, offering some relief from the intense heat of the sun.

"This looks bad," Sonia observed.

A flash of lightning was the only warning of the sudden rainfall that came down in sheets. Richard cursed, hit the wipers, and slowed.

"How is that for fast?" Richard squeezed Sonia's hand. She did not answer. She leaned forward looking through the torrents of rain for any sign of the road ahead.

Another flash of lightning lit the street for a moment and Richard steered for the next point he could see. Sonia tightened her grip on his hand, and he knew the conditions frightened her. He also knew he only needed to find somewhere to pull over and wait out the storm. He glanced at her and smiled his 'I have it all under control' smile. It worked every time. Unfortunately, this time it was his undoing.

7

Gradually opening his eyes, Richard saw an overhead light similar to those seen in office buildings, department stores, and schools illuminating the room. Confused as to why he would be sleeping under fluorescent lighting, he became aware of a dull ache in his head that increased to a deep throbbing and hindered his effort to concentrate.

A television was mounted near the ceiling of one wall. On another, a white board hung to one side of a handwashing sink. He saw something written in black, but even squinting would not allow his eyes to focus enough to make out the words. Next to him, a metal stand held various pieces of medical equipment. Richard knotted his brow. A familiar odor lingered in the air: the distinct smell of cleaner and sanitizer. He did not know why or for how long, but he was in a hospital.

He rolled his head in the opposite direction and the throbbing in his head intensified until it became almost unbearable. Next to his bed was an empty recliner, leaving him to wonder where Sonia was. The last time he was in the hospital, she had not left his side, except to eat and for a handful of other self-maintenance reasons. He supposed she could be getting a bite to eat at that very moment. God knew he was hungry. He tried to recall the last time he had eaten.

Letting his head settle back to a natural position, the pain receded to the constant ache he had awakened with.

Richard used his hand to search the space between his body and the bedside, finding nothing. Shifting his gaze, he found what he was looking for built into the railing that kept him from rolling out of the bed. Reaching to press the button with the symbol of a nurse printed on it, he did not immediately recognize his hand. Bandages covered most of the skin and what he could see was swollen and red. An IV tube protruded from another bandage on his forearm. He closed his eyes and began mentally assessing his condition.

The left side of his torso throbbed if he inhaled too deeply. That same arm was sore and had less range than his dominate right. Both legs ached. The left, wrapped in bandages and immobilized in a brace from thigh to calf, told Richard he had experienced some type of trauma that he could not recall. His mind raced, trying to retrieve a memory, but the last he could grasp hold of was the Halstead's party, and as far as he knew, nothing happened there.

The hinges of the door announced a visitor before Richard saw it swing into view. A young woman wearing dark blue scrubs crossed the room toward him, sporting a reserved smile. Her eyes darted between him and the monitors. She passed a hand sanitizing station and pumped a glob of the clear gel into her palm, finishing her journey while rubbing the substance over every crevice of her hands and forearms.

"Well, look who's awake." Her lips expanded into a broad smile as she took his wrist between two fingers. "How are you feeling?"

The question caused him to hesitate. "Been better."

His voice was weak, like a forced whisper.

The nurse's smile faded to a grin. "I suppose you have. How is your pain level on a scale of one to ten, ten being the highest?"

"Four." He lied. It felt closer to seven.

"Four?" the nurse repeated, skeptically checking the monitors. "That's not too bad."

"High tolerance." Not exactly a lie. "How long have I been here?"

"A couple of weeks." The grin faded, and a sadness took over her eyes. "For a while there, we weren't sure you were going to make it."

"Weeks?" It was his turn to repeat. He had lost two weeks of his life, and he still wasn't sure what had happened. He didn't even know which hospital he was in. What he did know was the one person who could tell him everything. "Where…," his voice caught in his throat. "Where is my wife?"

The nurse stepped up to the monitors and pressed a couple of buttons. "I'm going to let the doctor know you're awake. I'll see if you can have something to eat. Are you hungry?"

"Where is my wife?" He tried to sound demanding, but it made his whisper more raspy.

"The doctor will discuss everything with you." She did not look back at him as she walked out of the room at a fast clip.

Confused, Richard watched the woman retreat to the hallway. Voices carried into the room from beyond the door, but he could not make out what was being said. Taking a deep breath, the pain on his side screamed at him, forcing him to exhale in a huff.

Wanting answers, Richard tried to focus on the door, waiting for someone to return, hoping above all else, that it would be Sonia. He struggled to keep his eyes open until the wood slab swung inward again. He watched with anticipation for who coming in. A middle-aged woman of Indian descent who appeared to be going prematurely gray walked into the room wearing a lab coat. The nurse had said the doctor would explain everything, so he was anxious to hear what she had to say. She studied his face with what Richard could only describe as concern. The woman did not smile as the nurse had. Richard prepared for the worst. Instead of speaking, she reached into the pocket of her coat, retrieving a syringe. She pulled off the cap and injected the tubing that led to Richard's arm. His eyelids grew heavy and despite his effort to stop it, sleep took him.

8

Richard woke with a start, unsure where he was. His eyes moved in rapid motions, searching for what had awakened him. A woman of Indian descent stood to one side of his bed, studying a clipboard. She wore a long white medical coat with the telltale stethoscope draped over her shoulders, reminding Richard of a medical drama he and Sonia used to watch. It had been a little too soapy for his taste, but she loved it, and he loved holding her while they watched.

She had been the doctor who came into the room and gave him an injection of something. His eyes focused on the printing above the woman's breast pocket, identifying her as Dr. Rudra Paidi. Richard tried to remember if he knew the name. The sense of being watched caused the doctor to raise her eyes until they locked on his. The sadness was still there, and maybe something else.

"Mr. Jensen." The accent was thick, and her bedside manner could use some work. Her flat voice offered no comfort. "How are you feeling?"

"Been better." His reply was a harsh whisper. Richard frowned; positive he already had this conversation.

"Let's take a look, shall we?" The doctor stepped closer and took his wrist. Her own hand trembled, leaving Richard to wonder what kind of condition she might have.

The touch of her fingers on Richard's skin led to a feeling of déjà vu that faded into the memory of a nurse taking his pulse. It came to him then. The nurse had said he had been there for two weeks. He rolled his head to the empty chair on the other side of the bed. Still no Sonia.

The doctor listened to his heart and his breathing. She took a penlight from her pocket, pulled down on one of his eyelids, flashing the light into his pupil and away again. She repeated the process with the other eye. After checking his temperature with a digital thermometer to the forehead, she said, "Your vitals are improving."

"What happened?" Richard's raspy voice caught him by surprise.

"What do you mean?"

"Why am I here?" Richard asked. "In the hospital?"

"You suffered multiple lacerations and contusions," Dr. Paidi reported. "A sprained wrist, three broken ribs, a cut leg, a concussion and internal bleeding, which required surgery. The hospital is the best place for you."

"But what happened?" Richard repeated. "How was I injured? Was I attacked?"

"Oh, no." The doctor raised an eyebrow. "You were in a car accident."

"A car accident?" Richard's heart raced. "What about Sonia? My wife? Is she okay?"

"Your wife?" Doctor Paidi patted his shoulder. "I believe you were alone when you were admitted."

Richard pulled himself to a sitting position. The pain was almost unbearable, forcing him to lie back down. His mind was racing almost as fast as his heart. "Where is Sonia?"

The doctor glanced toward the doorway. "Listen, let's calm down. You don't need this kind of stress on your body."

"Calm down?" Richard grumbled. "Calm down? You just told me I was in a car accident but won't tell me if my wife is okay?"

"I'll look into it for you," the doctor promised. "Meanwhile, let's get you relaxed."

"I'm not going to relax." Richard argued. "Not until I see Sonia."

The doctor pulled a syringe out of her pocket. "This will help with the pain."

"I don't want that," Richard said, remembering the last time she had been there.

Despite his protests, the doctor pushed the needle into the tubing and Richard could only watch as she pressed the plunger, emptying the contents of the syringe into his system. She leaned over him and watched for a moment. Richard was convinced he saw a smirk on her face just before a fog clouded his mind.

Dr. Paidi smiled. "There you go."

Richard could hear the woman's voice as she continued to speak, but could not make out any words. Seconds later, he drifted off.

9

The third time Richard woke, the sense of confusion was only a fleeting moment. He opened his eyes slowly and looked at the chair at his bedside. A woman sat there with her head tilted to one side, her eyes closed. She was sleeping. He tried to focus, but the room was dark, and her face was in shadow.

"Sonia?" His voice was raspy but audible.

The woman's head snapped up as if someone had flipped a power switch. She was out of the chair in an instant, sitting on the edge of the bed, leaning over him. She took his hand in hers, holding it gingerly. A faint, sympathetic smile greeted him. The woman looking at him with sad eyes was not Sonia. If she noticed the look of disappointment on his face, she did not let it show.

"Mom?"

The last time he had been in the hospital, his mother had come, but she relented to Sonia. Of course, the situation had been much different. He had to have his appendix removed, nothing as serious as a car accident. He had never been in any real danger. The surgery had gone well, and they discharged him the next day.

His mother leaned forward and kissed him on the cheek. "Your father is in the waiting room. He and Nancy are eager to see you."

"Nancy's here?" The harshness of Richard's voice startled him when he spoke his sister's name. She lived halfway across the country and did not like to fly. He searched his mother's eyes for what she wasn't telling him. "How long have I been here?"

"I should get your father." His mother stood, looking toward the door. "He'll want to see you."

"Mom?" Richard tried again. She froze but did not look back. She was definitely hiding something. "Where's Sonia?"

His mother hesitated and looked back at him. The look of sympathy consumed her, but Richard saw something more. Fear? Maybe pain. Something had happened to Sonia. Something bad enough she did not want to say. "I'll be right back."

The door closed behind her without a sound. His mind ran through scenarios resulting from a car accident. The outcomes that his mother wouldn't discuss were outcomes he didn't want to consider.

Worried he might drift off again before she returned, he tried to stay focused. He calculated how long it would take for his sister to catch a flight. He knew he had been out for two weeks. Had she come right away?

The door opened again, and Richard raised his head, anticipating his father. Dr. Paidi walked in. She did not speak to Richard, did not even look his way. Stepping up to the side of his bed, she produced another syringe and pushed the needle into the tubing. He didn't even have time to protest. She only glanced Richard's way for a second before leaving the room again. Soon after, Richard's eyes grew heavy as he drifted to sleep.

When he opened his eyes again, the room was dark. He could see the outline of someone sleeping in the chair next to him, but again, it wasn't Sonia. Nor was it his mother. He squinted his eyes to sharpen his vision and recognized Nancy. The sister he had shared a room with until he was eight years old sat there as the woman she had become. They hated each other for two or three years as teens, making life hard for each other and their parents. But that was ages ago. Nancy had even been a bridesmaid at Richard's wedding. And now here she was asleep on a hospital recliner at his bedside.

"Nancy?" His voice was a harsh whisper.

She did not stir.

"Nancy."

Again, his sister did not react.

Richard took a deep breath and forced it through his lungs as hard as he could, saying her name as loud as he could.

She flinched, shifted her weight in the chair, and settled again. Nancy's eyes opened so fast it reminded Richard of one of those dolls his sister had as a child that appeared to be sleeping when horizontal and startled when vertical. Sitting up straight, her familiar soft voice greeted him. "Richard?"

"Hey, sis," Richard forced a grin.

"Jesus, you gave us a scare." Nancy leaned in and gave him a hug, squeezing as tight as she dared. "Mom's losing it."

"Nancy?"

"Yeah?"

"How long have I been here?" Richard asked.

Nancy grimaced and ran a hand over her eyes and then her mouth to stifle a yawn. She shook her head when she finally spoke. "You've been out for almost three weeks. We thought we were going to lose you. The doctor couldn't figure out what was going on."

"Three weeks?" Richard let the news sink into his mind. He had lost two weeks of his life. "What happened?"

"You don't remember?" Nancy looked away for a moment. "I guess you wouldn't. You were on your way to your lake house and there was an accident. Mom and Dad had you transferred back here so you would be closer."

"Where's Sonia?" Richard asked the question that ran his mother out of the room and half-expected Nancy to follow her lead. "Is she hurt too?"

Nancy grimaced and then quickly turned away, but not before Richard saw the tears welling up in his sister's eyes. Richard wished he had not asked, wanting desperately to take it back, lock it away. Nancy turned back to her brother, the tears now rolling down her cheeks, and she choked on the words. "She's gone, Richard."

"Gone?" Richard's face knotted. "What do you mean gone?"

"I mean, when the police arrived at the accident, she wasn't there," Nancy explained. "If it hadn't been for her purse being in the car, they wouldn't have even known she existed. They thought she might have been thrown from the car. They searched the area for hours, but there was no sign of her. She was just gone."

Richard's adrenaline surged as he tried to remember that day, but only pieces of it came. Nothing that would explain Sonia's absence.

"They even went to your house just in case. She was with you, wasn't she?" Sonia asked. "In the car?"

"Of course she was with me," Richard insisted. He searched his memory. "Wasn't she?"

Richard tried again to remember that day. Sonia had received a promotion. They were going to the lake house to celebrate. What happened after they left was beyond his grasp. But he was sure Sonia had been with him. He would not have gone alone, not with her purse and luggage. She had to have been with him. But where was she?

10

"What are you doing?" Nancy was clearly distressed.

Richard was sitting up, his legs dangling over the edge of the bed. She could see the pain in his expression as she tried to coax him to lie back down.

"I have to go find her." His eyes focused on the tubing attached to his arm, wondering what would happen when he pulled them out.

"Richard," his sister urged. "You're in no condition to go anywhere."

"And what condition is she in?" He snapped. "Someone has to look for her."

The door opened and a nurse walked in carrying a tray of food. Seeing what was happening, she set the tray down and rushed to Richard's side. "What's going on? You can't get out of bed without a nurse. You almost pulled out your I.V."

"I'm checking out," Richard informed her.

"No," she said. She looked at his lunch tray on the bedside table. "That's not a good idea."

His breathing labored, Richard felt lightheaded and wobbled. The nurse grabbed him and guided him back to his pillow. She checked the tubes and monitors to be sure everything was as it should be.

"I told you," Nancy said. "You need to get healthy."

"I have to look for her." He took deep, rapid breaths.

"You're in no condition to go anywhere," Nancy argued. "The police are looking for her. They'll find her."

"It's been three weeks, Nancy," Richard countered. "If they were going to find her, they would have by now."

"I'm sure they have a better chance than you do right now." His sister crossed her arms. "Where would you even start?"

Looking at her, he saw the defiant stance she used to take when they were kids and she wasn't getting her way. All the years that had passed and that stance remained the same. For a moment, Richard saw that young girl he had fought with so often in his youth. "I don't know. But I have to try."

"I know." Nancy's voice became soft, sympathetic. Tears formed in the corners of her eyes. "You just can't."

"You need to build up your strength, Mr. Jensen." The nurse pulled the side table towards the bed. "You need to eat something."

Richard fell silent, staring straight ahead without responding. The nurse paused a moment longer, looking to Nancy for support, before turning and leaving the room. Richard waited until he heard the door close before examining the food she had brought him. His stomach ached, telling him to eat, but he couldn't bring himself to do it. Sonia was missing. He did not want to eat. He did not want to talk. What he wanted were answers. He wanted to bring her home.

Nancy looked down at him with her hands resting on her hips, her jaw set and clenched. "You need to eat."

"I'm not hungry." He lied.

"Don't give me that." She pushed the food closer to him. "I can hear your stomach from here. If you want to get out of here so you can look for Sonia, you have got to eat. Or do you want to end up with a feeding tube? Then you'd never get out of here."

He stared up at her with wide eyes. Starving himself to death never even crossed his mind. He just didn't want to eat.

"Say something," she demanded.

Without taking his eyes from hers, he reached over and pulled the tray closer. "I'll eat."

She cocked her head, studying him before relaxing and pulling a chair closer to his bed so she could sit. She watched him pull the dome cover from his plate and examine the contents of his lunch. The food was pureed because he hadn't eaten solid food in two weeks. She looked down at it, her expression matching his. She said, "No wonder you aren't eating."

With that, he chuckled. She followed with a chuckle of her own. Within minutes, the two of them giggled uncontrollably. They continued until tears came to Richard's eyes.

When the nurse returned, Nancy slept curled up in the recliner. Richard lay on his back, face toward the ceiling, snoring softly. Next to the almost empty plate of food a note, scribbled on a napkin read: Nurse, I will give you $20 for a burger.

The nurse grinned and took the tray away, turning out the light as she left the room.

11

R ichard opened his eyes and looked around the room. Nancy was sitting in the recliner reading a book, unaware that he was watching her. She looked up while turning the page and smiled.

"Good morning."

"Morning," Richard said. "Do you ever get out of this place?"

"Sure," she grinned. "Earlier, I went all the way to the cafeteria to get some breakfast."

Richard rolled his eyes and shook his head. "You know what I mean."

"I do," Nancy said. "But you don't need to worry about that. Just focus on getting better."

"Not sure how to do that," he muttered.

"What?"

"Nothing."

A nurse walked in, verified that all the wires and tubes were connected, and changed out a bag that fed into his arm. She asked how he was doing and what level his pain was at. He lied. After writing something in his chart, she left the room.

"Why do you do that?" Nancy asked.

"Do what?"

"You told her your pain was low," she accused.

"So?"

"So, I've been listening to you moan all night," she said. "I know you hurt more than that."

"I'm fine," he said.

They locked eyes and held one another's gaze the way they did when they were kids trying to stare each other down. All those years ago, they considered it fun. Richard wasn't sure why.

A knock on the door broke their concentration, and they both looked to see who entered. A man, too thin for his height, peeked around the corner.

"You're awake." The man glanced at the monitor, then at Richard.

"Gavin," Richard greeted. "Thanks for stopping by."

"I've been here a few times," Gavin said, leaning against the bed. "You were out every time."

"Been doing a lot of sleeping," Richard acknowledged. "They've got me on some heavy-duty drugs."

"Sounds good," the man chuckled. "Can you share?"

"I'm sure we can work something out," Richard smiled briefly.

"Good to see you, Nancy." Gavin nodded to the woman. They had only met once, at Richard and Sonia's wedding.

"Gavin," she nodded. "How have you been?"

"I'm good," he answered. "Will be better when he quits slacking."

No one laughed.

"No, really," Gavin back tracked. "I've got everything under control, Richard. You take all the time you need. Get well. Whatever you need. Things will be fine."

"Sounds like you don't want me to come back," Richard commented.

"Don't be ridiculous," Gavin smiled. "You're why we're so successful. I'll be glad when you get back to work. I just understand if you need time."

"Thanks, Gav." Richard winced and inhaled deeply.

"I knew you were hurting more than you said," Nancy accused.

"I'm fine," Richard said. "Heavy duty drugs. Remember?"

"I don't believe you," Nancy squinted as if it would help her read his mind. She turned to Gavin. "See what I'm dealing with?"

"She's right, you know," Gavin said to Richard. "If you're in pain, you need to let them help you. That's their job."

"I'm fine." Richard held up a hand to hold them both at bay. "Honest."

"You're not worried about getting addicted, are you?" Gavin asked. "To pain meds?"

"No." Richard hadn't, although now the thought crossed his mind. He had seen the effects of addiction through the years, losing some friends far too young. "Listen, guys. If I was in severe pain, I would ask for something to help. I'm good."

Nancy squared off with him, willing him to change his statement. When he didn't, she let out a heavy sigh. "Okay. Just promise you're not punishing yourself for what happened."

"God, Nance." He hadn't used the nickname in years. "No. I promise."

"Any word on Sonia?" Gavin diverted his eyes when he asked. "Do they know anything?"

"Not yet," Richard muttered.

The room became silent as the three of them shifted uncomfortably.

"Well, I need to get back," Gavin announced. "I have a meeting with a possible client."

"That's good," Richard nodded. "Good luck."

"It's times like these I miss you the most." Gavin put his hand on his partner's arm. "Get better and come back. I'm nowhere near the salesman you are."

"You'll do fine," Richard offered encouragement.

"Get some rest," Gavin turned to the door. Just before leaving, he turned back. "I'll try to stop in again soon."

Richard nodded, watching his friend and business partner leave. When the door closed, he let his head fall back into his pillow. Exhaustion took over, which he didn't understand since all he had been doing the past three weeks was sleeping. Richard watched the door, expecting Dr. Paidi to come in and give him his pain meds, but she did not come. He turned to Nancy, grinned and drifted back to sleep.

12

B etween his parents and his sister, someone occupied the recliner at Richard's bedside almost constantly for two days straight. Whether through moral support, or his body finally taking charge, he was feeling better and only sleeping when necessary.

Nurses came and went, checking his vitals and bringing him meals and medications. Visits from Dr. Paidi ceased. He supposed even doctors had days off.

Richard and Nancy were reminiscing about their childhood when a young woman in scrubs, who Richard had not seen before, entered. She greeted the siblings from across the room as she stopped at the hand sanitizer. Working the gel into her skin, she continued her approach.

"My name is Shelly," the young woman announced. "The doctor has ordered some therapy and exercise."

"You mean I can get out of this bed?" Richard was hopeful.

"Just a short walk today," the therapist smiled. "We'll increase the time each walk."

"That's good news," Nancy sat up. "Let's get his sorry ass out of that bed."

"Some stretches first," the therapist rolled a stool to the bed and lowered the rail. "Let's sit you up with your legs over the side."

Even while she spoke, she was guiding his legs to her and pulling him into a sitting position. The brace on his left leg was heavy and threatened to pull him off the edge of the bed. Richard felt strange, lightheaded for a moment. When it cleared, the young woman was working his other leg into stretches and bends. His stiff muscles protested with each motion, bringing tears to his eyes.

"Since you've been lying down for over three weeks straight," the therapist said, "I don't think we're going to do much walking out first time. Your muscles are extremely tight. Maybe once around the room. Then later we'll see if we can go farther."

"I'm fine," Richard insisted. "I need to do this."

"Okay," she grimaced. Her eyes shifted to Nancy. "Will you follow us with a wheelchair? In case it's too much."

"Of course." Nancy assured her.

"I'll go get a chair."

The therapist stood and walked toward the door. Before she got there, it swung open to make way for a man and woman to enter the room. The man, tall and past middle-aged, appeared to like his pasta a little too much. Younger and leaner, the woman's expression depicted a failed attempt to appear intimidating. Shelly Backtracked, holding up a hand to stop them.

"If you're here to visit Mr. Jensen," she said, "you'll need to come back later. He's going to be doing therapy for a little while."

The woman shifted her jacket to expose the detective's shield she wore on her belt; her eyes locked on the patient. Richard watched on with concern and interest.

The man looked down at the small woman in scrubs. "We're here on official business. Therapy can wait."

"But …"

"Therapy can wait," the man repeated.

Richard watched on as the tiny woman stood her ground in front of the giant of a man. Reminded of a scene from a movie, he found it almost comical.

"Fine," the therapist huffed. "But first, I'm going to help him lay back down."

Shelly moved to her patient and helped guide Richard back to the position he had been in before her arrival.

"Thank you," Richard said.

"I'll be back in a bit," she patted his arm. "Then we'll take that walk."

"Sounds good."

Nancy settled back into the recliner and the newcomers stepped up to Richard's bedside. With one last glance, the therapist left the room.

"Mr. Jensen," the man said. "We've been waiting a long time to get the chance to speak to you."

"And you are?"

"Detective Theo Morris," he introduced. "And this is my partner, Detective Patricia Stevens. We're here on behalf of the Greene County Sheriff's Office. That's where your accident occurred, so they have jurisdiction over your case."

"My case?" Richard frowned. "What case? I thought we were in an accident. Are they looking for Sonia? Have they made any progress?"

"It was an accident," Theo said. "But the driver of the car that hit you fled the scene which makes it a criminal investigation. And since your wife wasn't in the car with you, we can only conclude that she never was, or she was abducted."

"Abducted?" Richard sat up. "You think someone took Sonia?"

"We don't know that." Theo held up his hand to stop the thought. "She may have been injured in the accident. She could have wandered off looking for help. No matter what, we need to find the driver that hit you."

"Why wouldn't they have stopped?" Richard thought aloud.

"It may have been a drunk driver," Theo suggested. "Or someone without insurance who didn't want to get caught. The sheriff just wants to track them down."

"We need to know what you saw." The female detective pulled out a recording device, turned it on, and held it between them. "Anything you can tell us about the vehicle that hit you would be helpful."

Richard looked past the woman to the man and back again. "Do you really think you'll find them now? After three weeks?"

"With your help, we hope so," Theo confirmed. "We would have talked to you sooner, but every time we stopped by you were unconscious. Now that you're awake, anything you can tell us to point us in the right direction will help. Tell us what you remember about the accident."

Richard looked from one face to the other without seeing them. Lowering his head, he studied the scars on the backs of his hands. "I don't remember anything about the accident. I didn't even remember being in one."

"You have no recollection?" Patricia asked. "Nothing at all?"

"I'm sorry," Richard shook his head. "I don't know what happened."

"Officers?" Nancy spoke up.

"Detectives, ma'am," Theo corrected. "And you are?"

"Nancy." She did not offer her last name. "I'm Richard's sister. Maybe, since he's the victim, you could tell him what you know. Maybe it'll jog his memory."

Theo let out a heavy sigh. "Yeah, okay."

"Theo?" Patricia turned to face her partner. "Can I have a minute?"

The two of them moved away until they were out of earshot of the patient and his sister.

"Are you sure about this?" Patricia challenged. "What if he did something to his wife before? She may not have been in the car at all."

"The woman's right," Theo answered. "He was nearly killed. He's not a likely suspect in the hit and run. That's the case we're talking about."

"And his wife?"

"We don't even know if a crime has been committed," Theo reminded her.

"Fine." Patricia crossed her arms in protest.

The two of them returned to the bedside.

"What do you know about what happened to Sonia?" Richard asked.

13

Detective Theo Morris had been a cop for almost thirty years, a detective for twenty, and awaited retirement with no small amount of anticipation. His former partner had been perfect for him. On the job a few years longer, the two of them complemented one another well and worked in harmony for more than a decade. They had developed a kind of shorthand for communicating, although they often seemed to know what the other was thinking.

His new partner, Patricia "Overachiever" Stevens, was young, ambitious, and questioned everything he did, like he didn't know what he was doing after all these years. Theo wanted to ask the chief what he had done to have her assigned to him. The thought of spending his final years on the job with her as a partner filled him with dread.

He could tell, despite her saying she agreed, she did not. She was ready to step in and take over, as if he would let her. With a side glance at Patricia, who stood with her recorder nested in the crook of her elbow, he stepped closer to the hospital bed.

"What we know," Theo said, "isn't much."

"It's more than I know," Richard said.

"A witness, driving in the car that was behind you on the highway, reported that," the detective referred to his notes, "a dark SUV came from an intersecting street and T-boned your vehicle, pushing it into a large tree on the side of the road. They said if you had been a few feet before or after, you would have missed the tree."

"And they just left us?"

"The witness was a distance away, maybe half a mile," Theo said. "And the rain was too heavy for them to see clearly. They weren't even sure what had happened until they got closer. They said when they slowed to see if anyone needed help, they saw figures moving away from the accident to the SUV and drive away."

"With Sonia?"

"They couldn't identify anyone," Patricia said. "With visibility being low and the fact that they were focused on your car, they didn't pay attention to them."

"You said it was a dark SUV?" Something tugged at Richard's memory.

"Given the rain and the distance from your vehicle," Theo said, "the witness couldn't tell if it was black, navy blue, hunter green, or any of a dozen other dark colors. However, the paint transfer suggests it was black."

"They hit us that hard," Richard adjusted himself for comfort. "And still managed to drive away?"

"The damage to your car suggests the SUV had an impact bar," Theo explained. "It likely sustained minimal damage."

"An impact bar?" Something in Richard's mind sparked.

"We used to call them cattle guards," Theo clarified. "Sometimes they're called grill guards. Police cars have them, as well as some trucks."

Richard knew what an impact bar was. But the mention of one made something that had been tugging at his memory jump to the front of his mind. His eyes widened. The SUV.

"Richard?" Nancy said. "What is it?"

"Did you remember something, Mr. Jensen?" Theo asked.

"It's probably nothing," Richard started. In his mind he was trying to gather every detail he could of the SUV that had passed them.

"Let us determine that," Patricia said.

"Yeah, okay." Richard closed his eyes for a second. "There was a dark SUV. I had seen on the highway."

"When and where?" Theo asked.

Bits and pieces of memories began breaking through the fog. Nothing about the accident itself, but the morning leading up to it became more clear. He and Sonia in the car, on the highway to the Lakehouse. They were talking, laughing. The SUV came out of nowhere and was gone again. Later, the rain started. And that was all. He remembered nothing after the rain began.

"It was about an hour out of town, I think," Richard said. "It came up behind us really fast. Scared us actually. Changed lanes just before hitting us, then passed us and was gone. Surely, it's not the same one."

"A reckless driver?" Theo argued. "Could be."

"It almost sounds like they were targeted." Nancy slid to the front of her chair. "Were you aggressive towards them in any way?"

"No," Richard shook his head. "I mean I probably cursed at them as they went by. But they wouldn't have heard it."

"But if it was the same SUV that hit you," Patricia said. "You may have been targeted. Like your sister said."

"Which brings us to the question." Theo's expression became very somber. "Mr. Jensen, do you know of anyone who would want to hurt you or your wife?"

14

The question was a slap in the face, and it took Richard a minute to let it sink in. The idea that someone wanted to hurt him or Sonia, that someone he knew had taken her from him, was overwhelming. The room spun like an amusement park attraction he had ridden when he was a kid. He didn't enjoy it then. And liked this even less. He closed his eyes tight in an effort to stop the ride.

"Mr. Jensen."

Richard could hear Theo's voice, though it seemed to be some distance away.

"Richard, are you okay?" Nancy's voice seemed much closer, but still at a distance.

Opening his eyes, Richard half expecting to be alone in the room. No one had moved from where they had been.

"Can you answer the question, Mr. Jensen?" Theo pressed.

"I just," Richard frowned. "I just can't think of anyone."

Since the day Richard met Sonia, no one had ever said a negative thing about her. She was one of the few people who could find common ground with anyone, admired and adored by everyone. He could not say the same for himself, but Richard couldn't think of anyone who disliked him enough to cause him physical harm. Not anyone in the last decade anyway. If asked the same question twelve years ago, his response may have been different. But Sonia had changed him and even she didn't know to what extent.

"What is it you do?" Patricia asked.

"I'm a programmer." Richard's mind raced, trying to think of possibilities. None of them seemed viable. "I own an internet security firm."

"No angry clients?" Theo asked. "Or maybe contractors?"

"There are always clients that feel they don't get exactly what they paid for," Richard said. "Sometimes they get hacked despite our efforts, because no system is impenetrable. If an experienced hacker wants in, they'll find a way. On the rare occasion that happens, clients are upset. But none were ever angry enough to threaten me. And in every case, our insurance covered any losses."

"What about employees?" Theo continued. "Did you fire anyone recently? Was there anyone who didn't get paid?"

"No." Richard shook his head. "Nothing like that. It's just me and my business partner. And if the reason was money, wouldn't there be a ransom demand?"

"You've been in the hospital, unconscious," Theo pointed out. "Who would they have made the demand to?"

"You're saying they may have been holding her all this time, waiting for me to wake up?" The news devastated Richard. "Where is my phone? What if they try to call?"

"It's being monitored," Theo said. "They haven't called."

"How do you know?" Richard demanded. "If they know me, they know my voice. And if someone else answers, do you think they'll admit calling for a ransom?"

"You're right," Theo said. "We'll get you the phone. But we've traced every call coming in. And nothing stands out."

The police going through his phone, tracing his calls, did not set well with Richard. He had nothing there to find, but he relished his privacy as most would.

"What about your wife?" Patricia asked.

"What about her?" Richard huffed.

"Could she have planned to get rid of you?"

"You think Sonia wanted to hurt me?" Richard couldn't believe what he was hearing. "Are you insane? She was the one who was taken."

"We have to ask," Theo put his hand up to stop the man's rant. "Now, to your knowledge, is there anyone who might want to hurt your wife?"

Richard calmed down. He knew they were just doing their jobs. He knew these questions were to give them an idea of who may have taken Sonia from him. The problem was, no scenario made sense to Richard, and he could not see where these questions would help.

"No." Richard was adamant. "Everyone loves Sonia."

"Does your wife work?" Patricia asked.

"Yes," Richard nodded. "Just the night before, we were at a company dinner at her boss's house."

"What does she do?" Theo asked.

"She's an account executive at Halstead Enterprises," Richard answered. "She received a promotion that night. To V.P. of Customer Accounts."

"A promotion?" Theo raised his head. "A good financial jump?"

"We never got that far," Richard admitted. "But I'm sure it would have been."

"Did she jump over any of her co-workers to get the job?" Theo asked. "Anyone who might have taken offense to her being promoted in their place?"

"I...I mean," Richard stumbled over his own thoughts. "I don't know them, really. But at the dinner everyone seemed happy for her."

"You said Halstead Enterprises?" Patricia asked.

"Yes."

"Who is her boss?" Theo asked.

Richard closed his eyes. "His name is... Stan ... Stan Webber."

He opened his eyes, looking at the others expectantly.

The door to the room opened, and all eyes turned to the tall man who entered. A few years older than Richard, the man wore a white medical coat with a stethoscope clasped around his neck like a tie. He stopped short when he saw everyone.

"Excuse me," he said. "I will need you all to leave. I need to examine my patient."

"We're detectives," Patricia announced.

"I don't care," the doctor grumbled. "Go detect something in the hall."

The female detective was about to say something when Theo put a hand on her arm and steered her away. "We can come back if we need more."

"But ..."

"Let's go, detective." No one would accuse Theo of denying medical treatment.

The doctor watched until the detectives had left the room and closed the door behind them. He turned to Nancy. "And who are you?"

"She's my sister," Richard answered for her. "She can stay."

"She can stay," the doctor repeated. He stepped up to the bed and, with skilled, efficient movements, started removing bandages and examining wounds. He made guttural noises from time to time but did not speak. When he finished the brief exam, he re-wrapped wounds he felt needed covering and tucked Richard under the blanket. "Well, you appear to be improving every day."

"And you are?" Richard looked at the empty space above the man's pocket.

"Oh, that's right," the doctor said. "You were unconscious every time I was here. You had me worried for a while. I'm Dr. Dean Avery. I'm the surgeon who patched you up. You had some internal bleeding we had to stop, and I put a plate in your leg."

"You were my surgeon?" Richard was confused.

"Yes."

"Then why has Dr Paidi been checking on me?"

"Dr. Paidi?" The doctor looked down at him with his head tilted to one side. "Dr. Paidi would have no reason to check on you. He's a gynecologist."

"Did you say, he?"

15

Richard explained to Dr. Avery about the female doctor of Indian descent, who claimed to have been his surgeon and had examined him on multiple occasions. The doctor listened to every word without interruption, nodding from time to time.

"Are you sure?" the doctor asked at the conclusion. "You were unconscious."

"I'm positive," Richard insisted. "Every time I woke, she came in."

"What was the detective's name?"

"Uh," Richard thought.

"Morris," Nancy said. "Theo Morris."

Dr. Avery moved to the phone at Richard's bedside and dialed. A moment later, an announcement came over the PA system requesting the detectives return to the patient's room.

Richard wondered why anyone would impersonate a doctor to keep tabs on him. The obvious answer was that Dr. Paidi, or whomever she was, had to be involved in what happened to him and Sonia. If that was the case, it meant that he had been in the same room with someone who might be able to tell him where his wife was being held. He concentrated on remembering every detail he could about the woman's face, a task he found hampered by a mind still filled with patches of fog.

Detectives Morris and Stevens walked back into the room with quizzical looks on their faces. Richard relayed once more the information he had just given the doctor. Like the surgeon, the detectives listened without interruption until he finished.

"And you're sure this doctor would have no reason to be in here?" Theo asked Dr. Avery.

"First of all, Dr. Paidi is an OB-GYN and would have no reason to examine Mr. Jensen," the doctor answered. "Second, Mr. Jensen said it was a woman. Dr. Paidi is a sixty-five-year-old man."

"And is there any chance that the medication he's on could have caused him to hallucinate?" Theo asked.

"Not impossible," Dr. Avery said. "But unlikely."

"I'm right here," Richard said. "It wasn't a hallucination."

"Mr. Jensen," Theo said. "We have to consider the possibility."

"I promise you, I wasn't hallucinating," Richard argued. "I felt the pain when she examined me. And besides, she knew everything about my condition. Told me about my injuries, the metal plate in my leg."

"But why?" Patricia asked. "Why would a fake doctor want to examine you?"

"I don't know. She was believable as a doctor," Richard said. "Dressed like one. And she talked like one. I believed she knew what she was doing when she injected my IV each time."

"Injected?" Dr. Avery stepped forward. "You didn't mention that. Injected with what?"

"How should I know?" Richard countered. "She examined me. Injected me. Then I would drift off again."

"What is it, doc?" Theo turned to the man.

"It would explain why it took him so long to wake up," the doctor shrugged. "If he was being drugged."

Theo studied the doctor's face a long time before turning to his partner. She was unusually silent. He turned to Nancy. "You ever see this mystery doctor?"

"No." Her voice was soft. "Sorry, Richard. Is this why you keep telling the nurses you aren't hurting? So, they don't give you something that knocks you out?"

"Yes," Richard shrugged. "Whatever it was, I didn't want it anymore."

"How about you, Mr. Jensen?" Theo asked. "Do you think you've ever seen the woman anywhere besides here? A client perhaps? Did you do work for anyone in the medical field?"

"I don't think I've ever seen her before," Richard shook his head. "We do have medical offices as clients, but to my knowledge there have never been any issues with any of them."

"Do you really think someone was wandering the hospital halls injecting patients at random?" Patricia scoffed.

"No, I don't," Theo rolled his eyes at her. "I don't think there was anything random about it."

16

What started out as doing a favor for another district, asking questions about a hit-and-run, had just taken a turn. While the accident had occurred in Greene County, the injections administered to Richard Jensen occurred in Theo's jurisdiction. The evidence presented itself less like an accident and more like a planned kidnapping and attempted murder, with the added charge of assault.

If Richard was supposed to die in the crash, it begged the question, why keep him unconscious for three weeks? It would have been easy for the Dr. Paidi impersonator to inject him with something that would kill him? Nothing made sense. Until it did, tracking down the person behind everything would be challenging. Detectives Theo Morris and Patricia Stevens needed to find out why the Jensens were targeted.

Unfortunately, because the Green County Sheriff's department did not know a second person had been in the car, hours passed before anyone started looking for Sonia. When the search turned up no sign of the woman, they wondered if the owner of the purse they found had been in the car at all. They focused on what Richard may have done to his wife prior to the accident. When Richard's parents insisted their son would never harm the love of his life, the search resumed. By then, the rain had washed away any evidence or prints there may have been.

Two theories rose to the top of the investigation. The first focused on the idea that Richard had harmed Sonia Jensen prior to being in the accident, planning to take a trip with her belongings to delay the discovery of her disappearance. The second was that Sonia had taken advantage of the accident to leave everything behind and run away. No one looked for suspects beyond the hit-and-run driver.

The results of the tox screen, showing Richard Jensen had been drugged, changed everything, leading the detectives to park their police-issued sedan in front of the Halstead Enterprises building.

"Someone is proud of what they do." Theo stood on the sidewalk, staring up at the combination of glass, metal, and stone that gave the building an ultra-modern appearance. A lot of money went into the design and construction of the business's home.

"I would be too," Patricia stood next to her partner. "If I made that kind of money."

"There's more to life than money," the senior detective offered his wisdom.

"Says the man who has none," Patricia returned the favor.

"Touché." Theo did not argue.

The duo walked side by side to the entrance, pushing on the brass plates that were imbedded in the glass double-doors. They swung open with ease and closed silently behind them.

The front lobby was wood and tile with metal accents. Close examination of the floor revealed it not to be actual marble, as the pattern suggested, but a more practical copy. Every effort was expended to impress their visitors, present company not included, as was evident by the scrutiny the security guard was paying the detectives.

Theo knew several security guards, many being formerly on the job. Some retired after their twenty years and worked to supplement their pensions. Others were released from duty for one reason or another and just needed the work. A few juggled their police schedules with their part-time gigs to make ends meet. The detective did not know the man giving them the once over.

They turned away from the guard and approached the attractive blond sitting behind the receptionist's desk. On the phone, the woman held up an exquisite, manicured finger in acknowledgement of their existence while simultaneously and silently asking them to wait. An effective maneuver, as they did just that. Finally putting the receiver in its cradle, the receptionist turned to them with a broad smile. "How may I help you?"

Theo held out his shield. "Detectives Morris and Stevens. We're here about one of your employees. A Sonia Jensen."

"Jensen?" The woman lowered her eyes to her desk.

Theo thought she was displaying sadness but soon saw that her eyes were moving. She was reading. Theo leaned forward to see a list of employees and their extension numbers.

"I'm sorry. There's no Jensen here." She looked up, surprised by how close the man's face was.

"How long have you worked here?" Patricia asked.

"I started last week," the woman answered.

"Well, Jensen hasn't been here for almost a month." Patricia pointed to the list. "Who would be her boss?"

"How would she know that?" Theo grumbled. "Can we talk to Stanley Webber?"

"Everything okay, Miss Terri?"

The security guard had moved to within inches of Theo's shoulder. He was taller than the detective thought, and broader.

"You mind stepping back?" Theo said.

"Yes, I do." The security guard did not budge.

"It's fine, Barney," the woman said. "They're just asking about an employee named…"

Her eyes shifted to Theo who still faced down the guard.

"Sonia Jensen," Patricia finished.

The concern the security guard was showing for the receptionist drained from his face. "Jensen?"

"Yes," Theo confirmed.

"Wait here." The man stepped away and pulled his phone from his pocket. Standing off to the side, he spoke in a hushed voice, his hand covering his mouth. A string of nods ended in him putting the phone away and returning to the receptionist's desk. "He'll be right down."

"He being?" Theo questioned.

"Mr. Halstead."

"As in the owner?" Patricia asked.

"Yes, sir," Barney said. "I mean, ma'am."

The detectives exchanged a glance and crossed the room to a secluded area where they could wait.

"The owner?" Patricia whispered. "Who is this woman?"

"Her husband said V.P. of Customer Accounts," Theo muttered. "Where does that fall on the food chain?"

"Evidently, pretty high," Patricia said.

Lost in their own thoughts, the detectives stared at the elevator bank in front of them, and the stairs just beyond. They watched the suits cuing up for the elevators and others disembark. The exchange took a matter of seconds before the process would begin again. They watched the cycle three times before one broke off to take the stairs.

In his younger days, Theo always took the stairs, keeping his legs strong and his fitness up to the required standard. Once he hit fifty, taking the stairs became less desirable, and elevators became a tool to help him get to where he was going.

"I understand you're asking about Sonia."

The voice came from behind them. The detectives spun on their heels to find a short, balding man facing them. Behind him, Theo caught sight of an almost hidden elevator closing.

"You must be Mr. Halstead," Theo said.

"Call me Charles," the man acknowledged. "Why are you asking about Sonia? She stopped coming to work three and a half weeks ago."

"That's why we're here," Theo said. "We have some questions."

"Questions?" Charles asked. "What kind of questions?"

"It's our understand," Theo said. "The last time she was seen was at a company party at your home. We would like to ask about that."

"What do you mean the last time she was seen?" Charles asked.

"The next morning, she disappeared during a road trip with her husband,"

Theo explained.

"What?" Charles frowned. "Why didn't Richard tell us? We thought she just quit without notice."

"Richard's been hospitalized," Patricia offered. "He wasn't able to call."

"You say she disappeared," Charles said. "What happened?"

"We have reason to believe she may have been abducted," Patricia answered.

"Seriously?" Charles took an involuntary step away. "Are you sure? Why haven't we heard anything about this before?"

"Positive," Theo said. "Honestly, we weren't positive she was missing until after Richard Jensen woke up."

"Woke up?" Charles was shocked. "How bad is he?"

"Let's concentrate on our questions," Theo took charge of the conversation. "We understand that Mrs. Jensen received a promotion recently."

"She did," Charles nodded. "We announced it at the party, actually. That's why we were so surprised she stopped coming to work."

"Did anyone try to reach out to her?" Patricia asked.

"Of course," Charles said. "We called. And when that didn't work, we tried to reach her husband. When neither answered our calls, we concluded she had moved on. I can't believe Richard's been in the hospital all this time."

"Was Sonia, by chance, promoted over a co-worker?" Patricia asked.

"She was promoted, detectives," Charles scowled. "That put her over all her co-workers."

"What we want to know is," Theo interjected, "whether there was someone else in line for the promotion who may have felt slighted by Mrs. Jensen getting it instead of them?"

"You think one of my people did what? Kidnapped her?" Charles' scowl deepened. "That's impossible. Everyone loved Sonia."

"We need you to answer the question just the same," Theo crossed his arms. "If you don't mind."

"I can't," Charles shrugged.

"You can't, or you won't?" Patricia pointed at the man's chest.

"I can't," he repeated. "I wasn't part of the promotion selection process. Nor did I make the final decision. I just signed off on it."

"Who made the decision?" Theo asked.

"The President of Customer Accounts," Charles answered.

"Would that be Stanley Webber?" Theo asked.

"Why, yes," Charles responded.

"Can we speak to him?" Patricia asked.

"I'm afraid that's not possible," Charles' demeanor became somber.

"Why not?" Theo pressed.

Charles Halstead looked from one detective to the other. "He's been missing since the night Sonia was promoted."

17

The smell of bacon lingered in the air even though the small restaurant had stopped serving breakfast nearly an hour before. Theo inhaled deeply through his nose and considered asking the server to bring him a couple of strips to put on his double cheeseburger. The words of his doctor warning him off fatty foods came to the forefront of his mind, causing him to decide against it as he lifted two fries to his mouth.

Detective Stevens sat across from him sipping at a murky green smoothie or energy drink. Even her eating habits got on the senior detective's nerves.

They were on a lunch break after spending half a day interviewing Sonia Jensen's coworkers and colleagues. The primary focus was to learn more about the missing woman and her mindset during the days leading to her disappearance. Secondary was looking into Stanley Webber, her missing boss. To get through the process more quickly, they had split the list and questioned the staff one on one.

"What did you learn?" Theo asked just before taking a bite that his wife would have said was too big. He chewed slow and methodical as his doctor had told him, watching his partner with expectation.

"I think I would hate Sonia Jensen."

The claim caught Theo off guard, and he almost choked. From all accounts, he had the impression Sonia was popular. He swallowed the rest of what was in his mouth. "Why?"

"Because everyone I talked to absolutely adored her," Patricia sneered. "Reminds me of the cheerleaders in high school."

"Let me get this straight." Theo pointed a thick finger at her. "You're basing a hatred for someone you've never met solely on the fact that everyone else liked her."

"That's right." Patricia sipped from her drink. "You know the type."

"The type?"

"Too good to be true," she explained. "Always butting in on the pretext of being caring and helpful."

"Maybe she is caring," Theo suggested. "And helpful."

"People like that don't exist." Patricia looked into her glass, her thoughts far away. "They're always hiding something."

Theo studied the woman's face, wondering what had happened in her past to create that mindset. "Did you learn anything that might actually help us with the case?"

"Well, aside from everyone liking her." She continued to sneer. "They were all surprised by the announcement of her promotion."

"That fits with what I heard too." Theo pursed his lips. "But no one would tell me why."

Patricia grinned.

"What?"

"Well, Susan Ashberry, one of the pool secretaries," the detective started, "said that everyone expected the promotion to go to Jeremy Griffin. He hadn't been with the company long, but everyone said he was outperforming everyone."

"Jeremy Griffin?" Theo pulled out his notes. "I talked to him. He didn't say anything about being up for the promotion."

"Maybe he didn't know," Patricia said. "Or didn't want you to know."

"Either way, We'll need to talk to him again," Theo said.

"What about you?"

"What about me?" Theo ate some fries.

"Did you learn anything?" Patricia prodded him.

"They all liked Sonia Jensen," Theo reiterated. "But no one was too fond of Stanley Webber."

"Stanley." Patricia closed her eyes and took a breath. "Webber."

"You didn't ask anyone about Webber?"

"I was focused on our victim," she answered. "And Griffin. Jeremy 'possible suspect' Griffin."

Theo took a turn closing his eyes, if only to keep from rolling them. He shouldn't have to make lists of questions for his partner to ask. It's just basic detective work to follow up on the topics discussed. Webber's disappearance was one of those things. He didn't understand how she failed to ask about him.

"What did you learn about Webber?" she asked.

"The story seems to be Stanley Webber went to the staff party with a date no one knew." Theo wiped his hands on a napkin. "Pretty woman, about ten years his younger."

"So?"

"So, he got sick and left shortly after arriving," Theo said. "But the woman stayed."

"That's odd." Patricia set her glass down. "Those events are usually boring for those who have to go. Why stay when you don't have to?"

"There's more," Theo smiled. "Stanley Webber is a married man. It was unheard of for him to bring someone other than his wife."

"He's been missing since then?" Patricia contemplated. "Maybe the wife killed him."

"Maybe," Theo chuckled. "We'll have to talk to her. But here's the strange thing."

"There's a strange thing?"

"Everyone agrees he left early, sick." Theo downed a handful of fries. He swallowed hard and continued. "But when I asked what time he left, no one knew. Guess why?"

"They were all too wasted to pay attention?"

"No." Theo lifted his burger. "Not one of them remembers seeing him at the party at all."

The detective took a large bite and chewed. He grinned ear to ear. The boring hit-and-run kept getting more and more interesting.

18

D o you think you can make it to the end of the hall this time?" The physical therapist held tight to the support belt that she had wrapped around Richard's waist.

This was their second venture out of the room. Not long after the detectives visited him, a uniformed officer appeared at the door. He stood guard to prevent Dr. Paidi, or whoever she was, did not continue to administer unknown drugs to Richard, as well as to deter any other kind of attack. He also made sure Richard didn't make a run for it. With that in mind, the officer trailed a few feet behind therapist and patient.

"I can make it." Richard stared at the painting on the far wall. A dull reproduction of a watercolor landscape. It reminded him of paintings he had seen in almost every doctor's office he had ever been in. Nothing like what anyone would purchase for their own home.

Given his size versus the small stature of the therapist, Richard couldn't help but wonder how she would prevent him from falling if that were to happen.

"Are you sure?" Shelly questioned. "We can turn around any time."

"I'm sure." Richard gave her a grin that almost masked the agony he was in. "I want to."

"Okay." She took a firm hold of the belt and guided him toward their destination. "If you change your mind, just let me know."

Richard knew the only way to get discharged was by building up his strength, getting the brace off his leg, and demonstrating that he could get around and care for himself. To that end, he took a deep breath and pushed past the pain shooting through his leg muscles where his stitches were. An occasional smile directed at the woman helping him was his way of assuring her he was doing fine.

"I think we should turn back," she said. They were still twenty to twenty-five feet away from the end.

"We're not there yet," Richard stated the obvious.

"And you're struggling." Shelly was not buying his assurances. "Don't forget, we still have to turn around and go back. The farther we go, the farther the trip back will be."

Richard stood still, looking at the cheap artwork ahead of him. It was meant to soothe the person looking at it. To Richard, it served as a symbol of the goal he hadn't reached. Contemplating his pain level and what another forty to fifty feet would do, he nodded his head to signal his defeat. "Okay."

The therapist guided him in a small arching U-turn and they were soon on their way back to his room, his head bowed to his feet as they went. No more smiles. He would not admit it, but he was glad she had shortened their trip. He was already faltering.

The officer, who had followed each step of the way, stepped past them in a take charge manner. Richard looked up and saw the man approach a couple walking their way. Any other day the scene would have warranted a chuckle. But fighting back the pain and knowing why they were coming; Richard could not muster the humor.

"It's okay," Richard said. "I know them."

The broad shoulders of the officer visibly relaxed as he stepped aside to allow the couple to continue.

"Hello, Charles," Richard greeted with no sign of cordiality. "Diane."

Richard and the therapist continued through the door to his room while the others stood and watched his retreat. Only after Shelly had her patient settled into the hospital bed did the Halsteads enter.

"Richard," Charles' voice was low and even.

"What are you doing here?" Richard asked.

"The police came by to talk to me," Charles explained. "We didn't know."

"Didn't know what?"

"We didn't know you were in here," Charles said. "Or what had happened to Sonia. We're so devastated by her loss. She was a wonderful woman."

"She really was," Diane agreed.

Richard adjusted himself until he was comfortable. Laying back onto the pillow until it all but covered his ears, he looked at his guests with more disdain than they probably deserved. They were speaking of his wife in the past tense. He was not willing to let her go just yet.

"What can I do for you?"

"We should be asking you that," Charles tilted his head. "After all, you're the one confined to a hospital room. Is there anything we can bring you? Some fresh clothes? Something to read? A decent meal?"

The last did have its appeal. The hospital food was fair at best. But at that moment, the two of them were just a reminder to Richard that Sonia wasn't there.

"I'm good," he said. "And unless you need something, my therapy wiped me out. I need to rest, don't I?"

He looked at the therapist. She looked at him and knew what he needed. She stepped up to the bed. "Uh, yes. He really needs to sleep."

"Okay, then," Charles raised his hands defensively. "Wouldn't want to hinder the man's recovery."

The couple exchanged a glance before making their way to the door. Walking away, they looked older to Richard than he remembered. Just before they stepped through the opening, Charles turned back.

"There is one thing," the man said.

"Of course there is," Richard muttered. Only the therapist could hear him.

"What was that?" Charles asked.

"I asked what it is you need," Richard lied.

"Well, when Sonia, uh . . .," Charles stammered.

"When she disappeared?" Richard snapped.

"Well, yes." Charles grimaced. "When she stopped coming to work, we, uh…you know, we tried to reach her. We even tried to contact you. And when, you know, we assumed she had quit without warning. I'm sorry."

"You terminated her," Richard said.

To Richard, it had been no time at all since they sat around the dining room table listening to the glowing speech Charles gave about Sonia and her contributions to the company. The man spoke of her future with them and what a pleasure it was having her on the team. No time at all since that speech and her termination. Job abandonment would be the official reason, but they had to know Sonia would never walk away from her position, especially after getting the promotion.

"Yes," Charles admitted. "It's just that, well, she had a company laptop and phone, maybe some files. We really need to retrieve them."

"You need to retrieve them?"

"Yes."

"Right this minute?"

"No." Charles smiled awkwardly. "Of course not. I just wanted you to know. You know. When you have time."

"I'll get right on it," Richard didn't hide the sarcasm. He grasped a handful of sheets and squeezed it with all the strength he could muster, while staring at the man's neck.

"Charles." Diane took her husband's arm and pulled him toward her. "You can worry about all that later. Let's go so he can rest."

"Okay. Okay." Charles followed her. "Get better, Richard. We're all thinking of you."

The couple walked out, and the door closed.

"I'm sure you are," Richard muttered.

"Who was that?" the therapist asked.

"My wife's boss," Richard said. "Thanks for the assist."

"No problem," Shelly said. "But honestly, you do need your rest."

19

Jensen and Barr Internet Security was housed in a renovated building that had once been a bank. Richard found the place, but it had been Gavin that fell in love with it. Being the perfect size and location, it had only needed minimal changes to make it fit their needs. Leaving the vault in the back corner was a decision they came to for both the unique aesthetics as well as financial. The cost of having it removed was more than Richard was willing to pay.

Detectives Morris and Stevens parked in front of the entrance and sat for a moment while Patricia finished a phone call. When she hung up, she turned to her partner. "The firm is having money problems. Some past due bills."

"Is it just from the past month?" Theo asked. "Or something ongoing?"

"I didn't ask," Patricia admitted.

"No worries." Theo released his seatbelt. "We can ask Mr. Barr."

They climbed out of the car and up to the sidewalk.

"This used to be my bank," Theo commented as he pulled the doors open.

Inside, the teller's counter and check writing tables the detective remembered were long gone, though the vault drew his eyes. He had a safe deposit box inside for several years and was pretty sure he still had the key. It surprised him to see the vault remained.

"May I help you?" The woman at the front desk was pleasant, contradicting the wide eyed, distressed expression on her face.

"We need to see Mr. Barr," Patricia said.

"Oh," the woman glanced over her shoulder. "Are you current clients? Or looking for a quote?"

Theo held his shield out. "Neither."

"Oh." The sound lingered on her lips. "Just a minute."

She pushed away from the desk and awkwardly pulled herself to her feet. She grinned at the detectives before crossing the room to the only other person in the building. The detectives concluded he was Gavin Barr. A hushed conversation took place between the two with the occasional finger point and glance. Gavin nodded repeatedly before she returned.

"He'll be right with you," she said.

The man was only a few feet behind her.

"Hello," he greeted. "I'm Gavin Barr. Is there something I can help you with? Bailey says you're detectives."

"Is there someplace we can talk privately?" Theo asked.

"Of course." He pointed to a glass enclosed space to their right. Theo remembered it as being the bank manager's office. "We can use the conference room."

The detectives followed the man through the opening. Theo pulled the door closed behind them. Documents spread across the center of the table represented their current project. Gavin slid them to the far side before they all sat. Surrounded by glass, Theo felt like he was in a fishbowl, being spied on from all sides.

"Now, what's this about?"

"As you probably know, your partner, Richard Jensen, was involved in a hit-and-run about a month ago," Theo said. "At which time his wife Sonia disappeared."

"Yes," Gavin said. "Of course I'm aware."

"What you may not know," Theo continued. "Is we now have reason to believe it was not a random accident."

"Not random?" Gavin frowned. "I don't understand."

"We believe the person who hit the Jensens did so on purpose," Patricia said. "Which would make Mrs. Jensen's disappearance a kidnapping."

"You mean someone took her?" Gavin said. "But why?"

"That's what we're trying to determine." Theo crossed his arms and leaned back. "First, we aren't sure if she was the target, or if it was Richard and for some unknown reason they took the woman, maybe for a ransom. Have you received any calls asking for money in exchange for her release?"

"No." The surprise on Gavin's face was unmistakable. "I would have called the police right away. Why do you think they would call me anyway?"

"With Richard in the hospital, they couldn't talk to him," Theo said. "But you have access to company funds. They might have thought you a viable option. We know you are in financial trouble. You haven't paid your bills. Is it because you paid a ransom but didn't get her back?"

"No," Gavin insisted. "Nothing like that. No one has called. And I haven't tried to pay any ransom."

"What about your money problems, then?" Patricia asked. "We know the firm is in debt."

"Well, yeah," Gavin hesitated. "I mean, we're struggling. But that's the nature of the business. We have good months and bad months."

"Is there anyone you owe money to that may have wanted to make a point?" Theo asked.

"It's not like we owe the mob or something," Gavin said. "We owe money to our landlord, some utilities, and the bank. We're making payments, trying to catch up. And when we get a few more clients, we'll be flush again."

"So this is a recent problem?" Theo asked. "And temporary?"

"Absolutely," Gavin assured them.

In Theo's experience, when people started talking about problems being temporary, they were hiding something, usually gambling or something like that. Gavin was showing signs of stress and was nervous in the detectives' presence. If he was using company funds to support an addiction, or just bad personal judgement and Richard found out, that might be a motive for wanting to get rid of his partner.

"What can you tell us about Mr. Jensen?" Theo changed the subject.

"About Richard?" Gavin smiled. "He's Richard. I mean he is liked by everyone. He's a brilliant programmer, a great partner and friend. I can't think of any reason anyone would want to hurt him. But then, I can't imagine anyone wanting to hurt Sonia either."

"What about unhappy clients?" Theo asked. "Surely not everyone is as happy as you say."

"I mean, sure," Gavin shrugged. "Some clients are impossible to please. But none of them are upset enough to try to kill Richard."

"What about people from their past?" Theo suggested. "Anyone that might hold a grudge for something against the Jensens?"

"Not that I know of," Gavin said. "But I don't really know anything about Richard's past. He doesn't talk about anything that happened before I met him. Really doesn't talk about much besides programming, oh, and Sonia. He's crazy about her."

"What about her past?" Patricia asked.

Gavin shook his head. "Sorry. I don't know much about her past either. I think she grew up out east somewhere. But I'm not even sure about that."

"Well," Theo sighed. "I guess that's all we have for now. If we think of anything more, we'll reach out. And if you think of anything, please give us a call."

"Of course," Gavin nodded.

The three of them stood and walked to the door. Theo stopped with his hand on the knob.

"One more thing," Theo turned to Gavin.

"Anything."

"Let's say Richard had died in that accident," Theo hypothesized. "What would happen to his part of the business?"

"God forbid," Gavin said. "Assuming Sonia was here, it would have gone to her. But I imagine she would have sold it to me. If not, I'm not sure."

"And his share of the debt?"

"Oh," Gavin said. "We both carry life insurance for that kind of thing."

20

After two days of walking the halls, Richard built his strength up to maneuver on his own, with the help of a cane and some pain meds. Tears came to his eyes when he reached the milestone of having the brace removed. The therapist walked behind him, the officer just behind her; a small convoy making their way around the hospital corridors.

Richard reached the point in their journey that was the farthest from his room, where going forward or turning back were the same distance. He pulled up short and stood still for a moment.

"You okay?" The therapist stepped up next to him and took his arm. "Do you need to sit?"

He looked down at the small woman and smiled. "I'm fine. Just thinking about what's next. Do I dwell in the past?" He hooked a thumb over his shoulder. "Or do I move forward? Move on?"

"That's a lot of pressure for a walk." The therapist patted him on the back. "Maybe just concentrate on the next step. Then the next. See where it leads you."

His smile grew a little larger. "You're right. It's not like I have to decide now."

"You kind of do," the officer interrupted. "We can't just stand here. It's too exposed."

Therapist and patient glanced at one another and chuckled.

The therapist stayed at Richard's side as they continued forward in a triumphant gesture that the officer behind them did not seem to understand. On two occasions, Richard looked at chairs they passed with a bit of longing. Both times he refocused his eyes on the far wall, took a deep breath and pushed on. Reaching his room again, Richard did not let on how much the last leg of the walk had hurt. The woman helped him back into his bed and, at his request, handed him the television remote.

Richard paid little attention when the door opened and Dr. Dean Avery walked in. The doctor checked his notes and took a brief look at the machines that Shelly reattached after returning to the room.

"You're progressing nicely," the doctor said. "Your wounds are healing. Your strength is returning. I'm considering discharging you."

"That would be great." Richard dropped the remote and faced the man. "What do I have to do to convince you?"

"Well, we have a decision to make." Dean clasped his hands together. "Do you go home? Or do we send you to a rehab facility?"

"I would prefer going home." Richard stated. "If it's up to me."

"What kind of support do you have at home?" the doctor asked. "You're going to need some help for a few days. Maybe even a couple of weeks."

"I can ask my parents and sister," Richard assured him. "I'm sure they'll help. And if needed, I can hire someone to cover any time they aren't available."

"Talk to your family," Dean nodded. "I'll have some documents for you that will give you an exercise regimen you will need to follow. Some restrictions."

"Sounds good."

"Barring any complications," the doctor said. "I don't see any reason we can't send you home in the morning."

Getting out of the hospital was the first step toward finding Sonia and bringing her home. Richard still needed to build up his strength more, but he wanted to do it his way on his time. He could also work on research at home, something he couldn't do in his current situation. He wanted out of the confining environment he was in, and he wanted out as soon as possible.

"Okay." Richard looked down at his shaking hands. He lay them in his lap to stop them. "In the morning then."

21

Detective Morris sat in one of the more comfortable chairs he had ever been in while looking around the Webber's living room. The chair adapted to his shape, allowing him to sink into the cushions while still offering much needed support, essentially giving him a full body hug.

His partner sat straight-backed on the edge of the sofa, giving the appearance that one wrong move would land her on the floor.

The woman of the house was in the kitchen, having insisted that beverages were in order, despite the detectives' assurances that they were unnecessary. The sound of glasses and dishes clanging suggested more than drinks were coming their way.

Moments later, their suspicions were verified as Valarie Webber walked in with a tray of iced tea and cookies, which she placed on the coffee table in the center of the seating arrangement. She nestled herself on the opposite side of the sofa from Patricia and clasped her hands together.

"Please." Her voice was soft and kind with a hint of a southern accent. "Help yourself."

Theo realized that freeing himself from the grip of the chair to reach the tray would take more effort than he felt he could expend. He chose instead to remain still. He watched his partner reach out, her hand hovering over the cookies before moving on to a glass. She straightened again and held the iced tea on her knee.

"Mrs. Webber," Theo said.

"Call me Valarie." She grinned at him. "Everyone does."

"Valarie." Theo gave her a single nod. "We need to talk to you about your husband, Stanley."

"Have you found him?" she asked, a hint of hope in her voice overshadowed by dread. "Is that why you're here?"

"No, Mrs., uh, Valarie," Theo pursed his lips. "The Missing Persons Unit is searching for your husband."

"Then why are you here?" Valarie tilted her head, confused.

"We, Detective Stevens and I," Theo explained. "We're investigating another case."

"Another?" Valarie clenched her fists. "Not Stan's?"

"No, ma'am," Patricia said.

"I don't understand," Valarie said. "What does this have to do with my husband?"

"Does the name Sonia Jensen mean anything to you?" Theo asked.

"Of course," Valarie said. "She works for Stan."

"Are you aware she was involved in an accident?" Theo said.

"I hadn't heard," Valarie said. "Is she okay?"

"We don't know," Patricia said. "She disappeared."

The detectives watched the woman for her reaction. Her hands clutched the hem of the apron she wore over her modest floral print dress. She seemed to weigh the information the detectives shared. Her eyes locked on Patricia for a long time before she spoke.

"You mean, like Stan? And you think they're connected?"

"We have reason to believe that the accident Mr. and Mrs. Jensen were in may not have been an accident," Theo explained. "We believe they were struck intentionally. That they were targeted, possibly for the purpose of taking Sonia."

"That's awful," Valarie said. "But I don't understand what that has to do with my husband."

"The night before Mrs. Jensen was taken," Theo said. "She and her husband attended a party held by Charles and Diane Halstead. A party you and your husband were to have attended as well."

"It's also the day your husband disappeared," Patricia added.

"Wait." Valarie looked from one detective to the other. "Are you suggesting that whoever took Sonia may have taken Stan as well?"

"We don't know," Patricia said. "But it's one possibility."

"You don't think that Stan took Sonia?" Valarie asked. "And what? Now he's hiding somewhere with her?"

"Do you think that's what happened?" Theo tried to shift forward. The chair's hold on him gave him the impression he was being swallowed.

"Of course not." Valarie was visibly shaken. "Stan would never hurt anyone. And why would he kidnap that poor girl?"

"Is there another reason Stan would have left?" Patricia held her tea by the rim and moved it in a circular motion. The ice spun around the glass wall, creating a clatter that earned the detective a stern look from her partner. Her hand froze, but the ice continued spinning for a short time.

"Stan would never leave me." Valarie was clearly offended.

"We're not suggesting that he left you." Theo put his hands on the arms of the chair and pulled himself forward. "We just need to know if he was under unusual stress, maybe receiving threats. Something that would make him go into hiding."

"I don't think so." Valarie's eyes swelled with tears. "I just know something happened to him. He would never go this long without calling me, unless he wasn't able to."

"So you think someone took him?" Patricia asked.

"Or worse," she lowered her eyes. "That's the only thing that makes sense."

"Mrs. Webber," Theo slid to the front of the chair. "The night of the party. You and your husband were to attend together. Why did you not go?"

Valarie took a deep breath and faced the detective. "Because Stan texted me."

"He texted you?"

"Yes."

"Saying what?"

"He said something came up at work and he was going to have to work late," she said. "He said he wasn't going to make the party. So I stayed home."

"What time was that?"

"It must have been around four." Her brow knotted tight. "I wasn't expecting him home yet."

"And was that the last time you heard from him?" Theo asked.

"Yes," her voice cracked.

Theo struggled to pull himself free of the man-eating chair and stood. "Mrs. Webber, thank you for your time. Would it be alright if my partner or I stopped by again if we have any more questions?"

"Are you going to look for Stan?" She looked up at him.

"We will," Theo promised.

"Then you can come and ask anything you like," Valarie said. "Anything to help bring Stan home."

The detectives showed themselves out, leaving the woman to sulk alone on the couch.

Once they were secure in their car, Theo said, "So, why, if Stanley Webber never went to the party, did everyone tell us he left early?"

"They said he was there with another woman," Patricia said. "Who was she? And if he didn't go, why was she there?"

"Maybe we should ask the Halsteads?" Theo suggested.

"Now we know the last time anyone heard from Webber was around four o'clock," Patricia stated.

"Do we?" Theo challenged. "We need to find out the last time anyone saw the man. Because if someone took him, his abductors may have sent that text."

22

Richard stood on the front porch of his home, most of his weight supported by the generic, bent tube cane the hospital supplied. He stared at the door, tapping his foot as he waited to go inside. His sister made her way up the steps, being careful not to bump him. The last thing she wanted was to be responsible for sending him back to the hospital. She fumbled with his keys until she found the right one and unlocked the solid oak door. A gentle push sent it swinging smoothly into the foyer. Nancy stepped back to give her brother room to enter.

Richard did not move, his gaze transfixed on the opening. He had carried Sonia over the threshold after their wedding. Richard's eyes fell to the porch, and he fought back the tears forming in the corners of his eyes.

"We could go to Mom's," Nancy suggested.

"No," Richard said, squaring his shoulders. "I have to do it some time. May as well be now."

"Richard." Nancy put her hand on his arm. "It doesn't have to be now."

He turned to her. Nancy was the nurturing type. Always had been. Always would be. Even when they were teens and hated one another, she would take care of him. She was married to a man who understood her need to help others and gave her the room and freedom to do what she felt she needed to. Despite looking years younger than Richard, she was the older sibling by two years. She felt a responsibility for him. If Richard allowed it, she would hold his hand from now until he was sixty, if that was what she thought it would take to get him through this.

"Yes it does," he insisted.

Unlike his sister, Richard believed getting through difficult times required a head on approach. Some situations were harder than others, but they were all essentially the same. To overcome them meant facing them alone and challenging them to defeat you. When they couldn't, you came out the other side, stronger for it.

Nancy knew him well, having witnessed firsthand his method of coping with his fears. His determination did not surprise her. And though she did not agree with him, believing instead that he needed more time to heal emotionally as well as physically, she did not press him further. She stood back and waited for him to make his move.

Inhaling through his nose, air filled Richard's chest, and he held it. Beyond the door was his home. He and Sonia had lived there for years. He had crossed its threshold thousands of times. This did not differ from any other time he had entered. Not exactly the same, since Sonia was not inside. And may never be again.

Richard lifted his cane and set it in front of him, only inches from where it had been before. He planted its base firmly and shifted his weight, worked his leg muscles, and stepped forward. It hurt. It hurt more than he let his doctor and the nurses at the hospital know. He led them to believe he felt almost nothing. It was the only way to get the doctor to sign the release, the only way to get out of that hospital room. Now, standing outside his home, Richard wondered for a fleeting moment if he had made the right decision.

Too late to change his mind, he took another step. And another until he was inside. He released his breath slowly through parted lips and looked down the hall toward the kitchen. Sonia was not there, he knew. But he couldn't resist looking for her in these familiar surroundings.

The blinds were closed, as they had been when they left for the lake house almost a month ago. The diffused light made the house look gloomy, an appropriate atmosphere in Richard's mind. He moved into the living room and stared as if lost while Nancy took his bags up to his room. Photos of Sonia were everywhere, something she had argued against. But he had been adamant about having at least one framed picture of her in each room. Sometimes she rearranged things so she wasn't front and center, but he always moved them back to a place of honor on the shelves. Somewhere along the line, it became a game for them.

Sonia's essence filled the house itself. Her tastes dominated the décor; an area Richard left to her. Many times, he arrived home from work to hear about an ideal piece she had found online. She sometimes gave a room a complete redo over a weekend because she no longer liked the way it looked. But to look at any room in the house was to see Sonia's personality.

"You want me to fix you something to eat?" Nancy called to him as she came back down the stairs. "Or I could pick something up? What would you like?"

"It's up to you." The monotone in his voice startled him. "I doubt I have much to work with here."

"I'll have to go out either way," she agreed. "What would you like?"

"I'm not really hungry," Richard said.

"You have to eat," Nancy used the tone she used with her kids.

"Yes, mother," he said.

"Don't 'yes mother' me," Nancy said. "The doctor told me to be sure you ate. Unless you want to end up back in the hospital."

"I'll eat," Richard walked to the kitchen where Nancy was throwing questionable food items she discovered in the refrigerator into a trash bag. She looked up at him and smiled when he entered the room.

"Hey," she said. "Hope you don't mind. I opened the blinds."

Sunlight poured into the kitchen, fighting against the gloom of the rest of the house. Richard could see the backyard and noted the grass needed to be mowed. A bird feeder his wife kept for the Cardinals was empty. Sonia would be upset. He considered making his way out to fill it, but the feel of the cane in his hand made him reconsider.

He turned away and watched his sister finish her assault on the contents of his fridge. Leftovers, expired meats, and not so fresh vegetables all made their way to the bag. Unsure what he should do, Richard stood lost in his own kitchen. Nancy closed the refrigerator and gave the trash bag a spin to close it. She looked at her brother with another smile at the ready but he was not looking at her. His gaze focused on a spot over her shoulder. She half turned, following his line of sight. A magnetized notepad clung to the top corner of the refrigerator door. A note on the pad, written in Sonia's handwriting read: 'Richard don't forget dinner tonight at the Halstead's. I promise I'll make it up to you. Love, Sonia.'

"How about a burger?" Nancy attempted to capture his attention. "Quick and easy."

"That would be fine." He returned his gaze to the backyard.

"Will you be okay while I go to the store?"

"I can handle being alone for half an hour," Richard assured her.

Nancy walked toward the front door, trash in hand. With her hand on the knob, she turned back to him. "Are you sure you'll be okay?"

"Nancy." Richard looked her square in the eyes. "I'm fine."

"Okay." She pulled the door open. "I'll be back before you know it."

He gave his sister a half-hearted grin and slight nod. She hesitated before stepping out and closing the door behind her.

Richard hobbled to a window overlooking his front lawn. He watched and waited until Nancy backed down the driveway. When he was sure she was gone, he made his way to a small room in the back of the house. Years ago, he and Sonia had gone through a healthy phase. They had cut carbs, salt and fat almost completely out of their diet. They also turned the room they seldom used into a mini gym. The phase only lasted a couple of months before they agreed the change was not for them. He stood in the doorway looking at the dust covered equipment. A weight machine filled the back wall. In front of it stood a treadmill, row machine, and stationary bike.

He limped to the bike, leaned his cane against its frame, and used his hands to lift his injured leg over the center bar. Putting his other foot on the pedal, he shifted his weight and pushed up to put himself on the seat. Taking a deep breath, he pulled his other foot into place, then leaned forward until his arms rested on the handles. Gritting his teeth, he used his good leg to start peddling, trying to ignore the pain as his other leg went along for the ride.

Richard worked his left leg while letting his right stretch and flex during the rotation. From time to time he tried to push down with the injured leg, only to relent to the pain and ease off, but it didn't prevent him from trying again. He continued for twenty minutes before letting the pedals slow until they stopped. He swung his legs to one side and slid off the seat to the floor. Grabbing his cane, he made his way to the living room, where he fell back into a recliner and stared at the blank screen of the wall-mounted television.

Moments later, Nancy opened the front door and walked in with two bags of groceries. Her heart sank as she grinned at her brother in his chair. "You should try moving around, Richard."

"I'm good," he replied.

She sighed, lifting her bounty. "Well, I'm going to make us some food. How hungry are you?"

Instead of answering, he closed his eyes and settled back in the recliner. The concern in her own eyes deepened and Nancy walked toward the kitchen, not sure what to do for him.

Hearing her walk away, Richard opened his eyes, letting his mind wander back to Sonia and the last night they shared. The party was better than Richard thought it would be. Or did it just seem that way, being his last evening with her? He tried to remember, letting his mind run through the sequence of events over and over again, always ending when they left the party.

The exterior lights on the Halstead's house were off, throwing the front lawn in darkness. Sonia smiled and laughed as they held hands. She tilted her head onto his shoulder, making him smile as well. They walked down the circular drive toward their car, talking. When they reached their car, he opened the door for Sonia, who kissed him before getting in. Soon they were driving down the twisting roads of the Halstead neighborhood. Exhaustion had set in by the time they arrived home. That was when they came up with the idea of going to the lake house for the weekend.

Richard opened his eyes, wondering how different things would be had they just stayed home. His eyelids grew heavy and he freed his mind to accept the sleep coming his way. Instead, he remembered.

They had been driving to the lake house when the SUV sped past them. The impact grill was hard to miss. And he was positive it was the same vehicle that had hit them and run them off the road. In his exhausted state, he remembered something else. The SUV. He had seen it before.

23

The receptionist at Halstead Enterprises informed the detectives that Charles Halstead was in a meeting and unavailable for at least an hour. Theo considered shoving his shield in the woman's face and demanding to speak to the man, but one phone call about harassing a witness would land him in hot water with his chief. Instead, he asked to see Jeremy Griffin.

The woman hesitated for just a moment before picking up the phone. She spoke in a hushed voice with her hand over the receiver and her mouth while her eyes bounced between the detectives, reminding Theo of the game Pong that he played as a child. When she lowered the phone and her hand, a fake smile greeted them.

"It'll be just a moment."

"Save it for your clients, sweetheart," Patricia scoffed.

The receptionist's smile faded.

Theo grinned and moved to the opposite wall where he could see both elevators. Patricia followed but kept her focus on her phone. The older detective rolled his eyes.

One elevator chimed, announcing its arrival to the ground floor. Theo watched the doors open. A stocky man of average height and no neck stepped out and into the lobby, running his fingers through his dark mane of hair. Theo recognized him as the man he interviewed the day before. He tapped his partner's shoulder and moved to intercept him.

"Detective Morris, isn't it?" Jeremy greeted. "What can I do for you?"

"Is there someplace private we can talk?" Theo asked. "We have some follow up questions."

"Sure, come with me." Jeremy walked toward a door to one side of the lobby.

They entered a small meeting room and sat around the small table in its center.

"So, you have more questions?" the man asked.

"We are wondering why you never told us you were up for the same promotion that Sonia Jensen ultimately got." Patricia rocked back in her seat and crossed her arms.

"And you are?"

"Detective Stevens," she introduced herself.

"Well, detective," Jeremy faced her. "While it's true I threw my hat into the ring, I knew I would never get the promotion. I didn't think it worth mentioning."

"Your coworkers seemed to think you might get it," Theo said. "And the fact you didn't mention it when the woman you lost out to vanished makes it look like you were trying to hide something. Like a motive."

"Wait, what?" Jeremy sat up straighter. "You can't honestly think I did something to Sonia because she got promoted."

"People have killed for less," Patricia said.

"Well, not me," Jeremy insisted. "Like I said, I wasn't ever actually in the running."

"Why do you say that?" Theo asked. "I heard your numbers were exceptional."

"Charles doesn't like me." Jeremy lowered his voice as if someone might overhear.

"Mr. Halstead told us he wasn't the one who made the decision on the promotion," Theo said. "He just signed off on it."

"Yeah, right," Jeremy chuckled. "Nothing happens in this building without Halstead's input."

"What about now?" Patricia sat forward.

"What?" Jeremy frowned.

"Well, obviously Sonia Jensen hasn't taken over the position. Who took her place? You?"

"Me? No." Jeremy chuckled again. "I was serious about Charles not liking me. The truth is, they haven't filled it. Something about showing Sonia respect. Plus, she might turn up."

"You sound skeptical," Theo said.

"Do I?" Jeremy thought about it for a moment. "Yeah, I probably am."

"And why is that?" Patricia asked.

"Come on." Jeremy spread his hands, palm up. "It's been a month."

"You think that's long enough?" Theo asked.

"She wasn't a family member," Jeremy said. "I don't care what Charles says. He doesn't think of us as family. It's business. You don't wait to fill a position. Unless…"

"Unless what?" Patricia bit.

"Do you know who the Vice President of Customer Accounts was before Sonia?"

"Who?"

"No one." Jeremy nodded like he was sharing a huge secret.

"She filled a new position?" Theo asked.

"You ask me," Jeremy whispered. "They created the position for her. She disappears and so does the position."

"Why do you think they would create a position just for her?" Patricia asked.

"Just guessing?" Jeremy shrugged. "Maybe she and Mr. Halstead were closer than they let on."

"You think they were having an affair?" Theo sat up. "Do you have proof?"

"No," Jeremy shook his head. "But it makes you think."

Jeremy's mannerisms reminded Theo of a conspiracy theorist, Brian Dugan, he had interviewed several years ago. The man's name had come up during an investigation into a missing person named Walter Phoenix. Walter had filed a restraining order against Brian, claiming he felt harassed and threatened. A week later, Walter went missing. Theo brought in the obvious suspect, Brian, who turned the tables by claiming Walter was part of a government organization that was taking innocent people off the streets to conduct experiments on them. Brian claimed these innocents were never seen again, though he never provided proof or names to be verified. He insisted Walter had arranged his own abduction to cover up his involvement. Brian also claimed the organization took Walter because he became too exposed and they didn't want him caught. They then experimented on him so he couldn't talk.

The conspiracy theorist's story came from a point of reality. Brian he had actually witnessed the kidnapping. He had actual photos of the event that led Theo to the people who had taken Walter. Theo was able to make an arrest because of the information Brian provided. Unfortunately, Walter had died of a heart attack shortly after being abducted. The fact that Walter never came home only reinforced Brian's conspiracy theory.

Theo sighed, shaking his head. "Let's talk about Stanley Webber."

"Stan?" Jeremy's eyebrows rose. "What about him?"

"Who was Mr. Webber to you?"

"Stan?" Jeremy frowned. "He's my boss. Why?"

"Your boss," Theo said. "And Sonia Jensen's boss as well?"

"Yes," Jeremy confirmed. "Mine, Sonia's and a dozen others."

Theo nodded. "And when was the last time you saw Mr. Webber, your boss?"

Jeremy studied the detective for a moment. "The day of the party. But he left early. Didn't feel well."

"So you saw him at the party?" Patricia asked.

"Well, no," Jeremy turned to her. "Like I said, he left early. I was a little late."

"You didn't see him before he left?" Theo asked.

"No," Jeremy said. "I didn't see him at the party."

"So, I'll ask again." Theo leaned forward. "When was the last time you saw Stanley Webber?"

"I guess it would have been earlier." Jeremy looked down at the floor. "Here at the office. You…you don't think he had something to do with what happened to Sonia?"

"Why would you ask that?" Patricia asked.

"They both vanished within a day of one another," Jeremy declared. "Stands to reason they went together."

"When exactly was the last time you saw Stan?" she asked.

"After lunch, I think." Jeremy nodded. "Yeah. That was it. He came by to remind me not to be late to the party. That's why I was surprised he left early."

"Why is that?"

"Arriving late and leaving early aren't like him," Jeremy explained. "He always did what was expected. Besides, he seemed fine at work that day."

"You're saying he wasn't sick?" Patricia demanded.

"No," Jeremy said. "I'm not saying that. I'm just saying he didn't seem sick when he was at work."

"And no one has seen him since that day," Theo said. "Nobody found that odd?"

"Are you kidding?" Jeremy looked at them like they were crazy. "Everyone found it odd. Sonia and Stan disappearing? It's practically all we've talked about."

"Do you think it could have been Sonia and Stan having the affair?" Theo asked. "He could have convinced Mr. Halstead to create the position for her."

"It's one idea circulating the office," Jeremy nodded. "But why get your mistress a promotion and then run away with her? Doesn't make sense."

"What about the woman?" Theo asked.

"What woman?"

"The one who supposedly came to the party with Stan that night," Theo said. "Had you seen her before? Do you know who she was?"

"I never saw her," Jeremy said. "I hate those parties and Stan wasn't there, so I left early. I only heard about the woman when I went in to back to work that Monday."

24

"You have to do your exercises," Nancy pleaded with her brother. "The doctor said it was the only way you would get better."

"The fastest way," Richard corrected her. "Not the only."

He sat in his recliner in the living room of his home. His feet were up, his cane resting in the nook created by the leg rest and the arm of the chair. He knew his sister meant well. He just didn't want her knowing what he was doing.

After they ate their burgers, Nancy had run to their parents' house to pick up some things. While she was gone, he was on the stationary bike. After she went to bed for the night, he spent another half hour pushing himself as far as he could go. He was up at five the next morning going at it again. He wasn't trying to avoid exercise; he just needed a break.

"Don't you want to get better?"

"Drop it, Nancy." He regretted his sharp tone as soon as he said it.

The shock in her expression told him he had hurt her. Tears formed in her eyes as she turned away and walked into the kitchen. Taking a seat at the dining table, she rested her head on her arms.

A half hour later, Nancy sat on the couch watching her brother watch the local news. The current story reported on a city council in a small town where three of the members had been arrested for accepting bribes and embezzling hundreds of thousands of dollars from city funds. Richard watched without actually listening. He wondered what story, if any, ran when Sonia disappeared.

"I'm sorry." He was still staring at the screen. "About earlier."

"It's okay." Nancy focused on her brother's profile. He looked so much older than she remembered.

"No. It's not." He turned to her then. "You're trying to help and I'm treating you like crap. I'm sorry."

"You snapped," she shrugged. "I get it. I was pushing and you weren't ready. That's hardly treating me like crap."

"I made you cry."

"You didn't make me cry," she denied.

"I saw your tears," Richard pointed out.

"Oh Richard." The corners of her lip curled up a little. "Lately, I cry all the time."

"Are you okay?"

"Fine," Nancy assured him. "Nothing to worry about."

The next news story started, and they both turned their attention to the television. Neither of them moved for more than half an hour. Not until the doorbell rang.

Richard reached for his cane and for the lever that would lower the recliner's leg rest. Before he could make much progress, Nancy was on her feet.

"I'll get it," she said as she passed by on her way to the front door.

After the third ring, she feared it might be their mother and if no one answered, the woman who raised them would fear the worst and call the police. To her surprise, when she answered the door, it was the police.

"Detectives Morris and Stevens," Theo greeted her. "And you're Nancy, the sister?"

"I am." Nancy stepped to one side to allow the two detectives room to enter. "If you're here to talk to Richard, he's in there."

She closed the door behind them, following on their heels. She considered telling them where to turn, but decided if they couldn't find her brother, they shouldn't be detectives.

They rounded the corner and found Richard, dressed in sweatpants and t-shirt, staring at the television. Theo had almost reached the center of the room before the homeowner seemed to notice he was there.

"Mr. Jensen." Theo greeted the man.

"Detectives."

"No offense," Theo studied his face. "You don't look so good."

"None taken." Richard returned the man's gaze. "You don't look so good yourself."

Theo frowned and glanced at his partner. Patricia shrugged. The man sitting in front of them was not the same man they had visited in the hospital. That man had been determined, but weak. This man appeared to be broken, yet something in his eyes made Theo reconsider.

"How's your recovery coming?" Patricia asked.

"What brings you here?" Richard ignored the question. "Did you find something?"

"We have questions." Theo moved to the couch. "Mind if I sit?"

"Knock yourself out." Richard waved his hand in a gesture to encompass all the seating in the room.

The detective sat where Nancy had been moments before. His partner leaned against the wall nearby. Richard sat back and focused on the screen in front of him.

"First, we have some questions about your business," Theo said. "And your business partner."

"Gavin?" he glanced to and away from the detective. "What about him?"

"Are you aware of the financial struggle your business is having?" Patricia asked.

"Financial struggle?" Richard frowned. "What kind of struggle?"

"The unpaid bills kind," the detective said.

"That shouldn't be," Richard said. "What did Gavin say?"

"He said that you were just one contract away from making it all right again," Theo answered.

"Well, if that's what he said." Richard's tone changed, though nervousness still registered in his eyes. "He would know."

"Did you know Gavin was in the same situation?" Theo asked.

"How do you mean?"

"He means, Gavin is broke and in debt," Patricia answered. "Behind on his bills. For a lucrative business, you're the only one who seems doing well."

"What is that supposed to mean?" Richard challenged.

Nancy saw a spark of life in her brother for the first time since his return home. After Sonia, his business was the most important thing in his life. Problems at work might give Richard something to focus on. It might get his mind off everything else.

"Were you aware of Gavin's money troubles?" Theo asked.

"No," Richard shook his head. "We don't discuss our personal finances. Only work."

"I have to ask, Mr. Jensen," Theo said. "Two months ago, before the hit-and-run, how were the company finances?"

Richard stared at the detective for a long moment. "They were good."

"Good enough that it surprises you to hear things have changed?"

"Yes." Richard's voice was soft.

"Gavin told us that both of you have life insurance policies listing the business as beneficiary," Theo said.

"That's right," Richard frowned again. "I have a separate one with Sonia as my beneficiary."

"So, your partner was having money problems," Theo said. "And had you died in the hit-and-run, he would have gotten the business and an insurance payout?"

"Gavin wouldn't…"

"But you lived," Theo continued. "And now, not only did Gavin's money troubles not go away, but the company has money problems as well."

"I'm sure there's an explanation," Richard defended his partner. "I always handled the money. He probably just over-extended, not realizing how long it would take to recover."

"Is that what you really think?" Patricia asked.

"Gavin wouldn't kill me for the money," Richard grumbled. "Not for anything."

"Maybe not," Patricia said. "But maybe he could hire someone to do it."

"I don't believe that," Richard insisted. "He wouldn't. We've been friends too long."

"I've seen people who have been friends much longer than the two of you kill one another for much more insignificant reasons," Theo said. "Or maybe he arranged your wife's kidnapping and has been waiting for you to wake up to make a ransom demand."

"No." Richard shook his head. "Not Gavin."

Looking into Richard's eyes, Theo could see that the man believed his partner had nothing to do with his wife's disappearance. His belief in Gavin wasn't proof, but the detective changed his questioning.

"Okay, we also need to talk to you about the night before the accident," Theo started.

"It was no accident," Richard muttered.

"Right," Theo acknowledged. "Now, at the party, it was announced that your wife was being promoted."

"Yes."

"We were told that her boss, Stanley Webber, chose her for that position," Theo said. "Is that your understanding?"

"Is that my understanding?" Richard faced the detective. "What does that even mean? My understanding? What does this have to do with Sonia's disappearance?"

"Just answer the question," Patricia directed. "I know some things we ask won't make sense to you, won't seem to have a reason. But the more information we have, the better the odds we find your wife."

Theo looked at his partner, dumbfounded. He had not found her very useful up to that point, but her argument for getting Richard to talk was spot on.

"Fine." Richard crossed his arms in a huff. "Was it my understanding? Yes. It was my understanding that Sonia was being promoted. It was my assumption that Stan, being her boss, was the one who made the decision."

"Did you see Mr. Webber the night of the party?" Theo asked.

"No," Richard pursed his lips, thinking back. "I think he went home sick."

"But you didn't see him before he left?"

"No."

"What about Sonia?" the detective asked. "Did she mention seeing him?"

"No." Richard shook his head. "We were together the entire evening."

"Are you aware that no one remembers seeing Stanley Webber that night?"

"No." Richard showed an interest for the first time. "How would I know that?"

"And no one has seen him since," Patricia added.

Richard shifted his attention to her. "No one?"

"No one," Patricia confirmed. "Not even his wife."

"And you're thinking what?" Richard asked. "Whoever took Sonia took him as well?"

"That's one possibility," Theo grunted. "The timing is quite a coincidence."

"But why?" Richard questioned.

"We don't know," Theo admitted. "That's why it's just a theory."

"And the others?"

"What others?"

"You said that was one possibility," Richard reminded the detective. "What are the others?"

"What was their relationship like?" Patricia asked.

"Whose?" Richard asked. "Stan and Sonia's?"

"Yes."

"Boss and employee," Richard said. After a pause, he added, "They got along. Why?"

"Did you ever suspect there might be something more between them?" Theo was blunt.

"No," Richard insisted. "There was nothing else between them."

"How can you be so sure?" Patricia asked.

"Because I know my ..." The words caught in his throat. "my wife."

"I assume she knew you," Theo said. "Are you saying you never kept secrets from your wife?"

Richard froze. He kept plenty of secrets from Sonia. "Secrets are one thing. Cheating is something else entirely. Are you suggesting the two of them ran away together?"

"Again," Theo said. "It's just a theory. We'll have to investigate it further."

"Look all you want," Richard said. "There's nothing to find."

The two men stared at each other as if they were trying to see who would blink. The detective broke first.

"I guess that's it." Theo pushed himself to his feet.

"I have something," Richard said.

"What's that?"

"I've been thinking a lot about the last moments I shared with my wife." Richard was somber. "I've replayed the night of the party over and over in my head. And I remembered something I think you should know."

"What is it?" Patricia asked.

"The SUV that hit us," Richard said. "The one that sped past us earlier that morning then hit us."

"Did you remember something that will help us identify it?" Theo asked.

"Not that, unfortunately," Richard said. "But I remembered seeing the SUV before."

"Before the day of the accident?"

"Yes." Richard looked at the detective. "It was parked behind us at the party."

25

Richard sat brooding after the detective's left. The suggestion that they thought there might be something going on between Sonia and her boss, Stan Webber, struck a nerve. Richard did not believe for a second that Sonia was having an affair. But they worked in the same department and vanished within twenty-four hours of one another. Richard remembered that as they were leaving the party, Sonia asked Charles Halstead if Stan had talked to him about something, then agreeing to discuss it later. Richard had to consider that there might be a connection between that conversation and their disappearances.

The apparent financial problems his firm was now facing did not even seem possible. The idea the business had taken a turn for the worst and had fallen on hard times in just a few weeks was absurd. Sure, he normally handled the finances, but Gavin couldn't have caused enough damage, in such a short time, to put them in danger of closing. He knew a quick talk with Gavin would be the best way to clear things up. With that in mind, Richard pulled himself to his feet with the help of the cane.

Nancy followed the detectives to the door, shutting and locking it behind them. She returned to the living room to check on her brother and almost collided with him as he stepped into the hall.

"I'm sorry," she apologized. "Did you need something?"

"I need to change clothes."

Richard limped to the foot of the stairs and stopped. He had been sleeping on the couch since coming home. Even with the exercises he had been pushing himself to do, he had yet to tackle stairs. He may as well have been looking at Mount Everest.

"Let me get them for you," Nancy suggested. "What do you need?"

He gave her a list of items and she raced up to his and Sonia's room on the second floor to retrieve them. Richard leaned against the wall next to the bathroom and waited for her. She returned, handing him a stack of clothes; jeans, t-shirt, socks and shoes. With a nod, he rotated and placed the items next to the sink as he entered.

Fully dressed when he came out again, Richard realized it was the first time since waking in the hospital that he had worn anything other than a gown or sweats. It felt good. Nancy watched on as he moved through the house, stopping at a table and tearing open the plastic bag he had been giving upon his discharge. From inside, he retrieved his wallet and the watch Sonia had given him for his last birthday. He admired the timepiece a moment before pulling over a box containing items retrieved from his car at the impound. At the bottom, he found what he was looking for. He pulled out the keys and dropped them into his pocket. Richard reached back into the box to retrieve his phone, complete with cracked screen and dead battery.

"Are you going somewhere?" Nancy did not hide her concern.

"To the office," Richard informed her. "I have to talk to Gavin."

"Okay," she grinned. He was doing what she hoped he would. Focus on the business and get his mind off everything else. "I can drive you."

"That's not necessary." Richard walked to the kitchen where he plugged his phone into a charger. When he was sure it still worked, he started pulling drawers open until he found a car charger.

Nancy followed close behind. "I really don't mind."

"Nancy, I appreciate it," Richard said. "I do. But I can handle a quick trip to work and back. I won't be long."

Reluctantly, his sister gave in and watched Richard limp out the door, cane in hand. He rounded the corner of the house to where the freestanding garage was located. The two-car structure was where he kept his car that was totaled in the collision. Behind the second door was Sonia's car. Not up to what memories that would stir, he went to the side of the garage, to an old pickup truck he kept for hauling. The last time he had driven it, he picked up a load of pickets when he redid the fence almost a year ago.

Sliding in behind the wheel, he put the key in the ignition and turned it. The engine turned over twice before catching. He gave it a minute to be sure it didn't stall on him before shifting it into gear and pulling out and down the driveway. He glanced back at the house before leaving and saw Nancy standing in the window, watching him.

Working the pedals with his injured leg proved painful, but he managed. His time on the stationary bike prepared him, though the angle of his leg was different and the muscles required still needed to be stretched more.

The drive to his office did not take long, one reason he had agreed to the old bank. He wasn't as enamored with the building as Gavin, but being only fifteen minutes from home sold him. If he worked on a weekend, he could run home for lunch or Sonia could bring it to him. In the early days of the company, when he worked more hours than he liked to admit, they had shared many meals in the conference room. As time passed, those days became fewer and farther between.

Richard steered into the small parking lot and guided the truck into the space directly in front of the sign for Jensen and Barr Internet Security. He killed the engine and sat for a moment, staring straight ahead. The company name and the subsequent sign took a long time to come up with. He, Sonia, and Gavin drank more bottles of wine than he could remember during their brainstorming sessions. One night they consumed so much all they did was make horrible suggestions and laugh. Unproductive but fun. In the end, they all agreed they were overthinking things and went for simple clarity. Staring at the sign, he knew they had made the right choice.

He grabbed his cane off the bench seat, swung his legs around, and lowered himself to the ground. The short walk to the front door took longer than it should. When he walked into the building, a place that so familiar, it felt somewhat foreign to him. The first thing that was out of place was the young woman sitting at a desk just inside.

"Hello," the woman said. After a brief pause, she added, "Oh. Sorry. Jensen and Barr Security. How may I help you?"

"Who are you?" Richard asked.

"Uh?" She seemed confused by the question. "I'm Bailey."

"Where is Gavin?" Richard asked.

"Mr. Barr is, uh," she stammered. "He's not available right now."

"Is he here?" Richard demanded.

"He is, but…"

"Then he's available," Richard interrupted. He walked around the desk into the space beyond, looking for his partner.

"I, uh." Bailey rose, unsure what to do. Finally, she called out, "Mr. Barr, sir!"

Richard was in the center of the building when Gavin walked out of the server room.

"Richard?" He was caught off guard. "What are you doing here?"

"Who is she?" Richard pointed at Bailey, whose face was still a portrait of confusion.

"She's Bailey," Gavin hesitated. "Our receptionist."

"Receptionist?" Richard exclaimed. "Gavin, she didn't even get the company name right. And since when do we need a receptionist?"

"Since you haven't been here," Gavin answered. "I've been the only one working on the servers, on bringing in new clients, coddling our current clients, the paperwork. I'm doing the work of two. I can't be answering phone calls too. So I brought Bailey in to help."

"Okay," Richard calmed down. "I get it. Could you make sure she knows the company name though?"

"I will." Gavin glanced at Bailey who lowered her eyes.

"Good," Richard said. He looked at the young woman, then back at Gavin. "Can we go to my office and talk?"

"Sure." Gavin led the way, holding the door open for his partner.

Inside, Richard sat behind his desk. He felt comfort in the familiarity. He felt himself. "So, listen. I had a visit from the detectives on Sonia's case."

"They've been here, too," Gavin said.

"They told me the company is having money problems," Richard said. "Is that true?"

Gavin froze. He looked as if he might speak but didn't. A moment later, he sat heavily in the chair across from Richard.

"Gavin?"

"I'm trying, Richard," he said. "With me being the only one here, I'm behind on some deadlines. So, the money isn't coming in as fast as normal, but the bills are still coming."

"Alright," Richard acknowledged. "So, it's not bad?"

"No," Gavin assured him. "We're just a little behind is all."

"So, I need to get myself back in here." Richard thought aloud.

"That would be great," Gavin said. "But only if you're ready."

"Not yet, but soon," Richard sighed. "Send me a list of active projects and how far along they are. I'll make some calls. Maybe I can get some extensions as long as they know I'll be back in a week or two."

"That would help."

Richard could see the relief in Gavin's body, like a weight had been lifted.

26

"D o you believe he suddenly remembered the SUV being at that party?"
Patricia sat with her eyes closed while Theo drove. "Or is it more likely
he thinks he remembers because we told him it was an SUV that ran him off
the road?"

"Doesn't matter what I believe." Theo turned onto the street that led to
their destination. "We still have to follow up. The killer could have been at the
party. Or maybe they were just following the Jensens. Or, as you said, there's
no connection. It's up to us to figure it out."

The detective made a quick turn into the parking lot of Halstead
Enterprises. He found a parking space that wasn't too far from the door and
pulled in. A few minutes later, they were pushing their way through the lobby
doors.

"Detectives Morris and Stevens to see Charles Halstead." Theo held his
shield in front of the receptionist as he had done the day before. "And before
you tell me he's too busy, understand that if I have to get a warrant, we will be
seizing every document in the building."

It was an empty threat. No judge in their right mind would sign off on
such a broad warrant. However, it did get the woman to pick up the phone.
She spoke in a hushed voice with her hand over her mouth. Her eyes repeatedly
locked onto Theo with a mix of concern and agitation. When she finished the
call, she did not address the detectives, choosing instead to return to what she
had been doing before their arrival.

The two of them had moved away from the desk and Patricia started back
toward the woman when a voice stopped her.

"Detectives?"

They both turned to find a tall, muscular man in a black button-down
shirt, black slacks, and shiny black shoes. The two details that caught the
detectives' attention were the bright silver security badge on his chest and the
gun belt around his waist. Theo resisted the urge to place a hand on his own
weapon. His partner did not.

"If you will follow me." The man took note of Patricia's hand but said
nothing. With a flick of his wrist, he indicated to them they would be going to
the elevators behind him.

Waiting for the doors to open, Theo asked, "Are you the head of security, by chance?"

"I am," the man answered. "Mathias Cunningham. Although everyone calls me Ty."

"Well, Ty," Theo said. "Mind if we ask you a few questions before we leave?"

"You can ask all you want," Ty said. "I'll answer what I can."

The elevator opened and Ty placed his hand on the doors so they would not close until the detectives had boarded. He joined them and pressed the button for the twelfth floor.

"Mr. Halstead has the entire top floor."

Theo did not know why the man offered the information, or what it mattered. To the detective, it seemed like a great waste of space.

Standing in a row, they watched the digital readout count each level as they approached their destination. When they finally reached the top, the lighted twelve was accompanied by a chime. All eyes lowered to the doors as they parted.

The trio stepped into an office with a desk facing them. A woman sitting there typed without looking up. When they came closer, she continued to type without addressing them. Not until they were standing over her did she acknowledge their existence by holding up a single finger to keep them silent as the receptionist had done when they entered the building the first time. Theo wondered if Halstead had the women go through training for this skill. Memories of his school librarian, Mrs. Wagner, when he was in fifth grade. She always held up a finger to silence students. A rumor suggested if you made noise in the library, Mrs. Wagner would whack you with that finger, leaving a bruise that lasted weeks. Theo never tested the rumor. Maybe Mrs. Wagner trained these women.

"Yes, sir," she said to no one in particular. "I'll get copies out immediately. Oh, and sir, those detectives are here."

The way she said 'those' gave Theo the impression that there had been some negative discussions at his and his partner's expense.

She tapped the nearly hidden Bluetooth in her ear and presented them with a choreographed, dazzling smile. "Welcome to Halstead Enterprises."

"Is he ready for them?" Ty asked.

"Almost," the executive assistant said. "Should be any minute now."

Theo rolled his eyes. Executives, especially those who claimed that time was money, had a habit of turning minutes into hours. He had one CEO who kept him waiting for three hours for an interview. Theo took a lot of satisfaction when he arrested the man for hiring the man who murdered his wife.

"He'll see you now," the woman declared while standing to open the door to the inner office.

The space beyond the door was large, though not as large as Theo expected, given the man had the entire floor. In front of them, a wall spread from exterior to exterior, containing multiple doors. To the right, a glass partition separated them from a conference table surrounded by two dozen or more seats. Similar to the room of the same function at Richard's business, this one appeared to be on steroids. To the left, Charles Halstead sat behind an executive desk the size of Theo's first car, a vehicle the detective had nicknamed 'The Tank'. The man rose to his feet to greet them.

"Thank you, Mathias," Charles said. "I'll let you know when I need you."

"Sir." Ty bowed and returned to the outer office.

"Detectives," the man turned to them. "What can I do for you today?"

"Thank you for taking the time to see us." Theo despised sucking up.

"We have questions about the night before Sonia Jensen disappeared," Patricia answered.

Charles took his seat and gestured for his guests to do the same. They did and found themselves looking up at the man. Given the man was about six inches shorter than Theo, the height difference in the chairs was too obvious to be ignored. "Anything I can do to help."

"That night," Theo said. "You held a party, during which you announced Sonia's promotion."

"I've already confirmed that," Charles said. "I hope that you're not here to waste my time."

"You also told me that the man ultimately responsible for choosing her for that promotion was Stanley Webber," Theo reminded. "Yet, Mr. Webber was not at the party."

"No, he wasn't."

"Didn't you find that odd?" Patricia asked.

"Yes," Charles nodded. "Although I was told he was sick and left early."

"You were told?" Theo repeated. "You didn't speak with Stan directly?"

"I never saw him."

"But you're positive he was there?" Patricia said.

"I was told he was there," Charles said. "Do I have reason to believe I was lied to? No. Would I bet my life on it? No. But why is any of it important?"

"Stanley Webber disappeared that day and Sonia Jensen disappeared the next," Theo said. "We find that to be quite a coincidence."

"Are you suggesting Stan had something to do with Sonia's disappearance?" Charles laughed. "That's ridiculous. Stan adored Sonia."

"Adored her?" Theo raised an eyebrow. "Romantically?"

"More like fatherly," Charles corrected.

"Stan is married, isn't he?" Theo knew he was.

"He is," Charles confirmed.

"Yet, his guest for your party was not his wife," Theo said.

"I wasn't aware of that," Charles said.

"You had an unknown guest and didn't find out who she was?" Patricia asked.

"There were more than four dozen people there, detective, "Charles addressed the woman. "I knew most, but not all. And no, I did not go out of my way to introduce myself to the ones I had never met."

"I would have thought you might have made an exception for this one," Patricia grinned.

"And why is that?" Charles was skeptical.

"Tall, auburn-haired woman," Patricia offered. "I believe they said she was in a blue pant suit."

"Oh, I remember her." Charles had an aha moment.

"Thought you might," Patricia said.

"You say she came with Stan?" The businessman asked.

"That's right," Theo answered.

"I would have sworn she was a guest of Sonia and Richard." Charles seemed lost in his thoughts. "She spent most of the evening with them."

"The Jensens knew her?" Patricia asked.

"It seemed so," Charles answered. "Like I said, they spent most of the evening together."

"And you had no idea she was Stan's guest?" Theo asked.

"I said I didn't."

"We need a list of everyone who attended that party." Theo knew they would have to check vehicle registrations for everyone to see who drove an SUV. Someone would have to make a visual check to see if any of them had an impact bar, or had one removed.

"I can have my wife send you a list of who was invited," Charles said. "But we didn't take attendance. And we don't have a list of anyone's plus one."

"Whatever we can get." Theo grimaced and studied the man's posture. He wasn't defensive, maybe agitated. "We need to talk to someone who knew Stan. Someone who worked with him closely, if possible."

"The ideal person would have been Sonia," Charles informed them. "But since that's not possible, I would suggest you talk to, Fiona, Stan's assistant. She probably knows him better than his wife. Ty can take you to her."

"That would be good," Theo said. "We need to talk to him too."

The detectives left the office and rendezvoused with the head of security. The man's fingers were working at high speed as he texted someone. He looked up to find two sets of eyes gazing at him.

"Done already?"

"Mr. Halstead said you could take us up to see Fiona," Theo said. "Stanley Webber's assistant."

"I can do that," Ty pushed off the wall he had been leaning against. "Follow me."

27

Talking to Gavin didn't fully alleviate Richard's concerns for his company, but it made him less stressed than he had been. As requested, his partner gave him a list of active projects, how far along they were and the contact information for each. Richard sat in the truck, scanned the information and noted who he felt would be most receptive to allowing them an extension on their deadlines. He set them on the seat next to him when he finished and lay his cane across the top.

He started the truck and pulled away from the building and into traffic. While he drove, his mind wandered to Stan.

In his heart, he knew there had been no affair between Sonia and Stan, but they might have been involved in something else. His former colleague, Caroline Winters, told him she was working with Stan Webber on a security matter, something he hadn't given a second thought. But the fact was, Stan worked with Sonia running client accounts. He was not involved in security. If Caroline had not lied, the only option for her to work with Stan was in a protection capacity. And if Stan went missing, she must have failed to protect him, unless she had moved him to a safe house where she could keep him out of harm's way.

Richard regretted not getting Caroline's business card. He wanted to know what threats Stan may have been facing and she would be the person to ask. If Sonia was facing the same dangers just because she worked with the man, he wanted to know why neither Stan nor Caroline had warned them. If Sonia's disappearance was connected to Stan's, a simple heads up could have kept her safe.

A horn brought him out of his thoughts. He checked his rearview mirror, concerned he may have cut someone off. Instead, he saw a motorcycle several car lengths back. An extended arm from the car behind provided a rude gesture and enough information for Richard to know the motorcycle had had been the offending driver.

Richard thought it might be a good idea to run to the store for supplies since Nancy had been refusing to let him pay her back. He turned away from his home, down an industrial street that would take him to his preferred grocery store. A less used route since many of the companies were closed. The sound of a motor had him checking his mirror again. Richard saw the reflection of the same motorcycle behind him.

Richard looked down at the folder on the seat. Even being behind on projects did not explain the company's money problems. He would make those calls first, giving assurances of payments before looking deeper into things.

The roar of the motorcycle speeding up brought his eyes up again. As the driver came around him, Richard watched, years of training kicking in. As he neared, the man on the cycle pulled a gun from his jacket and pointed it toward the truck. Richard's instincts took over as he pulled hard on the steering wheel and hit the brakes. The would-be killer was unprepared for the maneuver that brought the front fender of Richard's truck into his path. The man pulled to steer away, but with the gun in his right hand, he had no control. He sideswiped a parked car, losing control before hitting the front of the truck. He flew over the hood as Richard steered back toward the road. The truck struck the same car the motorcycle had before veering away. Richard felt the bump as he ran over what he could only be the gunman. Braking, Richard climbed out of the driver's seat.

The cyclist lay on the street, a pool of blood forming around his upper body. Richard knelt and checked for a pulse, finding none. He did a quick search of the man's pockets. Finding no identification, only a folded piece of paper, Richard opened it to find a photo of himself, along with his name and address. Someone had taken out a hit on him.

He stooped over and snatched up the man's weapon where it lay on the street and threw it into his truck. Looking up and down the street, he didn't see any witnesses to what had happened. He climbed back into his truck and sped away, deciding to skip the store and go straight home.

Someone wanted him dead. If that was the case, he may have been the intended target the day of Sonia's disappearance. Richard's mind raced. It didn't add up. If they wanted him dead, they could have finished the job at the accident. There was no reason to take Sonia. Trying to make it look like an accident, they may have panicked if Sonia saw them. But it didn't explain Stan's involvement.

What made more sense was if Stan and Sonia had stumbled onto something that put targets on them. That would explain their disappearances. But it didn't explain why someone just tried to kill Richard.

He drove the next few miles with his eyes darting from the road in front of him to the mirrors in search of following vehicles. Richard saw no more threats and hoped he was right. When he reached his home, he didn't slow turning into the driveway and racing to the back where the truck had sat for the past year. He climbed out, collected the papers that had come out of the folder Gavin had given him. He tucked the pistol into his belt before clutching his cane.

Entering the back door, he set the pistol on a high shelf before continuing. Nancy was coming down the stairs when Richard entered the kitchen. He tossed the folder on the counter and took a moment to calm his nerves.

"Did I see a dent in the truck?" Nancy demanded.

"It's nothing," Richard dismissed.

"Nothing?" Nancy challenged him. "Did you hit something?"

Richard moved past her, while she fell in step behind, insisting he tell her what happened. His mind was elsewhere. Charles Halstead visited him in the hospital, which Richard thought little of at the time. Before leaving, he had asked about Sonia's company phone and laptop. If she and Stan stumbled onto something, it might be on those devices.

Richard opened the door to Sonia's office, just off the living room, at the front of the house. A quick scan revealed no phone or laptop. The chargers to both were there, but not the devices. He started opening drawers and cabinets, rummaging through them as he went. With Nancy watching on from the doorway, he yanked open filing cabinets and searching inside. At times, he pulled handfuls of folders out and dumped them on any empty surface he could find. When the devices didn't turn up, Richard moved to the living room and started tearing it apart.

Years of Sonia's work decorating the house to make it the home they wanted was being undone. Finished with that room, Richard moved on to another, continuing with his newfound purpose, pulling open drawers and dumping their contents, emptying closets and tossing rows and rows of books from shelving to the floor.

"If you told me what you were looking for," Nancy pleaded, "I could help you find it."

His sister offered to help him for the third time. Richard used his forearm and swept another row of books onto the pile forming below. Nancy retreated to the far side of the room, fighting back tears as she watched her brother losing his mind.

Next on the shelf was a photograph of Sonia, taken early in their relationship. She was wearing a yellow sundress, the one she had been wearing the first time he had seen her, just a few months after Mexico City. He sat in his parent's home, unemployed, as they talked to him about the next step in his future. Nancy came home from college for the weekend with a couple of friends in tow. The moment Sonia walked into the room, he froze, unable to take his eyes off her.

Taking the picture from the shelf, he held it in both hands, his chest heaving as he panted from the exertion of his search. Richard stared at her beautiful eyes, so full of life. He longed to look into those eyes again, to feel her touch.

"I'm looking for her work phone and laptop," he said between breaths, continuing to stare at her face. "I need to see what's on them."

"Oh."

Richard's head snapped up. "Oh? What do you mean by, oh?"

"Richard, you have to understand," Nancy held her hands up. "I didn't know. And they belonged to Halstead. They even had 'Property Of' stickers on them."

"What did you do?"

"This guy stopped by," Nancy shrugged. "From Halstead. It was just after you were released from the hospital. And he asked for them. You were sleeping. So, I gave them to him."

"I can't believe you, Nancy," he yelled.

"How was I supposed to know?" she defended. "They belonged to the company."

Richard lowered his eyes to Sonia's photograph. "I can't believe you gave them the computer, phone and files."

"Files?" Nancy looked at her brother. "What files?"

28

Halstead Enterprises's head of security led the two detectives to Stanley Webber's office. Fiona Delaney, Stan's personal assistant, saw them coming, convinced she was about to be escorted out of the building. The inevitable next step after her boss's disappearance, she braced herself for the news.

Standing behind her desk, she looked like a teenager at only five feet tall. Freckles spotted the soft, smooth skin of her face, making her look much younger than her twenty-seven years. Despite wearing her jet-black hair pulled up in a bun to look older, she often had to show identification to prove she wasn't a minor.

When the trio reached her desk, she looked up at them, each one taller than average, like a child awaiting her punishment.

"Hey, Fi." Ty abbreviated her name the same way he did his own. "These detectives need to talk to you about Stan."

"What about him?" Her voice squeaked, a sound she had never made before. Her mind was racing. Were they going to tell her they found her boss? Was he dead? Did they think she killed him?

"I'm Detective Theo Morris. You're Stan Webber's personal assistant?"

"Yes."

"So, you keep his calendar up to date?" Theo asked.

"Of course." After a brief hesitation, she added. "But he didn't have anything about being gone like this."

"Okay," Theo said. "That's all right. Can you tell me about his schedule for the day he disappeared?"

Fiona glanced at Ty, who gave her a nod. The head of security walked away, putting distance between himself and the questioning. Turning to her computer, she brought up the date of the company party. "He had three meetings that morning. A lunch meeting off campus. And the afternoon was clear... Oh, he called to have me cancel his last meeting of the day because he couldn't make it back in time."

"You remember that?" Patricia asked.

"Oh, yes," she said. "It was a meeting with Mr. Halstead. He wasn't happy."

"Did Stan say why he couldn't make it back?" Theo asked.

"No," she shrugged. "Just said cancel the meeting. And when I asked if he wanted me to reschedule, he said, not yet."

"Not yet?" Patricia mused. "Almost like he wasn't sure when he'd be back."

"But he did come back," Fiona said. "And in time for the meeting. He just didn't go."

"He blew off a meeting with his boss?" Patricia said.

"It was very unlike him," Fiona said.

"Tell us about the meetings he did have that day," Theo said. "Who were they with? What were they about?"

Fiona turned back to the computer and clicked on the individual entries. "First one was an eight a.m. staff meeting. He had one every Friday to discuss what had happened that week and what he expected in the week to come."

"Was there anything unusual in that meeting?" Patricia asked.

"It was just a normal meeting," the assistant said.

"What was next?" Theo asked.

"At nine, he met with Sonia Jensen," Fiona said.

"What did they meet about?"

"I don't know," she shrugged. "I wasn't in the meeting, so…"

"That's all right," Theo assured her.

"I can tell you it got heated." Fiona sat up straighter.

"Heated how?" Patricia asked.

"At one point, they were yelling at each other."

"Was that out of the ordinary?" Theo asked.

"God, yes," Fiona lowered her eyes. "Stan and Sonia. Neither one of them were yellers. Especially not at each other."

"Could it have been a lover's spat?" Patricia asked.

"What? Ew, no," Fiona cringed.

"Why, ew?"

"For starters, Stan adores Valarie, his wife," the assistant said. "He would never cheat on her. And then there's Sonia and Richard. Oh my God. They are, um, the perfect couple. Just, no way."

"Then what were they arguing about?" Theo pressed.

"I don't know," Fiona shook her head. "Honestly. I could hear them yelling but couldn't make out the words. By the time the meeting was over, they had calmed down. They came out together, cordially. Sonia smiled and thanked him. She smiled at me. You would have never known they had just argued."

"And the third meeting?" Theo saw no point in continuing, knowing they couldn't question either participant.

"He had an eleven o'clock meeting with a prospective client." Fiona tapped the screen. "Now, that one was unusual because Stan didn't really bring in business anymore. That's more an Account Manager's job."

"How many do you have?" Patricia asked.

"How many?"

"Account Managers," the detective clarified. "How many are on staff?"

"I'm not sure," Fiona said. "Fourteen or fifteen, maybe."

"Were all of them booked that day?"

"I don't know," the woman said. "I don't keep their calendars. You would have to ask them."

"Do you remember when the meeting was scheduled?" Theo asked.

"Eleven o'clock."

"No," Theo smiled. "When was the meeting added to the calendar? Do you remember?"

"Oh, yes," she smiled. "Stan asked me to add it that morning."

"That morning?" Theo frowned. "He didn't ask you to try an Account Manager?"

"No." She shook her head. "He just told me to add it. Didn't even give me a name. Just said it was a prospective client."

"What can you tell us about them?" Patricia asked. "The prospective client?"

"Nothing," Fiona said.

"This is a murder investigation," Theo's tone darkened. "We're not trying to steal a client. You need to tell us everything you know about them."

"You don't understand," the woman became defensive. "Stan sent me on an errand. I never saw the client."

"What was the errand?" Patricia asked.

"Excuse me?" Fiona turned.

"Stan sent you on an errand," Patricia said. "What was it?"

"He asked me to go across town to pick up his suit from the dry cleaners," Fiona explained. "For the Halstead's party."

"Did he often have you pick up his dry cleaning?" Patricia sneered.

"It was the first time," Fiona said.

"Really?" Theo said. "How long were you gone?"

"About forty-five minutes."

"And this prospective client was already gone when you returned?" Patricia asked.

"That's right."

"Are you sure they actually made it to the meeting?" Theo asked. "Maybe they were a no show."

"Maybe," Fiona said. "Stan didn't say."

"So you came back with his suit," Theo said. "And then what?"

"I gave it to him and he thanked me," she said. "Then he told me he was going to a lunch meeting and left."

"Lunch meeting with whom?" Patricia asked.

"I don't know," Fiona grimaced. "There was nothing on the calendar. I only added it after he said he was going."

"Another last-minute meeting?" Theo thought aloud. "What about after lunch? What happened then?"

"Well, it was a Friday," Fiona tilted her head. "And the night of the party. He had cancelled his meeting with Halstead, so he was just alone in his office."

"What was his demeanor?" Theo asked. "Anything different about him when he came back? Did he seem nervous?"

"No," Fiona said. "He was just Stan. Cracked a bad joke. Told me I could leave early since there wasn't really anything to do."

"So, you left early?"

"Yes," she said. "About three forty-five."

"And that was the last time you saw Mr. Webber?" Patricia asked.

"Yes," Fiona confirmed, her eyes welling up.

"I think we've taken enough of your time," Theo said. "Thank you."

The woman nodded, still fighting tears.

The detectives walked away and approached Ty, where he leaned against the wall and typed into his phone.

"Unusual for security to walk away from an interview like that," Theo observed.

"Sonia was good people." Ty took a deep breath. "Her and Stan going missing like that, at almost the same time. There's something not right. You're looking for them and I'm not going to be the reason someone doesn't answer your questions."

"Would Halstead agree with you?" Patricia asked.

"Probably not." Ty pushed off the wall. "You said you had some questions for me?"

Theo admired the man for standing up for what's right over what his bosses might prefer. "I was wondering if you could tell us what time Stanley Webber left the building that day? He told his wife he was working late."

"Let's go to the control room." Ty was walking before he finished. "We can watch him leave on video."

The three of them backtracked through the building, riding the elevator to the basement level. A departure from the elegant decor of the floors above them, the halls were painted cinder block with drop ceilings. The fluorescent lighting reminded Theo of a hospital, which made him think of Richard Jensen. He was glad when they finally reached the security office.

"Welcome to my sanctuary," Ty said as he opened the door.

Inside, a man sat in a rolling desk chair watching a wall of screens, each representing a camera within the company grounds. Most of them were interior shots of empty halls. One covered the loading dock on the back of the building. There were several angles of the parking lot. But the two most interesting to the entourage covered the front entrance. One was an interior shot, catching anyone entering the building, and the other was from an exterior camera, catching anyone coming out.

"It's been a month," Theo commented. "You still have the footage?"

"We don't erase anything," Ty said. He put a hand on the shoulder of the man in front of the screens. "Pete. Take camera twenty-eight back to Friday, February third. Say five o'clock. Then fast forward, stopping on any male leaving the building."

"Yes, sir." Pete moved his hands and the image on the screen flickered. The date and time stamp showed them what Ty had requested. "Are we looking for anyone in particular?"

"Stanley Webber," Ty said.

"He's an easy one," Pete said.

"Why is that?" Theo asked.

"Mr. Webber walks with a limp," Pete explained. "Very distinct."

The four of them stared at the screen as the images zoomed past. Pete would slow the image down from time to time to show a man leaving the building. Once they knew it wasn't Stan, he would speed up again. The process took about twenty minutes until the image was dark, and the timestamp reported it being well after midnight.

"It looks like he never left," Pete said.

"Wait," Theo said. "His assistant said she left between three-forty-five and four. Can we find her leaving?"

"Sure thing," Pete typed, and the image jumped back to four o'clock.

He set the time at three-forty-five and moved the image forward until three-fifty-two, where he slowed it down to show Fiona walking out of the building.

"There she is," Ty said.

"Okay," Theo said. "Let's go from here until five, where we started."

Pete sped up the video, stopping it again almost immediately. The timestamp read four-sixteen. The image on the screen was a largish man limping through the door with a garment bag slung over his shoulder.

"He didn't work late," Patricia announced. "He left early."

29

No longer looking for electronics, Richard's search of the house slowed down considerably. With Nancy's help, they went back through rooms he had already destroyed, only this time they opened every file they came to and scanned the contents. The task was daunting because Sonia had hundreds of files at the house.

"Look for anything about Halstead," he told his sister again. "Particularly regarding Stanley Webber."

"I know," Nancy whined. "Let me read."

They sorted the files into three groups. One for anything non-work related like insurance papers, owner's manuals, personal taxes, car loans, the mortgage, etc. The second and largest group were Halstead files that, on examination, were too old to be a current problem, or had no reference to Stan or notes about issues. Leaving the third, and most important group for those files that involved Sonia's boss or notated an issue, no matter how small.

The process took hours, each more tedious than the one before. Nancy would normally complain about doing this type of work, but she was so happy to see her brother focusing on something that she didn't say a word. For his part, Richard seemed to grow more and more energetic as the day wore on. The dinner hour approached, and Nancy had to remind him they needed to eat. He resisted, wanting to complete the task at hand. But seeing the tower of files yet to go and the exhaustion in his sister's eyes, he relented, though he continued to work while she went to the kitchen to make sandwiches.

The sky was darkening by the time Richard shoved the last bite of his meal into his mouth. His body was sore. Despite the stationary bike, this was the most he had moved in a single day since leaving the hospital. Nancy was still working on her food, never having been a big eater, something Richard always teased her about. She looked up and caught him staring at her.

"What?"

"Thanks for helping me," he smiled. "And I don't mean with just this mess. Everything."

"You know I would do anything for you." She smiled back at him, letting it fade as she looked at the stacks of files. "What are you hoping to find in all this?"

Richard let out a deep breath. "I don't really know. Answers, I guess. I'm hoping I'll know it when I see it."

The look of sympathy she gave him made Richard uncomfortable.

"You know," he said. "It's getting late. You don't really have to keep doing this."

Nancy set her plate aside and pulled the top file off the stack closest to her. "It's going to take all night if you don't get busy."

With a chuckle, Richard got back to work. It took another two hours just getting through the initial sorting of the files. When they were done, they had a stack of about twenty meeting the criteria Richard had set. He stood, stretched, and snatched up the files, carrying them to the dining room, where he placed them at the head of the table.

Nancy followed, walking with her hand over her mouth to stifle a yawn.

"You should get some sleep," Richard told her.

"Are you going to bed?"

"No."

"Then neither am I." She walked through the dining room to the kitchen. "I'm making some coffee. Do you want some?"

"That would be good." He sat and slid the stack to the left corner. He took the top file and leaned back in the chair as he prepared to read.

The information in an Account Manager's files was confidential financial information pertaining to the clients of the company. They were not intended reading for the Account Manager's husband and sister-in-law. If anyone knew what the two of them were doing, Sonia would probably be terminated, if she ever returned.

With fresh coffee in hand, the siblings began reading through pages of spreadsheets, bank statements, transaction statements, internal memos, and copies of client letters. It was all very boring. But like highlighted passages in a textbook, sticky notes appeared throughout the files gaining scrutiny from the researchers.

Most were used to make finding the pertinent information from reports easier. Total costs, percentage of returns on investments, total losses incurred. They were just as boring as the files themselves. Richard focused on the other notes. The discrepancies, the glaring errors, the unexplained gaps. They identified three files that needed further scrutiny.

"What about this one?" Nancy presented a document like an auctioneer. "It looks like Sonia's handwriting on the note. It says, gain of nine actually loss of six."

"Let me see." Richard took the paper and skimmed through the contents. The letter sent to the client detailed the return on their previous six months' investments and projections for the next six. He held out his hand. "Give me the rest."

Nancy closed the folder and placed it in her brother's hand. She took the next one from the stack and settled in to read.

Richard reached for his now empty coffee cup, realizing it had been his second. Together they had gone through more than a dozen documents, and this was the fourth with notations of major issues.

He pulled the financial spreadsheets from the contents and checked the math line by line with a calculator. The eighteen-million-dollar investment now had a balance of $16,950,000, a net loss of six percent. Richard found the coinciding income report showing a balance of $19,650,000, an increase of nine percent.

Richard studied the two pages. The nine and the six had been inverted, resulting in a difference of two point seven million dollars on paper. It could have been a simple typo. But being the fourth example they had found, it looked like a deliberate deception to show greater success than was actual.

In each case, the signature on the spreadsheets belonged to Sonia Jensen, Richard's wife. And the signature on the financial reports was that of Stanley Webber, her boss. Richard felt sick to his stomach. It appeared that Stan was covering up losses to make Sonia look better.

Thinking back to that last night together, as they were leaving the party, Sonia had said something to Charles Halstead. She had asked him if Stan had talked to him about something. Charles had replied that he had, and that they would talk on Monday.

Richard shoved the papers back into the file and dropped it on the other three they had found. He closed his eyes and buried his face in his hands in a silent scream. The only thought racing through his mind was that Stan was behind whatever happened to Sonia to keep her from talking to Charles. Then he had run.

30

Detective Theo Morris set a fresh cup of coffee on his desk, removed his jacket to hang on the back of his chair, and picked up the inter-department envelope that had not been there the night before. He sat heavily and rocked back, tearing the seal on the envelope and pulling out the contents. He was still reading when his partner walked up with a small stack of papers in her hand.

"Toxicology report came back on Richard Jensen." Theo held up the pages.

Detective Stevens dropped her papers onto her desk and slid out of her coat. She draped the garment over the back of the chair, sat, and rolled forward until her elbows rested on the worn desktop. "What's it say?"

"He had Pentobarbital in his system," Theo reported.

"And that is?"

"A strong sedative," Theo said. "It wasn't on the list of medications that the doctor had him on."

"So, someone was coming to his room and pumping sedatives into his system?" Patricia questioned.

"That's what it looks like," Theo said. "But for what reason?"

"To keep him quiet," she suggested.

"We've talked to him twice," Theo was skeptical. "He doesn't know anything. Why keep him quiet?"

"Maybe we just haven't asked him the right questions," Patricia shrugged.

"If he knew something that would help us find his wife," Theo challenged, "don't you think he would offer the information regardless of what we asked?"

"Maybe he doesn't realize what he knows," Patricia said.

Theo let his mind wander as thoughts assaulted him from all sides. Something his first partner as a detective taught him when the clues didn't present themselves or seemed to point in random directions. Stop directing his thoughts and let them direct him. He closed his eyes for a moment and slowed his breathing. When he opened them again, he said, "What if Sonia wasn't the target?"

Patricia sat up straight. "You think Richard was the target?"

"I think we should consider it," Theo said.

"But that makes no sense," Patricia said. "If they wanted him dead, why sedate him? Why not just kill him?"

"The hit and run. It looked like an accident," Theo explained. "Green County thought it was an accident. We thought it was an accident. If he had died, no one would be looking for a murderer. We would be looking for a reckless driver. Killing him in the hospital would have risen suspicion."

"Taking Sonia rose suspicion," Patricia countered. "Sedating him solidified it. Why do that if you want to maintain it was an accident?"

"She could have left the scene on her own," Theo suggested. "If she hit her head, she could have been confused. She may have wandered off, got lost. Could be in a hospital somewhere with amnesia."

"That seems unlikely," Patricia said. "It's been a month. Surely her memories would be back by now."

Theo thought back to a case he had been on early in his detective career. An assault victim knocked unconscious. The beating had been brutal and when he woke up; he didn't even know who he was. He didn't remember being attacked, let alone who his assailant may have been. Two days later, it all came back to him. The man remembered walking down a side street and hearing a woman scream. He ran to help and found three men trying to drag her into an alley. When he tried to intervene, they jumped him. The woman escaped and called the police. Unfortunately for the man, the assault had broken his back and confined him to a wheelchair. It was rare for amnesia to last a month.

"True," Theo relented. He let his thoughts drift again. "Maybe she went looking for help but found trouble instead."

"You're suggesting someone crashed into them to kill Richard," Patricia said. "Then Sonia went to look for help and was picked up by an entirely different person, who then decided to keep her locked up in his basement?"

"A long shot," Theo said. "But possible."

"Two separate perps for one crime?" Patricia thought aloud.

"Technically, two separate crimes for one incident," Theo corrected. "But, yes. We should investigate registered sex offenders in a five-mile radius of the accident."

"It's a rural area," Patricia pointed out. "Should be a short list."

"Make it a ten-mile radius," Theo amended.

"I'll get a uniform on it."

"And if we think Richard may have been the target," Theo added. "We need to dig into his life a little deeper."

"Speaking of looking into people." Patricia lifted the papers she had been carrying. "It turns out that the detective in charge of Stanley Webber's case pulled his credit card information after he went missing."

"Saves us some time." Theo raised his eyebrows. "Anything interesting?"

"His last charge was at a restaurant the day he went missing," Patricia said.

"The mystery lunch meeting," Theo said. "What did they learn?"

"No one followed up," she said.

"What do you mean, no one followed up?" Theo growled.

"As far as I can tell," Patricia held up the papers. "No one did anything after the records were pulled."

"Let me see that." Theo held out his hand until she placed the papers in it. He flipped to the first page of the report until he found what he was looking for. "Oh. It was assigned to Sinclair."

"I didn't even notice," Patricia said.

Detective Sinclair had been on the case of a missing woman, Delia Ellington, the same time Stan's case had come to him. He had tracked Delia's movements for the day she disappeared and found himself at the door of a man she had been seeing after meeting on an online dating service. The detective knocked on the door, intending to ask some questions for background. There had been nothing to suggest any contact between the two of them for the week leading to her disappearance. The man wasn't suspect. The interview was just routine fact finding.

When Sinclair identified himself, the man pulled a gun and shot him right on his doorsteps. A neighbor called the police to report the shooting, and the suspect fled. Sinclair had been well liked, and every cop in the district wanted a piece of the killer. They brought the man in alive, but he didn't last the night. Suspicions circulated that officers stood guard while other prisoners beat him to death, but nothing could be proven. They found Delia chained in his basement, too late. She had been dead for at least two days. No one could fathom why he kept her after that.

"I guess we know why he didn't follow up," Theo sighed.

"No one's been looking for Stanley Webber?"

"Appears not," Theo sighed again. "You said his last charge was at a restaurant?"

"Yes."

"You up for an early lunch?"

"It's not even nine," Patricia argued. "Besides, I don't think we can afford to eat at this place."

"Where is it?"

"Stefano's Bistro."

"Bistro, huh?" Theo cringed. "That does sound expensive. Guess we'll have to settle for questioning them."

"It's been a month." Patricia put her coat back on. "Hope they still have something to give us."

31

Nancy always slept late. Her brother did not. Even as children, their parents would come downstairs to find Richard sitting in front of the television watching cartoons or playing with his toys, while Nancy slept until someone woke her. When she woke the next morning, Richard was not in his recliner, at the kitchen table or on the deck. She panicked. Knocking on his door softly at first, she increased the strength and repetition with her fear. Nancy finally opened the door, hoping to find him sitting on the edge of the bed, or maybe in the shower.

Shock and a whole new wave of panic hit her when she found the room empty, the door to the bathroom wide open. He was gone.

Nancy raced into the guest bedroom where she had been sleeping whenever she was able. Digging through her luggage, she found a pair of jeans and a t-shirt that didn't need to be washed quite as bad as the rest of her wardrobe, making a mental note to do laundry first chance she got. She shoved her limbs through the appropriate holes and stepped into a pair of shoes. Purse. Keys. Jacket. She was ready to go find her brother.

Nancy made it all the way to the front door before freezing in her tracks. She had no idea where to look. Since flying in, she had spent most of her time at the hospital or her hotel. After Richard had awakened, she dropped the hotel and moved into his home, but her horizons had not expanded. Hospital, hotel, Richard's home and a small grocery store at the edge of the neighborhood were the only places she had been.

She did not know where Richard might go. A doctor's appointment, to his office, a run for supplies, or a favorite coffee shop; Nancy had no clue where he had gone and wouldn't be able to find the places if she did. She stood motionless in her frustration until finally resigning herself to sit where she could watch the door and wait. Within just a few minutes, Nancy made her way to the kitchen to brew a pot of coffee.

She leaned back against the counter next to the coffeemaker, staring down at the floor, and letting her mind race with possibilities where her brother had gone. An object in the corner of her eye caught Nancy's attention, and she tilted her head to concentrate on it. Richard's cane came into focus and her panic renewed. He needed the cane to walk. The one possibility she had not thought of, until that moment, was that someone had taken him. They had taken Sonia.

What if they came for him? Pulling her cellphone out of her pocket, Nancy's hands shook. The police were just a phone call away. But if she was wrong …

She closed her eyes and inhaled deep into her lungs, trying to decide what to do. At the sound of the back door opening, her eyes popped wide open. Richard stepped into the kitchen and gave her a quick nod.

"Coffee smells good," he commented.

"Where have you been?" The panic could be heard in her voice.

"I went for a walk," Richard said. "Why? What happened?"

"What happened?" Her volume rose. "I woke up and my brother, who has barely moved since coming home from the hospital, was gone. You went for a walk? Without your cane?"

"I have to build up my strength again." Richard took two mugs out of the cabinet and poured the coffee. "And I don't really need the cane. It was just my way of not moving forward."

"Okay." Nancy accepted the offered cup and sat at the kitchen table. "I've been saying you need to move and get stronger. Why the sudden change?"

Richard sat across from his sister. She was not aware of the time he spent on the stationary bike. Hiding it from her was his way of keeping her from trying to limit how much he pushed himself. From her point of view, he hardly moved at all until he left the house just a day ago. He blew across the surface of his coffee and watched the ripples. They reminded him of fishing trips with his father. The bobber on the water's surface created the same ripples. "If I'm going to find Sonia, I need to get into shape."

"What?" Nancy became rigid. "Wait a minute. What we were doing last night was to find answers. You didn't say anything about trying to find her on your own. That's out of the question. It's too dangerous."

"Out of the question?" Richard almost laughed. "I don't need your permission."

"I think you do," his sister argued. "And I don't give it. No."

"Listen, sis," Richard's voice became softer. "I'm doing this. Just accept it. But you are right about one thing. It's dangerous, which is why you should go home."

"Go home?" Nancy looked as if she had been slapped. "Are you trying to get rid of me?"

Richard thought back to the motorcyclist who had tried to shoot him. The man had his name and address in his pocket. If they had his address, Nancy was in danger. Richard should have sent her away as soon as he found that paper. He would not wait any longer.

"Nancy. Listen." Richard's voice took a serious tone. "I meant what I said last night. I'm very grateful for everything you've done for me. I just want you to be safe. And I don't think it's safe here anymore. Besides, I'm sure David would like to get his wife back."

"Oh, Richard," Nancy moaned. "David and I separated six months ago."

"What? Why didn't you tell me?" Richard appeared to be slapped this time. "And don't you dare tell me it's because of my situation. That was long before the accident."

"I haven't told anyone," Nancy sighed. "At first, I thought it wouldn't last. We'd work things out. You know. Why tell everyone I'm separated if we were going to get back together anyway?"

"But now you don't think you'll be getting back together?"

"No."

"I thought David was this great guy," Richard said. "Understood you. Gave you space to help others."

"I thought so too," she grimaced. "Turns out giving me space just gave him more time to spend with his girlfriend."

"Oh, Nancy," her brother soothed her. "I'm so sorry."

"Don't be." Her imitation of confidence betrayed her. "I'm moving on."

"Then why haven't you told anyone?"

"Now it's old news," she said. "And I don't know how to bring it up in conversation."

"You said no one knows?"

"Just you."

"You haven't told Mom and Dad yet?"

"No."

"I don't envy you that one," Richard grinned. "Mom loves David."

"She doesn't love him," Nancy countered. "She just prefers him to me."

"Well, if it's any consolation, she prefers Sonia to me," Richard smiled.

"Everyone does," Nancy said.

The two of them laughed for a moment, forgetting about everything else. It felt good.

"You know," Richard said after the laughter stopped. "If you don't want to go home, you could always stay with Mom and Dad."

"After everything I've done for you," she crossed her arms. "This is how you repay me?"

Richard didn't respond.

"Wait." Nancy furrowed her brow. "You're serious about it not being safe here, aren't you?"

"If I look into this," Richard explained. "If I hit a nerve, they may come after me, I don't want you caught in the middle."

"What about you?" Nancy whined. She looked at him for an answer that wasn't coming. "You're really doing this, aren't you?"

"I am."

"Fine," she pouted. "I'll stay at Mom's. But if you get yourself killed, I'll kill you."

Richard smiled. "I'll keep that in mind."

32

Detectives Morris and Stevens arrived at Stefano's Bistro; a restaurant located on a stretch of road separating an upper-class neighborhood from a business district. They parked in the empty parking lot, having arrived before the posted hours of operation. Theo banged on the door with increasing repetition, drawing glances from staff members inside, but no one came to let them in. Growing angrier each time they ignored him, the detective grumbled as he power walked around the building to the delivery entrance. Patricia, amused, followed close behind.

A piece of cardboard between the back door and the frame prevented it from latching. Theo reached out and pulled the door open and held it out of his way as he walked into the backroom of the restaurant. To his right, a bulletin board hung, complete with acknowledgements, achievement awards and an employee schedule. Next to the board was a digital time clock that required an employee code.

To his left, a doorway opened into what appeared to be a break room. A small round table sat in its center, cluttered with dirty dishes and silverware. Soiled napkins and various food wrappers rounded out the decor. A young kid sat at the table, his face turned down to his phone. His fingers moved at lightning speed as he played a game, or texted. Theo studied the names on the schedule, broken into groups based on the positions the staff held. None of them stood out.

"Hey, who are you?" A man called out.

The two detectives turned toward the man at the end of the short hallway that spilled into the kitchen proper. When they did not respond fast enough, the man marched toward them with his jaw clenched. "How did you get in here?"

"The door was open." Patricia pointed.

"Open?" The man looked past them to the piece of cardboard still keeping it from latching. The man let out a heavy sigh, no doubt trying to decide who to fire. "What? Are you two selling something? Because you're wasting your time if you are."

"We're not selling anything." Theo reached into his pocket.

"You should really use the front door," the man said.

Theo pulled out his shield and held it up for the man to see. "We need to see the manager."

"Oh." The man focused on the detective's shield. "The manager's not here."

"And you are?" Theo asked.

"Jimmy," the man said. "Jimmy Nolan."

"Okay Jimmy," Theo said. "Where's the manager?"

"Late," The man tensed. "As usual."

"How late is 'as usual'?" Patricia asked. "Will he be here any minute or is it going to be a while?"

"Varies." Jimmy shrugged.

"So, who's in charge until he gets here?" Theo was growing weary of the man.

"That would be me, I guess." Jimmy gave them an insincere grin.

"Of course it is," Theo muttered.

"What?"

"Nothing," Theo said. "We're looking for information on a guest of yours."

"There's no one here," the man said. "We're not open yet. We don't have any guests."

"That's okay," Patricia said. "Because the guest we need information on was here about a month ago."

"A month ago?" Jimmy grumbled. "Are you serious?"

"We have a date." Theo pulled out his phone.

"Don't you need a warrant or something?"

"We will get one if we have to," Theo said. "But we're hoping you might help us."

"Why would I do that?"

"The man we're looking for is missing," Patricia explained. "And he may be responsible for a woman's disappearance."

"A real winner then?" Jimmy sighed.

"Exactly."

"Fine," Jimmy agreed. "What can I do?"

"I don't suppose you have security video of your dining room," Theo began.

"No." Jimmy shook his head. "And any video we do have records over itself every two weeks."

"Okay," Theo shifted his focus. "Can we look at your credit card receipts for February 3rd?"

"They'll be in the office." The man turned and walked away.

The detectives hesitated before following Jimmy through the kitchen, filled with staff members prepping various food items for the day. One man they passed had four large clear containers at his station. Two, filled to the brim with sliced onions and one with slivered onions, were covered with lids and labeled. The last, partially filled with diced onions, sat closest to the prep-cook who worked at lightning speed, chopping the vegetables on the cutting board before him. Having worked in a kitchen as a young man, Theo cringed at the sight.

Arriving at a door with a nameplate identifying it as the office, Jimmy produced a key to unlock it, revealing a cramped room. To the left, a small desk occupied the near corner, with a table wedged between it and the far wall. A small safe tucked underneath looked old and well used. Opposite them stood a chrome coated wire rack, common within the restaurant industry, its shelves loaded with dozens of boxes marked with dates and identifiers written in permanent marker. Jimmy focused his attention on them.

"Hey, boss." A short, stocky Hispanic man wearing a chef coat stepped into the small space between Patricia and the door. "Didn't you want to run the Mahi Mahi special today?"

"Yes," Jimmy barked. "What kind of question is that?"

"Well," the chef grimaced. "We don't have any Mahi Mahi."

"What?" Jimmy growled. "I ordered three cases."

"Yea," the chef muttered. "They sent Swordfish instead."

"Swordfish?" The man sighed and looked up to the ceiling. "Okay. Prep the Swordfish. I'll get you a recipe. And tell Angie to change the special board. We'll have to double the price."

"Will do, boss." The chef smiled, his head bobbing as he backed out.

"Boss?" Theo turned to Jimmy.

"Yes," Jimmy muttered. "I'm the manager. Wasn't sure why you were looking for me."

Theo frowned. "The receipts?"

Jimmy scanned the boxes until he found the one he was looking for. Holding the boxes above it with one hand, he pulled the one he wanted out, letting the others fall to fill the vacant space. He placed his find on the table and lifted the top. "Here you go. February. They're bundled by day."

Theo looked inside. Hundreds of bundles of receipts, each bound by a small rubber band, filled the box.

"I was expecting thirty," the detective said. "Why so many?"

"Each server handles their own receipts," Jimmy explained. "So, I guess they're bundled by server, by day. Now, if you'll excuse me, I have a Swordfish crisis to handle."

The detectives glanced at one another before positioning the box between them. They began the meticulous task of pulling out each bundle and checking the date in search of February 3rd.

33

With Nancy's things packed into her rental, Richard stood on the front porch of his home, using his cane to support most of his weight. The walk he took had been what Sonia used to call a power walk. Now his leg muscles were reminding him how long it had been since he had performed such an exercise, and that he was still recovering from the damage of the hit and run. He forced a smile while waving to his sister as she backed out of his driveway.

Once she was gone from view, the smile faded, and he went inside. He propped the cane against the nearest chair and walked to the kitchen.

He and Sonia spent almost a year looking for the right house to call home. His wife fell in love with the modern-Victorian and Richard had bid over asking to insure its purchase. The house was two stories and had a finished basement. Since returning from the hospital, Richard had not left the main floor. The few changes of clothing he had, Nancy retrieved from his bedroom for him.

In the kitchen, he stood at the top of the stairs that led to the basement. His head bowed, he studied the steps that would take him to the entertainment part of their home. He started down, holding firm to the rail. The bottom of the steps ended in the game room with a pool table, a foosball table, a card table and more. A door to the left led to the media room, with projector television and theater style seating. Next came Richard's home office, purposely located away from Sonia's office on the main floor. Otherwise, he would get nothing done.

On the opposite wall was a single door. Richard walked over and opened it, reaching for the light switch just inside. Fluorescent bulbs came to life to reveal the utility room and storage. Lining the walls were shelves and stacks of tubs, each labeled with large, bold lettering.

The rigorous organization, driven by Sonia, had taken weeks to complete. In the thick of it, Richard thought the work was too much effort and a waste of time. Since then, he turned out to be the one maintaining the detailed system. He could not help but grin as he walked through the space, remembering his small wife barking orders at him as they worked. Directing and redirecting him on where things should go.

Her obsession with organization was only one quirk Richard discovered about Sonia during the early months of their courtship: a relationship that Richard knew only came to be by chance.

He wasn't supposed to be there when Nancy brought her college friend home for a weekend visit. Richard was sitting in the living room with his parents, discussing his future. Days after Mexico City, he left his job and was unsure what to do with his life. His parents were discussing just that while he tried to look interested. In the middle of him not listening to their advice, his sister walked into the room with her ever-present smile. Behind her, a petite girl of the same age strode through, wearing a yellow sundress. Sonia's dark brown hair, pulled back in a ponytail, swayed from side to side as she followed Nancy through the room.

To Richard, she was the most beautiful woman he had ever seen, and he could not take his eyes off her. He could no longer hide the fact that he wasn't listening to his parents as his gaze followed her through the room. Sonia carried herself in a way that was filled with confidence and grace. Her smile captivated him, being the only one Richard had ever seen that made Nancy's seem insignificant. When he realized he was staring at her, he also realized Sonia was staring back at him. There had been a third girl with them that day who, to this day, Richard couldn't remember anything about. He thought she was at their wedding, though.

Reaching the end of the shelving, Richard rounded a corner and came to a door secured by a padlock. He dug into his pocket for the key, thinking back to the first time his wife encountered the door. Sonia asked him what was so important it had to be locked away, even joking about him having another woman tied up in a secret room. They both laughed at the idea. He assured her nothing behind the door would be of interest to her, explaining that he had sensitive information from past jobs that needed to be kept secure. Though partially true, he felt that conversation had been the greatest lie of his marriage.

Richard slid the key into the lock. Holding steady, he considered what opening it would mean to his life. Once he turned the key, there would be no turning back. A few months ago, the idea of going through the door would have never crossed his mind. But now, Sonia was missing and someone was responsible. He twisted the key and let the lock drop to the floor.

Pulling the door open, Richard smelled the dust that had accumulated in the room over the years. He coughed and turned on the lights, which flickered to life and illuminated the small room. On one side, a worktable with various tools dominated the space. To the left were neatly arranged crates he hadn't touched since placing them there. Richard lifted a crate and moved it to a bench in the center of the room. He flipped the lid up and stared at the contents; a life he had left far behind.

34

Standing in the narrow office of Stefano's Bistro, the detectives sorted their bounty of credit card receipts. After collecting the ones dated February 3rd, they returned the rest to the box from which came. A popular restaurant, they still had hundreds of pieces of paper. Patricia muttered her disappointment at the obvious absence of the customer's name sometimes printed below the signature line.

The kitchen was growing louder. The manager and some of the staff stepped into and out of the office from time to time. Occasionally, employees would begin asking questions as they entered, stopping short when they saw the detectives rather than their boss, and retreating in confused silence.

The detectives paid them no mind, as they began looking for payments matching the dollar amount that appeared in Stan Webber's credit card statement. Theo had learned years ago that the time printed on the receipt did not always match the time on the credit card statement. If a customer added a tip, the time stamp would update to when the server entered it into the system. There might be a delay in the transfer between the restaurant's machine and the bank, a fact that almost cost Theo a case. A restaurant's internet blinked out and sent the data an hour later, giving a killer an alibi. Luckily, the detective found video of the man walking into his victim's home, still carrying the to-go bag.

After finding more than a dozen receipts with the matching dollar amount, the detectives spread them out to examine the signatures. It seemed many of the patrons considered themselves to be doctors or just didn't care about legibility. The one they zeroed in on was impossible to read, but for the first letter of each name. Written with flair were a capital 'S' and 'W'. It had to be Stanley Webber.

The next cumbersome task was checking the server identifier, the table number and the timestamp to identify who Stan had lunched with that day. When they finished, one possibility stood out. Patricia went in search of the manager while Theo boxed up the remaining papers.

"Are we out of walnuts?"

Theo leaned against the table with his head down. The voice brought him out of his thoughts, and he looked to the doorway where a woman wearing a chef's coat stood. "What?"

"Walnuts," the woman repeated. "I can't find any. Are we out?"

Theo furrowed his brow, remaining silent.

"Are we out or not?" She put her hands on her hips. "I need to get the banana bread in the ovens."

"Maybe you should ask Jimmy," Theo suggested. "I don't work here."

The woman appeared confused. "What are you doing in here then? Are you interviewing for the assistant manager's job?"

Before Theo could respond, the woman spun on her heels and walked away. Seconds later, the detective could hear the woman arguing with Jimmy. Apparently, she thought she should be up for the assistant's job. She didn't understand why he was interviewing outsiders. At no time did she ask about the walnuts. Then everything went silent. A moment later, Patricia walked into the office.

"Someone's getting an earful." She hooked her thumb over her shoulder.

Jimmy appeared a short time after. "Sorry about that. Some people forget their place."

"No worries." Theo pushed off the table. "Can you get the customer information off of this receipt?"

"Uh, no." Jimmy took the offered paper. "I can't get it. And you won't be able to without a warrant, I'm pretty sure."

"That's what I figured," the detective nodded, reaching for the receipt.

"We could check the reservation log," the manager suggested.

"How would that help?" Patricia asked.

"We write in the log what table they were taken to," Jimmy explained. "That way we know they aren't still waiting to be seated."

Theo looked at the manager with a mixture of hope and disdain. Hope that they might be able to retrieve the name of the person Stan had his mystery lunch meeting with. Disdain that Jimmy had mentioned nothing earlier. They could have saved an hour of searching through receipts.

"Where's the log?" Theo asked.

"Follow me." Jimmy led the two detectives through the kitchen and dining room to the front desk. He pulled out the reservation book and flipped through the pages until he came to the one with the February third entries. He looked at the receipt. "Table thirty-seven."

He scanned the page for the table number until he found an entry about an hour and a half before the time on the receipt. He turned the book to face the detectives and pointed.

"Parker Belton," Theo read, somewhat relieved that it was the only name on the reservation and he had not wasted the time going through the receipts. He wrote the name down in his notes. To the manager, he gestured with the notepad. "Thank you."

"No problem," Jimmy shrugged. "Hope you find the guy...and the woman."

35

Richard stood in his bedroom looking into the same mirror where he had seen Sonia applying her makeup hundreds of times before. The memory of his last time being in the room stirred up an assault of emotions that threatened to overwhelm him.

He gathered himself and examined his reflection. His signature suit and tie hung in the closet. He owned dozens of them, encouraged by his wife to look the part of the consummate professional anytime he left home. Sonia's advice had helped him land more contracts than he had before. In time, it became his natural choice of attire for all occasions. Current circumstances compelled him to forgo his usual look for something more conducive for adapting to anything that might come up.

He wore clothing he had not seen in years and had not worn in more than a decade. They still fit, though a little more snug than he remembered. The black leather jacket had aged in storage, making it stiff and brittle. It would do for now but would need to be replaced. He could not go without it, as it hid two features he did not want known. One was the bullet-proof vest he wore beneath his shirt. The second was a pair of pistols, one nestled in a shoulder holster, the other tucked away in his belt at the small of his back. After all these years, it still felt natural for them to be there.

Years before programming, before Sonia, and before Mexico City; Richard had worked for a private security firm that worked off book jobs for the government. Recruited from the army where he served as a Ranger, the money wasn't what swayed him to give up a job he had no intention of leaving. The money was extreme, but the offer of having the freedom to conduct missions the way he determined, rather than by officers who put him and his team in harm's way, was too much to pass up. It gave him the opportunity to do a lot of good things, a lot of important things. And everything went well until that last assignment, the Mexico City job.

He sighed and returned his attention to the mirror, wondering if he might be over thinking the situation he was moving toward. He shook his head at his reflection. The man on the motorcycle was not a random attack. He had Richard's name and address. He needed to be prepared in the event of another attempt. Bending at the waist, he brushed at the crease in his pants, the result of being folded in a box for twelve years. It had no effect.

Making his way downstairs, he grabbed his cane on the way out the door. Though he still limped, Richard didn't need the support. He took the cane for the added sympathy it might invoke. Likely to cause others to underestimate him, it also gave him an immediate weapon if the need arose. Richard didn't think he would need to defend himself where he was going, but until he knew who was involved in Sonia's disappearance and who wanted him out of the way, he would remain cautious. On the more practical side, if the pain grew in his leg more pronounced, he would have it with him.

Richard made it all the way to the garage before the reality hit him that since his car was totaled in the accident, he would have to take Sonia's Mercedes. Clicking the remote he carried, the garage door rose, revealing the car his wife had not wanted when she first saw it. After the test drive, she wouldn't consider anything else. He remembered the smile on her face when they drove it home. He missed that smile.

A deep breath to still his nerves and he was on his way. A half hour later, he was pulling into the parking lot of Halstead Enterprises, looking for a place to park. The parking sticker in the window would allow him to use employee parking, but he decided against it. Instead, he found a space near the center of the main lot. He stepped out, clutching the cane as if his life depended on it and stood by the Mercedes, scanning the lot. There seemed to be more cars than usual, not that he spent much time at the building.

Conscious to lean on the cane as he limped to the entrance, he kept his head bowed and his cap pulled down to obscure his face. Underneath the bill, his eyes darted about, looking for any sign of threat. What he thought a bunch of finance executives were going to do he wasn't sure.

The front door opened just before he reached it and a young man in business attire walked out clutching a small case. He did a double take when he saw the injured man approaching and reached back to catch the closing door, holding it for him to enter. Richard thanked him as he passed.

The lobby, like the parking lot, was more crowded than he remembered. The seats were filled with people waiting for their names to be called. Richard ignored them, stepped up to the receptionist and waited for her to finish a phone conversation.

"Are you here for the interview?" She dropped the receiver onto its cradle. Without waiting for an answer, she continued. "Name and appointment time?"

"Richard Jensen," he introduced himself. "No time."

"You can't just walk in for an interview." The woman looked up and gasped. "Oh, God. You said Jensen. You're Sonia's husband."

"That's me."

"I'm so sorry," the receptionist said. "Why are you here? I mean, what can I do for you?"

"I thought I might pop in and see Charles." Richard gave her a sad, half smile. "If he's available."

"Oh, uh," she stammered. "Let me see what I can do."

She picked up the phone and made a quick call. Richard grinned and leaned on his cane while he waited. When she finished, she looked up at him. "Mr. Halstead will see you."

"Thank you." He nodded and started limping toward the elevators.

"Mr. Jensen."

Richard ignored the woman's attempts to call him back. No doubt she intended to have someone escort him through the building. He had been there enough times to know where he was going. Though he had never stepped onto the top floor, he felt he could find his way.

One elevator opened and Richard stepped forward only to back pedal seconds later to allow space for a young woman in a suit stepping out. As soon as she was clear, he darted inside and chose the twelfth-floor button to close the doors. No one stopped him.

Th elevator was nothing special. It looked like any other of the thousands of elevators Richard had been on. But knowing that the last time he had been in this one was with Sonia struck him hard. He closed his eyes, took a deep breath, and held it.

It had been about six months before the Halstead party, on a Friday. Sonia had taken the day off so the two of them could go to the Lake House for a three-day weekend. Unfortunately, she had forgotten some papers that she wanted to work on while they relaxed on the deck. She had insisted on Richard accompanying her to the office to minimize the chance someone would stop her for questions. The plan worked well until the ride back down. A new account manager ended up on the same elevator and would not stop talking until he disembarked several floors later. Sonia apologized to her husband and the two of them had a good laugh.

The memory, like most of Sonia, reminded him how much he missed his wife. Richard opened his eyes and checked the number displayed above him. He focused on the eight and then the nine as he controlled his nerves. When the emotion subsided, he let the air out through his lips. The elevator stopped and he lowered his eyes as the doors slid away.

Richard felt like he was stepping into a different building. In stark contrast to the bright lighting of the office spaces, the décor floor was a mixture of warm colors and stained woods. Speakers in the ceiling filled the air with soft music, giving off a sauna vibe, or maybe a doctor's waiting room.

Clutching the cane tight in his hand, Richard stepped off the elevator. A woman sitting behind a desk looked up at him with an expectant smile. He nodded at her and forced a grin.

"Charles?"

The woman held her smile. "Mr. Jensen. He's ready for you."

She gestured toward the door behind her.

Inside, another drastic change in decor greeted Richard. The dark stained wood was almost black. A conference table behind a wall of glass stretched across the room next to floor-to-ceiling windows. Across from it, behind an enormous desk screaming dictator, he found Charles, sitting in a room designed to make him look powerful, but made him appear quite small. Deeper into the space was a lounge area, leather seating and ambient lighting. A fireplace gave it a lodge feel.

"Richard." Charles stood and came around the desk to meet him part way with a firm handshake. "What brings you here?"

"I wanted to talk to you," Richard repeated what he had told the receptionist downstairs. "If you have a few minutes."

"Of course." Charles gestured toward the lounge as he eyed his guest's cane. "Let's sit in here, where you'll be more comfortable."

The men chose two chairs separated by a small table. After Richard declined the offer of a drink, Charles poured himself a tumbler full of a dark alcoholic beverage from an unmarked decanter. He dropped two ice cubes into the liquid and swirled the glass in his hand as he walked back to sit.

Richard settled into the softest leather he had ever felt and for the first time wondered how much the man sitting with him might be worth.

"Before we begin." Charles sipped at his drink, seeming to savor it. "Has anyone reached out to you about Sonia's death benefits?"

"We don't know she's dead." Richard frowned. Death benefits. The term seemed to be an oxymoron. What benefit was there in dying?

"No one has seen her for a month," Charles said. "I just assume."

"Well don't," Richard snapped. "I have to believe she's alive."

An awkward silence fell between the two. Richard inhaled deep into his lungs to calm his nerves. Charles took a long drink attempting to do the same.

"So, tell me." Charles sat back with glass in hand. "What did you want to talk to me about?"

"Well." Richard suddenly wished he had accepted that drink. "I wanted to ask you about Stan."

"Stan?" Caught by surprise, Charles choked on the name. "Stan Webber?"

"That's right."

"What on earth for?"

"He vanished the same time Sonia did," Richard explained. "One theory the police have is that they were having an affair that went wrong. Stan took Sonia out of jealousy or something and has her locked away somewhere."

Charles laughed. "That's absurd. The idea that Stan would kidnap Sonia is ridiculous. But the idea that the two of them were carrying on some kind of relationship is beyond laughable."

"That's what I thought," Richard nodded. "But since there isn't much evidence, and because of the timing. I thought maybe her disappearance and his might be related."

"I guess that makes sense." Charles sipped.

"The night of the party," Richard said. "When we were leaving, Sonia asked you if Stan had told you about something. Something you said you would discuss with her on that Monday. Do you remember what it was?"

"You can't possibly think I had something to do with all this?" Charles defended.

"No." Richard held his hands up. "Of course not. I just wanted to get an idea of what they may have been working on. Just to give me a starting point."

"I promise you it wasn't anything worth kidnapping Sonia over," Charles said. "You know Sonia. Newly promoted, she had some ideas for the department. Just business stuff."

"And Stan wasn't threatened by that?"

"Are you kidding?" Charles grinned and took a long drink. "Anything Sonia did just made Stan look better. He was far from threatened."

"Just had to ask," Richard said. "Is there anything you can tell me about Stan that might help me?"

"I don't know what I could tell you," Charles said. "But I'll try."

The two of them chatted for a few minutes about Stan, about Sonia, about the work they did together. The men discussed what the future looked like for them both without the dynamic personality of the woman taken from them might look like.

"Well, I should go," Richard announced. "I've taken far too much of your time."

"Nonsense," Charles said. "It was good getting to know you better."

"Still."

"I do have some things to get back to," Charles sighed. "Listen. As much as I hated doing it, we had to clear out Sonia's office. Business doesn't wait. Let me have Ty meet you. He can help you get her belongings."

"Ty?"

"He's our Head of Security," Charles explained. "Nice man, if not a little intense at times."

Charles pulled out his phone and made a quick call.

"Okay." Charles put the phone away. "All set. Just head back out. He'll meet you."

Richard stood, making a show of stretching his back and working the kink out of his leg. With the support of the cane, he returned the way he had come.

It had been an interesting conversation. He learned things he didn't know. But the one detail that stood out was what Charles claimed to be the topic of his interaction with Sonia as they left the party. Sonia did not know the promotion was coming before the party that night. She wouldn't have discussed her ideas for changes in the department with Stan ahead of time. Charles Halstead had just lied to his face.

36

How is this for luck?" Patricia looked up at her partner. "There is only one Parker Belton in the entire metro area."

Theo sat at his desk, rubbing his eyes to alleviate the strain of staring at the computer screen for too long. His own search for who Parker Belton had taken a detour into the life of Stanley Webber. The man had an interesting story. A straight 'A' student throughout high school, his GPA was blemished by a single 'B' from a gym class. Apparently, he was not athletic enough. Stan spent his college years on the coast where he continued with his high marks while majoring in Finance and minoring in music. He was an accomplished saxophone player. After graduating top of his class, he took a job with a fledgling company, Halstead Enterprises. He had spent his entire career with them. Theo lowered his hand to his coffee mug and his eyes to his desk.

"That's good." He did a quick scan of the names on the guest list that Mrs. Halstead had finally sent to them. "He wasn't at the party, unless he was someone's plus one. What do we know about him?"

Patricia moved the computer mouse and clicked on the man's name. She scanned the information until she found what she was looking for.

"It says he's a lawyer," Patricia said.

"Is he a corporate lawyer?" Theo asked. "Does he work for Halstead?"

The younger detective opened a search engine and typed in the name. Far too many results appeared. She added the word lawyer to the search field narrowing the results to just a few. She selected the one that lived locally and the man's photo filled her screen. The image was from a website for the offices Friedman and Bouche Law.

"No." She shook her head. "And no."

"Don't tell me he's a divorce attorney," Theo said.

If he met with a divorce attorney, the theory that Stan Webber left his wife and ran away with Sonia would come back to the forefront. Not really a crime, unless he took Sonia against her will. Although the hit-and-run and the drugging of Richard in the hospital were crimes. Both suggested some level of foul play was involved.

"He's a criminal lawyer." Detective Stevens looked up from her reading.

"Really?" Theo shifted his weight in his chair, causing it to squeak in protest. "Why would Stanley Webber be meeting with a criminal lawyer?"

"Maybe he's under investigation."

"Could be why he ran," Theo suggested.

"Do you know anyone in White-Collar Crimes?"

"I know just who to call." Theo picked up his phone, scrolled through his contact list until he came to the one he needed, hesitating just a moment before clicking the call button. Answered after the first ring, he said, "Hey, Evie. It's Theo."

"This can't be Theo," the woman argued. "Theo's dead."

"What?"

"That's the only reason I can think of for him not to have called me like he said he would."

"Right," Theo said. "And I'm calling."

"It's been six months, Theo!" Evie raised her voice loud enough that Patricia heard.

"True, but..."

"And I bet you're not calling to apologize," Evie accused.

Theo did not answer.

"I knew it," she snapped. "What is it? Why are you calling?"

Theo took a deep breath. "It's about a case I'm working on."

"Of course it is," Evie grumbled. "Well, what is it?"

"We're working on a possible kidnapping," Theo said.

"Possible?" Evie snapped. "You call yourself a detective and you don't even know if your victim was kidnapped or not?"

"You're not going to make this easy, are you?"

"Why should I?"

"Point taken," Theo acknowledged. "Okay. One of our suspects has disappeared. And we just learned that the last day anyone saw him, he met with a criminal lawyer."

"And you want to know if we have an open investigation on him?"

"If you don't mind."

"What's his name?" She let out an audible sigh.

"Stanley Webber," Theo answered. "I appreciate it."

"Whatever."

Theo could hear the clicks of her keyboard. When they went silent, she said, "No open investigations."

"Any closed?"

"No investigations."

"Then why was he meeting with a criminal lawyer?" Theo thought aloud.

"How would I know?" Evie said. "Maybe they knew each other. Maybe, since he's a suspect, he wanted to get ahead of the legalities of the crime he was about to commit. Why don't you just ask the lawyer? If it was about a case, he'll tell you he can't discuss it. If not, he might be of help."

"Thanks, Evie," Theo said. "I owe you one."

"One?"

"Two?"

"Not even close," she said. "I have to go."

"Thanks again."

The line was dead.

"I take it Evie's not a fan," Patricia smirked.

"Not at the moment," Theo confirmed. "Where is Parker Belton's office? We're going to pay him a visit."

37

"So, you're Sonia Jensen's husband?" Ty Cunningham pressed the basement button on the elevator panel.

"I am," Richard looked up as the doors closed. The numbers above the door counted down their descent.

"Sorry for your loss," the man said. "She was a great lady."

Richard didn't respond. Everyone assumed Sonia was dead, that her body would be discovered in a shallow grave somewhere. Richard refused to let his mind go there. They rode the rest of the way down in silence. The doors opened, and the men stepped out into a stale concrete hallway. The head of security led the way to the room where Sonia's things were being stored.

"Why the basement?" Richard asked as they entered.

"Excuse me?" Ty asked as he pulled a box from the shelving and set it on the table in the center of the room.

Richard pulled the box to him and looked inside. Along with various office supplies she had purchased over the years, he saw a snapshot of her career. Her framed diploma and various certificates stood on end to one side, held in place by the several awards presented to her over the years. Richard saw a portrait of himself that he couldn't remember posing for. His appearance and darker hair suggested it was taken early in their relationship. He made a mental note, when all of this was behind them, to get her something more recent.

"Why are Sonia's things down here?" Richard asked. "In the basement."

"It's been a month," Ty explained. "They're interviewing for a replacement. Had to have the office cleared."

"What about Stan?"

"Stan?" Ty frowned. "You mean Webber?"

"Yes," Richard nodded. "Are his belongings down here?"

"Well, no."

"Why not?" Richard asked. "It's been a month."

"True," Ty agreed. "But they aren't interviewing for his replacement. Not yet anyway."

"What if she comes back?"

"I don't know," Ty admitted. "It's not my call. I clean out the offices they tell me to clean out."

"How well did you know them?" Richard searched through the smaller items in the box.

"Sonia and Stan?"

"That's who we're talking about," Richard said. "I mean, you said Sonia was a great lady. So, you must have known her."

"I knew her," Ty confirmed. "I don't know that I could say I knew her well."

"What about Stan?"

"I knew him," Ty said. "I know all of the execs."

Richard finished looking through the items in the box and packed them back into place. "One theory the police are looking at is that they were having an affair and Stan took her before running off. Jealousy or something."

"Seriously?" Ty was shocked. "I would have never thought that."

"So, you never saw signs of them being a couple?"

"Hell, no." Ty shook his head. "All Sonia ever talked about was you."

Richard grinned at that. "As Head of Security, you would be the one to arrange any kind of protection detail, right?"

"Protection detail?" Ty laughed. "We aren't dealing with movie stars or politicians here. We don't do protection details. Why would you ask that?"

"Just curious."

The night of the party, Carolyn said she was working with Stan on something to do with security. Stan was the President of Customer Accounts, nothing to do with security. Richard didn't know if Carolyn was lying to him, or if Stan had hired person protection. Whatever the reason, Richard believed it less likely Stan had taken Sonia and more likely his wife became caught up in whatever danger the man was in.

"It's all there." Ty pointed at the box.

"I'm sure it is." Richard had been standing motionless, staring at Sonia's things. "I guess I should be going."

"Stan and Sonia together," Ty laughed again. "Now, had you asked about Stan and Fiona, I might have believed it. I always wondered about them."

"Who's Fiona?"

"Stan's assistant," Ty said. "They were pretty close."

"With him gone, whose assistant is she now?" Richard asked.

"No ones," Ty said. "As of this morning, she's on leave."

"Can you tell me her last name?"

"Delaney," Ty said. "Fiona Delaney."

Richard lifted the box and had to adjust to keep it from pressing against his shoulder holster. Ty looked at him, his eyes narrowing.

"Mr. Jensen," Ty said. "Why would you come into my building armed?"

38

Theo and Patricia stepped out of the elevator on the fourth floor of the office building that housed the law office where Parker Belton worked into a short hallway. Although the directory showed the law firm as the only occupants of the floor, they faced three doors. The closest one identified Friedman and Bouche Law. The ornate glass entry listed the named partners, six in all. Belton's name was not among them.

The detectives pushed the doors open and walked into the simple yet elegant lobby. The name of the firm stretched across the wall behind the receptionist. She looked up when they entered, assessing their appearance with her eyes. Two men passed from one doorway to another, dressed in expensive tailored suits. Theo was very aware of how the off-the-rack suit he wore looked, but didn't care. He pulled his shield out as he approached. His partner did the same.

"Detectives Morris and Stevens," he announced. "We need to speak to one of your employees. A Parker Belton."

"Mr. Belton?" Surprise registered on her face. She turned to her computer and typed. "Mr. Belton is with a client. If you can have a seat, I will let him know you are here, when he is finished."

"Listen, we don't ..."

Theo's hand on her arm cut Patricia short.

"Does your computer tell you how much time is blocked out for this client?" The detective pointed at the monitor.

"Yes."

"And how much longer will he be?" Theo asked.

"About ten minutes," she said.

"Let us know when he's finished." Theo thanked the woman and wandered to a chair where he could sit.

Patricia grunted and followed her partner.

"We need to talk to him now," Patricia grumbled. "So we can move on."

"He's a lawyer," Theo reminded her. "He's going to be reluctant to talk to us. There's no point in agitating him before we ask the first question."

The woman crossed her arms and maintained a frustrated appearance standing over him.

Theo had dealt with more than his fair share of lawyers over the years. From prosecuting attorneys arguing with him about evidence, defense attorneys trying to get the criminals he had arrested released from jail, to civil attorneys trying to sue him for things he hadn't done, the detective had a disliking for lawyers. But he had no greater disdain than he had for his ex-wife's divorce attorney. That lawyer, above all others, was the one Theo hated the most. All that aside, he had, over the years, learned how to deal with the over-inflated egos of the suited pests. Rule number one was to always let them think they were in control.

They waited in silence, Patricia brooding and Theo using his phone to check his emails and messages. A small parade of suits and briefcases filed past them and out the doors. They mumbled amongst themselves and did not give the detectives a second glance. To be honest, most didn't even give them a first glance.

"He'll see you now," the receptionist called out to them.

Theo pulled himself to his feet and the two detectives followed the woman's directions to an office on the interior wall, spacious but sorely in need of the windows it did not have.

"Come in." The man behind the desk was standing. "Take a seat."

Parker Belton did not project the refinement Theo expected. A man of average height, he did not wear the usual high priced, crisp attire. Rather, he sported a pair of dark brown slacks with a pale green jacket that hung on him like a baggy sack. It made Theo think of a child's drawing of a tree.

The lawyer directed them to the chairs across from him, holding his position until the detectives sat. Theo noticed the man's belt cinched tight across his waist, causing the material of his slacks to bunch up. It appeared the tree had recently lost several pounds. As Parker settled into his seat, Theo noted the gauntness of the man's face, leaving him to wonder about the lawyer's health.

Parker sat back, resting his elbows on the arms of his executive chair that swallowed his frame, and clasped his hands together. He watched guests with anticipation. "I understand you're detectives. Are you in need of legal counsel or are you on detective business?"

"Detective Theo Morris and my partner Detective Patricia Stevens," the detective introduced. He glanced down at the nameplate on the front of the desk. "You are Parker Belton?"

"That's what they call me," the lawyer grinned. "What is it I can do for you? I don't have much time before my next meeting."

"We need to ask you about a client of yours," Patricia said.

"Well," Parker frowned. "You both should know that I can't discuss my clients."

Theo held up his hands. "What my partner meant to say is … We don't even know that he was a client. But we know you met with the man for lunch.

And we need you to tell us anything you can about him and what the meeting was about."

"Even if it was just a meeting to discuss whether I would take him on as a client or not," Parker said. "I can't discuss it with you."

"Listen," Theo sighed. "I'll give you his name. Then you can tell us if you can talk to us about him."

"Fine," Parker nodded. "Who are we talking about?"

"The name's Stanley Webber," Patricia responded.

"Stanley Webber?" Parker searched his memory for the familiar name.

"You had lunch with him at Stefano's on February third," Theo said.

"Oh, wait." Parker pulled a date book to him and flipped through the pages. "Right. I remember him."

"Can you talk to us about him?"

"I'm not really sure," Parker hesitated.

"What does that mean?" Patricia asked.

"Our conversation was hypothetical," Parker explained. "A series of 'what if' scenarios about a 'friend' of his." Parker made quote marks with his fingers. "I knew it was him we were discussing, but he never confirmed it."

"So, technically," Theo surmised. "You could talk to us."

"I would prefer to get approval from the man," Parker shrugged.

"That won't be possible," Theo said.

"It won't?" Parker sat forward. "Is he dead?"

"Missing," Theo corrected.

"Is that why he never followed up?" Parker asked. "When did he go missing?"

"As far as we can tell," Theo answered. "He met with you, returned to work. But after he left for the day no one ever saw him again."

"He went missing that same day?"

"That's right," Theo clarified.

"That was a month ago," Parker declared. "It's taken you this long to talk to me?"

"The original detective on the case was killed in the line of duty," Theo explained. "My partner and I just found out about it yesterday."

Parker sat back in his chair and focused on a point above their heads. "Well, given the circumstances, I think I can talk to you."

"Thank you," Theo grinned. "What was the purpose of your meeting with him?"

"Hypothetically," Parker reiterated. "Mr. Parker wanted to know what his friend's options might be."

"Options?" Theo asked. "Options for what?"

"He suggested a friend of his had uncovered some information," Parker said. "Very damaging to another individual but potentially damaging to themselves as well. I had the impression that he wasn't sure who was responsible, but knew he was at risk if the information came out."

"What kind of information?" Patricia asked.

"Remember," Parker said. "Our conversation was hypothetical. He was rather vague. We didn't get into specifics. I assumed we would do that when he hired me."

"Well, you're a criminal lawyer," Theo pointed out. "So, something illegal?"

"The hypothetical friend had come across some information about his company," Parker said. "I assumed illegal or he wouldn't have come to me. He suggested it could cost the company its reputation and a fortune. Jobs were on the line. He didn't seem to know who was responsible, didn't know who he could trust. He just knew he couldn't ignore it."

"So, he wanted to become a whistleblower?"

"I suppose so," Parker nodded. "Mostly, he wanted to protect his friend who, like I said, I assumed was actually him."

Even though Parker thought Stan wanted to protect himself, Theo wondered if the friend might be Sonia. He may have been trying to protect them both. Their disappearances might boil down to survival. If their intention was to expose someone's illegal activity, that person may have found out. Stan and Sonia may have gone into hiding for their own safety. The other option was the person they were going to expose took them both, making it unlikely either of them would still be alive.

"Did he say anything about being worried for his life?" Theo asked. "Or if he felt he needed to go into hiding?"

"No," Parker said. "Nothing like that."

"Okay," Theo said.

"But we were being watched," Parker said.

"Watched?" Patricia asked. "At the restaurant?"

"Yes."

"By whom?" Theo asked.

"There was this woman," Parker said. "I noticed her because she was very attractive."

"Of course you did," Patricia sneered.

"Anyway, she came in right behind Mr. Webber," Parker continued. "She kept looking our way. I don't exactly draw the attention of beautiful women. So, I could only guess that she was watching us. Or at least Mr. Webber. When he got up to leave, she followed him out."

"Can you describe her?" Theo asked. "Other than beautiful?"

"It's been a while," Parker said.

"Try."

"Okay," Parker thought a moment. "I remember she was on the taller side and had reddish brown hair."

39

The walk back to the elevator was more tense than when they had made their way to the basement. Richard carried the box of Sonia's things under one arm and clutched his cane with his other hand, to assure Ty that he was no threat. The Head of Security followed a step behind with his hand resting on the handle of his own weapon.

"You haven't answered me," Ty said to Richard's back.

"I know," Richard sighed. "It's just that, when the police talked to me, they suggested Sonia may not have been the target."

"Not the target?" Ty stepped closer. "Why would they have taken her if you were the target?"

"It's just one theory," Richard said. "They said I may have been the target, and that they grabbed Sonia out of convenience."

"So, you're packing because . . ."

"If I was the target, they may try again, right?" Richard said. "So, I bought a gun for protection."

"You bought a gun for protection," Ty chuckled. "You know how to use a gun, dude? If you don't, it's a good way to get yourself hurt or killed."

"I've had a couple lessons," Richard lied. "Although it's been a few years."

"Been a few years?" Ty raised an eyebrow. "Think about a refresher course, if you're going to carry that around. And do me a favor. Next time you come to Halstead's, leave the gun in the car."

Richard nodded. "I understand. No problem."

They stood in front of the elevator, waiting for the car to arrive.

"You mentioned that one theory is that Stan might be responsible for what happened." Ty stared up at the numbers. "I just don't see Stan doing anything like that. I've always considered him to be more of a victim."

"It's one theory they have," Richard said. "In case Sonia was the actual target."

"Who would want to hurt Sonia?" Ty muttered.

"No one," Richard said. "Which is why the police think they may have been after me instead."

A chime announced the elevator's arrival. The two men waited for the doors to open. Ty let Richard step inside before following. Inside, they maneuvered to stand side by side. The head of security pressed the ground floor button. Both men turned their attention to the display above the door.

Ty pushed the button again. "Who wants you dead?"

"I have no idea," Richard sighed. "But they better finish the job before I find out."

Ty turned to look at Richard's profile. He wasn't sure if the man was issuing a threat, but it sure sounded like one. They reached the lobby and Ty escorted Richard all the way to the exit, holding the door for him. As Richard stepped out of the building, Ty said, "Remember what I said. About the . . ."

"I won't," Richard said. "And thanks."

"Of course," Ty nodded. "You take care. And don't accidentally shoot yourself."

"I'll try not to," Richard grinned before turning away and making his way through the parking lot to Sonia's car. He popped the trunk and dropped the box inside.

Sitting in the driver's seat, he pulled out his phone and searched for the name Fiona Delaney. Several options appeared. Narrowing the search down to only those with local ties still left him with more possibilities than expected. Using various sources, he soon had a list of a half-dozen women with that name, along with addresses. Putting the address of the nearest woman with that name, he left the Halstead Enterprises parking lot for what he hoped would be the last time.

It took him twenty minutes to find the house he was looking for. A modest home in a modest neighborhood. He parked across the street for a few minutes before approaching. He rang the doorbell and stepped back, not wanting to make the woman nervous.

A short time later, the door opened, and a woman stood staring at him.

"What do you want?" she asked.

"Are you Fiona Delaney?" Richard asked.

"Yes," she answered. "Who are you?"

"Do you work for Halstead Enterprises?"

"No." The woman frowned. "Why?"

"Thank you for your time." Richard turned and walked back to the car. Behind him, he could hear the woman throwing questions and colorful expletives at him. He ignored her and drove away.

The exchange at the second house on his list proved similar to the first. At the third, no one answered. He made a note to swing back to it later. The fourth address was an apartment on a third-floor walk-up. He climbed the stairs, forcing himself to use the cane as he went. By the time Richard reached the landing he needed, he was glad he had brought it.

Richard rang the bell and waited. The door opened and a tentative woman peered out at him. She was small in stature, with freckles across her cheeks. At first glance, Richard thought a teen had opened the door, but something in the woman's eyes revealed the truth. She stood silent, her body hidden by the door, as she looked up at Richard, confused.

"Fiona Delaney?" Richard asked.

"Who are you?" She asked. "Did they send you?"

The woman seemed nervous. Richard did not detect fear, but she did not want a visit from anyone.

"Did who send me?"

"Halstead Enterprises," she clarified. "Did they send you?"

"No," Richard assured her. "They did not send me."

"Then who are you?"

He pondered the reason the woman might think Halstead's had sent him and why she thought they might visit her at her home? And why the possibility made her so anxious.

"I'm Richard," he introduced himself. "Richard Jensen."

"The husband?" Fiona seemed to relax a bit. "Right?"

"Yeah, the husband," Richard grimaced. "I'm sure you know Sonia."

"I do," she grinned. "I like her. She's always so kind. Do they have any news?"

"Not yet." Richard let the grief he felt show.

"May I ask why you're here?" The change in Fiona's demeanor was so slight, Richard almost missed it; cautious curiosity.

"I need to ask you some questions." Richard decided the direct, honest approach would be best.

"What kinds of questions?"

"I'm having a hard time wrapping my head around the fact that Stan disappeared within a day of Sonia," Richard explained. "It just doesn't feel like a coincidence."

"The police already asked me if I thought they were having an affair," Fiona offered. "They weren't."

"I didn't think they were."

In Richard's heart, he knew there had been no affair, but hearing such an adamant dismissal of the idea struck him in a way he did not know he needed.

"They argued that day, you know," Fiona said.

"Who argued?"

"Stan and Sonia," Fiona replied. "It wasn't like them at all."

"What did they argue about?" Richard asked.

"I'm sorry." Fiona pursed her lips. "I couldn't hear what they were saying. Just the raised voices."

"They were angry with one another?"

"No." Fiona shook her head. "When the meeting ended, they were all smiles. Like it never happened."

"Really?" Richard knew Sonia was normally a positive. He also knew that when she was angry, it could be days before you could step back into her good graces.

"They must have resolved it," Fiona suggested.

"I guess," Richard agreed. "Can you tell me what else the police asked you about?"

"Mostly about Stan's relationship with Sonia," she said. "And they wanted to know who he had meetings with that day, you know, the day he disappeared."

"Did any of those meetings stand out to them?" Richard asked. "Or to you?"

"No," she said.

"Okay."

"Except that one," she corrected.

"That one?" Richard frowned. "What one?"

"Stan had me put a meeting in the calendar, to show he was unavailable," she said. "When I asked for a name, or an account to attach to it, he said not to worry about it. And that was weird because Stan always attached something to the meeting, so he would have a record."

"But he didn't this time."

"Right," she said. "And Stan was organized. He scheduled his meetings weeks out. This one was last minute."

"What did they look like?"

"I don't know," she shrugged. "Stan sent me on an errand before she arrived and she was gone before I got back."

"She?" Richard asked. "Did Stan say it was a woman?"

"I don't think so."

"Then why do you think it was?" Richard pressed.

"You know, I forgot about this when I was talking to the police," Fiona said. "But there was the scent of perfume in Stan's office when I came back."

"Couldn't it have been from an earlier meeting?"

"No," Fiona was adamant. "I didn't smell it before I left on the errand. Only when I came back. Oh, and I found a red hair on the guest chair."

"A red hair?"

"Yes," Fiona nodded. "I was going to ask about it, but then Stan left for his lunch meeting and I forgot about it."

"Lunch meeting?" Richard's head snapped up. "Who was that with?"

"I didn't even know he had a lunch meeting until he told me he was leaving for it," Fiona said. "So I don't know who it was with."

"Two meetings in one day without names?" Richard asked. "Is that unusual?"

"Yes," Fiona lowered her eyes. "It was the first time I thought he might be having an affair."

Richard thanked her for her time and walked back to his car. Sitting inside, he considered everything Fiona said. Although he wanted to know what Stan and Sonia had argued about, and who Stan had the lunch meeting with, Richard focused on the eleven o'clock mystery meeting.

Under his breath he muttered, "Carolyn."

40

As a young beat cop, Theo partnered with an older, more experienced officer tasked with showing the rookie how things were done. While Don Caraway taught him the basics, the main thing Theo learned from the soon to retire officer was avoidance. Primarily, being near the end of his career, he wanted to avoid dangerous calls. If dispatch sent such a call their way, Caraway did not respond. He also avoided anything that drew attention to himself. "Best to be invisible," he would say. The lesson Theo took to heart centered on avoiding any task deemed tedious. The aging officer would pass those jobs on to others, usually Theo. Which is why the now detective had given Patricia her current assignment.

"Do you know how many of the guests from the Halstead party own SUVs?" Patricia leaned on her elbow and rubbed her eyes.

"I'm guessing more than one." Theo was reading through police reports, witness statements, and his notes on the case to see if he had overlooked anything.

"Eleven." She gazed at him the way his first wife used to.

"That's a lot of territory to cover." He averted his eyes, not wanting any more thoughts of his ex coming to mind. "We should get some uniforms to check for collision bars and front-end damage."

"I'll ask them to check for mounting brackets in case the bars were removed," Patricia added.

"Good thinking," Theo nodded. The detective picked up his phone and called to make his argument for having officers assigned to a task amounting to a shot in the dark. To his surprise, they approved the request with little resistance. Without a warrant, they could only make visual examinations of vehicles that were on the street or in driveways. Garage doors with windows could provide a quick peek to determine if they might need a more thorough search later.

"Did you come up with anything?" Patricia sat back in her chair.

"Stanley Webber's mystery guest for the Halstead party had red hair." Theo sat back as well. "And the lawyer said Stan was being followed by a red-haired woman."

"You think it's the same woman?" Patricia asked.

"I think there's a possibility," Theo said. "And I'm wondering if maybe she had something to do with his disappearance. Could be the SUV was hers."

"And she's not on our list," Patricia rolled her eyes.

"We'll need to figure out who she is and track her down," Theo said.

"Didn't Charles Halstead say the woman knew the Jensens?" Patricia asked.

"He did." Theo shifted forward and started flipping through his notes. "Here it is. Charles thought she was with the Jensens because they spent the evening together."

The detectives fell into silence. Stanley Webber disappeared on Friday before the party, followed by the disappearance of Sonia Jensen the next morning. Occurring in such a brief timeframe suggested a connection between the two events. Common sense would reason that since the victims knew one another; it would be too much of a coincidence for there not to be. But no evidence tied one to the other. Besides working together, the only link between them seemed to be the mystery woman.

"What if the mystery woman knew Richard," Patricia offered. "She wanted to get rid of Stan and he wanted to get rid of Sonia, so they worked together?"

Theo contemplated what his partner said before raising his eyebrows. "Then who was drugging Jensen in the hospital?"

"I don't know." Patricia shrugged. "Maybe they had a falling out and...Never mind. What's your idea?"

Reading through his notes, Theo was trying to form a theory that might direct their investigation. Removing Richard's victimization in the hospital, and everything pointed to the disappearances of two employees of the same company, one of whom visited a lawyer just before he vanished. Every detail of the case pointed to Halstead Enterprises.

"I think the case is about Stan or Sonia or maybe both of them wanting to become a whistleblower," Theo said. "The fact that one of the last things Stan did was visit a lawyer suggests it."

"But to throw your own question in your face," Patricia said. "Who was drugging Richard Jensen and why? He wasn't a Halstead employee. He wasn't going to be a whistleblower."

"That's the part that doesn't add up."

Patricia threw her hands up. "There's just no scenario that accounts for every piece of this case."

"We need to find the red head." Theo stood. "If we can identify who she is and get her to talk, it might be the break we need. She was supposed to be security for Stan. Why did he need security and why wasn't he kept safe?"

"How do we identify her?"

"We pay Richard Jensen a visit and ask him who she is," Theo said. "He spent the evening of the party in her company. Even if he didn't know her before, he should at least have her name."

"And what do we do if he lies?"

"If he lies, we rethink our case," Theo said. "And ask why an innocent man who wants to find his missing wife would lie."

41

There had been a time when Richard considered Carolyn to be a friend. Her being at the Halstead party had been a pleasant surprise, and he enjoyed seeing and talking to her again. His discussion with Fiona Delaney left him filled with doubt. He wondered if their chance meeting had been less of a coincidence and more an arranged encounter.

It had been Carolyn who found him at the party. She called his name out in the crowd. Despite her saying he looked the same, the past decade had seen him change in numerous ways. He wasn't sure he would recognize himself. That Carolyn knew who he was when she saw him seemed impossible. The idea forming in his mind was that she knew he would be there, even sought him out.

She claimed to be at the party as a guest of Stan, who wasn't even in attendance. She may not have been invited to the Halstead's home. Carolyn did not mention meeting with Stan in his office the day he disappeared. The reason Stan had not told Sonia he was hiring security may have been because he never did. The information had come from Carolyn, who just as likely met with him to assess his security, something they would have done back in the day. Richard's old colleague may have played him. She may have been responsible for Stan's disappearance, as well as Sonia's. The idea did not set well with Richard. He knew what Carolyn was capable of, having witnessed it first-hand.

It seemed too late for her to be getting revenge for what happened on the Mexico City operation. But there was nothing else he could think of to bring her back into his life. The thought had him reevaluating the entire evening they had spent together, considering every sentence she had spoken, looking for clues of what she had planned. The thought ignited an anger inside that he hadn't felt in years. But most of all, the thought had him distracted.

With pure luck, Richard looked over his shoulder just as a black sedan tried to overtake him on a nearly deserted stretch of four-lane road. The driver's sudden acceleration was enough to pull Richard from his trance, allowing his instincts to kick in.

Richard slammed on the brakes and watched the sedan speed past him. He spun the steering wheel and stepped down on the accelerator, sending the Mercedes on a trajectory toward an alley. He raced down the narrow passage, watching for obstacles while checking the rearview mirror for the pursuing vehicle. It did not take long for the sedan to appear, confirming that he was indeed being chased.

Considering where he was and what direction he was heading, Richard weighed his options for losing or confronting the car behind him. The alley was coming to an end and, unlike the street he had just left, the one ahead was an intermittent string of traffic. He checked behind him and saw the sedan gaining on him, eliminating the option of slowing down. He accelerated, putting a little more distance between them. Reaching the end of the alley, he braked hard and spun the wheel to the right as he cleared the buildings. His tires screeched in protest as he slid into traffic, hugging the sidewalk, just missing a passing car. The driver laid on the horn as Richard raced past.

The sedan emerged from the alley a couple car lengths behind him, steering to continue their pursuit. A longer, heavier vehicle, it fishtailed through the turn, clipping a heavy-duty pickup which lost control. It veered away before over-correcting and slamming into the driver's door of the sedan. The last Richard saw of the sedan was the collision pushing it off the road and into a wall.

Richard considered returning to confront the driver and demanding answers but did not want to chance getting into a gunfight surrounded by bystanders. He decided instead to continue home. He spent the rest of the trip checking his mirrors and watching any vehicle that looked suspicious. Twice he made unnecessary turns to be sure he wasn't being followed.

Once home, he checked the front again and again, glad that he had sent his sister to their parent's. Satisfied no one was watching the house, he relaxed a bit while remaining alert. That diligence allowed him to see the detectives turning into his driveway.

He quickly pulled his shoulder holster off followed by his shirt. Releasing the bullet proof vest's straps, he yanked it off and tossed it into a closet. The weapons he crammed into a drawer as the doorbell rang. He was still shoving his arms through the appropriate holes of his shirt when he opened the door, remembering too late that his cane was still in the car.

42

Detectives?" Richard greeted with feigned surprise. He worked at tucking his shirt into his trousers as he watched them with anticipation. He couldn't help but glancing toward the street for unknown vehicles.

"Mr. Jensen, how are you doing?" Theo noted the absence of the cane he had never seen the man without.

"Getting better." Richard breathed heavy from the adrenaline. "Sorry, I've been doing my exercises. But I'm sure you're not here to check on my recovery."

"No. We're not," Theo said. "Can we come in? We have some more questions."

"Sure," Richard stepped back. "But you'll have to excuse the mess."

The homeowner held the door open as his guests stepped through and into the main room of the home. They stopped short as they scanned the scene. Once neatly arranged shelving stood empty. Drawers pulled out of their places, lay in haphazard stacks. Framed photos and other items littered tables and countertops. Papers were everywhere. Nothing looked as it did the last time they had been there.

"Were you robbed?" Theo asked, noting the piles of books and home decor in various parts of the room, in stark contrast to the bare surfaces.

"What? Oh, no," Richard said. He crossed the room to the dining table where the files he and Nancy had gone through still covered the surface. He scooped them together and slid them to one corner. "Let's sit in here."

Theo eyed the couch, which was serving as a low table, piled high with more items once perched in prominent locations around the room. He glanced at his partner, who seemed to think the same thing he was. Sonia Jensen had only been gone a month, and for her husband, it had only been a few days, far too soon to be packing up her things.

Richard circled the table to sit on the kitchen side next to the files he had just moved. The detectives took seats across from him and adjusted themselves until they were comfortable. An awkward silence followed.

"You have more questions?" Richard finally asked.

"Do you mind telling us what happened here?" Patricia turned to the living room to be sure he knew what she meant.

"Oh, that," Richard grimaced. "I was looking for some papers. Couldn't remember where Sonia told me she had put them."

"Did you find them?" Theo asked. "The papers."

"Not before tearing the whole place apart," Richard sighed. "As you can see."

"Must have been important," Theo commented.

"Health insurance documents," Richard explained. In truth, he knew where those documents were for both he and Sonia, filed away in his own office downstairs. "As you can imagine, spending a month in the hospital isn't cheap."

"I see." Theo gave the room another glance.

"Your questions?" Richard tried to draw their attention away from what they must be thinking.

"Yes," Theo shifted in his seat. "We want to talk about the night of the Halstead's party."

"What about it?"

"You know, Stanley Webber, your wife's boss," Theo continued. "He didn't show up for the party. And it's my understanding he was the one who chose Mrs. Jensen for the promotion she received."

"That's my understanding as well," Richard confirmed. "But I'm not hearing a question."

"The thing is," Theo said. "While Mr. Webber was a no-show, his plus one for the evening, not his wife, was there. Don't you think that's odd?"

"I suppose so." Richard's thoughts returned to Carolyn. "That's your question?"

"No." Theo dismissed, changing gears. He thumbed through his notes. "Mr. Webber's plus one was described as a tall, fit, redhead. And we were told that you and your wife spent most of the evening with her."

"We did." Richard closed his eyes for a moment as images of Sonia flooded his mind.

"So, you know her?"

"Yes," Richard admitted. "We worked together, years ago. Carolyn Brechenstanch. No. Wait. She married. It's something else now."

"What is it?"

"Uh." Richard reached into the depths of his memory. "Winters. Carolyn Winters."

"Do you know how we might get in touch with Mrs. Winters?" Theo asked.

"Sorry," Richard frowned. "That was the first time I had seen her in years."

"And you didn't get her number or email?"

"I wasn't looking to reestablish old friendships," Richard said.

"I find that strange," Theo observed.

"I don't."

"Did she introduce herself as being Stan's guest?" Patricia asked.

Richard locked eyes on the detective and noted how unlike Sonia she was. The tall woman sat rigid with her limbs at sharp angles. His wife was always a symbol of grace and calm. He thought back to the night of the party, what seemed a lifetime ago. In a way, he supposed, it was.

"She said she had arrived with Stan, but that he had gone home sick." Richard shrugged. "She stayed for the free food. At least that's what she told us."

"You didn't find it odd a plus one would stay after the person she came with left?"

"I really thought nothing of it."

"Did she mention why she was his plus one rather than his wife?" Theo asked.

"I didn't ask," Richard admitted. "She mentioned she was working with Stan on something. She's in security."

"Security?" Patricia repeated.

"Yes."

"You're saying," Theo leaned forward in his chair and placed his arms on the table. "An old friend, you hadn't seen in years, shows up out of the blue. She tells you she's working with Stanley Webber. Something to do with security. On the same day Mr. Webber disappears. And you didn't think that was worth mentioning during our first conversation?"

"To be fair." Richard placed his hands on the edge of the table as if to hold it in place. "I was unconscious for a month and had just learned my wife had disappeared. I didn't make the connection between the two events."

Theo sat back again. "Okay, then. Tell us everything you know about Carolyn Winters."

"There's not much to tell, really," Richard said. "Before that night, I hadn't seen her in twelve years. I didn't even recognize her."

"But she recognized you?"

"Yes." He felt his eye twitch.

"After twelve years?" Patricia asked. "Have you not changed in that time?"

"Some," Richard admitted. "I doubt I would have recognized me. Especially out of context. My younger self would never have thought I would be attending upscale parties."

"I need to ask," Theo said. "Is it possible the reason she so easily recognized you was because she knew you were going to be there?"

"How would she have known that?"

"Maybe the reason she was at that party was because she was looking for you," Theo suggested.

"No." Richard shook his head, knowing he was thinking the same thing. "She was there because of Stan."

"Are you sure?" Theo questioned. "She's the one who told you she was there with him. She also told you he went home because he wasn't feeling well.

But no one else saw him at that party. But she was there, and she spent the evening with you."

"With me and Sonia," Richard clarified. "Yes."

"What did you talk about?" Theo asked. "The three of you?"

"About the past, a little," Richard said. "But mostly about the twelve years since we last saw each other. Where we were in our lives. My company. Hers. My life with Sonia."

"What about her husband?"

"I think she said he died shortly after they were married." Richard closed his eyes, thinking back to that night. "She didn't say anything else about him."

The three of them sat, studying one another.

"If that's all," Richard was the first to break the silence. "I have a mess to clean up."

Theo glanced at the living room before pulling himself to his feet. "Okay. Well, if you remember anything else about Mrs. Winters, call us."

Patricia followed her partner's lead and stood. "It would help us if you remembered something."

"I understand." Richard pulled himself out of his chair. "I will call if I remember anything."

Richard escorted the other two out of his home and watched from the door as they made their way to their car. Once hidden from view, he pushed the door closed.

Settled into their vehicle, Theo turned to his partner. "What did you think?"

"I think there's something off about his story," Patricia answered.

"I agree." Theo looked up at the house. "There's something he's not telling us."

"It looked like he was getting rid of everything related to his wife," Patricia said. "We should consider the possibility that he was involved."

"Or that he may have been the intended target." Theo saw the curtains move in the main window of the living room. He was sure Richard had his eyes on them. "Either way, we need to do a deep dive into Mr. Jensen's life."

Inside, Richard stood watching the detectives' car. They sat in his driveway much longer than he thought they should and he thought they would be returning to the door soon, perhaps with more questions. He waited and prepared himself for what was coming. He was surprised when the car started backing down the driveway toward the street. When he could no longer see them and convinced they would not be returning, Richard considered what they had said about Carolyn.

A few minutes later, he sat behind the desk in Sonia's office, searching the internet for the name Carolyn Winters. Her name gave him thousands of results, which he scrolled through as quickly as he could. The profiles included doctors, teachers, cashiers, and business executives. Stories of awards, marriages, retirements and obituaries filled his screen. Thousands of faces from hundreds of women appeared with each click of a link. None of them proved to be his old co-worker.

He changed his search to look for security firms, opening the company websites and skimming through them for information on their origins and personnel. After the first hundred or so, Richard began regretting not getting Carolyn's contact information.

He rubbed his eyes and sat back. Given enough computer power and the right software, Richard knew it would only take a few minutes to find what he was looking for. His current method would take hours, if not days, and may still not produce a result. He had one option he could use that would provide him with the information he wanted within minutes. The idea of going that route would take him even further into his past. Unfortunately, he didn't see that he had a choice.

He took a deep breath and held it for as long as he could before picking up his phone. Scrolling through the contacts until he came to the one he was looking for, he paused for a moment. Many times, he considered deleting the entry that was simply listed as "Dog", always talking himself out of it. Now, his finger hovered over the call button for a long moment before he pressed it.

It rang once.

A familiar deep voice said, "Wondered when you were going to call."

43

Theo sat at his desk unwrapping a Philly cheesesteak that had his mouth watering. On the way back from Richard Jensen's house, the detective had stopped at a small diner that had been a favorite of his when he was a patrol officer. After the original owners retired, the children had taken over the business and ran the place into the ground. It had broken Theo's heart. Recently, the diner changed hands, and the new owners promised to bring it back to its old glory with a revival of many items from the original menu. Theo couldn't resist picking up an order to go. He took a bite and savored the experience while he watched his partner, sitting across from him, picking at the grilled chicken sandwich she had ordered.

"You need to learn to eat," Theo said after swallowing. "Your food choices have no flavor."

"My food choices are healthy," Patricia countered. "And have plenty of flavor."

"Then why are you picking at your food?"

"It has pickles," she grumbled.

Theo laughed and took another bite.

A young officer appeared at Theo's side and handed him a large envelope. Reluctantly, the detective set his sandwich down, wiped his hands, and opened the offering. Laying the contents on his desk, he scanned the documents.

"We got the background check back for Richard Jensen," Theo announced.

"That was fast." Patricia rolled her chair around her desk until she was sitting next to her partner, who rolled a few inches away. She did not seem to notice. "What've we got?"

"It's more about what we didn't get," Theo said.

"How do you mean?"

"Okay." Theo pointed at the report. "It gives us the date and city of birth. There are records for every school he attended through high school. Sports. Medical records. It even lists summer jobs."

"That's a thorough report," Patricia commented.

"Yes," Theo agreed. "But everything stops when he graduated high school."

"Stops?" Patricia frowned. "What do you mean stops?"

"I mean," Theo said. "From the day he graduated high school until he enrolled into tech school eleven years later, there is nothing about Richard Jensen."

"How is that possible?"

"There are only two ways I know of," Theo said. "Either Richard Jensen died after high school and we're dealing with a case of stolen identity..."

"Which would mean he's a criminal, possibly capable of murder to protect his true identity," Patricia surmised.

"Or those years have been scrubbed from his record," Theo added.

"Meaning what?" Patricia asked. "Sealed records? Witness protection? Government coverup?"

"Sealed records are sealed from the public, not law enforcement," Theo responded. "Witness protection is a possibility. He may have been placed with a new identity and years later, when there was no longer a threat, he returned to his past life."

"Or maybe he missed his family and walked away from the program," Patricia suggested.

"That's an interesting theory," Theo said. "It might explain some of what has occurred if the person or persons he testified against has found him."

"They may have been released from prison recently," Patricia added.

"As for a government coverup," Theo continued. "That would be hard to prove. Unless we know who scrubbed the records or why, it won't be easy to find anything."

"So, we may never know."

"Possibly."

Theo returned his attention to his sandwich, taking a good-sized bite and deeming it as good as he remembered the original to be. Patricia rolled her chair back around to her side of the desk and her lunch as well.

"Richard Jensen is a programmer." Patricia was halfway through her food. "Is it possible he hacked in and erased himself?"

"Erasing that much data would take a lot of skill and time." Theo was cleaning up the remains of his meal. "Especially on your own."

"He's an internet security specialist and owns his own company," Patricia said. "I think he could do it."

"Let's say he did," Theo relented. "Why just those years?"

"Obviously, something happened during that time that he doesn't want us finding out about."

"If that's the case." Theo tapped his desk. "We need to figure out what he's hiding."

"We talk to his parents, his sister and his business partner," Patricia concluded. "They must know something."

"What about the guest list for the Halstead's party?" Theo asked. "Did you find anything on the SUVs?"

"The visual inspections of any SUVs registered to a guest has come up empty," Patricia said. "We need to know who the plus ones are to know what they drive."

"Did you check the name Carolyn Winters?" Theo asked. "To see what she drives?"

"I haven't found anything on a Carolyn Winters working in the security field," Patricia said.

"What about her maiden name?" Theo asked. "Brechenstanch?"

"I haven't looked into it yet," she admitted.

"Okay." Theo closed the report. "You do that. I'm going to reach out to some contacts to see if I can get more on Jensen. Then we can revisit his family and Gavin Barr."

44

Bulldog."

Richard sat in a corner booth of a small cafe where they agreed to meet. The large man sitting across from him appeared uncomfortable from squeezing into his seat. He was a man who spent most of his time in a room filled with computers and screens. Not opposed to being out in the world, he just preferred not to be. Adjusting his position from time to time, he glanced about as if paranoid.

"Money." The man replied.

"I don't go by that anymore," Richard corrected him.

"You'll always be Money to me," Bulldog's deep voice was intimidating. "But I can call you Richard, if that's what you want."

"That's what I want." Richard glanced over the big man's shoulders. "You were expecting me to call. Why?"

"I heard what happened," Bulldog said. "And have been monitoring the case. I thought you might want assistance. So, how can I help?"

Benny Davenport had been part of Richard's team. His big stocky stature, his deep gravelly voice and his initials being B.D. all contributed to the canine nickname given to him. If anything, the past twelve years had resulted in the man being bigger.

The two of them had run into one another about six years ago at a restaurant where Richard was having lunch during an installation job. Richard had recognized him immediately. Men Bulldog's size did not disappear into the shadows. Their presence was apparent as soon as they entered a room. But it had been the voice. Unable to speak in soft tones, Richard identified the owner from halfway across the room.

Even then, their face-to-face encounter had only been by chance. As Richard exited the restroom, Bulldog was standing there. The interaction between them had been awkward, each trying to walk away without being rude. Richard had learned that Bulldog had just moved to town. Bulldog had learned about Sonia and Richard's company. They had exchanged numbers that day, but today was the first time they had spoken.

"I only need to know where to find Carolyn Winters," Richard said.

"Carolyn who?"

"Carolyn," Richard said. "From the old team."

"Aces?" Bulldog raised an eyebrow. "Why did you call her Winters?"

"That's not her name, is it?" Richard shook his head. "Of course she lied. I should have known. So, she never married?"

"Sure she did," Bulldog said. "Married Teeter. But he got himself killed about three years ago."

"Teeter's dead?" Richard looked pained. David "Teeter" Green was the team sniper, one of the best Richard had worked with. On their first mission after David joined the team, they all met at an extraction point. When the others arrived, David and his spotter were on a teeter-totter next to a burned-out school. That was how he earned his nickname. His partner was called "Totter the spotter", until he stepped on a landmine about two years later.

"It was sad." Bulldog inhaled until his lungs were full, then let it out in a huff. "Served all those years. Tagged in on I don't know how many operations. Then taken out by a hit-and-run."

"I didn't know."

"How would you?" Bulldog shrugged. "Once you're out, you're out."

"So, you're still...?"

"Nah," Bulldog said. "Been out for years. But I kept track of everyone. Even your sorry ass."

"That makes her Carolyn what?" Richard thought. "Green?"

"It was," Bulldog bobbed his big head. "But after Teeter bit it, she had it changed to Watts."

"Watts?" Richard was confused. "Why Watts?"

"Don't know," Bulldog shrugged again. "I just know she was trying hard not to be found."

"Is she even in security?" Richard asked.

"She is," Bulldog confirmed. "And she's good at it. Not that I would expect anything else. We didn't call her Aces for nothing."

"I saw her the night before my wife vanished," Richard said.

"That's when she told you her name was Winters," Bulldog concluded.

"Right," Richard confirmed. "She said she was working with Sonia's boss on a security issue. Now the boss is missing. I need to know where to find her."

"You don't think Carolyn had anything to do with your wife's disappearance, do you?" The big man's eyes filled with concern.

"I don't know," Richard said. "I hope not. It's been over a decade. But she may still hold a grudge."

"Maybe," Bulldog agreed. "She only stayed a few months after you left. Teeter stuck it out a couple of years."

"Including Lance," Richard said. "That was half the squad. Hard to run operations that way."

"Yeah," Bulldog said. "Everything changed after Mexico City. Jackson struggled for a while. He even brought in Lance's brother, Lucas."

"I hadn't heard," Richard said.

"He was some kind of math wiz," Bulldog said. "Like a human computer."

"Really?" Richard said. "Why would he want to be an operative?"

"Don't know," Bulldog sat back. "But he shouldn't have. Lucas was nothing like his brother."

"Well, Lance was a hard act to follow," Richard said.

"He was."

The two of them paused for a minute.

"Can you help me?" Richard finally asked. "Tell me where to find her."

"I'll be honest," Bulldog spread his hands. "I can see you're packing. But I also know you've been out of the game for a dozen years. And Carolyn. Well, she scares the hell out of me. So, the best I can do is reach out and let her know you would like a meet. See what she says."

"If that's the best you can do," Richard nodded. "I'll take it."

"Now," Bulldog stared at Richard. "Do you think it's her? I mean when you really think it through."

Richard had thought it through dozens of times. He wasn't sure if Carolyn was behind everything. He wasn't sure if she had taken Sonia. But he was positive she knew something, something that would help him find his wife and bring her home.

"I don't know to what extent," Richard answered. "But I know she's involved."

"It's just that," Bulldog said. "The times she and I have talked, she's not once ever asked where you were. And I don't care how angry she might be at you; she'd never harm an unarmed civilian. I don't see her taking Sonia."

"In the past two days," Richard squeezed his hands into fists. "Two attempts have been made on my life."

"Are you serious?" Bulldog frowned. "Why haven't I heard anything?"

"I didn't report it." Richard relaxed his hands.

"Why?"

"Because, if I do," Richard lowered his voice. "The police might try to put me in protective custody. I don't need to be hindered in my efforts to find Sonia."

"If people are trying to kill you," Bulldog's attempt to lower his voice only seemed to make it louder. "Maybe you need to be in protective custody."

"What I need," Richard snarled. "Is to talk to Carolyn."

"Okay." Bulldog raised his hands defensively. Then he slid his large frame toward the edge of the booth. "I'll be in touch."

"Tell me something, Bulldog." Richard stopped him.

"What's that?"

"Do you think it's her?" he asked. "Could Carolyn be after revenge after all these years? An eye for an eye thing?"

"I don't know," Bulldog stood and towered over Richard. "But if it is, you'd better be careful."

45

"Detective Theo Morris." He gave his name for the third time, and the frustration was clear in his voice. He listened to the person on the other end of the phone. "Why couldn't you have just said that to begin with?"

He hung up, throwing the business card in the trash. Over the years, he had exchanged cards with people from various branches of law enforcement. This was the fourth one that had either died or retired. It only proved to remind him that his days were closing in on him.

Picking up the next card, he read the information presented there. Agent Lucy Newton of the FBI. Theo stared at the card trying to remember when he had acquired it and the face of the person who gave it to him. He failed on both counts. Theo almost discarded it, but decided, at worst, they would have nothing to offer him. He dialed.

"Newton." The woman answered on the first ring.

"Agent Lucy Newton of the FBI?" Theo asked.

"Who is this?" Her voice sounded of a reserved caution.

"Detective Theo Morris." Theo thought there was something familiar in her voice. "I believe we met on a case."

"Must have been a long time ago," Lucy said. "I haven't been in the FBI for five years. I'm ATF now."

"Sorry," Theo sighed. He wasn't sure she would be of any help. "I didn't know."

"I still have contacts," she offered. "What is it you need?"

"If you don't mind," Theo said.

"Not at all," she confirmed.

"I have a suspect," Theo explained. "And his background check is missing seven years. I was hoping to find someone who could check and see if it was erased by the government, or someone else."

"That's a tall ask," Lucy said.

"I understand."

"You also understand that if the government erased it," Lucy said. "I wouldn't be able to tell you what was in those years, why it was erased."

"I do."

"Give me the name."

"Richard Jensen," Theo said, adding the date of birth and other details he knew.

"Can I reach you at this number?" she asked.

"Yes."

"Give me an hour."

Theo stared at his phone for a moment after she disconnected the call, trying again to remember where and when he had come to have Lucy Newton's business card. Something about the woman's voice, or maybe her accent, sounded so familiar. He just wasn't sure why. Then it came to him.

The case had been seven or eight years ago, or rather cases. A couple of brutal murders had fallen into Theo's lap. He felt he was making some headway when the FBI swept in to take over, claiming the murders tied to a case they were working on. Lucy Newton had been a junior agent in the background, treated like an outcast by her fellow agents. When they shoved him aside, Theo found himself next to the young agent. That's when they exchanged cards. He always wondered why they treated her with disrespect, and hearing now that she left the bureau did not surprise him.

Theo also wondered what had happened with the case. The detective had collected a ton of evidence from the murder scenes, pursued dozens of leads. He had narrowed the suspect pool to a manageable few before the FBI took the case from him. Yet, with all of that, the murders were still unsolved.

When he looked up, his partner was staring at him.

"What?"

"You're not going to believe this." Patricia was almost giddy.

"And again, I ask, what?"

"I ran a background on Carolyn Brechenstanch," Patricia informed him. "Every little detail until…"

"Until she graduated high school," Theo finished.

"Right."

"For how long?" Theo asked.

"That's it," Patricia said. "After high school, Carolyn Brechenstanch doesn't exist."

"What about Carolyn Winters?"

"Nothing. She's a ghost."

46

After an hour, Richard had made little progress in returning the items in his living room to where they had been before he had torn it apart in search of the Halstead laptop. He stood in the center of the room, his leg throbbing from the repeated squatting to pick things up. Sonia would not be happy at all with him for making such a mess. She was very particular about where things went.

He retrieved his cane for support as he made his way to the kitchen hoping to find something to eat. Nancy had stocked his fridge for him before leaving for their parent's home. He was grateful to her for that. The problem was, she tended to buy things she thought he should eat rather than things he would eat. He chuckled to himself as he scanned the contents.

Closing the refrigerator, Richard grabbed his cane and the keys to Sonia's Mercedes and headed out the door. He was in the mood for some proper food and he wasn't going to get that at home. He considered for a moment going to his parent's house, but he knew they would have questions he wasn't ready to answer. And he didn't want to lead trouble to their doorstep.

He steered, instead, toward an Italian restaurant he and Sonia frequented. They had great food and privacy, the two things he needed most. He kept an eye on his mirrors and double checked every vehicle that passed by. As far as he could tell, he was not being followed. He also knew that a professional would be difficult to spot. The fifteen-minute drive was tense. After parking, he watched for any car that stopped in the area. He still didn't see anything.

The staff at the restaurant knew him as half of the happy, friendly couple. Disappointment showed on the hostess's face when he asked for a table for one. Giving him a forced smile, she picked up a single menu and a roll of silverware.

"We haven't seen you in a while, Mr. Jensen." The manager approached with his trademark smile, slowing at the sight of the cane, before continuing. "Your wife won't be joining us today?"

Richard hesitated. "No. She won't be joining us."

"Very well," he smiled. "Alecia, take him to table forty-four. I believe you will like it there, Mr. Jensen."

"Thank you," Richard nodded and followed the hostess to a small table in the back of the dining room where he purposely sat facing the entrance while still having a view of the door to the kitchen.

He held the menu open before him without seeing it. He and Sonia had been there dozens of times and he knew what he would order before he even arrived. His mind wandered to the many meals they had shared, the conversations they had, all in this building. The server brought him water, took his order and the menu, promising the food would arrive in short order. A basket of bread and a small plate with a mixture of olive oil and seasonings sat on the corner of his table. Richard pulled them to him, tearing a piece of crusty roll to dip.

The roll was gone by the time his food arrived. He pushed the basket and oil aside to make room. The server placed the plate before him and the aroma reminded him of Sonia. She loved this place. Thanking the server, Richard ate. Though delicious, he took little notice of the food. Eating for sustenance rather than enjoyment, he could have chosen fast-food. His plate was empty in no time and when the server came to collect it, Richard asked for a dessert menu.

Richard looked up to watch the server's retreat when he saw a familiar face. Sitting at a table on the far side of the restaurant, there was no mistaking who he was looking at. He would recognize her anywhere. She was sitting with two other women, smiling, laughing. She was enjoying herself. And for Richard, that would not do.

The server returned with the dessert menu and Richard waved her off.

"I've changed my mind." He handed her his credit card. "Process it. Add a twenty-dollar tip for yourself."

"Are you sure, sir?" she asked. The meal had only been thirty.

"Hurry, please."

"Yes, sir."

Ten minutes later, Richard was sitting in the Mercedes after moving it to face the building. He watched every patron exiting the restaurant looking for the face he had seen, looking for Dr. Rudra Paidi.

47

D etective Theo Morris pressed the doorbell at the home of Mr. and Mrs. Harold Jensen and took a step back. Waiting, he looked back at Patricia, who was finishing a phone call. She walked up to join him and was just about to speak when the front door opened.

Richard's sister, Nancy, opened the door and looked out at them with a small amount of disappointment in her eyes. The senior detective picked up on it while his partner seemed oblivious. Richard's sister forced a smile.

"What can we do for you, officers?"

"Detectives," Patricia corrected.

"Pardon?" Nancy turned to the woman.

"Officers are in uniform," Patrica explained. "We're detectives."

"She doesn't care," Theo interjected. "Nancy, isn't it? Do you mind if we come in? We need to ask you and your parents some questions."

"You've already talked to us," Nancy protested.

"Questions are part of the process," Theo said. "The more information we have, the closer we come to finding your sister-in-law."

"Well," Nancy mumbled. "This is my parents' home. I'll have to ask them."

"Are you visiting them?" Patricia asked. "Your parents?"

"I'm staying with them for now," she called back over her shoulder. "Giving Richard some space."

Patricia leaned closer to Theo, keeping her voice low. "She's giving her brother space? The man is still recovering. He doesn't need space. He needs help."

"Maybe she got tired of cleaning up after him," Theo suggested. "Remember the mess he had? Maybe that's what she's been dealing with."

"I could see that," Patricia said.

Nancy appeared again and walked to the door. She pushed it open farther and waved them in. "They're down the hall on the left."

"Thank you." Theo stepped into the house, with Patricia close behind.

Nancy closed the door behind them and followed.

The Jensen's home was modest and clean, but a staleness hung in the air that made Theo think of houses left locked up for extended periods of time. Almost no outside light penetrated the closed curtains. Inexpensive artwork and family photos hung on the walls. Theo noted a cluster of wedding photos featuring Richard and Sonia, Nancy and her husband, and one older picture that could only be the parents. He also noted none of the photos featured grandchildren.

The detectives joined the homeowners in the living room, where the walls appeared much the same. Richard's parents were sitting side by side in matching wing-backed chairs, watching their unexpected guests walk in. Theo and Patricia sat on a small sofa next to them while Nancy leaned against the wall behind her parents, followed by a fast exchange of greetings.

"Do you have news for us, detective?" Richard's father asked.

"Not yet, I'm sorry," Theo apologized.

"Then why are you here?"

Theo glanced Nancy's way. "When we have a case like this, it helps if we can establish possible motives to identify suspects. That involves looking into the victims' backgrounds to see if anything stands out."

"And you learned something?" Richard's mother asked. "In Sonia's background?"

"No," Theo said. "We didn't find any red flags when we looked into Sonia."

"What are you saying?" Richard's father asked. "There's something in Richard's past? What is it?"

"Not exactly," Theo admitted. "The truth is, when we looked into your son's background, we found a gap."

"What kind of gap?" Nancy asked.

"From the time he graduated high school until he enrolled into the tech college," Theo said, "there is nothing. No employment records. No financial records. Nothing showing where he was living or what he was doing. It's like, for seven years, he did not exist."

"That preposterous," Richard's father grumbled. "Of course he existed."

"But where was he?" Patricia asked.

"He joined the army right out of high school," Richard's father said. "How could there not be a record of that?"

"The army?" Taken aback, Theo said, "Are you sure?"

"Of course I'm sure," Richard's father snapped. "There's a picture of him in his uniform right there."

The detectives turned in unison to where Harold's outstretched arm directed them to the mantel above the fireplace. There, next to another wedding picture of Nancy and her groom, was a portrait of Richard as a young man in military dress.

Theo and Patricia exchanged glances of shared confusion. A military record should have shown up in a background check.

48

Richard sat in a chair in the corner of the master bedroom of the small house, watching the woman who slept there. From the restaurant, he had followed Dr. Paidi to her home where she appeared to live alone. After the lights went out inside, Richard waited half an hour before approaching, another twenty before entering. With no security system and no video doorbell, getting in was as easy as if he had been carrying the key.

Richard took his time looking around, searching for details of the woman's life. Her real name was Gina Stuart. She was single or divorced. From framed photos cluttering her shelves, he learned that Gina's mother was from India while her father was American. She had two siblings, a brother and a sister, both younger. Richard saw a photo of a dog but no sign of one in the house, suggesting a pet from her childhood.

The mail was also revealing. He learned she was not a doctor, but worked as a paramedic for a private ambulance company. A stack of past due bills on the kitchen counter told him she didn't make enough at her job, she had a problem with spending, or perhaps gambling. Nothing explained why she came into Richard's hospital room to sedate him.

He quietly searched her nightstand and gently checked beneath her pillow. There were no weapons at the ready. For her to have done what she had, he would have expected some kind of protection.

"Stuart." Richard held a pistol in his hand but not pointed at her.

She flinched, but did not open her eyes, did not stir.

"Stuart!" This time his voice was loud and sharp.

Gina sat up straight in a full panic. Someone was in her room. She scanned the darkness, waiting for her eyes to adjust. "Who's there?"

"You tell me, Dr. Paidi." He used the alias. "Who do you think I am?"

"Oh, God. Oh, God." The fear in her voice shown on her face. "No. No. No. Please."

"Gina." Richard snapped. "I want you to very slowly reach for your lamp and turn the light on. Can you do that for me?"

"Please, don't hurt me," she pleaded. Tears streamed down her cheeks.

"Gina," Richard repeated. "Turn on the light."

The woman reached out and twisted the knob. A soft click was followed by the room being flooded with light. Seeing Richard sitting there with gun in hand, Gina began to sob.

Richard sighed. "Gina, I'm not here to hurt you."

It was hollow assurance coming from an intruder with a gun. Just the same, Gina's breathing began to even out and the tears slowed to a trickle.

"I'm going to ask you some questions," Richard informed her. "And you are going to answer them. Understood?"

She nodded.

"Good." Richard leaned forward, elbows on his knees, the gun angled toward the floor. "Now, first one. Why were you sedating me?"

Gina did not respond. Her chin quivered and the tears began anew.

"Do we know each other?" Richard asked. "Did I do something to you?"

Gina shook her head.

"Then why?"

It was a reasonable question, deserving of an answer. All Gina could do was close her eyes and fight back the sobs that tried to escape her. The woman's entire body began to shake as she cried.

"Gina!"

"I was paid." The words burst from her, followed by sobs. "I'm sorry."

"The past due bills." Richard began to see what happened. "Gina, get control of yourself. I told you I'm not here to hurt you and I won't. But I need you to answer my questions. Do you understand."

Gina sniffed and nodded her head. Taking deep breaths she began to calm.

"Good," Richard said. "Now, the person who paid you. Did you seek them out? Or did they approach you?"

"They came to me," Gina said. "I didn't want to do it. But I needed the money. And they promised no one would get hurt."

"No one hurt?" Richard frowned. "You stole a month of my life."

"I'm sorry," she cried. "Please, don't hurt me."

"I'm not going to hurt you," Richard assured her again. "The person who hired you, tell me about him."

"Her."

"Her?" Richard asked. "The person who hired you was a woman?"

Gina nodded.

"Describe her."

Gina closed her eyes and took a deep breath. "She was tall, thin, beautiful."

"Hair?"

"Blond," Gina said. "But she was wearing a wig."

"You're sure?"

"I'm a paramedic," Gina explained. "I've seen my fair share of wigs. She definitely wore one."

Richard's mind went straight to Carolyn. Bulldog had been wrong. She was involved. She wore a wig to hide her red hair. She paid this woman to keep him sedated and in the hospital. She was behind Sonia's disappearance.

"So this woman came to you, promising a lot of money," Richard said. "To do what?"

"To keep you sedated." Gina's tone seemed to say, 'you know this'.

"What were your instructions?" Richard asked. "What did she say? Word for word?"

"It was weeks ago," she said. "I can't remember word for word?"

"You were offered a sum of money to keep me sedated," Richard said. "I'm assuming that doesn't happen every day. I'm also sure you remember the conversation with some clarity."

Gina took another deep breath. "You're not wrong. But not word for word."

"As close as you can get." Richard prompted.

"She said I needed to make regular visits," Gina said. "And I was supposed to give you something to keep you sedated."

"That's it?"

"Yes," Gina insisted. She used her eyes to plead with him. There was a sudden shift in her line of sight.

"What?"

"There was something else," Gina offered.

"And what was that?"

"She said to keep you sedated," Gina repeated. "But I had to be careful not to harm you."

"She wanted to keep me sedated, but alive," Richard thought aloud.

"And no brain damage," Gina added. "Or anything permanent."

"How considerate," Richard mocked.

"Listen, mister," Gina pleaded. "I'm sorry. If I wasn't in desperate need of money, I would never have done it. But…"

"Desperation is a powerful persuader," Richard said.

"What are you going to do?" She looked down at the sheets covering her legs. "Are you going to kill me?"

"Kill you?" Richard raised an eyebrow. "Lord no."

"Turn me in to the police then?"

Richard looked at the woman's face. She was filled with regret and fear.

"You ever going to do anything like this again?"

"You couldn't pay me enough," Gina declared. "The stress of trying not to get caught, not to mention the guilt I felt for what I was doing, it was all too much. Never again."

"Good." Richard stood. "If I hear otherwise, I will be back. Do you understand?"

"Yes, sir." She swallowed hard.

"I suggest you take some of the money she paid you and invest in an alarm system." With that Richard left her room and made his way out of her house.

49

"This is Colonel Sutton."

Theo had called first thing in the morning only to learn the colonel was in a meeting. He called twice more before being placed on hold. Almost a half hour passed and Theo considered hanging up when the Army officer answered.

"Colonel, I'm Detective Theo Morris. I don't know if you remember me."

"Detective Morris," the colonel said. "You investigated the murder of one of my soldiers last year."

"That's right." Theo was glad he didn't have to remind the man who he was.

Fifteen months ago, a dishwasher found the body of a corporal in the alley behind the bar where he was last seen. Someone had beaten the soldier before stabbing him to death. The killer took his wallet and watch. Being the dead of winter, heavy snowfall obscured the body for three days before being discovered. Surveillance video showed the drunken soldier picking a half dozen fights with even more patrons. Being inebriated proved to be good and bad for the corporal. He lost every altercation, sometimes badly. Watching it all made Theo question whether the corporal was trying to get killed. It also made him question why the bouncers never put a stop to it. At one point, the soldier disappeared down the hallway to the restrooms and never came out. The investigation led Theo into a dark backstory of a man trying to punish himself for his part in losing the woman he loved when he cheated on her with a married woman. Whether he intended to die remained unknown.

In the end, Theo arrested a bouncer who convinced himself the woman the corporal claimed to sleep with was his wife. He pulled the corporal out the back door to the alley when no one was looking. After a brutal beating, the bouncer realized the soldier was dead and took his things to make it look like a robbery. A solid plan, had he not thrown the wallet into the back of his own truck. He also made comments later about how he had 'taken care of that guy' and 'he won't be a problem again'. Theo didn't know it at the time, but the guy had left a virtual roadmap in forensic evidence as well.

Unfortunately, the corporal was not the man who his wife had cheated with. He had killed the wrong man and was now spending the rest of his days in prison. His wife even came to court to testify against him, escorted by a man in military fatigues, the man she had actually been sleeping with.

"What can I do for you, detective?"

"I have a question about a military record," Theo explained. "And you are the only officer I know."

"I'm not sure I can help you with anyone's military record without written authorization," the colonel replied. "Dates and rank are probably the best I can do."

"That's just it," Theo said. "We did a background check on a suspect and turned up a seven-year gap."

"And you think he was in the military?"

"His parents say he was," Theo confirmed. "They even have a portrait of him in uniform."

"Are you sure it's real?" the colonel asked. "A background check should turn up any military record."

"That's what I thought," Theo said. "But I don't know why he would lie to his parents about it. And go as far as having a portrait made."

"Give me the name," the colonel said.

"Richard Jensen." Theo followed the name with his social security number.

Over the phone, Theo could hear the clicking of a keyboard as the colonel entered the information into the system. Unlike running a background check, the high-ranking officer should have direct access to whatever records existed. Occasional typing and vocalized frustration broke the long silence.

"This makes no sense," the colonel finally said.

"What's that?"

"When I search on your man's name," the colonel explained. "Nothing comes up. But when I search on the social security, I get a record with no name attached."

"No name?" Theo said. "What would cause that?"

"Nothing," Colonel Sutton muttered. "Shouldn't happen."

"Yet it did," Theo pointed out.

"You're talking about a human error that causes a man's record to disappear," the colonel said. "The military doesn't make those kinds of errors."

"Everyone makes errors," Theo said.

"First of all," the colonel explained. "A soldier's record isn't just created and ignored. Anything that happens goes into that record. Training completions, promotions, disciplinary actions, requests for leave. Everything goes in. If the record isn't there to be found, someone would notice as soon as it needed to be updated. And second, without a record, that soldier can't be paid, and if a soldier isn't paid, they are going to demand to know why. There is just no way a record doesn't exist."

"Could it have been erased?" Theo asked.

"The military doesn't erase anything," the colonel scoffed. "Let alone personnel records."

"Could they have been hacked?" Theo asked. "Erased by someone on purpose?"

"Our system is one of the most secure in the world. You don't just hack in and erase files with no one noticing." The colonel seemed lost in his thoughts. "I'm going to look into this. Give me your contact information and I'll call you if I learn anything."

Theo gave the colonel his phone number and email. He disconnected the call and shared with Patricia everything he learned, or hadn't.

"So his military record has been erased," Patricia said. "Who would do that? CIA?"

"Maybe," Theo shrugged. "Or he had someone erase it for him."

"But why?"

"No idea." Theo stopped for a moment. "I wonder if Carolyn Brechenstanch, or Winters, was not in the military the same time Richard Jensen wasn't."

"You think they served together?"

"A woman in the security industry," Theo said. "She has to be an ex-cop or a veteran."

"But why were their records erased?" Patricia asked. "And why did Jensen resurface when Brechenstanch didn't?"

"Million dollar questions," Theo said.

"I still say, CIA," Patricia said.

"Could I get you to go talk to Gavin Barr?" Theo asked of his partner.

"Sure."

"Find out if he knows anything at all about Richard's missing time," Theo said. "I know he said the man didn't talk about his past. But maybe he mentioned something. Anything at all would be more than we have."

"What are you going to do?"

"I'm going to dig deeper into both their backgrounds," Theo said. "See if I can tie them together."

50

Richard returned home from his impromptu visit to Gina Stuart's house close to two in the morning. He lay in bed another hour thinking about what she told him about being paid to keep him sedated by a woman in a blond wig.

He woke to sunlight streaming through the windows. Sleeping half the day away was not part of his plan. But terrorizing women in their bedrooms in the middle of the night hadn't been either.

Richard sat up, stretching and rubbing the ache from his muscles. A quick shower had him feeling almost normal. Throwing on the clothes he had worn the day before, he fixed a simple breakfast with a big cup of coffee. His phone rang while he was standing at the sink, washing the dishes.

The caller ID reported an unknown caller. He lay his phone on the counter and answered on speaker. "Hello."

"Hey, Money." Bulldog's distinct deep voice filled the kitchen.

"This isn't your number," Richard said.

"Oh, sorry," the big man said. "I use a program that generates random incoming numbers on caller ID. I don't like call backs."

"What do you have for me?"

"You know," Bulldog said. "I always remembered you as being the polite one. I don't even get a good morning? You've changed, my friend."

"Good-morning, Bulldog." Richard was not sincere. "What do you have for me?"

"A polite wiseass," Bulldog chuckled. "Now it's coming back to me."

"Bulldog."

"Sorry," the man said. "I spoke to Aces."

"And?"

"She's agreed to meet you."

"Great." Richard picked up the phone. "When and where?"

"She wants to meet somewhere public," Bulldog clarified.

"I would expect nothing else," Richard said.

"Food court at the mall."

"That's public all right," Richard said. "When?"

"Noon."

"Noon?" Richard looked at his watch. "Today noon?"

"Yes."

"That's in thirty minutes," Richard complained. "You couldn't call me earlier? I barely have time to get there."

"This was what she wanted," Bulldog answered. "She didn't want you to have time to plan anything."

"Plan anything?" Richard's voice was tense. Could Carolyn already know he had found the fake doctor? "Why does she think I would plan something, Benny? It's getting harder and harder to believe she didn't have something to do with my wife's disappearance."

"Hey, now," Bulldog said. "Let's not think that way, Money."

"I told you I don't go by that anymore," Richard snapped. "She wouldn't think I would be planning something unless she did something to make me want to."

"Just meet her," Bulldog suggested. "Ask your questions. She'll answer. We're family, Money, eh, Richard. She wouldn't do anything to harm the family."

"We were family," Richard agreed. "But that all changed after Mexico City, didn't it?"

Bulldog was silent.

"That's what I thought," Richard said. "Anyway, thanks. I owe you one."

"You owe me two," Bulldog countered. "But who's counting?"

"I've got to go." Richard disconnected the call, dropped the phone into his pocket, grabbed the keys to the Mercedes, and walked out the door.

It took twenty minutes driving well over the speed limit for him to arrive at the mall parking lot. It was unusually busy for a weekday, forcing Richard to race down the aisles in search of a space. A car backing out allowed him to park near the food court and in a matter of minutes, he was jogging to the entrance. Taking a moment to catch his breath, he pulled the doors open and walked in like he didn't have a care in the world.

The dining area was filled with families and groups of friends. Fast food establishments had lines of patrons cued to place their orders or waiting for their food. Music playing over the mall's speakers mixed with dozens of conversations to create an almost unbearable volume of noise.

Richard scanned the bodies standing in the lines, sitting at the tables and those just passing through. None of them resembled Carolyn. The food court spilled out into the rest of the mall, where store fronts vied for the business of shoppers. Doorways led to the back halls of the mall and a hallway that led to the restrooms. Too many vantage points to watch them all, Richard picked a table in the center of the space, giving him ample time to see anyone approaching him.

Bulldog had admitted Carolyn did not want him to have time to plan anything. He knew that if she was planning something of her own, leading him to a trap, it would have been in place long before he received the call where to go. Richard turned in his seat regularly, twisting his neck, watching every angle for his old friend and co-worker. He also knew she may not be the one who came. With that in mind, Richard also assessed possible threat levels of anyone who caught his eye or those looking his way. As the minutes ticked away, he added glancing at his wristwatch to the routine.

A man of average height, average build caught his eye. There was nothing special about him, other than the long coat he wore and the way the man walked straight toward Richard with a determined stride.

Slipping his hand under his jacket slowly, Richard grasped the handle of his pistol. His eyes shifted to track where everyone was and their movements. Families and friends on a normal day at the mall could easily turn into collateral damage if he wasn't careful. Returning his focus to the man who was almost upon him, Richard pulled his weapon free, keeping it below table level.

Richard was about to make his move when the man looked past him, curled his lips into a huge smile and said, "Been waiting long?"

The man passed by and Richard spun in his seat to watch his every move. Oblivious to Richard's stare, he stopped at the next table, where he was greeted by a woman about the same age. The two of them embraced and sat, diving into conversation immediately.

Focusing on the man, Richard had taken his eyes off the rest of the dining room. He spun his head and body in a smooth motion, scanning the entire space in one sweep. Still nothing. A glance at his watch told him the time was twelve-ten. She may have changed, but the Carolyn he knew was a very prompt woman. He gave her five more minutes before he stood and made his way out of the building. Taking his phone out, he picked a number from the 'recent' list and waited for Bulldog to answer.

"How'd it go?" the deep voice rumbled.

"It didn't," Richard replied. "She didn't show."

"You're kidding," Bulldog said. "That's not like her. She promised to be there."

Richard scanned the parking lot in a similar manner he used inside. "Well, she isn't."

Disconnecting the call, he shoved the phone into one pocket while digging his keys out of another. He took long strides walking toward the car, constantly searching for any threats in the area. None presented themselves. He couldn't help but wonder why Carolyn had agreed to meet if she had no intention of showing. Reaching the Mercedes, the thought crossed his mind that it may have acquired a bomb if she actually wanted him dead. He hesitated before unlocking it with the key fob. No explosion. Opening the door, he slid in behind the wheel. He hesitated again before starting the engine. He gave a sigh of relief and pulled the seatbelt across his body.

"You forget something?" The familiar voice was behind him.

He looked into the rearview mirror to see Carolyn rise to a sitting position.

51

Entering the offices of Jensen and Barr Internet Security, Detective Patricia Stevens could see Gavin Barr through the glass walls, sitting in an office with his elbows on the desk, his head in his hands. He did not look up to see who was entering.

The receptionist smiled. "Welcome, to …"

"I need to speak to Gavin Barr." Patricia interrupted the young woman while simultaneously holding out her shield and pointing at the man.

Bailey glanced over her shoulder before leaning forward to whisper, "He's been like that since he got here."

Patricia nodded to the girl and walked past her. Bailey made no protest nor any attempt to stop her. Not that the young girl could have done anything. Patricia was halfway across the building before the receptionist knew what was happening.

The office door stood open, and the detective walked right in with only a slight knuckle tap on the glass.

"Not now, Bailey." Gavin held his head in his hands, elbows on his desk, studying the sheet of paper in front of him.

"Mr. Barr," Patricia said. "I have some more questions for you."

Gavin raised his head, lowering his hands to cover the paper he had been staring at. "Oh, uh, Detective, uh, sorry I don't remember."

"Stevens," Patricia reminded him. "Are you okay? You look awful."

"Me?" Gavin said. "Sure. I'm fine. What can I help you with? Have you made progress finding Sonia?"

"I can't discuss the details of our investigation," Patricia responded. "I'm here to ask you some questions about is Mr. Jensen."

"Richard?" Gavin frowned. "What about him?"

"You mentioned he didn't share too much of his past with you," Patricia said.

"That's right," he confirmed.

"Can you tell me what he did share?"

"Like what?"

"Anything you remember," Patricia said. "Particularly the years just before you met him."

"Uh, he told me he was from around here." Gavin searched his mind for memories of the personal conversations he had with his partner. "He has a sister. She introduced him to Sonia."

"Anything not about his family?" Patricia interrupted.

"Oh, uh, let's see," Gavin closed his eyes and dug deeper. "He's a football fan. Used to travel a lot. He's been to a ton of places."

"Travelled?"

"I asked him how he could travel so much," Gavin said. "And he told me some of it was from being in the military."

"He told you he was in the military?"

"Yes. Army, I think."

"Did he say how long he was in the service?" Patricia asked.

"I don't think it ever came up," Gavin said. "Wouldn't there be a record you can check?"

"Did he ever tell you what he did in the Army?" Patricia ignored him. "Infantry? Artillery?"

"Sorry," Gavin shrugged. "He only mentioned it that one time. Never talked about it again."

"The business." Patricia hooked a thumb over her shoulder to the main room of the building. "You needed financing to open. Where is the loan through? Did he fill out loan papers? Something with his work history and the like?"

"No."

"He didn't?" Patricia could not disguise her surprise. "The loan's in your name?"

"No."

"What do you mean, no?"

"There is no loan," Gavin said. "Richard financed everything. I mean, we're partners, but he owns everything."

"You work for him?"

"No," Gavin shook his head. "We're partners."

"How does that work?" Patricia asked.

"It's the way Richard wanted it," Gavin said. "I told him he should be the boss and I would be happy working for him. He insisted we be partners. He said when we started growing I could pay him back half the investment. Like an interest free loan."

"Sounds like a nice guy," Patricia said.

"Richard's the best," Gavin smiled, but it quickly faded. "Which makes it all the worst that I'm letting him down."

"Letting him down?" Patricia asked. "How are you letting him down?"

"Richard doesn't even need me," Gavin confessed. "I can code. But he's much better than me. He's the brains of the operation. He's the salesman. He's the financial wizard. I contribute little to the business. I had to hire a girl to answer the phones."

"Surely you offer something," Patricia said. "He wants you as a partner. There has to be a reason."

"He's loyal," Gavin said. "Most loyal friend you could have."

Patricia didn't know what to say to that.

"But now." Gavin moved his hands from the paper on his desk. "I'm losing it all for him."

"Losing it how?"

Gavin lifted the paper and handed it to her. She took it and skimmed the page.

"You haven't paid the utilities?"

"Utilities, rent, nothing." Gavin looked like a broken man.

"Why?" Patricia asked. "And why don't you pay them now?"

"There's no money," Gavin lowered his head. "It's just gone."

"What do you mean gone?" Patricia asked.

"I mean, it was there one day," Gavin gestured to the ceiling. "And gone the next."

"What happened to the money, Gavin?" Patricia asked. "Did you spend it on something?"

"No." Gavin looked her in the eyes. "It's just gone."

"That makes no sense," Patricia said.

"Tell me about it," Gavin said.

"Money doesn't just disappear," Patricia said. "How much was in the account?"

"Last time I checked, before it vanished," Gavin said, "there was almost two-hundred-fifty thousand."

"And it's all gone?"

"All of it." Gavin's voice cracked.

"Is it possible Richard accessed the account?" Patricia asked. "Took the money out?"

"No." Gavin was adamant. "Richard wouldn't do anything to harm the company."

"What did he say when you told him?"

"I haven't." Gavin was somber.

"I think you should," Patricia advised. "I have no more questions at this time. Call him and explain what happened."

Gavin grimaced and nodded. He watched the detective leave the building before pulling out his phone and scrolling to Richard's name.

52

Looking at her in the rearview window, Richard said, "Carolyn."

"Richard," she grinned. "You wanted to see me?"

"I did."

"You waited for me a lot longer than I would have waited for you." Her eyes shifted to the mall entrance and back.

"What can I say? I'm a patient man." He studied her reflection, though he could only see from the collarbone up. He was certain she wore Kevlar under her jacket and that she was undoubtedly armed. "Thought we might do this in a more friendly setting."

"Is that what we are?" she asked. "Friends?"

"We were once," Richard said. They had been close friends all those years ago. The entire team spent their free time together. He and Carolyn had been half of a core group that had been inseparable. "Seemed like it that night."

In the mirror, he watched her eye movements and body language for a reaction to his reference of the Halstead party. To the credit of her training, he saw no clear indicator of her feelings on the matter.

"I heard about Sonia," she said. "I honestly liked her."

Without the benefit of being face-to-face, he could be mistaken, but he sensed sincere sympathy in her.

"Everyone does," Richard replied. "So, you didn't take her?"

"Me?" She seemed wounded by his words. "Why would I take her?"

"I know who you are," Richard said. "What you do. A job is a job, right?"

She had used those very words on an operation back in the day. The mission was to breech a compound where a known weapons runner lived. The objectives were to eliminate the runner and anyone who got in the way, destroy the weapons cache, and confiscate any electronics or files that might lead to identifying suppliers and buyers. They made extensive plans with contingencies for anything that might go wrong. The night they chose was moonless, giving them ample cover. Entry went as planned. They found the weapons runner in a storage building along with two of his top men, discussing the shipment they had just received. They were down before they even knew they were in danger. While Lance and James set up the explosives for the weapons, Richard and Carolyn broke into the main house in search of documents and computers.

They were rummaging through a home office, making a pile of what they would take with them when a woman walked in. She recoiled at the sight of the two intruders, staggering backward with a panicked expression. Her hands near her face, she took a deep breath, which could only be for an epic scream that would wake the entire household. Both Richard and Carolyn fired to keep that from happening. Their silencer equipped pistols kept the sound to a minimum. Later, after the mission was complete, Richard felt distressed about shooting an unarmed woman, and Carolyn shared her words of wisdom.

"I could say the same of you," she frowned.

"You show up out of the blue," Richard reported. "The next thing I know, Sonia's missing. And her boss, who you said you were a guest of, is missing. It's hard not to draw conclusions."

"You really think I would kidnap your wife?"

Asked that question six months ago, Richard would have responded with an adamant negative. The problem was, he had not seen or spoken to Carolyn in a decade. He did not know her any longer, not like he did. Although part of him wanted to believe the woman he once trusted with his life, the events that put them together in a car, in a parking lot, pushed him in the opposite direction.

"Dr. Rudra Paidi." Richard watched her face, seeing a slight twinge.

"Who?"

"Maybe I should say Gina Stuart?"

Resignation softened her expression. "You know about that?"

"Why, Carolyn?" Richard demanded. "If you didn't take Sonia, why did you keep me sedated?"

In the mirror, Carolyn watched the veins on his forehead and temples expand. He was justified in his anger, she knew. The road to making it right would be long and difficult.

"I could sure use a drink." She visibly relaxed. "How about you?"

"What?"

"Alcohol?" Carolyn said. "Maybe you've heard of it. You drink it and it makes you feel warm and fuzzy. Too much and it makes you stupid and brave."

"You want to go out for drinks?" Richard questioned.

"Yes." Carolyn became flustered. "There's a bar just up the road. Have a drink with me. I'll tell you everything."

"You kept me drugged for a month," Richard reminded her. "And what? I'm supposed to trust you?"

"Yes." Her eyes shrugged.

He studied her reflection. In her, he saw strength and resolve. Then, for a moment, he felt she was pleading with him.

"Fine." Richard started the car. "But I'll get my own drink."

"You can get mine, too." She sat back with her arms crossed. "If you want."

53

The glow from the computer screen on Detective Morris' desk illuminated his face in a pale light, giving him a similar look to the victims in the morgue. He did not move, did not blink. If not for the slight rise and fall of his chest, someone may have taken him down and put him in a drawer of his own.

Theo stared at a point well beyond the screen in front of him, his mind free flowing with thoughts of what Richard Jensen may have been doing during the missing years of his background check. The possibilities seemed endless. He could go to the source, but the widower could tell him anything. Theo wanted to have something a little more concrete before approaching the man.

His ring tone snapped the detective out of his trance. He patted his pockets until he located his phone, shifting his body to dig his hand in to retrieve the device. He missed the days when calls came over land lines. Finding a moment's peace proved difficult being reachable twenty-four seven.

He put the phone to his ear. "Morris."

"Detective."

The woman on the other end of the call sounded familiar.

"Yes."

"This is Agent Newton," she introduced. "I'm calling you back about Richard Jensen."

"Agent Newton," Theo said. "Thanks for getting back to me."

"Please, call me Lucy," she said.

"Okay, Lucy," the detective acknowledged. "You can call me Theo."

"Well, Theo," Lucy said. "I called some old contacts and did some additional digging on my own, trying to find out where your boy was during those missing seven years."

"Were you able to turn up anything?" Theo asked.

"My colleagues and I concluded those years had been scrubbed from Mr. Jensen's records," Lucy said. "It's as if, for seven years, the man did not exist. It was done so long ago, we have no way of tracing who scrubbed it."

"So, a dead end." Theo sighed, his frustration clear.

"I didn't say that."

Theo perked back up. "You found something? But you said the records were scrubbed."

"They were. But what I found was not in his records," Lucy clarified. "There was a mention of him during those seven years."

"A mention?" Theo asked. "What kind of mention?"

"About twelve years ago," Lucy said. "Right at the end of the missing time, a tracer was placed on his name."

"A tracer?" Theo said. "What does that mean?"

"Basically, if anyone does a search on his name, someone else gets notified," she said.

"Who put it there?"

"We don't know," she said. "The notification was set up to go to an email address. We tried to track its owner, but all the information tied to it came back as fake."

Theo hoped for something more conclusive to direct his questioning of Richard Jensen. But this proved beyond a doubt that the man had been in the military. Theo had what he needed.

"Twelve years?" Theo considered. "Do you think anyone is still monitoring the email?"

"That's a good question," Lucy sighed. "Not long after we discovered the red flag notation, it disappeared. So, yes. It was still being monitored. But we have no way of tracing it to who that might be, or who placed it there to begin with."

"So, back to zero."

"Not exactly," Lucy reassured him. "Finding the tracer tells us two things. First, that during those seven years where we find no trace of him, someone knew he existed. And second, although we don't know who put the tracer on his name, we know where it originated."

"Wait," Theo said. "You know where it came from?"

"Yes."

"Where?"

"Your local army base," Lucy said.

54

Richard sat across from Carolyn in a corner booth in the back of The Shot Glass Bar and Grill. Voices around them raised in volume to compete with the music being piped through strategically placed speakers throughout. Not a conducive environment for intimate conversation, it served well to prevent those conversations from being overheard.

The server flew in with their drinks before bounding away to the next table. The two former colleagues watched the young woman, trying to remember if they had that level of energy at her age.

"You were telling me why you felt it necessary to keep me sedated for four weeks," Richard reminded her.

"Was I?"

"Can we drop the games?" Richard growled. "Someone kidnapped my wife, and her abductors have a month head start because of you."

"Because of me?" Carolyn raised a hand to her chest. "How do you figure?"

"Are you kidding?" Richard shifted in his seat. "Sonia was gone a month before I even knew it. No one has been looking for her, not the way I would have."

"First of all," Carolyn defended, "you were unconscious when you arrived at the hospital. You remained that way for days with no help from me. Second, even if you knew weeks earlier, what would you have done? You couldn't walk. You couldn't even sit up. And you're still using a cane."

"I could have been researching." Richard gripped the cane tight enough to turn his knuckles white. "I would be further along than I am now."

"Maybe."

"Why does it matter?" Richard demanded. "You still haven't told me why you were keeping me sedated."

Carolyn let out a long sigh, sat back in the booth, and pulled her drink to the edge of the table. Lifting the glass, she said, "To old friends."

Richard stared at her, at the glass she dangled in front of him, and shook his head. With a show of his frustration, he lifted his drink. "Old friends."

Carolyn took a drink and set the glass down. Richard lowered his drink to the table.

"Now that was rude," Carolyn accused. "You can't even drink to friends?"

"Just answer the question."

Sitting in silence, she stared at him. The lines of his face were deeper than she remembered. She needed to know whether Richard had changed, or if he was still the man he had once been. She let out a long sigh.

"The night of the Halstead company party, I wasn't expecting to see you." Carolyn moved her glass in tight circles on the table. "You could say that you caught me off guard."

"So?" Richard said. "The same could be said for me about seeing you."

"But I was on the job," Carolyn explained. "And knowing your background, I had no way of knowing if you were too."

"I left that life," Richard said. "You know that."

"I know that's what you told me," Carolyn said. "What you told all of us. But…"

"Wait," Richard sat forward. "So, the only reason you approached me that night was to see if I was your competition?"

"Not the only reason." Carolyn shook her head. "But a big reason."

"And after spending the evening with us," Richard said. "You still thought I was working?"

"I didn't know," Carolyn admitted. "And after your accident, I couldn't take the chance. I took advantage of your situation to protect my client."

"To protect your client?" Richard scowled. "Who, exactly, is your client?"

"You know I can't tell you that," Carolyn said.

"Did your client take Sonia?"

"No," Carolyn said. "Absolutely not."

"You sedated me to protect your client," Richard thought aloud. "You thought I was on a job. Did you think I was there to take out your client?"

"I thought it was a possibility," Carolyn said. "Yes."

"And now?" Richard asked. "Telling me what you have, you must have concluded I'm not."

"I have."

"Your client," Richard said. "Is it Halstead?"

"Richard." She gave him a slight smile. "You know I can't tell you."

"Did he want me dead?"

"No." Carolyn insisted. "No one wanted anyone dead."

"Do you?"

The question stunned her for a moment. "Of course not."

"Well, someone does." Richard watched her face. He saw a slight change.

"What does that mean?"

"I had a man with a gun pull up beside me on a motorcycle." Richard answered.

"How did he miss?"

"Thought he could hit a moving target," Richard explained. "Didn't take into account that the moving target might hit him."

"You still have the moves then," Carolyn said.

"Maybe." Richard looked at the contents of his glass. "I also had a dark sedan chasing me. I didn't wait to see if he was going to try to shoot me too."

"Then you do still have the moves." Carolyn smiled as if she were proud of a child's grades.

He lifted his glass to his lips for the first time. It occurred to him that the last time he had alcohol was the night of his wife's company party. His eyes shifted to Carolyn as a memory invaded his thoughts.

"You did tell me," he said.

"Told you what?"

"Who you were working for." Richard sat the glass down and sat up. "When we talked that night, you told me you were working with Stan, Stan Webber."

Carolyn did not speak.

"If you thought I was on the job," Richard frowned. "If you thought I was an actual threat to your client, why would you tell me that? Was it some kind of warning for me to stay away?"

"I think we've shared enough." Carolyn slid to the edge of the booth.

"Wait," Richard put a hand up. "Stan went missing before the party, but you were there. So, either you have him hidden somewhere, or you've already failed your assignment."

Carolyn sighed. "I haven't failed."

"You know I've been looking for him?"

"I thought you might be."

Richard tapped the table. "Let me talk to him."

"I can't help you." Carolyn stood. "It's been good seeing you, Richard."

She moved away, and Richard turned. "Tell me something."

"What?" she huffed.

"That night at the party," he looked up at her. "When you were so nice to me, to Sonia, that was all an act, wasn't it? You were only trying to assess whether I was a threat to your client. You weren't happy to see me. You're still holding a grudge."

"A grudge!? Really?" she yelled.

The bar fell silent, and all eyes turned to them. Carolyn looked around, then sat back down.

Her voice became a harsh whisper. "Do you really think I'm still holding a grudge? After all these years?"

"I don't know, Carolyn," Richard said. "If I don't find Sonia, I imagine I will hold a grudge for a long time."

"Not the same thing," Carolyn huffed.

"It feels like it is," Richard said.

"You didn't kill him." Carolyn's jaw clenched.

"I may as well have," Richard narrowed his eyes. "That's what you told me at the time."

Operation Mexico City, codenamed for the location where they planned the mission, took place two hundred miles southeast of the capital. Fulfilling the mission objective meant infiltrating a drug lord's compound, eliminating the top man and as many lieutenants as possible, destroying the lab and getting out alive. A highly skilled eight-man squad went in and completed all the objectives. All but one.

"At the time," Carolyn's anger faded. "That's what I believed."

"You made that very clear," Richard said. "The fact is, I believed it too."

She tilted her head. "Richard. He was ten years old. None of us would have pulled the trigger."

"A ten-year-old with an AK-47," Richard reminded her. "It was my job to protect the team. We lost three men because I didn't pull the trigger. Three good men, including Lance."

Carolyn flinched at the sound of their squad leader's name. Richard had been Lance Brody's first recruit for the new team he was forming, convincing him to leave the army and join him, with the promise of making a difference. They had served together for three years. Carolyn became one of them two years in. Together, they had accomplished a lot of things. They had indeed made a difference.

"You couldn't have known the kid was capable of doing what he did," Carolyn reasoned. "None of us would have believed it."

Richard was the only one who knew Lance and Carolyn had become a couple. In the field, the two of them remained professional. Richard only guessed what was going on because he had a keen sense for body language and had noticed a slight change between them.

"It didn't matter what I believed," Richard grumbled. "Had I neutralized the threat, Lance would still be alive."

"Maybe," Carolyn looked down at the table. "But no one blames you for not wanting to shoot a kid."

They were in the final moments of the operation, having eliminated all the targets on their list. They had gathered in the lab to set explosives before leaving the compound. Richard was one of two members watching the doors, watching the team's back. He was the lucky one to have the drug lord's son step into the room.

"Didn't matter in the end," Richard sighed. "Still had to do it."

The images from that day still haunted his dreams. It was Richard's last mission. Losing a third of their team, the anger of the rest of the squad, and the killing of the young boy all played a part in his leaving. He couldn't face any of them. And for six months he vanished off the face of the earth, hiding from everyone and drinking his memories into oblivion. No one knew where he was or what he was doing for six months. Part of that time, he didn't even know.

Drinking, fighting and sex. Anything to take his mind off what happened. He was on a dark path.

At the end of that path, he woke with a terrible hangover, in a room he didn't recognize, with a woman he had never seen before and a broken finger he couldn't explain. A week later, he was sitting on his parent's couch, listening to them offer solutions to his future, without knowing his past. What saved him was the girl walking through the room behind his sister. Some light out of the darkness. When his and Sonia's eyes met, his world changed.

"Who wants Stan dead?" Richard asked.

"You know I can't discuss my client with you," Carolyn said.

"Who and why?"

"I can't tell you that."

"Sonia worked for Stan," Richard pointed out. "Someone took Sonia. And apparently, someone wants Stan dead. Seems to me it must be the same person."

"I considered that," Carolyn admitted. "But I couldn't find a connection."

"They worked together," Richard said. "That's the connection."

"It's a connection," Carolyn said. "But it's not enough."

"But you looked into it?"

"Of course."

"And did you learn anything?" Richard asked. "Anything that might help me?"

"Richard." Carolyn's voice softened. "Sonia hasn't been my priority."

"What has been your priority, Carolyn?" Richard asked. "Keeping Stan hidden from the world?"

Carolyn shifted and looked down at the drink in front of her.

"Wait." Richard sat up straight again, his sense of body language kicking in. "You're lying to me. What are you lying about, Carolyn?"

She raised her eyes to meet his. "Stan started receiving death threats. He thought it might be someone in the company. That's why I went to the party; to scout out likely suspects."

"And Stan?"

"He insisted he needed to run an errand before the party," she said. "He was supposed to meet me at the Halstead's home."

"But he didn't show," Richard concluded. "He was receiving death threats, and you let him run errands alone."

"It was against my wishes," Carolyn defended. "But you're right. We both thought he would be safe. Honestly, I wasn't convinced the threats were even real."

"So, you didn't stash him away somewhere?" Richard's hopes sank.

"I haven't seen him since that day," Carolyn confirmed.

55

"I want to thank you for taking the time to see us." Detective Morris sat in one of the two chairs positioned in front of the colonel's desk while his partner took the other.

"Of course," the colonel said. "What can I do for you? I thought I had answered all your questions."

"Something came up that I'm hoping you can help us with." Theo clasped his hands before him. "Having to do with Richard Jensen."

"The same name you gave me before," the colonel observed.

"Yes."

"I'm not going to get different results, detective."

The colonel reminded Theo of a conversation he had with one of his college professors in his third year. He had just posted scores for a research paper that was to be half the semester grade. Theo received a C for his efforts, prompting him to go to the professor's office to challenge the grade. Theo argued the merits of his research, the validity of his argument and the reasoning behind his conclusion. He followed his rant with a demand for an A, or a B at the very least.

The professor listened to every word with the patience of a parent listening to a child rationalize their need for a toy. He then pointed out the flaws in Theo's research, the errors in his argument and the holes in his conclusion. Though he praised his student's passion, he explained the resulting grade would not change. To his surprise, Theo and the professor had become friends by the end of the semester.

"I have a connection who did a deep dive into Jensen," Theo said. "And while they agree there are no records showing Jensen was in the military, they did find something."

"What would that be?"

"It seems someone put a," Theo turned to his partner. "What did she call it?"

"She called it a tracer," Patricia answered.

"That's right," Theo nodded. "Someone put a tracer on Jensen's name."

"A tracer?"

Patricia started, "That's where ..."

"I know what a tracer is, detective." The colonel cut her off.

"The thing is," Theo continued. "Whoever put the tracer on his name, did it from this base. I'm wondering why someone would do that. You know, when there are no records of him even being in the military."

"I'm curious how they were able to find this tracer," the colonel said. "Seeing how it was on a secure military computer."

"I don't know computers," Theo shrugged. "What I don't understand is how they found it, but you didn't."

The colonel stared through Theo to a point far beyond him.

"You did find it, didn't you?" Theo accused.

"I can't help you, detective." The colonel focused on Theo's eyes.

"You noticed the tracer." Theo thought aloud. "Which proved Richard Jensen was a soldier."

"I can't help you."

"His records have been scrubbed," Theo continued. "Why?"

"I think it's time for you to go," the colonel said.

"Colonel, this is a murder investigation," Patricia said.

"I'm aware of that and I'm sorry," the colonel said. "But I can't help you."

"We could get a warrant," Patricia warned.

"You could," the colonel agreed. "But even if you were to find a judge that would sign off on a broad warrant for a military base, it wouldn't help you."

"Because the records have been scrubbed," Theo nodded.

"If that's what you want to think," the colonel said.

"Hypothetically," Theo tilted his head and narrowed his eyes. "Why would a soldier's records be erased?"

"Seems unlikely," the colonel said. "But hypothetically, I would guess someone did not want anyone to find a connection between the man and the military."

"I can't think of any good reason for that," Theo said.

"Neither can I," the colonel admitted.

The detective sighed and stood. "Thank you for your time, colonel."

"Theo?" Patricia pleaded. "He knows something."

Theo looked down at his partner. "It's time to go."

With a huff, Patricia stood and followed Theo out of the office. As they reached their car, she turned on him. "What was that? He knew something he wasn't telling us."

"I know that." Theo climbed into the driver's seat. "I also know he wasn't ever going to tell us."

"You know that?" Patricia pulled her seatbelt across her chest.

"I do," Theo grimaced. "I think someone outranking him had warned him not to."

"Then why accept our request to meet?"

"Probably to learn how much we know," Theo said. "And now they know."

The detective turned the key until the engine started, then drove off the base.

56

"Let me get this straight." Richard pointed at Carolyn. "Your mission was to protect Stanley Webber."

"Yes."

"And you haven't seen him in what?" Richard said. "A month."

"That's right."

"Yet you told me you hadn't failed your mission."

"Until I have proof that he's dead," Carolyn crossed her arms. "My mission remains to protect him. Only now, I need to find him."

"If you thought I was working a mission," Richard asked, "a mission to kill Stan, why did you keep me sedated? Why didn't you interrogate me? Find out if I knew where he was? Or if he was even alive?"

The corner of Carolyn's mouth curled. "Do you remember The Needle?"

Richard flinched. Operation Thread the Needle was a mission to slip into an enemy camp and eliminate the top leaders and slip out again, undetected. The camp was a series of caves and tunnels, and the enemy was a group building an empire on gun running and human trafficking. It marked the first time a mission had not gone as planned. "Of course I remember."

"The background they gave us turned out to be wrong," Carolyn recounted. "You and, what was his name?"

"Peters," Richard lowered his eyes. "Maxwell Peters."

"Max," Carolyn smiled. "Always liked him."

"Yeah," Richard sighed. "Me too."

"So, you two go left," she continued. "Left was supposed to take you to where one of our targets slept. Only it didn't."

"No," Richard inhaled. "It didn't."

"How many were there?"

"Fifteen." Richard finished his drink. "Guarding a storeroom of weapons. All armed and not happy to see us."

"How long did they have you before we got you out?" Carolyn asked.

"Six hours," Richard said. "But you knew that."

"Six hours." Carolyn nodded. "What did they do to you during those six hours."

"They tortured me," Richard said. "Trying to get me to tell them who we worked for and why we were there."

"And Max?"

"You know."

She looked down at the table. In their attempt to get Richard to talk, they started torturing Max in front of him. When he refused to talk, they increased the torture. In the end, Max died and Richard did not break.

"And you thought I was going to try getting information out of you?" Carolyn looked up at him. "What good would that have done me?"

What she didn't know, what he never told anyone, was that moments before his rescue, he had almost broken. Would he have talked? Even he didn't know. But the thought had wormed its way into his mind.

"I'm not the man I was then," Richard dismissed. "But the fact you kept me sedated, you understand why I might think you did that as some kind of revenge?"

"I can see why you might think that." Carolyn crossed her arms. "But it's been a decade. I moved on, got married. I have no interest in revenge."

"About that," Richard perked up. "Bulldog told me you married Teeter."

"I did." She grinned.

"How did that happen?"

Carolyn's grin became a full smile. "It was funny. After everything happened, I left. Went off on my own, taking security jobs when I could get them. And it must have been two or three years later, I'm working a security detail for this wannabe star when I feel something poke me in the back and a man's voice says, 'Don't move'. I'm thinking someone's about to shoot me in the back. So, I do a quick maneuver and put him on the ground."

"Teeter?"

"Teeter being Teeter." She let out a soft laugh. "Always playing games. Fool could have gotten himself killed. Which, in the end, I guess he did."

Her smile faded.

"Anyway," she continued. "Turns out he had just left Jackson's group and was looking for something. It was only by chance he saw me that day. The two of us started our own company, started dating, got married. Then he took a bullet on a crap job for crap pay."

"Sorry."

"Thanks," she said. "It's the line of work we're in. You know, he told me Jackson hired Lance's younger brother just before he bailed."

"Bulldog mentioned that." Richard nodded. "You ever meet him?"

"Once." She frowned. "Lance took me to meet his parents. Lucas was sixteen, I think. Adored his big brother."

"I didn't even know he had a brother." Richard's voice drifted. "How did I not know that?"

"Well, if it helps," Carolyn said. "I didn't know you had a sister."

Silence lingered in the air between them. All those years they worked together, been friends, and they knew very little about each other.

"Anyway, Bulldog said he was some math prodigy," Richard said. "Why would a math nerd become an operative?"

"Like I said," Carolyn answered. "He adored his brother. Probably wanted to follow in his footsteps."

The two of them nodded a silent acknowledgment, as if they had answered the question of what someone else was thinking a decade earlier.

"So what now?" Richard asked.

"Now," Carolyn said. "I am on a mission to find and protect Stanley Webber. You are on a mission to find Sonia and those responsible for taking her. I believe whoever took Stan also has Sonia. In that respect, our missions align."

"I suppose they do," Richard said.

"And in light of the fact that someone is trying to kill you," Carolyn added. "It seems you're pushing the right buttons."

"It would seem so," Richard agreed.

"Then, I would like to propose a joint venture." Carolyn opened her arms. "We work together to find what we're looking for. Like old times."

"And if I refuse?"

Carolyn frowned. "Why would you refuse?"

"The last time we worked together things ended badly," Richard reminded her. "Besides. You want to find them and rescue Stan."

"That's right," Carolyn confirmed. "And you want to rescue Sonia."

"I won't be on just a rescue mission."

"What do you mean?"

"I intend to end them." Richard's expression hardened.

"End them?" Taken aback, Carolyn said, "You were always the voice of reason. The moral compass. We used to change mission plans to avoid unnecessary bloodshed. All because of you. Since when have you taken the stance of killing them all?"

"Since they took Sonia."

57

Detectives Morris and Stevens sat at their respective desks reading through everything they had so far. The accident report from when Sonia Jensen disappeared offered little. The original investigation concluded the accident a hit and run. No one even knew Sonia had been in the car until later, so interviews with friends and family took place later than they should have. Speaking to Richard Jensen took place a month after the fact because of the drugs administered to keep him unconscious. No one interviewed friends or colleagues since the need hadn't been established. They didn't know what they were looking at, so they never asked the necessary questions when they should have.

Concerning the investigation, Theo and Patricia started from scratch weeks after the fact. They might as well have been handed a ten-year-old cold case. No one gathered evidence from the scene. Police, rescue personnel, the tow-truck driver and the staff at the scrap yard, all touched the vehicle. The chances of isolating a suspect after so much time had passed were slim.

"Sonia Jensen was a normal, hardworking, happily married woman." Theo closed the folder he had been reading from and sat back. "Richard Jensen is a mysterious individual with a gap in his history, possible military training and who knows what other secrets."

"He seems like the obvious target." Patricia dropped the file she was reading to her desk. "Yet, she's the one taken. Not him."

"Let's suppose he was the target," Theo suggested. "Suppose someone from his past decided they wanted him dead, someone from those seven years."

"Then why isn't he dead?" Patricia asked. "He was a sitting duck at the scene of the accident. Not to mention the time he was in the hospital."

"And why take the wife?" Theo added.

"Unless that was the plan," Patricia perked up. "What if taking his wife was some kind of punishment? A way of hurting him?"

"Death is too easy," Theo ran with it. "Make him suffer by taking what he cares about."

"But then why would they keep him sedated?" Patricia deflated. "He wasn't really suffering since he didn't know she was gone."

Theo tried to think of any scenario where it made sense to keep Richard unconscious for a month. It only made sense if the person who took Sonia knew her husband had military training and feared he might come after them. The problem Theo had with that line of thinking was that if the person knew Richard's past, then Richard had to be the target, and taking Sonia was a way to harm Richard or a mistake.

A plan to harm Richard should include taunts to the husband, including unobtainable ransom demands. If taking her was in error, it would need to be fixed. They would have released her, in which case Sonia should have turned up somewhere a short time after the abduction. Or they eliminated the problem, and she would turn up in a ditch or shallow grave.

Theo sighed. "Did we check to see if there were any reports of stalkers or restraining orders?"

"There wasn't anything," Patricia said. "No stalkers. No threats."

The idea that someone took Sonia Jensen just to have her was bittersweet. It would mean that she was likely still alive. On the other hand, abductions of that nature seldom ended well. The victims disappear forever or turn up years later. The perpetrators hide them away in windowless basements, sometimes moving them out of state. With a month head start, they could be anywhere.

Theo rubbed his eyes. He was missing a large piece of the puzzle other than Richard's seven years.

"Richard Jensen is hiding things from us." Theo stood. "And it's time we find out what they are."

58

Richard drove the speed limit and checked his mirrors often, trying to spot a tail, if he had one. According to Carolyn, neither the man on the motorcycle nor the one in the black sedan worked for her. If she were to be believed, he was in no danger from her. He just wasn't sure he was ready to trust her. Keeping him sedated for the better part of a month didn't exactly instill trust. And her explanation fell a little flat considering it prevented him from looking for Sonia.

He had agreed to at least consider Carolyn's offer to join forces, a proposition that wasn't without merit. Having worked together in the past, Richard knew what an asset she could be. Being on the same team would allow them to have each other's backs. They could cover more ground, combine knowledge, and share thoughts and ideas. If not for that question of trust.

Years ago, the two of them, along with Lance, depended on one another. They each had the other's backs, relying on the team to complete missions and get home safe. With one another's lives in their hands, they felt confident and secure. There had never been any doubts.

That all changed with the Mexico City operation. Lance's death not only broke the team, it also broke the trust. It tore apart the relationship Richard had with Carolyn. He and Lance had been like brothers, making Carolyn family. Richard expected to be the best man at their wedding. He knew what losing Lance meant to her. What she never seemed to understand was what it meant to him to lose his best friend. It destroyed him. He didn't leave the team all those years ago because he failed his team. There's always a risk. They had lost men before. He left because he couldn't look at the team without seeing Lance's face staring back at him. He left because the loss he felt devastated him, and a decade later he still felt the hurt.

Richard's phone rang and he pulled it out of his pocket. He checked the screen and saw his partner Gavin's name. He scanned the area, checking his mirrors. Convinced no one was following him, he relaxed and answered.

"Hey, Gav. What's up?"

"Hey, Richard," Gavin said. "How are you doing?"

"Better. Thanks." Richard could hear a nervousness in his partner's voice. "And you?"

"I'm good," Gavin faked a nonchalance.

"Uh, Gavin?" Richard prodded. "Did you need something?"

"Yeah, so," his voice cracked. "Listen, Richard. There's something I need to talk to you about."

"About the business?"

"Yeah."

"Okay," Richard sighed. "Well, do you think it could wait? It's not really a good time."

"Yeah, sure," Gavin said. "I understand."

Richard heard a relief in his partner's voice that caught him by surprise. Concerned, he said, "Gavin? Is everything okay?"

"Uh," Gavin let the sound linger a moment. "Not really."

"What's going on?"

"Uh, well," Gavin stammered. "You see. Well, it's like…"

Richard looked in the rearview mirror and saw a car he thought he had seen before. Searching his memory, he remembered it had been at the cafe while he was talking to Carolyn. He turned at the next street and watched. The car turned as well.

"Richard?" Gavin said. "Are you still there?"

"I'm here," Richard assured him. "But I have to go."

"What?"

"Are you at the office?"

"Yeah."

Richard turned again. The car followed.

"I'll come to you." Richard thought about where he was and where he could go. "You stay there. We'll talk when I get there. Okay?"

"Yeah, sure," Gavin agreed.

Richard disconnected the call. His eyes moved from mirror to mirror trying to determine if the car he spotted was the only one following him. He couldn't see how many occupants were in the car. But the presence of other vehicles increased the odds against him. Nothing stood out to Richard, but he knew someone else could be nearby.

An abandoned bowling alley came to mind. Near his current location, Richard could lead his pursuer away from innocent bystanders. All he needed to do was put some distance between him and his tail to give him time to defend himself if needed. Seeing an opportunity, he accelerated into a left-hand turn in front of oncoming traffic.

Ignoring the blaring horns of angry drivers, Richard sped down the street as the car following him waited for an opening to make the same turn he had. The next turn he made put him on a path toward the bowling alley.

Having been around for years, Richard had bowled there as a kid. The place had been old then. When it shut down about eight years ago, there had been talk of refurbishing the place and opening with a new name. Nothing ever came of it, and years of standing vacant had taken its toll on the already failing structure. Questions had been raised about the building's stability as it had become a favorite nighttime hideout for kids looking to party. That told Richard that he would find access into the shuttered business while leaving him to hope no one would be there when he arrived.

Hitting the brakes and spinning the steering wheel sharply to the right, Richard skidded into a turn that took him through the entrance to the parking lot. He raced up to the entrance, turning away when he could see that the front was boarded up with thick chains securing the doors. Remembering an emergency exit on the side of the building, Richard continued there. He slid to a stop near the door. The plywood was lying on the ground, chains dangling loose from the handle. This was his way inside.

He rolled forward and parked the Mercedes, jumping out and jogging back to the unsecured opening. Pulling the gun from the small of his back, he stood to one side as he pulled the door open. Stepping through the doorway, the stark contrast in lighting blinded him. As his eyes adjusted to the change, he held the weapon ready and scanned for danger. He was alone inside.

Outside, he could hear the roar of a car engine approaching. Unfortunately, he soon heard a second. Following the same path he did, they sped up to the front door before moving on to the side of the building. They came to a stop at the side door, clearly identified by Richard's car being parked nearby. Richard waited as they tried to determine if they were about to be ambushed when they left the relative protection of their cars.

Richard considered where the best place to be when they came through the door would be. An obvious place would be behind the counter where patrons would pay and pick up their shoes to bowl. With two assailants, it would be a decent plan. Close enough to assure hitting his targets, while having the benefit of whatever protection the counter provided. However, if there were more, it left him too close to the enemy with nowhere to go. He needed to have maneuverability.

The racks that once held bowling balls ran the length of the bowling alley with breaks in between. They would provide similar protection as the counter would with the added benefit of being able to move from space to space with minimal exposure. It would also give Richard a place to initiate a conversation without giving away his location. He moved to the second rack from the door and readied himself for what was to come.

It didn't take long for things to happen. Richard could hear the door open followed by steps made by men trying to make as little noise as possible. He waited for the door to close behind them before speaking.

"That's far enough." He faced the far wall to make it harder for them to pinpoint where he was. "What do you want?"

Richard listened to cautious footsteps as the men tried to better position themselves. He calculated three separate movements. The man who spoke was a fourth.

"Oh, Mr. Jensen," the man said. "It's not about what we want. It's what our client wants."

"Your client?" Richard pulled his second pistol free of the shoulder holster, listening intently to pinpoint where the men were. "Who is your client?"

"That's not how these things work," the man answered. "We don't know his name. And wouldn't tell you if we did. Now, why don't you show yourself so we can get this over with."

Richard had an idea where three of the men were. The fourth was more elusive. "And what exactly is 'this'?"

"Mr. Jensen." The man sounded humored. "You're not really that naive are you?"

"I guess not."

Richard shifted to the left, gun in hand, and fired a single shot. Before he moved back to cover, he saw his target fall to the ground clutching his chest.

"He's armed!" The shout did not come from the man who had been speaking.

Footsteps became louder as they moved for position and cover. Richard pivoted and fired twice. A second man, running for the cover of a support post, did not make it. Richard moved away, using the cover of the racks to hide his actions.

"Who is this guy?" The elusive fourth man spoke.

Richard calculated the man's location and rose to his feet, both weapons over the top of the rack. He spotted the man and fired multiple shots in that direction while also trying to locate the original speaker, the obvious leader of the group. Return fire forced him to take cover again. This time he moved back the way he had come, toward the men who had come for him.

A single shot struck one rack as he passed between it and the next. Richard stopped, dropped to the ground and slid into the opening once more. He fired two more shots and the fourth man fell back into a display case, breaking what little glass remained. Three down. One to go.

The leader did not speak again. He moved in measured steps, trying not to give away where he was while he searched for his target. Richard did the same, keeping low and listening. Richard stopped behind one of the racks to slow his breathing and heighten his senses. That is when he heard the breathing of the other man, just on the other side of the same rack. Then the breathing stopped.

Richard raised his weapons to the rack and fired a row of shots through the wood. He heard the man drop. Not taking chances, Richard moved around the rack with caution, jumping out with weapons ready if the man was about to shoot. The man lay on his back holding his side, trying to stop the bleeding.

He saw Richard and stared at the guns pointed at him.

"Who are you?" The man spoke between gasps. "The client warned me to be ready. Which is why I brought backup. But..."

"Who is your client?" Richard demanded.

"I wasn't lying," the man said. "I don't know."

Richard snarled. He had hoped to get information that might help him find Sonia.

"There...There was a message," the man gasped for air. "I was supposed to give it to you if I had the opportunity, you know, before you died."

"What's the message?"

"I was supposed to tell you." The man took a deep breath and coughed. Blood appeared on his lips. "To tell you, when the time came, she wouldn't suffer."

"She's alive?" Richard demanded. "Where is she?"

The man shook his head. "Don't even know who she is."

Richard patted the man down until he found his phone. He dug it out of the man's pocket and put it in his own. He stood up again and put one gun back into his holster.

"Aren't you going to finish me?" The man asked.

"Do you want me to?" Richard asked as he walked to the closest of the bodies. He knelt and took his phone as well.

"Not really."

"Okay then."

Richard walked out of the building to the Mercedes. He drove out of the lot and drove back to a busy road. Once there, he used the dead man's phone to call 9-1-1 about hearing shots at the old bowling alley. He powered off the phone, drove to a bridge and tossed it out the window to the river below.

59

Richard's adrenaline was pumping, and his mind raced. Someone had taken Sonia. And now, that same person, presumably, had hired hitmen to take him out. What he wanted to know was why they hadn't killed him when they took her. And if killing him hadn't been the plan, what had changed?

The police would be all over the scene he just left. Richard would need to switch out weapons to prevent the bullet casings from being tied to him. But that could wait.

Richard checked his mirrors. He was confident that no one was following him now. He needed to swing by the office and talk to Gavin while he was sure he wouldn't put his partner in danger. While he drove, his heart rate slowed, as did his breathing. By the time he arrived, he was calm and in control again. He stepped out of the car, closed his jacket and walked into his business.

"Gavin?" Richard said upon entering. He looked at the receptionist. "Is he in his office?"

She nodded.

Richard walked past her without slowing. His partner sat behind his desk studying at his laptop, a worried look on his face. He saw Richard and gave him a half-hearted wave. Richard returned the gesture down to the lack of sincerity. He walked into the office, closing the door behind him.

"What's going on, Gav?" Richard sat heavily in the chair across from him. "What do you need to talk to me about?"

"Richard, I want you to know," Gavin said. "I tried everything I could think of to solve this without bringing you into it. I know you need your rest."

"I appreciate that," Richard dismissed. "Now what's the problem."

"Well." Gavin looked up, and his nervousness shifted to concern. "Is that blood?"

Richard followed his partner's line of sight to his own sleeve. He raised his arm and turned it so he could see. A red stain adorned the cuff of his shirt. "Oh, yeah. It's fine. It's mine."

"Who else's would it be?" Gavin asked. "Are you okay?"

"I'm fine," Richard assured him. Thinking fast, he added, "I had a nosebleed earlier. Didn't realize it got on my shirt."

"And you're sure you're okay?"

"I'm fine," Richard repeated. "Now, what did you need to tell me?"

Gavin sat back and took a deep breath. "I think someone is stealing from us."

"What do you mean by stealing from us?" It was Richard's turn to look concerned. "Stealing what?"

"Money," Gavin sighed. "Someone's stealing our money."

"What?" Richard exclaimed. "How?"

"I don't know," Gavin shrugged. "It's just gone."

"Gone?" Richard frowned. "How much, Gavin? How much is gone?"

Gavin looked at the screen of his laptop, let out a heavy sigh, and turned the machine to face his partner. "All of it."

Richard looked at the bank statement that filled the screen showing several transfers over the course of the past four weeks. A single transfer posted daily for thousands of dollars each, starting the Monday after Sonia's disappearance. The remaining balance of the account was less than two-hundred dollars.

"There was three-hundred thousand dollars in this account." Richard said it to himself, but his partner responded.

"I know."

"Who authorized these transfers, Gavin?" He looked up at his partner with a harsh stare.

"I don't know," Gavin whined. "Only you or I could have, and I know I didn't. And you, you were unconscious when they started."

"What did the bank say?" Richard's tone was firm. When Gavin did not answer right away, Richard added. "You did call the bank, didn't you?"

"Yes." Gavin blurted. "I called."

"And what did they say?"

"They said…," Gavin struggled. "It just makes no sense."

"What doesn't make sense, Gavin?" Richard could tell his partner was holding something back. His own involvement, maybe. "What did they say?"

"They said." Gavin took a deep breath before finishing. "They said Sonia authorized it."

Richard froze. Gavin was right. It didn't make sense. Sonia had nothing to do with the business. She would never take money out of the company accounts. He wasn't even sure she was authorized to do so. He thought back to when they started the business. Sonia was in finance. She helped Richard set up the accounts. She even helped with the books in the early days, before her own career took off. She was on the paperwork. She had the authority to do whatever she wanted. The question was, why.

Richard pulled out his phone and logged into their personal bank. Between them, they had three accounts. Richard's, Sonia's and a joint account they used for paying bills, making household purchases and the like. He opened the accounts page and was confused. His account and Sonia's were nearly depleted. The joint account, which usually only had a few thousand in it, had eighty-thousand and change.

On the surface, it appeared Sonia had left him and was cleaning out the accounts. But if that were the case, why did the joint account have more money than it should? Was she capable of setting up the accident that started everything? She could have easily been killed. And if she planned everything, how did he not see the signs? It made more sense to him that whoever took Sonia had been forcing her to help him take the money. Which brought up the question of what happens when the money is gone. Did the message from the would-be assassin, 'When the time comes', refer to that?

"Listen, Gav," Richard's tone had softened again. "I need you to call the bank. We need to set up another account that only you and I can access. Then we need to divert all incoming deposits to the new account. Can you do that?"

"Of course," Gavin said. "I'll get right on it. But what about the missing money?"

"I'll look into it when I get a chance." Richard thought back to when they first opened their business. He sank his rainy-day fund into the startup, and the two of them spent months going door to door dropping off flyers. The first technology conference they went to became the turning point where they made meaningful connections with others in the field as well as future clients. Now, years later, they were established and financially secure. Being on shaky ground again was not where he wanted to be. He wanted nothing more than to understand the situation and fix it. To do that, he needed to find Sonia. "Listen, Gavin. I have to go. I have something else to take care of right now."

"What?" Gavin frowned. "Uh, okay?"

"I will look into it. I promise." Richard patted Gavin on the back and started out. He skidded to a stop, turning back. "Don't forget to call the bank."

"Will do," Gavin gave him a thumbs up.

"Thanks for taking care of everything, Gav," Richard said. "You're a good friend."

"Just come back soon," Gavin said.

The drive home seemed to take longer than usual. Richard's thoughts kept going to the financial crisis he and his company were experiencing as well as what role Sonia did or didn't play in putting them there. He just couldn't reconcile with the idea that Sonia would harm him. And cleaning out the bank accounts didn't sound like her at all. Sure, comfort and stability were nice, but their marriage had never been about acquiring things. It had always been about them.

Richard turned onto the street where he and Sonia had lived for so many years. He saw a car out of place in an instant. The black sedan with tinted glass parked across from his house, just far enough down the street not to be too obvious. But Richard's training and knowledge of his neighbors' vehicles helped him spot the intruder. Without slowing, he steered into the driveway and up to the garage. Out of view of the street, he jumped out and used the back door to get inside. Making his way through the house, he leaned against the wall next to the main window. Pulling the curtains just enough, he peered out. To his surprise, the detectives were making their way up to the porch.

"Oh, crap." He was relieved no one was coming to kill him. But at that moment, he was wearing Kevlar under his jacket, along with two weapons. And he had left his cane in the car.

Richard moved away, yanking his jacket off. He tossed it over a chair as he passed and started unclasping his shoulder holster. Making his way through the kitchen, Richard shoved it and the pistol from his belt into the freezer. He left the house again the way he had come, pulling the vest off as he went. When he reached the car, he tossed the vest into the back seat and retrieved the cane. Shutting the door without making a sound, he returned to the kitchen, caught his breath and waited for the doorbell.

60

Detective Stevens pressed the doorbell and stepped to the side; her shoulder pressed to the wall. Theo shook his head and stood in front of the door, far enough back to allow for the swing of the screen. They had watched Richard Jensen return home, so they knew he was there. After a minute passed, Theo gestured to his partner to press the button again. Patricia raised a finger to do just that when the man of the house appeared.

Richard opened the door with one hand, clutching the cane with the other. He feigned surprise at seeing his guests and invited them in. Favoring his weaker leg, he limped his way down the hall, leading them to the living room.

The detectives settled onto the sofa, and the homeowner perched on the front edge of a matching chair. They all took a moment to observe and assess.

"Do you have news?" Richard broke the silence.

"No breakthrough, as of yet," Theo replied. "Just following leads where they take us."

"You have leads," Richard said. "That's good. Anything promising?"

"That's why we're here," Patricia said.

Richard knotted his brow.

"What she means is," Theo said. "We were doing some background on you and your wife. You know, looking for connections to someone who might want one or both of you dead."

"You found something?"

"Well, it's what we didn't find that we want to talk to you about," Theo said.

Richard closed his eyes. He knew exactly what they wanted to discuss. Necessary for what he did, Richard always knew it might come back to bite him someday. He wasn't even sure he could tell them what they wanted to know.

Richard grinned and nodded. "My military record."

"That's right," Patricia said.

"It was sealed," Richard explained.

"No," Theo challenged. "I've seen sealed records before. Yours aren't sealed. Yours are gone. Erased from existence."

"Erased?" Richard looked from one detective to the other. "Are you sure?"

"You didn't know?" Theo asked.

"How could I?" Richard asked. "I've never checked my records. I still receive my benefits. How could they be erased?"

"All we know is that there is a seven-year gap in your background," Theo said. "We're hoping you might fill in the blanks. Were you in the military for seven years?"

"Only three, to be honest," Richard responded.

"You said you thought they were sealed," Patricia said. "Is there a reason your records would need to be sealed?"

"There is," Richard gave a nervous smile. "But I'm not able to discuss it."

"And the circumstances of your discharge?" Theo asked.

"Not able to discuss it." Richard threw the excuse at them again. "Sorry."

"And if we get a subpoena?" Patricia asked.

"If the records have been erased, like you say," Richard answered. "I don't see how that would help you."

"The gap in your records is seven years," Theo said. "What about the other four?"

Richard fell silent for a moment; a reaction that made the detectives take notice.

"When I left the service, I was a bit lost," Richard lied. "So, I took some time off the grid, traveling Europe, particularly the Nordic countries."

"For four years?"

"Have you ever been?" Richard brightened. He and Sonia had spent two weeks in northern Europe on vacation. "Beautiful place. I didn't want to leave."

"What did you do for money?" Patricia asked.

"The occasional odd job," he answered. "Spent time on the farmlands. Was given food and lodging in return for a hard day's work. It was rather satisfying."

"If you didn't want to leave," Patricia asked. "Why did you?"

Richard smiled. "Couldn't live like that forever, now, could I?"

"I suppose not," Theo said.

"Besides," Richard said. "It was the best decision I ever made. I returned home and met Sonia."

Richard's thoughts turned to Sonia walking through his parent's living room, following his sister. So many years ago, yet it seemed like it had only just happened.

"You didn't make any enemies during that time, did you?" Theo asked.

"While traveling Europe?"

"Or in the military?" Patricia added.

"Well, I never had any issues while I was in Europe," Richard said. "So, I don't think I would have made enemies there."

"And the military?" Theo asked.

"Now, that was a whole other ballgame." Richard sat back. "I'm sure I had enemies. That's kind of the point of the military, isn't it?"

"I suppose it is," Theo agreed. "But typically, you're not on a first name basis with them. Did you make any enemies who knew who you were?"

"None that I'm aware of," Richard said. "But if they did learn my name, I would have no way of knowing who they were. It's not like I introduced myself to them."

Another lie. Some assignments required him to work closely with a target to gain their trust. Other times, he interrogated prisoners. But in those cases, he never used his real name. At best, they could pick him out of a lineup. He couldn't see how they could have tracked him down a decade later.

The detectives exchanged looks.

"Okay, Mr. Jensen," Theo said. "Thank you for your time and clearing up what you could."

"No problem," Richard said. "May I ask a question?"

"Of course."

"Stanley Webber," Richard began. "Have you found him? Or figure out what happened to him?"

"Stanley Webber?"

"Yes."

"You see," Theo said. "I would have thought you would ask something about your wife's case."

"Well, Stan was her boss," Richard explained. "And he disappeared the same time as Sonia. I can't help but wonder if there is a connection."

"We're looking at all possibilities," Theo assured him.

"So, you haven't found him?"

"No," Patricia confirmed. "He hasn't been found."

Richard nodded his head, looking from one detective to the other. "Say, you couldn't tell me the last place he was seen, could you?"

Theo became silent for a moment. When he spoke, he said, "Why would you need to know that?"

61

Richard stood in the doorway, watching the detectives drive away until they were out of sight. When he was sure they were gone, he tossed the cane onto the couch and cursed.

It had been a mistake to ask about Stanley Webber. He could not come up with a justified explanation for wanting to know the man's last known whereabouts. And when the detective asked why he wanted to know, his answer of just being curious wasn't even believable to him.

Richard wanted to talk to Stan about Sonia. He could only do that if he could find the man. To find him, he needed a starting point for his search. That meant knowing where he had been before he disappeared. Not having a badge that would open doors and get him answers or the resources of the police department at his disposal, Richard hoped he might get something from the detectives. Even as he asked the question, he regretted it.

He grabbed what gear he felt he would need and returned to the car, where he put the vest back on. He backed out of the driveway and drove about two blocks, checking to be sure no one was following. Pulling over, he selected a name on his phone and pressed call. The first ring hadn't even finished when he got an answer.

"I'm in," he said.

"I knew you would come around," Carolyn smiled at the phone.

"Where was the last place you saw Webber?"

"We should meet again," Carolyn said. "Work out the details."

"Where did you see him?" Richard was firm.

"Okay," she conceded. "I met him in the parking lot of a grocery store. Corner of 127th and Grand. But we already checked it out. Let's meet up and discuss a plan."

"If you want to meet, fine." Richard put the car in gear. "I'll be at the corner or 127th and Grand."

"Richard." When Carolyn did not get a response, she added, "I forgot how stubborn you could be."

Richard disconnected the call and pulled into traffic. He knew the grocery store she mentioned. Located on the edge of a residential neighborhood, across from a light industrial zone and about two miles from Halstead Enterprises, it made a good place to meet if the objective was not to be noticed. If spotted, though, it became a logistical nightmare with almost nowhere to run.

It took fifteen minutes to arrive, choosing a space on the outskirts of the lot. Stepping out of the car, he tucked the second pistol into his belt at the small of his back, pulled his jacket down to cover the grip and zipped up the front to conceal his vest. Taking long strides, Richard walked the length of the parking lot perpendicular to the road, keeping his eyes on vantage points as he went. Too many of them to be sure no one was watching, he didn't understand why Carolyn had met with Stan in such an exposed location.

With a disappointed shake of his head, Richard started toward the store. As he walked, he scanned the building for cameras. Identifying two that might have caught something useful, he hoped they kept records for more than a month.

Richard walked between two rows of cars parked in the angled spaces. A dark sedan racing into the lot far too fast drew his attention. It slid to a stop, steered in his direction and sped up again. Instinctively, his hand went to his weapon. Another sliding stop brought the vehicle to a rest just a few feet away. The driver's window lowered, and Richard tightened his grip on the pistol.

"Is this how it's going to go?" Carolyn's face appeared in the opening.

"How what's going to go?"

"I'm going to tell you my opinion," Carolyn said. "And you're going to ignore me and do what you want."

"I don't do what I want," Richard defended. "I do what I need to do."

"Why are you always so difficult?" Carolyn grumbled.

Richard relaxed, but did not release the weapon. "Why did you meet him here?"

"Pardon?"

"You were hired to protect your client." Richard waved his free hand to encompass the parking lot. "Yet, you meet him in one of the most exposed places possible. Why?"

"Now you're criticizing how I do my job?" She tightened her grip on the steering wheel. "For your information, we didn't set this up. He left work early, before we were there. He called, asking me to meet him here."

A car rolled to a stop behind Carolyn and honked. She gave them an annoyed glance. "Where are you parked?"

"By the street." He pointed.

"I'll wait for you there." She sped away in the same manner that she had entered.

Richard looked at the building and, with a frustrated sigh, turned back toward his car. By the time he got there, Carolyn was out of her vehicle, leaning against the front fender. "You never struck me as a Mercedes type."

"It was Sonia's," he explained. "Mine was totaled in the crash."

"Right." She grimaced and looked away. "Sorry."

"You said Webber asked you to meet him here." Richard scanned the parking lot again. "Why here?"

"He was here to buy a bottle of wine for the party," Carolyn said. "A gift for the hosts."

"I'm guessing he didn't want your advice on what wine to buy." Richard leaned against the dark sedan next to its driver.

"No," Carolyn confirmed. "He did that all on his own."

"Then why here?" Richard asked again. "Why would he want you to meet him here rather than somewhere more protected, like his home or any one of a hundred other places."

"I don't know, Richard." She became defensive. "The man called me. Told me he was here and asked me to meet him. When I arrived, he said he was getting nervous. Felt like someone was watching him."

"Someone was watching him?" Richard frowned. "He said that?"

"He thought he was being followed," she said. "I never saw anyone. But he was concerned about having his wife with him. He wanted me at the party in her place."

"That's why you were there?"

"We were supposed to meet there." Carolyn crossed her arms and looked down at her feet. "I argued that if he thought he was being followed I should stay with him. But since I had to change into something more party appropriate, that wasn't really an option. So, I suggested I pick him up from his house. He nixed that idea because he didn't want his wife thinking he was going to the party with another woman. That's when I gave in and agreed to arrive ten minutes early."

"He thought he was being followed." Richard's head snapped in her direction. "And you left him alone?"

"I'm not stupid," she growled. "I put a team on him with instructions to follow him until he met up with me at the party."

"Wait." Richard stood and turned to her. "You had someone tracking him and he still disappeared? What did they say happened?"

"They didn't know."

"How could …" Richard brought his hand to his face. "They lost him, didn't they?"

"Yes," Carolyn said. "But…"

"Your team lost him," Richard repeated. "And that's when he vanished."

"A delivery van cut them off," Carolyn explained. "By the time they could get around, Stan's car was nowhere to be seen. They went to his home and to the office. He was gone. I went to the party as planned, hoping he just went somewhere to lay low."

"You show up ten minutes early," Richard said. "What then?"

"You know what happened next," she said. "Stan didn't show."

"Right, but…"

"But what?"

The two of them stood face to face. Richard tried to think back a decade, to remember if things had been the same then. Were they at odds with one another all the time? Was Lance a buffer between his best friend and his girlfriend? Richard couldn't remember.

"You stayed at the party," Richard stated the obvious. "Your client went missing and you stayed."

"First of all," Carolyn gritted her teeth. "At that point, I only knew he wasn't there. I didn't know he was missing. He could have been running late."

"And second?"

"Stan wanted me to be at the party because he was feeling nervous," she said. "If something had happened to him, my suspects were at that party."

"Did he tell you who he was scared of?" Richard asked. "Or why?"

"You ever meet him?"

"Stan?"

"Yeah."

"A few times."

"Then you know what he's like." Carolyn folded her arms across her chest.

"I don't know what you mean," Richard frowned. "What's he like?"

"Paranoid."

"You don't think the threat against him was real?" Richard asked. "Then where is he?"

"No," Carolyn said. "It was real. Someone was sending him threatening letters."

"Letters?" Richard raised an eyebrow. "As in handwritten?"

"Not handwritten," she said. "Typed. Sent to him at work and home."

"Then why did you say he was paranoid?" Richard asked. "It sounds like he had reason to be."

"I was hired to protect him." Carolyn pushed off the car. "But his paranoia kept him from trusting me fully. He didn't want to share too much."

"He wanted you to protect him with one hand tied behind your back."

"Pretty much."

"What about the letters?" Richard asked.

"What about them?"

"What were they like?" Hearing steady footfalls, Richard turned to watch a man pass by, wondering why anyone would want to jog through this area. "Were they general threats? Or did they get specific?"

"Most were general," Carolyn responded. "You know. 'Stop, or you'll regret it.' 'I know what you're up to.' But it was the last one that made him change plans for the party."

"What was different about it?"

"It said if he continued, he would die," she said.

"That's a bit more direct," Richard pursed his lips. "And that was the last one?"

"That I know of," she nodded.

"When was that?"

"The morning of the Halstead party," she answered.

"And when did he get the first one?" Richard looked off into the distance.

"About two weeks before that."

Richard stood silent for a moment before turning back to her. "Did he tell you what he was doing? What they wanted him to stop?"

"No." She raised a hand between them. "And before you ask. Yes, I questioned him. He either didn't know or didn't want to share. I assumed, between the letters going to his home and office and the fact he was nervous about going to the company party, it had something to do with Halstead's."

"We should look at the surveillance footage from the store," Richard said.

"I have the footage," she admitted. "There wasn't anything to see. Just Stan driving away."

"I want to see it," Richard demanded.

"I told you; there's nothing to see."

"Do you know all of the Halstead employees?" Richard asked.

"No," she said. "Do you?"

"No," he rolled his eyes. "But I'm guessing I know a lot more than you. I might spot someone who looks perfectly normal but is actually following him."

"Fine." She gave in. "I'll send it to you."

"Thank you." Richard shifted his weight. "Now, what do you want to do about the black SUV."

"The one that's been watching us for the last fifteen minutes?"

"That's the one."

62

Detective Morris sat at his desk, taking a third look at the Halstead party guest list. They had tracked down everyone in attendance, but none of them stood out as a threat to anyone, let alone to the Jensens. Truth be told, Theo wasn't even looking at the list anymore. He was only staring at the page as his mind wandered.

"Why did he ask about Stanley's last known location?" Theo looked up at his partner, who sat opposite him looking into the financial records of anyone who had made it high enough on the list to warrant an extra look. There weren't many.

"What?" Patricia looked up.

"Jensen," Theo clarified. "Why does he want to know where Stanley Webber was last seen?"

"Maybe he wants to look for him," Patricia suggested.

"The man can barely walk," Theo dismissed.

"He has money," Patricia said. "Could be he's hiring a private detective and wants to have as many details as possible."

"Just what we need," Theo groaned. "A private eye in the way. And if he's looking for anyone, wouldn't it be his wife?"

"Maybe he thinks the two are together and he's hoping Stan's trail will be easier to follow," Patricia said.

"He made it clear he doesn't believe there was an affair," Theo said. "Why would he think they're together?"

"They disappeared at the same time." Patricia sat up with a jerk. "What if he just wants us to think he's looking for them? What if Richard Jensen is the reason Stan and Sonia disappeared? He may just want to know what we know. To see if we're on to him."

"If he didn't believe there was an affair," Theo said, "why would Jensen make Stan disappear?"

"He could have lied," she suggested. "If he thought they were having an affair and killed them because of it, he wouldn't want us knowing he knew about it. It would give us his motive."

"True," Theo grimaced. "And it might explain why Sonia was missing from the accident scene and Richard was left behind."

"See."

"But it doesn't explain why Richard was kept sedated so long," Theo continued. "I think we still need to look at Halstead Enterprises."

Patricia thought for a minute. "Finance can be a cutthroat business. Maybe someone at Halstead's is taking out their competition. Literally cutting throats."

"You think they're dead?"

"I think no one's heard from them in over a month," Patricia stated. "No ransom demand. Nothing. They either ran away together or they're dead."

"Everyone we talked to said Sonia Jensen was a wonderful person," Theo countered. "You really think one of them killed her?"

"Unless the whole 'wonderful person' is what they were told to say," Patricia offered.

"A conspiracy theory involving everyone in the company?" Theo discounted. "I don't buy it. Too many pieces to control. We're missing something."

The two of them froze in deep thought. It seemed obvious they were missing key evidence. Like a recipe made without a key ingredient. Something wasn't right, but it just wasn't obvious what the problem was.

"Who stood to gain from the removal of both Stan Webber and Sonia Jensen?" Theo broke the silence. "Who is running that department now?"

"Webber still holds the title," Patricia said.

"True," Theo said. "But with him not there, someone is running it."

"That would be Jeremy Griffin," Patricia looked at her notes. "The man who said he didn't know he was even in the running for the promotion."

"Maybe he knew he was in the running," Theo suggested. "And he knew he lost out to Sonia Jensen. If he didn't like the outcome, could be he decided to change it."

63

Richard and Carolyn shook hands before retreating to their respective cars. They pulled up to the nearest exit, the black SUV creeping after at a respectful distance. The first order of business was to determine who the vehicle was following. To that end, Richard turned right, and Carolyn left. The SUV increased speed to get to the exit ahead of another car and fell in behind the Mercedes.

"Tag. You're it," Carolyn said into her phone. "Give me a minute and I'll turn around."

"I'll stay on this road until you catch up." Richard held his phone to his ear. He wished he had the Bluetooth he had kept in his own car.

"Are they on your ass?" Carolyn asked. "Or keeping their distance?"

"Two cars back," Richard answered. "It would be easy to lose them on these streets."

"But that's not what we want," Carolyn reminded him.

"No," he agreed. "It isn't."

When they worked together in the past, if they felt they were being followed, they would do anything to lose their tail. The first strategy was to lose them without appearing to try, a technique that usually involved an interference car that would 'accidentally' cut them off. Screaming would ensue until a successful escape. Often, this tactic allowed for turning the tables and putting a team in place to pursue the vehicle that had been following them. The result allowed them to locate safe houses and hideouts of their enemies.

The second strategy was more aggressive, taking sharp turns, making fast lane changes, racing down stretches of streets, and blowing through red lights and stop signs. The possibility of accidents running high made it a dangerous choice. Adding to the danger, the enemy team became more likely to pull weapons and engage if they noticed the swap. Even under the best conditions, they faced a risk of injury during a shootout.

Carolyn made some quick maneuvers to reverse direction. She sped up, cutting in and out of lanes, leaving angry drivers in her wake. One prominent finger directed towards her brought a grin to her face. She slowed again to avoid bringing attention to herself, finally matching the speed of the SUV as she fell in behind it.

"Alright," Carolyn said. "I'm in position."

"Good." Richard checked his rearview. "There's an alley up ahead. Get ready."

"I was born ready," Carolyn chuckled.

"You haven't changed a bit."

"Nope."

Approaching the alley, Richard accelerated without warning and spun the steering wheel hard to the right, narrowly missing the curb as he turned. He drove forward about thirty feet before stomping on the brake and jerking the wheel back to the right. The Mercedes slid to a stop, blocking the alley. It crossed his mind that scratching the car would not make Sonia happy.

The SUV, caught by surprise, hesitated before increasing speed to follow. Unlike Richard, it jumped the curb as it went around the corner. The large vehicle bounced and wobbled as the driver fought for control. By the time he realized he had nowhere to go, he had to slam on the brakes to stop before crashing into the car that blocked their path.

Carolyn took the corner slower than either of the other two and rolled to a stop at an angle behind their prey. The tinted windows obscured her view, but she could make out movement inside. The two occupants seemed confused about what to do next. She and Richard were already out of their cars, weapons in hand, as they had trained to do so many times before.

On missions, stopping cars in this manner was always dangerous. With no way of knowing what weapons were inside, the threat of bullets spraying through glass was very real. On one operation, they lost a man because he approached the vehicle too close. Shots fired through the rear window without warning killed him. It did not end well for those inside.

As she neared the back of the vehicle, Carolyn produced a knife and plunged it into the driver-side rear tire. The quick release of air dropped that side of the vehicle about ten inches.

"Get out!" Richard shouted. He had his pistol aimed at the passenger. "Slowly."

Carolyn tapped her gun on the driver's door glass and gestured for him to exit the vehicle.

Both doors opened in unison, slow and easy. The driver said, "Don't shoot."

He stepped out onto the pavement. On the passenger side, a woman slid to the ground. Both held their hands in clear view. Both wore dark suits and sunglasses.

"Are you kidding me?" Richard grumbled.

Only a handful of organizations dressed this way. The FBI and the Secret Service were the most obvious, but these two were clearly neither of those. Of the others, only one would spy on Richard and his old crew, at least when they were stateside.

Carolyn choked on a laugh and lowered her weapon. Following her lead,

Richard hesitated only seconds before doing the same.

"Richard Jensen," the driver said. "I'm…"

"I don't care." Richard put his gun away and walked toward his car. "Tell Jackson you need more training."

Carolyn chuckled and retreated to her car as well. "Sorry about your tire."

64

"Keep this up and I'll have to issue you employee badges." Ty guided the detectives to the elevators, where they waited for an available car.

"Hopefully, we won't be here enough for that." Theo gave the head of security a half-hearted smile.

"Who is it you need to see?"

"Jeremy Griffin." Patricia stared up at the numbers as they counted down to the ground floor.

"Good 'ole Jeremy," Ty nodded.

The elevator opened, and the man who stepped out looked the detectives over before moving on. Theo supposed took it as as a silent comment about the way they dressed and gave the man his own silent opinion. They stepped inside and waited for the doors to close.

"What can you tell us about Mr. Griffin?" Theo asked.

"Jeremy? He's okay," Ty said. "He's one of those people who you either love or hate."

"Where do you fall?" Theo raised an eyebrow.

"Oh, I don't love or hate anybody." Ty shrugged. "Always neutral."

"Do more people love him or hate him?" Patricia asked.

"Oh…" Ty leaned against the wall. "I'd say it was fifty-fifty. Which is why Sonia beat him for the promotion. Everybody loved her."

"But he got the promotion after all, didn't he?" Theo asked.

"Kind of."

"Kind of?" Theo cocked his head. "What does that mean?"

"He's acting head of the department," Ty grinned. "No official change has been announced."

"What does he think of that?"

"I doubt he's happy," Ty said. "But it's only been a month. If Stan and Sonia turn up, I'm sure they could get their jobs back."

"Does that mean Halstead doesn't believe they left on their own?" Patricia asked.

"Well, no one knows about Stan, I mean that's a big paycheck to walk away from without a word." Ty pushed off the wall. "But with Sonia, the circumstances and all, everyone pretty much thinks someone took her. Just hope she's okay."

The elevator came to a stop, and the doors opened. The three of them filed out onto the third floor. With the wave of a hand, Ty steered them toward Jeremy's office.

"I thought Stan's office was the other way," Theo observed.

"It is," Ty confirmed. "Oh. You thought… Apparently, acting head doesn't get you the big office."

"I see." Theo fell in step with the man, a task that only served to remind him of the weight he should lose.

"How long will they wait before deciding they need to make him the official head?" Patricia asked.

Ty looked around to be sure no one would overhear. "I figure another week or two and they'll figure they need to make a permanent change. But it's going to be a long time before Griffin could convince Mr. Halstead he's the man for the job."

"So, Halstead really isn't a fan?"

"Not in the least." They came to a door and stopped. Ty lowered his voice. "He did move into what would have been Sonia's new office."

Ty knocked, waited about a second and then pushed the door open. A large desk sat centered in front of the back wall. Behind it sat Jeremy Griffin, with an anguished look on his face. Seeing his guests, the muscles shifted to non-expressive.

"What can I do for you, Ty?" Jeremy's voice was weak, filled with resigned defeat. When he saw Theo and Patricia enter the room, he perked up and stood. "Detectives. What brings you here?"

Theo turned to the head of security who seemed to take the hint. Ty raised his hands. "I guess I'll leave you to it."

The detective waited for the click of the door latching behind him before continuing. "You remember my partner, Detective Stevens?"

"Yes, of course." Jeremy turned to the woman. "Hello."

"We need to talk to you further about Stanley Webber and Sonia Jensen," Patricia said.

"I didn't think you were here to talk finance," Jeremy smiled. "Please sit."

The detectives settled into the chairs across from the man. Jeremy returned to the position he had been in when they entered, minus the anguished expression.

"When we last spoke to you," Theo started. "You told us you wouldn't be promoted, because Halstead didn't like you."

"That's right."

"Yet, here you are," Patricia said.

"Temporarily, detective," Jeremy protested. "They made me acting head because they had to have someone in charge. They didn't even let me have Stan's office. If they were going to give me the job, they would have."

"Whether he likes you or not," Theo said. "With Stan and Sonia out of the way, you're King of the Mountain, are you not?"

"King of the Mountain?" Jeremy's face knotted. "Do you think this is a game? Because it's not. It's a business. A ruthless one at that. And I am good at what I do, detective. But that doesn't matter, because Halstead doesn't like me. I'll never be promoted."

"Why?"

"I just told you why."

"No," Theo corrected. "You said Halstead doesn't like you? I want to know why. Did you do something to make him hate you?"

Jeremy fell silent, his eyes shifting from one detective to the other. It reminded Theo of one of those vintage cat clocks from the forties and fifties. His grandmother had one in her kitchen. He grew up afraid of cats because of it.

"Mr. Griffin," Patricia said. "Answer the question."

"You have to understand," Jeremy began.

"We can't understand anything until you tell us," Theo crossed his arms across his chest, resting them on top of his belly. "What did you do, Mr. Griffin?"

"I dated Emily." Jeremy blurted out.

"You dated Emily?" Patricia glanced at Theo. "And who is Emily?"

Jeremy closed his eyes. "Emily Halstead."

"You dated the bosses daughter?" Patricia laughed. "No wonder he hates you."

"No," Jeremy raised his hands and waved the idea away. "I dated her before I worked here."

"I get it," Theo nodded. "You dated the daughter until the father gave you a job. Then, what? You dumped her?"

"No." Jeremy sighed. "I dated her. She talked her dad into hiring me. Then things changed."

"Changed how?" Patricia asked.

"You know," Jeremy shrugged.

"We don't know," Patricia said. "Tell us."

"I was working all the time," Jeremy insisted. "I didn't have the time to spend with her like I had before. And then Trisha came along."

"Trisha?" Theo said. "You dumped the girl who got you your job for someone else?"

"It didn't happen like that," Jeremy denied. "You see, Emily was great. But she had a big personality. Energetic and adventurous. She wanted to do things like partying and dancing. I just couldn't do it anymore, not with the long hours at work. When I met Trisha, she was a calming force. She enjoyed staying in and taking quiet walks. I was drawn to that."

"You just said it didn't happen that way," Theo pointed out.

"It didn't," Patricia said. "He didn't dump the girl. Emily dumped you, didn't she?"

"I had told Emily I was going to stay home to rest and then she walked into the coffee shop where Trisha and I were talking." Jeremy looked up to the ceiling. "She broke up with me right there. Then she accused me of using her to get to her dad. When I denied it, she told me to prove it and quit."

"You obviously didn't quit."

"I needed the job."

"So, Halstead hates you because you broke his daughter's heart," Theo concluded.

"That might be part of it," Jeremy agreed.

"Part of it?" Patricia asked. "What else is there?"

"Emily," Jeremy said. "She, uh…"

"She didn't kill herself?"

"Oh, God. No," Jeremy said. "She was supposed to be groomed to take over her father's company. When I didn't quit, she moved away. Emily's working for another company in another town. Because of me. That's why her father hates me."

"What about Trisha?" Patricia asked.

"What about her?"

"Was she the one?" Patricia asked. "Was it all worth it?"

"It only lasted a couple of months," Jeremy sighed. "So, no. Not worth it."

"What I don't get," Theo said. "If Halstead's daughter won't come work here because of you, why doesn't he just get rid of you?"

"I told you," Jeremy said. "I'm good at what I do. He hates me, but I make him money. And he loves money. Besides, I'm not the only one he's mad at."

"You mean Emily?" Patricia asked.

"She left him," Jeremy explained. "Left the company. What's worse is she did it for emotional reasons."

"He's mad at her for that?" Theo asked.

"One thing Charles Halstead excels at," Jeremy lowered his voice. "Is holding a grudge."

65

Richard and Carolyn agreed to meet at his home to discuss their next move. Dealing with the black SUV had been child's play. But what it represented had far greater ramifications. They would have to tread lightly going forward.

On the drive home, Richard pulled his phone out and called Gavin. He had promised his business partner he would call him back. He also promised to come up with a plan to take care of things.

"Hello?" Gavin's voice seemed distant, his mind elsewhere.

"Gav," Richard said. "It's me. Richard. Calling you back."

"Oh, sure," Gavin perked up a bit. "Sorry. I was just looking at our financials."

"Don't worry about it," Richard assured him. "I'll figure it out."

"Figure it out?" Gavin said. "Three hundred grand is a lot to figure out."

"I know it is, Gav," Richard said. "I'll handle it. I promise."

"Wait," Gavin said. "Do you know what's happened to it? Do you know where it is?"

"No, I don't know where it is," Richard said. "But I'm going to find out. As soon as I know something, I'll let you know."

"Richard," Gavin pleaded. "Are we going to lose everything?"

"Did you set up the new account?" Richard asked.

"Yes," Gavin answered. "Took care of it this morning."

"Good," Richard said. "Today, you need to contact all our clients with the new details. With their deposits going into the new account, no one can access them."

"Okay," Gavin sighed. "I'll get on it."

"Listen, I have to go," Richard said. "We'll talk again soon."

Richard could hear Gavin protesting when he disconnected the call. He turned into his driveway, half expecting to find several black SUVs. Richard was relieved to find nothing there and parked in front of the garage. He was almost to the door, keys in hand, when he saw movement out of the corner of his eye. He tossed his keys from hand to hand and spun, pulling his weapon free. There was no one there. He grinned and let out a small chuckle. Paranoia was getting the better of him.

Walking through the house, he removed his shoulder holster and laid it on the dining room table. Peeling the vest off, he draped it over a chair. The paranoia pushed him to check the front, to see if anyone had followed him home. He entered the living room and started for the large plate-glass window that covered most of the wall next to the front door.

"Hello, Richard."

For a second time, he spun on his heels. The voice had come from the left. Richard dropped to one knee, snatching his other weapon from the small of his back as he went.

"No need for that," the man held his hands out in plain view. A tall, broad man in his sixties, he sat in an accent chair that Sonia had found at an estate sale a couple of years back. Richard was reluctant to get blood on it.

"Jackson." Richard lowered the gun and rose to his feet. "What are you doing here?"

"Can't I just stop by to say hello?" Jackson lowered his hands to his lap.

"Sure you can," Richard answered. "But we both know you don't do that kind of thing."

"That's true."

"Now, really," Richard said. "Why are you here?"

The man became solemn. "I'm here to offer my condolences for your wife. Sorry for your loss."

"Don't do that." Richard waved him off.

"What?"

"Did you have her killed?" Richard asked.

"Of course not."

"Do you know she's dead?"

"No."

"Then I don't need your condolences." Richard put his gun away and sat facing the man. "Tell me why you're really here? And why are you having me followed? We didn't bruise their egos too bad, did we?"

"Probably," Jackson smiled. "But it was my fault. I gave them a name and a photo. I didn't tell them who you were. It's good for them to have some practice and to learn to not underestimate anyone. But that does bring up the question. Who was the woman?"

"That would be me." Carolyn entered the room. She held her gun lowered to her side.

"Carolyn." Jackson's smile grew. "What is it now?"

"Winters."

"That's right." Jackson shifted in the chair. "The two of you together. Now, that's interesting. Not to mention, totally unexpected."

"Don't you have some new recruits to train?" Richard asked.

"As I recall," Jackson said. "Your first assignment didn't go so well either."

"It went just fine for me." Richard took a seat. "Just not so much for that punk-ass kid you paired me with."

"I haven't heard this one." Carolyn joined Richard on the couch. "What happened?"

"Richard here and, what was his name?" Jackson started.

"Simms," Richard sighed. "Douglas Simms."

"That's right," Jackson smiled. "Dougie. Anyway, Richard and Dougie were supposed to enter an enemy camp, all stealth like, and reclaim a certain briefcase that had been lost."

"Sounds easy enough," Carolyn said. "What happened? You get caught?"

"Dougie happened," Richard moaned. "Idiot set off an alarm. Had the entire camp on us."

"About two dozen armed and angry men," Jackson laughed.

"You think it's funny?" Richard said.

"Well, now I do." Jackson straightened up. "Certainly not at the time."

"You're alive. So, you must have pulled off the mission somehow," Carolyn said. "Wait. Dougie didn't die, did he?"

"No, Dougie didn't die," Richard assured her. "And yes, we pulled off the mission."

"Sort of," Jackson added.

"What does that mean?" Carolyn questioned.

"They returned with the briefcase," Jackson was grinning. "But it was full of bullet holes. The contents were practically useless."

"They weren't useless," Richard protested.

"Whatever happened to Dougie?" Jackson changed the subject.

"He washed out," Richard said. "Last I heard he was a security guard somewhere."

"Good for him," Jackson said. "Landing on his feet."

"Enough about Dougie," Richard snapped. "Why are you here?"

"Can't a guy stop by to see a friend?"

"A guy can," Richard said. "But we're not friends."

"Now that just hurts." With a hand on his heart, Jackson feigned a pained expression.

"Why are you here?" Carolyn asked.

"Okay. I'll tell you." Jackson held his hands up in surrender. "I'm here to ask what you're doing here."

"I live here."

"I know that." The grin faded. "But what are you up to?"

"What do you mean?" Richard sat up.

"Someone searched for your name in the military database, Richard," the man said. "I want to know why."

"Oh, that."

"Yes. That."

"My guess would be that the search was made by the detective investigating my wife's disappearance." Richard frowned. "You didn't have anything to do with that did you?"

"Do you really think I would kidnap your wife?" Jackson huffed. "You don't think any more of me than that?"

"It's hard to know what to think," Richard said. "Tell me, Jackson. Why was my military record completely erased?"

"You know why."

"No." Richard challenged. "I know why part of it needed to be erased. But I have family that knows I was in. They have photos of me in uniform. Don't you think it might seem strange to someone looking into my background not to find any record at all?"

Jackson did not respond.

"If my basic record had been left intact." Richard stood and moved to the window, looking out. "Detective Morris would have no reason to look any further. Now he just thinks I'm lying about my record. That I'm hiding something."

"Well, you are hiding something."

"Shut up, Jackson," Carolyn said. "You know what he means. Now, tell us the real reason you're here."

"I just told you," Jackson argued.

"Yeah, I heard. Someone searched for Richard's name." Carolyn was dismissive. "That would bring someone. Someone who would quietly investigate things and then be gone with no one the wiser."

"What are you suggesting?" Jackson asked.

"A simple search wouldn't bring you in person," Carolyn explained. "Would it?"

"No, it wouldn't." Richard watched a boy riding his bicycle down the street, reminding him that he and Sonia had been talking about having kids. "Why are you here?"

"I told you."

"Jackson!" Richard snapped. He spun and pulled his gun out for the third time since arriving home, pointing it at the man. "Why are you here!?"

"Easy, Richard." Jackson raised his hands to show he was no threat. "We're all friends here."

"I thought we already established that wasn't true," Richard said. "Answer the question."

Jackson glanced at Carolyn.

"I'd do what he says," she said. "He's not in the best mood."

"Fine." Jackson gave in. "I'll tell you. Just don't shoot me."

"No promises." Richard narrowed his eyes and held the gun steady.

"I don't remember you being so irrational," Jackson commented.

"Keep avoiding the question and you'll see how irrational I can be."

"Okay," Jackson leaned forward and rested his arms on his legs. "What I'm about to tell you is not to be shared. It stays between the three of us. Is that understood?"

"Just talk," Richard barked.

"First of all," Jackson looked up at them. "I've gone private, like you."

"Not like me."

"Like Carolyn, then," Jackson corrected.

"When did that happen?" Carolyn asked.

"Not long after you left," the older man explained. "They disbanded the team. Put me out to pasture."

"Why did they disband?"

"Officially, to cut costs," Jackson laughed. "But the reason I was given was because they considered us a liability."

"Wait," Richard stood. "He's lying."

"I'm not," Jackson denied.

"You got a notification about the search on my name," Richard reminded him. "How did that happen if you're out?"

"That I can explain."

"We're listening," Carolyn prodded.

"Before I left, I wiped out all our records." Jackson sat back. "Except where it counted. Everyone still gets their veteran's benefits, their pensions. But I got rid of everything else. So, the notification came to me, because that's the way I set it up."

"Why?" Richard asked.

"In the end, they were treating us like the enemy," Jackson explained. "I didn't want anyone coming back on the team with allegations. I did it to protect all of you. All of us."

"Why did things go so bad?" Carolyn asked.

"Truth is," Jackson said. "I hired Lance's brother, Lucas."

"What was wrong with that?" Carolyn frowned. "I heard he didn't last. A lot of people wash out."

"Lucas was nothing like his brother," Jackson shook his head and sighed. "Angry, undisciplined. He kept going rogue. Too aggressive, violent. He's the reason we were considered a liability. He's the reason we were disbanded and discharged."

"So, you went private," Richard said. "I guess that explains the under-trained goons."

Carolyn tilted her head. "But doesn't explain why you are here."

"You have to understand," Jackson's voice took a serious tone. "I didn't have all the information. It was a rush job, and we were given very little background."

"You're here on a job?" Richard asked.

"My team was," Jackson nodded. "But, like I said, I'm here because you the search of your name. That's when everything clicked."

"What clicked?" Richard demanded. "What was the job?"

Jackson closed his eyes, took a deep breath, and let it out slowly. "The job was Sonia Jensen."

66

The detectives sat in comfortable leather chairs, waiting to see Charles Halstead. His assistant assured them he would be available in ten minutes. They had already waited twenty.

"Let's run down what we've got," Theo suggested.

"Do we have anything?" Patricia asked.

Theo wasn't sure if she was joking or not. "Suspect number one, Richard Jensen."

"You think he staged an accident to cover the fact he killed his wife?" Patricia asked. "Putting himself in a coma for a month?"

They only had Richard's word that Sonia was even in the car when the accident occurred. Forensics found some of her blood, but that could have happened when he killed her. He could have gotten rid of her body and hired someone to crash into him as part of the cover story. It required him to risk his life to sell it. Unless the plan was to go to their lake house and report her missing. The hit and run may have been a random incident that he had to adapt to. Richard claimed seeing the SUV at the Halstead party and again when it passed them on the highway. But with no other witnesses, the detectives could not corroborate the claim.

"Suspect number two," Theo moved on. "The mystery doctor who kept him in that coma. It's possible she killed Sonia then kept him sedated."

"But we don't know who she is," Patricia said. "It's hard to follow up on a suspect we can't find."

Richard was the only one who saw the woman. It's possible they couldn't find her because she didn't even exist. Although the drugs in his system were real. It would be impossible for him to administer them himself and not have the vials lying around. It also made no sense for him to keep himself sedated. Someone had to be giving him the shots. An enemy of his or Sonia's, Richard would recognize. Unless he gave an incorrect description on purpose, leaving the police to search for the wrong suspect. Could be he knew her and wanted to go after her himself, maybe the woman from the Halstead party.

"Who is number three?" Patricia asked.

"I think that would be Charles Halstead." Theo glanced to the assistant. If she heard, she did not show it. "According to Richard, Sonia talked to him the night of the party about something she and Stan Webber wanted to discuss with him. Then they both end up missing."

"They may have been getting ready to expose something he didn't want the world to know," Patricia said.

"We should look into the finances of Halstead Enterprises."

Patricia nodded her agreement. They both glanced at the assistant, who remained focused on her computer as she typed.

The idea that a finance company may be involved in shady business dealings or creative accounting was nothing new, almost commonplace. That the head of the company would kill, or order the killing of, whistleblowers was also not unheard of, though not as prominent. Theo had a difficult time picturing Charles Halstead getting his hands dirty in such a way. But Mathias Cunningham, the head of security, had to have military training. It would be easy to see him cleaning up Charles' problems for him. The question was, would Ty be willing to kidnap or murder on his boss's behalf?

"Number four," Theo continued. "Stanley Webber."

"No one thinks he and Sonia were having an affair," Patricia pointed out. "So, what's his motive?"

"Same as Charles Halstead," Theo said.

If Sonia stumbled onto something, uncovering shady business going on in the company, she may have taken the information to the one person she trusted, Stan. Instead of discussing the situation with his boss, as he said he would, he killed Sonia instead. The theory had holes, of course. Stan vanished before anything happened to Sonia. If he felt concerned about what she might reveal, it would have made more sense for him to make her disappear before the party to minimize her chance of talking to Halstead. And if he got rid of his problem, why didn't he return to work? Of course, they still couldn't confirm that Stan and Sonia weren't having an affair.

"Number five is Valarie Webber," Theo announced.

"Why?"

"If there was an affair between her husband and Sonia," Theo said. "That's her motive."

"I thought we ruled out an affair?" Patricia challenged. "Besides, do you honestly see that woman being able to pull any of this off?"

"She could have hired someone," Theo suggested. "A look at her finances should tell us."

Valarie Webber seemed an unlikely suspect. However, Theo once arrested a ninety-year-old woman for having her sixty-eight-year-old boyfriend killed because he snored. Apparently, her sleep was more important to her than the companionship he provided. When Theo asked her why she didn't just break it off with him, she said she had, but he thought she was joking.

"What if Richard was the one that found out?" Theo suggested. "That would be another motive for him."

"Assuming there was an affair," Patricia said. "We haven't found any proof. Who's next?"

"I would say number six would be Gavin Barr," Theo answered.

"Richard's business partner?" Patricia raised an eyebrow. "What's his motive?"

"Money."

Richard and Gavin started the business together, but Richard's money made it happen. If he was getting the lion's share of the profits, it may have upset Gavin. Not to mention the nice home in the great neighborhood or the beautiful wife. Gavin may have decided he had had enough, that he wanted the business all to himself, and maybe the wife as well. He may have taken Sonia and tried to get rid of Richard. Only in the end he couldn't bring himself to kill his partner, so he hired someone to keep him drugged and out of the way.

Theo added. "And we can't forget Mister Griffin."

"Jeremy makes seven," Patricia said.

Jeremy Griffin's motive seemed to be power. He may have made a desperate move to get promoted to a position that he felt overlooked for. However, every indication was that he would never get the promotion, and he knew it. So, making his superiors disappear seemed to be a lot of work and risk with no reward.

"What about the woman at the Halstead party?" Patricia suggested. "Stan's supposed plus one. According to Mrs. Webber, Stan canceled because he was going to work late rather than go to the party."

"But he left early," Theo reminded.

"How can we be sure the mystery woman was his plus one?" Patricia asked. "Maybe she got rid of Stan and then crashed the party."

According to Richard Jensen, the woman was an old colleague of his, a Carolyn Winters. If she kidnapped or killed Stan, and then took his place at the party, she wanted to be there for a reason. Maybe her goal was to get close to Richard and his wife. Someone could have hired her to remove Sonia from the equation, if she was a hired gun. It would be a matter of determining who paid her for the job. The obvious being Richard since he knew her. It just made little sense for him to offer that information since it would connect them.

The one thing that stared them in the face was that none of the scenarios explained why Richard spent a month in the hospital under an unprescribed sedation.

"I'd like to have a sit down with Stanley Webber," Theo said. "If he's still alive."

"I thought you wanted to leave him to Missing Persons," Patricia said.

"I did," Theo admitted. "But I'm thinking he's the key to this case. Or at least one of them."

The detectives fell silent and waited another five minutes.

"He'll see you now," Halstead's assistant announced.

"It's about time." Patricia rose to her feet and headed for the office door. Behind her, Theo pulled himself up and stretched before following.

"Sorry to keep you waiting," Charles greeted them. The owner sat behind his desk, gesturing for them to sit across from him. "Stanley and Sonia did a lot for this company. My days are filled at the moment."

"I thought Jeremy Griffin was covering Stan's position." Theo sat in one of the chairs Charles indicated.

"Jeremy still has his own work to do." Charles waved his hand dismissively. "He's not ready to take on much more."

"Jeremy is why we're here actually," Patricia said.

"Really?" Charles raised an eyebrow. "What has he done?"

"We don't know that he's done anything," Theo said. "But we are looking at a lot of individuals and their possible motives."

"You think Jeremy had a motive?" Charles asked.

"He tells us," Patricia continued, "that you would never give him Stan's job. Or even the position Sonia was meant to take. Is that true?"

"It is." Charles crossed his arms.

"So, he has no real motive to cause either of them harm?" Theo asked.

"Not professionally," Charles said. "Personally? I don't know the dynamics of their relationships outside the office."

"Do you suspect they socialized outside of business?" Patricia asked.

"As I said," Charles said. "I don't know."

"Is there anyone in the company who would gain from the two of them not being here anymore?" Theo asked.

"I mean, I suppose some of the staff gained from taking over Sonia's clients," Charles said. "But we dispersed them evenly. And that was going to happen eventually anyway, given her new position."

"So, no one?" Patricia said.

"No one."

"You don't have anyone in mind for Stan's job?" Theo asked. "From within the company?"

"No," Charles said. "We're looking outside. For Sonia's position as well."

"What about your daughter?"

"What about her?"

"Might you offer her one of those positions to get her back into the company?" Theo asked.

"If you're suggesting I had Stan and Sonia killed to make room for my daughter, it's ludicrous." Charles chuckled. "There is always room for my daughter in this company. But she won't come as long as Griffin is here."

"So, why do you keep him?" Patricia asked.

"Griffin?"

"Why not fire him and bring her in?"

"Because, as much as he isn't ready for an executive role," Charles said. "He's damned good at what he does."

"Surely, family is more important than money?" Theo suggested.

"Of course it is," Charles agreed. "But loyalty is even more important. She should have joined the company. She chose not to. I will not bow to her wishes to get her to work for me. She has to make the choice."

"Even after what he did?" Patricia asked.

"He won't be welcomed into our family," Charles stated. "Business and personal lives are separate things. They should be independent of one another."

"Isn't not giving him a promotion a personal decision?" Theo asked.

"No," Charles huffed. "The man is not executive material. Even if he had married Emily, he would not get the promotion."

"What about you?" Theo said.

"What about me?"

"Did you gain anything from them being removed from the company?" Theo asked.

"More workload?" Charles said. "Why?"

"It's been suggested that one of them may have had information on the company you didn't want to have exposed," Theo said. "Is that true?"

Charles' lips curled into a slight grin. "I think we're done here."

67

"What do you mean, Sonia was your job?" Richard loomed over Jackson, still holding the gun. "Did you take her?"

"No. We were hired to monitor her," the man explained. "It was a rush job. Came in one day, started the next. And the information I was given was thin. I did not know she was your wife."

"What was the assignment, exactly?" Richard demanded.

"We were asked to keep her under surveillance," Jackson said. "And report back to the client who she was meeting, where, and what was being discussed."

"You had her under surveillance?" Carolyn asked.

"Yes." Jackson nodded. "Now, could you put that thing away?"

"Twenty-four, seven?" Richard tucked the weapon into his belt.

"Yes."

"And you didn't recognize me?"

"I wasn't here," Jackson said. "It was a simple, boring, low risk job. I sent a small team. They did all the groundwork. You were listed as 'the husband' on the reports. I didn't make the connection until your name was searched. That's why I'm here now."

"Your men saw who took her?" The realization made Richard's voice crack.

"They were there, yes." Jackson raised his hands as a barrier. "But they stopped at a distance, not wanting to blow their cover. The rain was heavy, and they assumed it was just an accident. The driver of the other car appeared to be helping. It wasn't until the car left, they realized something was wrong. That's when they approached. They discovered Sonia was gone. But they never got a good look at who took her."

Richard looked down at Jackson with disgust. It seemed his team's training was lacking in more than one area. Jackson had taught him, years ago, that nothing is insignificant until proven so. Not identifying players introduced, even for a short time, could be costly. In this case, it had cost Sonia her freedom. Had Jackson's people approached, it's possible they would not have risked taking her. At the least, they could have had a lead as to who took her.

Richard took a deep breath and let it out. He felt his nerves calming. "Who hired you?"

"I knew you would ask that," Jackson's voice was solemn.

"Don't say you're not going to tell me," Richard warned. "I don't care about protecting your client."

"That's not it," Jackson said. "I had a name and an email. I sent the reports to the email. Payments came by courier. I never met them."

"Give me the name," Richard said.

"When I realized the connection to you," Jackson went on. "I ran a background check to find out who the client was and how they might be connected to you."

"And?"

"They gave us a fake name," Jackson answered. "The email had been set up the day we received the order. All payments were certified checks, dropped off to the courier via a drop box. I couldn't find anything on them."

"When were you hired?" Carolyn asked.

"What?" Jackson turned to her.

"When did you get the email to hire you?" Carolyn asked again.

"About a week before the accident," Jackson said. "Why?"

"When I was hired," Carolyn said. "It was by email. Thin on information. A week before the accident."

"You said Stan Webber hired you." Richard turned.

"No. I said I was hired," Carolyn said. "When I met with Stan the first time, he seemed surprised. But, since he was concerned about his safety, he started talking to me. After that, I just never thought about it again."

Richard looked from one to the other. "So, of all the agencies in the country, the two of you were hired, at the same time, for jobs in the same place? A place where I happen to be living?"

"That doesn't sound like a coincidence," Carolyn concluded.

"But why?" Jackson asked.

"To get us to the same place, obviously?" Richard offered.

"But that didn't work, did it?" Carolyn said. "I came, but Jackson sent a team."

"And taking Sonia was a mistake," Jackson said. "I withdrew the team because there was nothing else to be done. We weren't hired to protect her, so we left it to the authorities. I notified the client and have had no contact with them since."

The two men turned to Carolyn.

"Same here," she said. "There was no contact after Stan vanished. I didn't have a client to protect anymore."

"Yet you're still here," Jackson said.

"It didn't sit well with me that he disappeared," Carolyn explained. "I still want to know what happened to him. But I'm on my own time. As far as the client knows, I left town weeks ago."

"If this had nothing to do with Stan and Sonia," Richard said. He felt a pit in his stomach. "But rather, a ploy to get the three of us in one place, isn't it likely we're being watched? Our movements tracked?"

"It seems likely," Jackson agreed. "It's also possible they gave up on me and are working on Plan B."

"What I don't get," Carolyn said, "is how did they found Richard. He isn't even in the same field. He's a tech nerd for crying out loud."

"Hey," Richard defended. "I'm not a nerd."

"You make a living doing nerd stuff," Carolyn clarified. "You're a nerd."

The three of them went silent. They felt tension in the air. In the past, they knew who their enemy was and had the upper hand. They would be the ones planning to make a move, whether it be getting intel, or capturing a target, or eliminating one. They had what information they needed to get the job done. It came down tof executing the mission.

"We agree that whatever is happening," Jackson broke the silence, "it has something to do with an operation we were on?"

"Has to be," Carolyn agreed. "There's nothing else to tie us all together."

"Some kind of revenge then?" Richard crossed his arms and leaned back. "The family of one or our targets, or even a government we interfered in? But how did they get our names? Could the military have sold us out? Maybe as a peace offering?"

"Not the military." Jackson shook his head. "But an individual in the military or in our government. That's possible."

"If they wanted us together," Richard said. "They've achieved that. We should stay vigilant of our surroundings. Without knowing their intentions, anything could happen."

"Isn't it obvious?" Jackson said. "They already tried to kill you once."

"If they just wanted us dead," Carolyn said, "why bring us together? Why not pick us off one at a time where we were? We're stronger together."

"And if they were trying to kill me," Richard said. "Why didn't they finish me at the accident, or while I was in the hospital and vulnerable?"

"Maybe because I was keeping you sedated," Carolyn shrugged. "They may have thought you wouldn't to make it. My keeping you drugged may have saved your life."

"Wait," Jackson looked from one to the other. "You were keeping him sedated?"

"She was," Richard fumed. "For a month."

Jackson let out a long whistle. "I'm surprised she's still walking."

"Believe me," Richard said. "No one is more surprised than me."

"Let's worry about what I did or didn't do later." Carolyn changed the subject. "We should be trying to figure out who is behind this. Jackson, if you erased our military records. How could anyone find us?"

"I erased our individual records," Jackson said. "Operational records still exist."

"Even so, someone would have to know the name of the operation they wanted to look up," Richard said. "And that would only get them our names which, without our records, wouldn't get them what they needed to find us. It must be someone who knew the members of our unit."

"You think it's an inside job?" Jackson grumbled. "Because the number of people who had the access to the records and knew who we were is very small."

"That would mean a high-ranking official double-crossed us," Carolyn said. "But who? And why?"

They remained silent, each waiting for the other two to offer ideas. None of them did. This time Carolyn who broke the silence.

"What we're saying is someone took the time to figure out who we are, then tracked us all down," she said. "Made a connection between Richard and Sonia, then somehow connected Sonia and Stan."

"Seems like a lot of work," Jackson said.

"Furthermore," Carolyn continued. "They started threatening Stan and arranged to have me come to be his protection without knowing if he would accept."

"Which didn't work out for Stan," Jackson quipped.

Carolyn shot him a look that silenced him. "They also hired you under the pretense of spying on Sonia."

"Which didn't achieve their goal of getting Jackson here," Richard added. "Only his team."

"Then what?" Carolyn asked. "They went to a lot of trouble planning something but it's like it started a month ago and then was put on hold, until…"

"Until now," Richard finished. "We're all together now."

For a moment, they all froze, as if waiting for something to happen.

"Why threaten Stan but not Sonia?" Richard asked.

"Because of you," Carolyn said. "If she told you she was being threatened, you would have acted. Bringing Jackson in would have been even more difficult."

"Since we think we know what's going on, now," Jackson said. "What's our next move?"

"If they want us together," Richard said. "Maybe we should split up. You could go home, Jackson. There's nothing keeping you here."

"I think I should be here to help," Jackson argued. "If someone comes for you, it might be helpful to have an extra gun hand."

"Uh, guys." Carolyn was looking out the window. "We've got company."

68

Detective Morris sat at his desk studying crime scene photos while Patricia stood behind him looking over his shoulder. The images of four men found shot to death in an old, abandoned bowling alley did not have any similarities to the case they were working on. Evidence suggested that one person had killed all four victims, not that they hadn't put up a fight. Shell casings from multiple weapons covered the floor. However, it wasn't the evidence that had brought Detective Mark Downing, who had caught the case, to talk to Theo. It was the witness, Brian Thomas Jones.

A delivery driver had been sitting in his truck across the street when a vehicle raced up to the bowling alley and around to the side of the building. Moments later, two more cars joined the first. The driver thought little of it at the time and went on with his route. Later that day, after he heard about the bodies being found, he mentioned to his wife what he had seen. She convinced him to call the police.

During the witness statement, the detective learned of the third vehicle, which was not at the scene when police arrived. Brian remembered raising his head to the sound of screeching tires. He saw the Mercedes speeding toward the front entrance. He couldn't remember the plate number, but he recalled the first three digits, but only because they were his initials, BTJ.

A search for Mercedes with license plates starting with those letters came back with two results. One belonged to a ninety-two-year-old woman who no longer drove her car. The second was registered to Richard and Sonia Jensen.

Now, examining the photos of four victims killed by one suspect, the detectives tried to reconcile what they were looking at with what they knew of the man who, until recently, was in the hospital and currently walked with a cane.

"What do you think?" Patricia looked down at her partner. "Is Jensen capable of this?"

"I suppose that depends on what he did in the military," he shrugged. "At the very least Mark needs to talk to him."

"I'm thinking maybe we do to." Patricia circled the desks to her seat. "There's obviously a lot more to the man than he's told us."

"But why?"

"Because he doesn't want us to know the truth," Patricia said.

"No." Theo shook his head. "Not why is he keeping things from us. But why would a man in the middle of a police investigation suddenly shoot down four men?"

"Self-defense?" Patricia offered. "The witness said he arrived first. The others followed. And with all the shell casings, it looks like they intended to kill him."

"Why was he there to begin with?" Theo countered. "And he had to go in there armed. He must have been expecting trouble."

"Maybe he's into something illegal," Patricia said.

"Or he's trying to find Sonia?" Theo suggested. "What if he knows who took her? Or at least has an idea. He may be trying to get her back on his own."

"Something else he's keeping from us," Patricia grumbled. "Hindering our investigation. We should charge him with obstruction."

"At the very least we talk to him," Theo said. "We confront him with what we know and see what he says. He can either tell us what he knows or face arrest."

The detectives agreed on their course of action. Twenty minutes later, the two of them were walking up Richard Jensen's driveway.

69

"That was fast." Jackson rose to his feet, pulling a pistol from under his jacket. "How many are there?"

"Two." Carolyn remained focused on the front lawn.

Richard stepped up next to her and peered through the blinds. "Those are the detectives. Put your guns away. Hide if you don't want to be questioned. Especially you, Carolyn. I know they want to talk to you."

"I'm going to the back," Jackson said.

"I should stay," Carolyn said. "If they have questions, they'll keep looking for me until they find me. May as well get it over with."

"You sure?" Richard questioned.

"Yes," she assured him. "It's okay."

Jackson disappeared through a doorway on his way to finding a quiet place to wait them out. Richard shoved his gun into the coat closet next to the front door and grabbed his cane. Carolyn took a seat in a chair, trying to look as relaxed as possible.

When the doorbell rang, Richard waited a moment before answering the door. Theo Morris and Patricia Stevens stood on the porch. Without a word, Richard waved them in, stepping aside to let them pass. To the detectives' surprise, a woman sat on the far side of the room.

"Mrs. Winters?" Theo asked.

"Ms." Carolyn corrected. "Widow."

"Sorry for your loss," the detective said.

"Thank you."

"What brings you?" Richard waddled past and fell onto the couch, leaning into the corner.

"More questions," Patricia answered.

"For you too," Theo continued addressing Carolyn.

"Of course," Carolyn smiled. "Whatever I can do to help."

"Detective Stevens, I'll take Mr. Jensen to the kitchen," Theo said. "You can question Ms. Winters here."

"Okay," Patricia said. "Sounds."

Richard grimaced as he stood again, and with a glance toward Carolyn, walked toward the kitchen. He had left his other gun and vest there. Things were going to get messy fast. Patricia nodded at Theo just before he turned to follow the man he would interview. Patricia waited until they were out of sight.

"What would you like to ask me, Detective …what did he call you?"

"Stevens," Patricia said. "So how long have the two of you …"

"The two of us?" Carolyn laughed. "Oh, detective, there is no two of us."

"You understand why I might think there is?" she asked.

"You mean because you found the two of us together?" Carolyn laughed again. "That hardly proves anything more than we know each other. And you already knew that."

"I did."

"Let me help you here." Carolyn shifted in her seat. "Richard and I have known one another for a long time. We worked together years ago and ran into each other about a month back. I heard about his wife and stopped by to see how he was doing. Why don't you ask the questions you wanted to ask?"

"Okay." Patricia took a seat on the couch. "Let's start with…Why were you at the Halstead company party as Stanley Webber's plus one, when he wasn't even there?"

"Wow," Carolyn said. "That's a good one."

"Would you answer, please?"

"Of course," she grinned. "I was supposed to meet him there and I had already arrived when he canceled."

"He canceled?" Patricia perked up. "He called you to cancel?"

"Well, no." Carolyn shook her head. "I suppose canceled was the wrong word. He didn't show up."

"Why were you there instead of his wife?" Patricia asked.

"You would have to ask him," Carolyn dodged the question.

"You know I can't," Patricia said. "That's why I'm asking you."

Carolyn shrugged. The two of them sat in silence for a moment, sizing one another up. Carolyn enjoyed a good game of cat and mouse, especially when no harm could be done. Patricia, on the other hand, was not humored in the least.

"When Stanley didn't show," Patricia continued. "Why didn't you leave?"

"I was going to," Carolyn admitted. "But I ran into Richard. We started reminiscing and I lost track of time. When they said the food was ready, well, who says no to free food?"

"What is it you do, Ms. Winters?"

"I run a security firm," she answered.

"Is that why you were with Mr. Webber?" The detective asked. "Security?"

Carolyn hesitated before answering. "I was assessing his situation."

"Assessing?"

"Yes."

"And your conclusion?" Patricia asked.

"I would have to say there was a viable threat," she said without emotion.

"I would have to agree," Patricia said.

"I don't know how you couldn't," Carolyn said. "Of course, it's much easier in hindsight."

"You're not from here, are you?" Patricia asked. "I mean locally."

"No, ma'am."

"If you were only assessing," the detective asked. "Why are you still here? Seems to me that, without a paying client, you would want to move on. To home. To the next client. Somewhere."

"Who said I didn't have a paying client?"

"You said you were assessing Stan's situation," Patricia reminded her. "Since you weren't watching him, I can only conclude he wasn't paying you yet."

"That's right."

"I'm confused," Patricia frowned. "Was Stanley Webber your client or not?"

"That is a difficult question," Carolyn said.

"How hard could it be?" Patricia asked. "Yes, he was your client. Or no, he wasn't your client."

"I would have to say." Carolyn looked up to the ceiling as if in deep thought. "Yes and no."

"Would you care to explain that?" Patricia grunted.

"I was hired to assess the danger level to Stan," she said. "But I don't know who hired me."

"What do you mean, you don't know?"

"It means, I don't know," Carolyn explained.

"How can you not know who hired you?"

Carolyn took a deep breath. "I thought Stan hired me. Now, I'm not sure."

"What changed?"

"That's not something I can discuss."

"Can't?" Patricia asked. "Or won't?"

"Does it matter?"

"I could take you down to the station," Patricia threatened. "Keep you there."

"You and I both know that won't change anything," Carolyn said.

Theo stared at the woman for a long moment.

"Is there anything you can tell me that might shine a light on who kidnapped Stanley Webber?"

"No."

"What about Sonia Jensen?" Patricia asked.

"No."

"Or who was drugging Richard Jensen while he was in the hospital?"

"No," she lied.

70

Richard walked into his kitchen as he had done countless times over the years. This time, he expected the detective behind him to spot his weapon and vest, bringing the full weight of the law down on his shoulders. But when he stepped in, they were nowhere to be seen. Apparently, Jackson had snagged them and put them somewhere out of view.

With a sigh, he opened the refrigerator and pulled out a bottle of beer. He hooked the cane over his arm and twisted the cap off. Turning to the man who had followed him, he reacted as if surprised to see her.

"Sorry, detective," he said. "Can I get you something? Water? Cola? I can make some coffee."

"I'm good." Theo eyed the bottle in his hand. "Shall we sit?"

Richard pulled out the chair nearest him and lowered himself onto it, setting his beer on the small kitchen table in the center of the room. Theo sat opposite him, arms crossed, studying him for a time.

"You had questions," Richard reminded him.

He grumbled. "I do."

"And they are?"

"Let's start with," Theo unfolded his arms and leaned forward. "How long have you and Ms. Winters been an item? Did it start before Sonia vanished?"

"Me and Carolyn?" Richard grinned. "Are you serious?"

"Answer the question, please."

"Listen," Richard said. "She and I have history, but not that kind. Besides, she's still pissed at me for something that happened years ago."

"What was that?" Theo asked.

"That was personal and has nothing to do with Sonia," Richard said.

"Could be motive," the detective suggested.

"It's not." Richard took a drink. "Now, you obviously didn't know she would be here, so these aren't the questions you came to ask."

"No," Theo admitted. "They aren't."

"So, ask."

"The last time we spoke," he began, "you asked where Stanley Webber was last seen. Why would you want to know that?"

"I was curious," Richard said.

"You see, I don't buy that," Theo challenged. "Why would it matter? Even if, as you say, you were curious. Why would you care?"

"He was Sonia's boss," Richard explained. "He disappeared like she did. It made me curious."

"You know what I think?" He asked.

"Why don't you tell me." Richard crossed his arms.

"I think you're trying to find your wife," Theo said. "I think you know who took her. And I think you know, or believe, Stanley Webber was somehow involved. And instead of telling us what you know, you're conducting your own investigation."

"You think Stan was involved, then?" Richard narrowed his eyes.

"We don't know." Theo said. "But you obviously know more than you're sharing with us. Why don't you tell me if he was involved or not."

"How would I know?"

"Because you're trying to find him instead of your wife," Theo said.

"Why would I do that?" Richard asked.

"Because you think he will lead you to her," Theo argued.

"It sounds like you have it all worked out, detective," Richard grumbled. "I assume you're looking for Stan for the same reason."

"Leave the tracking to us, Mr. Jensen," the detective said. "As far as we know the last place Mr. Webber was seen was at Halstead Enterprises. If you know otherwise, tell us and let us do our jobs."

Richard glanced up at him. They didn't know about the grocery store parking lot where he met with Carolyn. Which meant Stan paid cash for his wine. He could tell them, but he would have a difficult time explaining how he knew. Maybe Carolyn would tell them. He grimaced. "I don't know anything."

"Are you sure about that?"

"I'm sure."

"Tell me about the bowling alley." Theo watched his face for a reaction.

To his credit, Richard gave him nothing. But his mind raced, wondering how they had tied him to the crime scene. "Bowling alley?"

"Your car was seen at the bowling alley," Theo clarified.

"First of all, detective, I don't bowl," Richard said. "And second, my car was totaled when that SUV rammed us off the road."

"We know you own more than one car, Mr. Jensen," Theo said. "Your Mercedes as seen."

"I don't think so, detective." Richard was going to make the detective tell what he knew. "Like I said, I don't bowl."

"The abandoned bowling alley where four men were found shot to death," Theo demanded. "What were you doing there?"

"That sounds awful." Richard couldn't imagine there being working cameras at the run-down building. "But I wasn't there."

"We have a witness," Theo informed him.

"Well, I don't know what they told you," Richard argued. "But they were either mistaken, or they lied."

"Why would they lie about that, Mr. Jensen?" Theo demanded.

"I don't know," Richard raised his voice. "Why would someone take Sonia? Why would someone drug me to keep me in the hospital? I don't know. Aren't you supposed to be finding these things out?"

Theo fell silent.

"Are we done here?" Richard sat up.

"Not quite," Theo shifted. "Tell me. Gavin Barr."

"What about him?" His voice was still tense.

"Have you ever known him to lose his temper?" the detective asked.

"Everyone loses their temper, detective," Richard said.

"True," he agreed. "But have you ever noticed him lose it, say, unexpectedly? You know, over something small. Something where he seemed to overreact?"

"Not that I recall," Richard frowned. "Why?"

"Just looking at all options," he said.

"Gavin?" Richard shook his head. "You're wasting your time with him."

"Until we know who has Sonia, or attempted to kill you," Theo said. "We're following through with all possible suspects."

"First you accuse me of, what?" Richard frowned. "Killing four people. And now you think Gavin did something? Do you know anything yet? Because from where I am, it seems you're still grasping at straws."

71

Richard closed the door behind the detectives when they left and stood there waiting in case they returned. Carolyn moved to the window where she watched their retreat just as she had their approach. Neither of them seemed to breathe until the detectives' car was out of sight.

"Is it all clear?" Jackson appeared from the hallway leading to the bedrooms.

"And if it isn't?" Carolyn said. "What are you going to do now?"

"It's clear." Richard leaned his cane against the door frame and made his way to a chair. "Where are my vest and weapon?"

"When I heard you coming to the kitchen, I grabbed them and used your back hallway to get to the small bedroom back there."

"Thanks for that," Richard nodded.

"No problem," Jackson nodded. "What did they want?"

"They were fishing," Richard answered. "Wanted to know if Carolyn and I were a thing. Asked me about my business partner."

"He asked me about four dead men in an abandoned bowling alley," Carolyn said. "What do you think that was about?"

"That was about me," Richard confessed. "They came after me. I had no choice."

"And this is the first I'm hearing of it?" Carolyn snapped.

"We just discussed that whoever is behind all this wanted us together," Jackson jumped in. "We were going to split up to defuse that. Them going after you alone changes everything."

"Well." Richard looked from one face to the other. "I still don't know who to trust."

"Are you serious?" Carolyn growled. "If you can't trust us, who can you trust?"

"I don't know," Richard responded. He stood in silent defiance. "What now?"

"You figure out who you can trust," Carolyn sneered. "And we figure out who is behind all of this so we can find Stan and Sonia."

"There aren't many options," Jackson said. "It obviously goes back to the time we worked together. Either it's the government wanting to erase more than just our files …"

"Do you really think they would do this?" Richard asked. "Especially after all these years?"

"Or," Jackson continued. "It's a family member of one of our targets looking for revenge."

"Equally unlikely," Richard said.

"They would have to know it was us who did whatever it is they think we did," Carolyn argued. "Then they would have to access secure files to get our names, track us down with only names to go on, and what, create an elaborate scheme to get us all together? I don't think so. If someone like that was after us, we would have been targeted individually. Taken out one by one."

"So, the government?" Jackson said.

"What if someone watched their father, or some relative, die?" Richard asked. "And now they want to make us watch each other die?"

"That's a morbid thought," Jackson said. "I still say it's the government."

"Why would they want us all together?" Carolyn countered. "No. We're missing something."

"We're ignoring the connection between Stan and Sonia," Richard said. "And what I found in Sonia's notes."

"Sonia's notes?" Carolyn's head snapped in his direction. "What did you find in her notes?"

Jackson sat in the same chair he had been in when Richard came home. "Do tell."

"Okay, so when we were leaving the Halsteads' party, Sonia asked Mr. Halstead if Stan had told him about something they wanted to discuss," Richard explained. "After I got out of the hospital, I found something in her notes suggesting that someone was falsifying results on accounts to show they were making money when they were, in fact, losing."

"Why didn't you mention this before?" Carolyn asked.

"When would I have?"

"So, this may all be legitimate?" Jackson said. "Some one-in-a-million coincidence that put us all together?"

The three of them looked at one another.

"We're definitely missing something," Carolyn said what they were all thinking.

72

"How did it go with Jensen?" Patricia asked. "Did he give a reason for wanting to know where Stan Webber was last seen?"

"According to him." Theo guided the car out of Richard's neighborhood. "He was just curious."

"Right," Patricia scoffed.

"I asked him about his business partner, Gavin Barr," Theo pulled the wheel hard to avoid a large pothole. Straightening out again, he continued. "He thinks we would be wasting our time pursuing him."

"Protecting his partner?"

"He either believes there is no way Barr is involved." Theo said. "Or Barr helped him get rid of Stan and his wife."

"I don't see that, do you?"

"Not really," Theo admitted. "But open mind. I also asked if he and Carolyn were in a relationship."

"I asked her, too," Patricia said. "What did he say?"

"He seemed humored by the idea," he said. "Denied anything was going on. And her?"

"She actually laughed," Patricia said. "I'm pretty sure there's nothing there."

"Agreed," Theo nodded. "Now for the big one. The bowling alley."

"What did he say?"

"Denies being there," Theo said.

"Did you tell him we had a witness that puts him at the scene?"

"I did."

"What was his answer to that?"

"Says the witness lied," Theo answered. "He thinks the people who took his wife are setting him up for it."

"Seems like a stretch," Patricia said.

"It does. What did Ms. Winters have to say?" Theo asked. "Did you learn anything from her?"

"She runs a security company, like Richard told us," Patricia said. "Says she was doing a threat assessment on Stan to determine if she was going to take him on as a client. He disappeared before she completed the assessment."

"I wonder what the conclusion of the assessment was." Theo couldn't help but smile.

"I think she claimed to be in the early stages to reduce her liability," Patricia said. "Not to mention, if she claims he wasn't a client yet, the failure doesn't go onto her success rate."

"Clever," Theo said. "Do we think she knows what happened to Webber?"

"I don't know for sure," Patricia said. "She went to the Halstead party alone, as Stan's plus one. Claims he was supposed to meet her there and didn't show. But I think she already knew he was missing."

"Because she disappeared him?"

"Possibly," Patricia said. "Or she was providing him protection and lost him. She may have thought going to the party might give her insight into what happened to him."

"I could see that, I guess," Theo said.

"But get this," Patricia grinned. "She also said she doesn't even know if Stanley Webber is even the person who hired her to protect him."

"What?" Theo looked at his partner. "How does that work?"

"According to her," Patricia explained. "She was hired through email. Paid by courier. And when she reached out to Stan, he seemed surprised. The fact that he was being threatened made him accept the help."

"Would you?"

"Would I what?"

"Okay, you're Webber and I'm Winters," Theo said. "I come up and say, hi, I'm the person you hired to protect you. But you didn't hire me. You're going to say what? Okay, sure?"

"Does seem odd," Patricia agreed.

"It could be he was just surprised to find she was a woman," Theo said.

"What does that mean?"

"Don't get defensive," Theo rolled his eyes. "Yes, women can be bodyguards. Some are better at it than men. But if you're Stan and hired someone through email, you might just assume a man will show up."

"That's probably true." Patricia settled into her seat. "What if it's all a lie?"

"How do you mean?"

"Protecting or assessing," Patricia said. "Why doesn't she know what happened to Webber?"

"Good point."

"We only have her word that she was protecting him. What if Carolyn Winters wasn't hired to protect Stan at all," she said. "Maybe someone hired her to kill him and make the body disappear."

"Like his jealous wife?" Theo said.

"Or Sonia's jealous husband," Patricia said. "Could be instead of going to the party for clues, she was there for payment."

"We need to narrow down the time that Stan was taken, if he even was,"

Theo said. "Then we could start checking alibis and eliminating suspects."

"We know when he left work," Patricia said. "And when he was supposed to show for the party. We could check alibis for that time frame."

"It's a three-hour window. But it's the best we can do, for now." Theo slowed and made a U-turn. "Let's start with Jensen and Winters."

73

W hat do we do now?" Richard sat on the couch rubbing his injured leg. Though the pain improved every day since his time in the hospital, it still reminded him he had been in an accident.

They had debated at length who would have the motive and the resources to find them and orchestrate the events that had put them together in the same room. No names came to the top of the list. Someone waiting a decade to exact revenge on the team seemed implausible. With the mission records sealed, and the personnel records erased, it would be impossible for someone to know who they were looking for.

"What's this 'we' business?" Jackson responded. "I just came to see what was going on with you. I'm done with this place."

"You were hired to follow a woman who was kidnapped on your watch," Carolyn said. "Don't you owe it to Richard to help find her?"

"Richard chose to leave the team," Jackson countered. "I don't owe him anything."

"Then do it for me," Carolyn said.

"For you?" Jackson raised his eyebrows. "You aren't my wife. Why would I do it for you?"

Carolyn turned to Richard. "You talk to him."

"Forget him," Richard dismissed. "We don't need him."

"Fine," Carolyn rolled her eyes. "He's probably doesn't have it anymore anyway. What are you thinking?"

"I know what you're doing," Jackson said. "Reverse psychology won't work on me."

"The way I see it," Richard spoke to Carolyn, "we have two investigations to conduct. The fraud at Halstead Enterprises. They may have been the reason Sonia and Stan disappeared."

"And the possibility of an affair between them that ended with Stan taking her and running," Carolyn said. "One for each of us."

"What about the revenge angle?" Jackson offered. "You can't ignore the fact that someone may have gone to great lengths to get us together just because it's unlikely."

"Like I said," Carolyn smirked. "One for each of us."

"Wait." Jackson waved his hands between them. "I'm not ..."

The other two gave him a look of disappointment.

Jackson huffed. "Fine. I can look into our past assignments and see if anyone connected to them has traveled to the states recently."

"You can still access the files?" Richard asked.

"I still have my clearance," Jackson admitted.

"That's the spirit," Carolyn smiled at him. To Richard, she said, "I'm assuming you don't want to track down the possibility your wife was cheating on you."

"Good assumption," Richard said. "I'll dig deeper into the financial aspect of Halstead Enterprises. Maybe Bulldog can help me."

"I'm sure he will," Carolyn said. "I think I'll talk to Stan's wife and assistant."

"Fiona Delaney," Richard said.

"What about her?" Carolyn asked.

"She's Stan's assistant," Richard said.

"I know," she said. "I've done my research."

"I've already talked to her," Richard said. "She said there was no affair."

"You're the husband," Carolyn said. "Of course she would tell you nothing happened."

"She's got you there," Jackson grinned.

"I believe her," Richard said.

"I know you do," Carolyn lowered her voice. "I'm still going to talk to her."

"So, we have a plan." Richard stood. "Let's get this over with."

Richard put his vest back on, positioned his weapons, and pulled his jacket over them. Moving to the front of the house, he hesitated, considering whether he should take the cane. Deciding the optics of an injured man might play to his advantage, he snatched it up, twirling it like a baton as he pulled the door open. The three of them stepped onto the porch and Richard closed the door behind them. Only a few steps into the yard they found themselves looking up at a car as it pulled into the driveway.

Inside, the detectives gazed at the three of them, confusion in their eyes.

74

Richard planted the end of the cane into the ground as soon as he saw the car. With his free hand, he tugged upward at the zipper of his jacket, hoping it sufficient to hide what was beneath. His two guests eyed one another as the detectives climbed out of the car.

"Mr. Jensen," Theo greeted. His eyes were on the older man standing behind and to the left of Richard, trying to assess if he was a threat. The detective also realized that unless he had just arrived, the man might have been in the house while he and his partner were conducting interviews. Theo chose to consider him a danger until he knew if Richard was being held against his will.

"Detective," Richard responded.

"Ms. Winters." The detective nodded to her.

"Hello again." She returned the nod.

Theo shifted his gaze to the other man. "And you are?"

"The gardener," Jackson lied. "If you'll excuse me ..."

"Where are your tools?" Patricia asked.

"Oh," Jackson looked down. "I'm a new age gardener. Don't use tools. I like the feel of the dirt in my hands."

"Do you?" Theo asked. "Why don't you give me your name? For my records."

"Brian." Jackson offered his hand. "Brian Andrews."

Theo ignored the hand as he wrote the name down. "What are you doing here, Brian?"

"Gardening?" Jackson shrugged.

"In the house?"

"Oh," Jackson said. "Mr. Jensen was kind enough to let me use his restroom. You know, when nature calls, and all."

"Aren't you a little old to be a gardener?" Theo asked.

"Aren't you a little old to be a detective?" Jackson countered.

The two men stood about a yard apart, staring at one another. It would have been humorous, but for the fact that both men carried weapons. Out of the corner of his eye, Richard could see Carolyn side-stepping to add to the distance between her and the impending shootout. Richard considered doing the same, deciding on de-escalation instead.

"Is there a reason you came back, detectives?" Richard asked.

"There is," Patricia answered. "The day of the Halstead party, you both attended. Can you tell us where you were from about four to say eight?"

"I was at home with Sonia," Richard said. "Getting ready."

"Your alibi is your missing wife?" Patricia asked.

"You asked where I was," Richard said. "That's where I was. Alibi for what, may I ask?"

"Stan's disappearance," the detective explained. "And you, Ms. Winters?"

"Me?" Carolyn had met with Stan during that window, though she decided it would be best to keep that fact to herself. "I had a business meeting. Had to pick up my dress, get ready. And of course, I drove to the house, you know, where the party was being held."

"Can anyone corroborate any of that?"

"Afraid not," she said. "Didn't know I would need an alibi."

"What about your meeting?" Patricia asked. "Surely there were others that could vouch for you."

"Sorry," Carolyn shrugged. "Clients are confidential. They wouldn't want to be involved in such things."

"What about you, Brian?" Theo said. "Where were you?"

"I don't even know what a Halstead Party is," Jackson said. "So, I don't know when it was. Therefore, I can't tell you where I was."

"February third," Theo said.

"Oh, that's easy," Jackson said. "I was in the Bahamas."

"Gardening?" Theo snarled.

"Vacationing." Jackson gave him a broad smile. "Have you been? Beautiful place."

"I don't suppose you have any proof?" Theo asked.

Jackson's smile faded to a grin. "No. Now, since you have no cause to detain me, I need to be going. Richard. Carolyn. Good to see you."

The large man started down the driveway. He pulled out his phone and tapped a string of keys. By the time he reached the street, he had put the phone away. A large SUV pulled up, and Jackson climbed in. As it drove away, Richard recognized the woman in the front passenger seat as one of the two who had followed him from the grocery store.

Theo directed his attention to Richard. "That man was no gardener. Who was he?"

"Brian?" Richard said. "I've never met Brian Andrews before today."

"Then why was he here?" Patricia asked.

"Sales," Carolyn answered before Richard had the chance. "He was trying to get Richard to sign up for a lawn care package."

"You're not going to convince me that man is really a gardener," Theo scoffed.

"I don't think he does the work," Carolyn grinned. "Just the sales."

"If there's nothing else," Richard interrupted. "We really need to go, too."

The detective stared at Carolyn, as if he were trying to bore his eyes through the lie to find the truth. When he finally looked away, he stared at Richard with the same intensity. "Have you put on weight?"

Richard became conscious of the vest under his jacket. "Uh, yeah. Starting to get my appetite back. Spending a month in a coma is a great diet plan, by the way."

"What's that supposed to mean?" Theo asked.

"I, uh," Richard stammered. "Nothing."

Patricia grinned. "We should go, Detective Morris."

Theo nodded. "We'll be checking into your friend."

"Not a friend," Richard clarified.

Theo waved a dismissive hand. He turned to walk away with his partner close on his heels. So much so that she almost ran into him when he stopped and turned back. "Richard? Do you know Valarie Webber?"

"Stan's wife?" Richard thought back. "We've met a few times, at past Halstead parties."

"The two of you never met," Theo asked, "for say, lunch or coffee?"

"No," Richard said. "Why would we?"

"I don't know," Theo said. "To plan the demise of your cheating spouses, maybe."

"Sonia wasn't cheating on me, detective," Richard argued. "If someone is telling you otherwise, they're lying."

"My experience with married people having affairs is that they keep them a secret. Maybe you just didn't know about it," Theo suggested. "Like Sonia didn't know about your military history."

"She knew I was in the military," Richard said.

"But did she know what you did?" Theo asked. "I mean your records weren't just sealed; they were erased. That doesn't happen to people who just serve their time in the military."

"Were you in the military, detective?" Richard asked.

"Marines," Theo responded.

"Does your wife know what you did while you were serving?"

Theo did not answer.

"I'll take that as a no," Richard said. "We don't talk to our spouses about what we did in the service. Not because we're keeping secrets, but because we want to spare them the details. And we don't want to relive those moments. So, no, Sonia did not know what I did in the military. But I did not keep secrets from her, nor she from me. There was no affair. Now, if you'll kindly leave, I have somewhere I need to be."

75

Jackson slammed the door closed and slumped back into the seat of the SUV. With a wave of his hand, the driver sped away. He hated having the police in his business. Hated even more the idea of burning a perfectly good alias on the likes of that detective. He let out a low, audible growl, drawing the attention of the female in the passenger seat.

She twisted to face him. "Do you need something, sir?"

Richard was right. They needed more training. She should be watching the road, looking for threats, not looking at him and asking questions. Jackson shook his head. "No. I'm fine."

"Where to, sir?" The driver called back.

"Take me to the hotel," Jackson ordered. "I want to get everything packed up. And call Louie. Tell him to prep the plane. I want to leave sometime this evening."

"Yes, sir," the driver said.

Jackson sat back and stared at the buildings as they passed by. He was angry with himself for letting Richard and Carolyn snare him into their little investigation. He wanted no part of it. His interest lay in keeping the old team safe and their names clear.

He had agreed to look into the past missions they had completed, in search of anyone connected to the targets who might hold a grudge. The past was the very thing he wanted to keep buried. No good would come from digging things up. Besides, as far as he was concerned, anyone connected to a target would have reason to want revenge, though not all of them would have the resources to track them down.

"Dutch," he turned to the front of the car.

"Sir?" the woman responded.

"There is something you can do for me," he said. "That kid we use for hacking. What's his name?"

"Brady?"

"That's the one," he nodded. "Get him on the phone. I have a job for him."

"Yes, sir."

Jackson sat back again. He couldn't remember being called sir so much in his life. Richard and Carolyn almost never called him that, even when they were new to the team. He closed his eyes and let the rhythm of the car soothe him.

He missed the days before Mexico City. Prior to that operation, the best team he had ever commanded was whole. He had lost men before, and two of the ones he lost that day had been good men but replaceable. Losing Lance was different. And when Richard left, followed by Carolyn, Jackson saw it as the beginning of the end. Replacing operatives like them wasn't a matter of picking names out of a stack of files. The dynamics of a crew like that took time to build. The training needed to turn a new team into a unit that could trust every other member to have their backs would have taken months. Not that he didn't try.

Three of the new members fit into place as well as could be expected. But he had lost five in a matter of weeks. The remaining two were another matter. One interviewed well. His paperwork projected an exemplary soldier, his evaluations excellent. But the day he arrived, Jackson knew something was off. The man, Christopher Stone, was arrogant, insisted on sharing his thoughts at every opportunity and challenged decisions at every step. Valuable qualities to have in their line of work except for one problem. Chris had no clue what he was talking about. His ideas were too basic or too dangerous to be successful. His decisions, if not kept in check, could get people killed. Years later he learned Chris's father was a senator that no one wanted to rub the wrong way. They gave him high marks and moved him on to be someone else's problem. Until he landed in Jackson's lap.

The last new member Jackson brought on turned out to be that type of decision. He thought he had found the perfect replacement for Lance in his brother, Lucas. He was intelligent, self-assured, talented; just like his brother. Everything needed to be the team leader Lance had been. Lucas reminded Jackson of the man he had lost.

Jackson was hopeful for a smooth transition. Unfortunately, that wasn't the case. One significant difference stood out between Lucas and his brother. Lance had been a leader of men, well liked, trusted. He made every decision with the welfare of his men in mind. Lucas was a loose cannon. He shot from the hip and worried about the consequences later. But the most damaging difference was Lucas's anger. He flew off the handle without warning, did not like being challenged, and had almost no filter.

Lucas and Chris hated one another. Putting them together was like building a bomb. Chris was the fuse, Lucas the dynamite. They just needed someone to strike the match. When it finally came to a head and the match finally lit could have been predicted in retrospect.

They were on mission, a time when everyone had to be at the top of their game. Follow the plan to the letter, have one another's backs, and get out. Five minutes in, Lucas and Chris were arguing about something trivial. Jackson had to pick up the radio and shut them down.

When they neared the target location, Lucas unexpectedly had Chris take point. Jackson almost picked up the microphone again, but they weren't arguing, and he allowed Lucas to lead his team. They approached the first corner of concern, where keeping hidden from the enemy would be more difficult. It required precise timing. Then it happened.

Watching body-cam footage later, it was obvious what had happened, though Jackson couldn't prove it wasn't an accident. But he knew. Chris was at the corner waiting to make his advancement across the hall when Lucas bumped him, hard. Chris was leaning in preparation to run across, so the bump caused him to lose his balance, sending him sprawling into the opening. He was in full view of three enemy combatants. Before he could even raise his weapon, he was dead. Lucas had killed him without pulling the trigger.

The mission had to be scrubbed. Lucas became the 'hero' who killed the enemy and recovered Chris's body to be sent home. Anyone who knew Chris blamed him for his own demise, assuming he had started his run too early. Only Jackson knew the truth. He just couldn't prove it. The video would only show Lucas had bumped his teammate. It could not prove intent.

Three days later, Jackson dissolved the team and started his current company. In looking for suspects who might want revenge and have the access and resources to carry it out, he might consider Chris's father, but the senator died of a massive coronary upon hearing of his son's death. The senator's wife became a senator as well, winning her husband's seat. She had lost her son and husband in a matter of days and could want someone to pay. It just wouldn't explain why Richard and Carolyn were being targeted. They left the team long before Chris's death.

"Sir?"

His eyes snapped open to Dutch holding a phone in front of him. He looked at the offering as if wary of it.

"Brady, sir." She shook the phone at him. "He's on the phone."

"Oh, thank you." He snatched up the device. "Yes. Brady. Is that you?"

"You called me."

Brady never called him, sir. In fact, Brady never said much at all. "You remember when I had you hack into that secure facility to erase some things a while back?"

"The military personnel database?"

"That's the one," Jackson acknowledged.

"You want me to erase something else?"

"No. No," Jackson said. "I'm going to give you a list of missions. Then I need you to find every living person connected to the targets of those missions and tell me if any of them have the resources to carry out an elaborate revenge scheme. And if any of them have traveled to the states within the last year."

"Is that all?"

Jackson wasn't sure if he was being sarcastic. "I need you to rush this if you can. I'll text you the mission code names."

"Can't wait."

The line went dead. Jackson was glad he would be retiring soon. This younger generation got on his nerves. He handed the phone back to Dutch and pulled out his own phone. Scrolling through his contacts until he came to the one tagged 'Hacker Nerd', Jackson typed a quick text with the list he had promised. He sat back again, eyes closed. The hotel was still ten minutes away.

76

Carolyn had been to Stan's home once, when she first introduced herself to the confused man. It had been obvious at the time that he did not know why she was there. After explaining that she was to provide him with protection, he accepted the help so fast that she put it out of her mind. The question of who hired her was now at the forefront.

Pursuing the idea that Stan and Sonia were having an affair was one way of explaining the events that took place a month ago. But if that was the catalyst, and Stan had taken her and run, why would he need protecting? The fear she sensed in him at their first meeting was genuine. For that fear to originate from an affair, he would have to think his wife or Richard wanted him dead.

Either Richard had become a much better liar since she knew him, or he was unaware of any affair, denying even the thought of it. That left Valarie Webber, Stan's wife of twenty-seven years. Carolyn stood on the couple's front porch and rang the bell.

The wait stretched long enough she began debating whether she should ring the bell again or move on and return later. The arguments for each were just forming when the door opened. Valarie stood in the doorway, wearing an apron and wiping her hands on the towel she carried. She gazed at her unexpected guest with curiosity.

"May I help you?" she asked.

Carolyn wondered what made people, when opening their doors to strangers, feel obligated to offer assistance. "Valarie, you don't know me, but I would like to talk to you about your husband."

The woman's demeanor changed from cautious curiosity to guarded paranoia. "Do you know where he is? Is he alive?"

"I'm sorry …"

"Oh, no." Valarie's hand covered her mouth. "No. No. No."

"Mrs. Webber." Carolyn was sharp. "I don't know where Stan is. He hasn't been found."

The small amount of optimism Valarie had, fell away. Carolyn knew the woman was vulnerable. A good person would console her and be sure she was alright. Carolyn took the opportunity to pounce.

"Valarie," she said. "Did you believe your husband was having an affair?"

"What?"

"Do you believe Stan was capable of kidnapping Sonia Jensen and disappearing?" Carolyn continued.

"Listen …"

"Did you hire someone to kill your husband and Sonia Jensen?"

"Absolutely not." Valarie's demeanor changed again. Anger flashed in her eyes. "I think you need to leave."

"Did you kill your husband, Mrs. Webber?" Carolyn asked again.

"What is wrong with you?" Valarie questioned.

The anger on Valerie's face was intense. Carolyn had a hard time connecting this woman with the one Stan had described to her during the initial background questioning, the one she did with all new clients.

"So many things." Carolyn gave the woman a half-hearted smile. "But I need you to answer the questions."

"Who are you?" Valarie demanded.

"I'll tell you what," Carolyn bargained. "You answer my questions and I'll tell you."

Valarie sized the woman up. "The truth?"

The words surprised Carolyn. Had someone told Valarie lies? Carolyn softened. "The truth."

Valarie invited her guest inside and led her to a sitting room. They sat across from one another and sized each other up. Carolyn glanced around the room. Nothing had changed in the month since she had been there. A framed family photo hung above the fireplace. Father, mother, son and daughter; they were a handsome group. Stan had talked about his family when she had met with him. The portrait was not recent, maybe twenty-years old. The son, about five in the picture, lived overseas somewhere with a wife and two kids of his own. He came home for the occasional holiday.

The daughter lived on the coast with her second husband. She had one child from the first marriage and two from the second. Stan did not approve of his son-in-law, considering him bad for his daughter, and the girl knew it. So, visits from them were scarce. There had also been another son that Stan and Valarie had lost at a young age to leukemia. They had been a happy family before that. Afterward, they had just been sad. The sadness was clear in the eyes staring back from the portrait.

"You have questions," the homeowner said. "Ask them."

"Okay." Carolyn turned back to the woman. "Do you have any reason to believe your husband was having an affair with Sonia Jensen?"

"No." Valarie was adamant.

"Thinking back," Carolyn said. "Do you think it might have been possible?"

"Of course not."

"How can you be sure?"

"Nearly three decades of marriage," Valarie declared. "That's how."

"Plenty of marriages end with infidelity, even after that many years," Carolyn pointed out.

"You look at those couples," Valarie said. "You'll find there were struggles throughout their marriages. Stan and I are best friends. He would never cheat on me because he wouldn't have wanted to. Next question."

Carolyn smiled. There had been struggles in the Webber's marriage. Stan had told her during their interview. Losing their son was not the only issue, just the worst. "Was Stan capable ..."

"... of kidnapping or killing Sonia?" Valarie completed. "Not in a million years. He didn't have a violent bone in his body. And he would never hurt a woman."

"Okay," Carolyn nodded.

"And as to whether I killed him, or hired someone else to do it," Valarie said. "I've already answered that. I would never. He is my best friend. I love him. I want him home."

"Do you know anyone who might want to do Stan harm?"

"No," Valarie insisted. "He's a wonderful man. Everyone loves him. Now, I've answered your questions. Tell me who you are."

Carolyn pulled out a card and laid it on the small table between them. Valarie picked it up and examined it, turning it over and back.

"My name is Carolyn Winters," she said.

"Professional Securities, Inc.?" Valarie read.

"My company," Carolyn said.

"I don't understand."

"I was hired to protect your husband, Mrs. Webber," she explained. "To protect Stan."

"Protect him?" Valarie's brow tightened. "Protect him from what?"

"I wish I knew," Carolyn admitted. "Then he might be here with you today."

"He hired you to protect him," Valarie said. "But didn't tell you why?"

"Stan seemed to know he was in danger but wasn't clear on where the threat was coming from," Carolyn said. "But I don't believe he was the one who hired us."

Valarie started to speak, then closed her mouth and pursed her lips. When she started again, she said, "I don't understand. Who else would have hired you?"

Carolyn sat back, clasping her hands in front of her. "We're not sure."

Valarie sat back, frowning as she spoke. "You don't know who hired you? You don't know why Stan needed protection. And you don't know what happened to my husband. What do you know?"

"My company was approached through our website," Carolyn explained. "After that, a series of emails gave the details of the client's needs."

"Protection for my husband."

"Exactly," Carolyn confirmed. "As far as we were concerned, we were communicating with Stanley Webber. A date was set, a price. Payment arrived through a courier service."

"That's odd."

"Yes," Carolyn agreed. "But not unprecedented. However, when I met Stan face to face for the first time, he was surprised. He wasn't expecting me. However, when I explained why I was there, he accepted."

"But you didn't protect him, did you?" Tears formed in the corners of her eyes, her voice accusing.

"No, I didn't," Carolyn admitted. "We had only arrived the day before. We were starting our assessments to determine how viable the threat was and in what form it would come. There was no sign that things would escalate so quickly."

Valarie lowered her eyes. "I'm sorry. I know it wasn't your fault."

"I met with Stan the day he vanished," Carolyn moved on. "He told me he wanted me to go to the company party in your place. Thought it would be safer for you and that I might learn something there. Then he mentioned he needed to run an errand. I wanted to go with him, but he insisted I meet him at the party. Do you have any idea what the errand might have been?"

"He told me he couldn't go because he had to work late," Valarie looked up at the family portrait. "I knew that wasn't true. Charles wants everyone at his parties. I guess he said that so I wouldn't be upset about him taking you."

"He wanted to keep you safe," Carolyn offered.

"Right." She turned back to her guest. "Anyway. In answer to your question: No. I don't know what errand he may have been running."

"I understand."

"If you were hired to keep him safe," Valarie said. "And now he's missing …"

"I know." Carolyn closed her eyes. "We failed. I'm sorry."

"But that was a month ago," Valarie said. "Why are you still here?"

"Whether or not he was the one paying," Carolyn said. "Stan was my client. I'm trying to find him, or at least what happened to him."

"Thank you for that," Valarie tried to smile. "If there's anything I can do to help."

"Stan's assistant," Carolyn said.

"Fiona?"

"Right," Carolyn said. "Fiona Delaney. Do you know where she lives?"

"Hold on." Valarie stood and left the room. When she returned, she handed Carolyn a piece of paper with the assistant's address and phone number.

"Thank you." Carolyn stood to leave.

When they reached the front door, Valarie stopped her. "If you find out that someone's killed him…"

"We hope that isn't the case," Carolyn tried to reassure her.

"But if you do," Valarie looked around at her neighbor's homes and leaned closer. "Can I hire you to, you know, kill them?"

Carolyn's eyes widened. "Mrs. Webber, we aren't that kind of company. And I would recommend you think long and hard before doing anything like that."

77

Richard sat in the back of the same diner where he had met with Carolyn. The server refilled his coffee for the third time and eyed the plate that held the sandwich he had ordered. An hour later, he had taken only one bite. He smiled at her and waved her off, suggesting he might still finish the meal.

Between him and his lunch were financial records and income reports from more than a dozen files in which Sonia had noted discrepancies. The differences totaled in the millions, and he began to suspect that Stan had taken Sonia to keep her quiet. He wanted to find the man and ask him to his face.

The waitress returned much sooner than expected. His coffee cup was still more than half full.

"My shift is ending," she informed him. She put his ticket on the table next to him. "I need to close out your table."

"No problem." Richard checked the total, just shy of twenty-one dollars. He pulled out his wallet, withdrew two twenties and laid them on top of the ticket. "Keep the change."

"Thank you, sir." The server smiled as she tucked the money into her apron.

When she was gone, Richard turned his attention to his phone. Scrolling through his contact list, he clicked on the one he wanted and waited.

"You keep calling me and I'm going to think you're back in the game." Benny Davenport's deep voice greeted him.

"Hey, Bulldog," Richard acknowledged. "I guess I am for now. I was hoping you might have a few minutes to help me with something."

"Of course," Bulldog said. "What do you need?"

"Before Sonia disappeared," Richard explained. "She found some differences between actual and reported returns on investment on several of her clients."

"Sounds shady," Bulldog said.

"It is," Richard agreed. "I was hoping you could hack into Halstead Enterprises and see how widespread the problem is."

"That's more than a few minutes," Bulldog grumbled.

"I'm sorry," Richard apologized. "If you can't …"

"I didn't say I can't," Bulldog cut him off. "I'm just saying it will take a while."

"I appreciate it," Richard said.

"Anything for you, Money. You know that," Bulldog assured him. "I'll call when I have something."

Richard ignored the use of the nickname this time. When the team was between operations, they often got bored. They came up with several activities to occupy their time. Card games, drinking games; anything to entertain themselves. One activity was shooting games. They would set up targets at different distances and angles. Then they would bet on who would get the closest to the bullseye. Richard always won the pot, being the most accurate shot on the team. After a while, when his turn would come up, someone would say, 'Here comes the money shot.' From that came his nickname, but they wouldn't bet against him anymore.

He dragged his plate closer and took a second bite of the sandwich. As he chewed, he contemplated the papers before him. If Stan was behind the fraudulent reports and he kidnapped Sonia to keep her from exposing him, why run? Running only linked her disappearance to his. Instead of being a man of interest in the case, he could have just gone on as if he knew nothing about what happened. He would have been safe to continue his misdeeds unhindered. Running made no sense.

The alternative was that when Sonia reported what she had found to Stan; he didn't know about it. He would have reported what she found to Charles Halstead. Consequently, Stan disappeared and then Sonia. Charles owned the company, so a report of fraud would have been very damaging. And if he was behind the fraud, trying to keep his company looking good to investors, Charles stood to lose everything.

Someone falsified the reports to show increased income rather than losses. Reporting a lower income would allow someone to skim the excess off the top, making millions in ill-gotten gains. To report higher income levels would only make the person managing the account look better. But Sonia was managing the accounts, and she reported it. She was not behind it.

Richard gathered his papers. Taking another bite of the sandwich, he shoved it to the far side of the table. The only other possibility was that someone was trying to make the company itself look better. It all came back to Charles Halstead.

78

Stanley Webber's assistant stood in the doorway of her home looking her unexpected guest up and down. "Do you need something?"

Carolyn gave the woman a broad smile. "My name is Anita Brown. I have been asked to follow up on the disappearance of…" She glanced at the notepad in her hand that had nothing on it. "Here it is…Stanley Webber. Are you…" She glanced at the pad again, "uh, Fiona Delaney? Mr. Webber's assistant?"

"Yes." Fiona let out a loud huff. "I've already talked to the police."

"Of course you have." Carolyn smiled again. "My agency has read the reports, but we like to pay another visit. Especially after the victim has been missing so long."

"Victim?" Fiona asked. "I thought they said he left."

"Until we can confirm he left on his own," Carolyn said. "We will refer to him as the victim."

"You don't think he's dead, do you?" Fiona asked. "He's such a pleasant boss."

"We don't have enough to suggest whether he is dead or alive." Carolyn wanted to establish a rapport with the woman but was tiring of answering questions. "Did you ever know Mr. Webber to lie?"

"Mr. Webber?" The question humored Fiona. "Never. He was a good man."

"Even good men lie," Carolyn said.

"Not Stan," Fiona defended. "Never."

"Were you sleeping with him?"

"What?" The woman put a hand to her chest. "Of course not."

"It wouldn't be the first time a boss slept with his assistant," Carolyn said. "I wouldn't judge you."

"It didn't happen."

"Was it because he was sleeping with Sonia Jensen?" She finally asked the question she came to ask.

"No," Fiona stiffened. "Stan was a happily married man. He wouldn't cheat on Valarie."

"How can you be so sure?"

"I know." Fiona was adamant. "I was his assistant. I knew everything."

In Carolyn's experience businessmen's assistants usually knew more about them than their wives. If Fiona was so convinced that there had been no affair, there probably wasn't one. Although exceptions to the rule always existed.

Early in her private career, she had taken a job for a wealthy client who wanted her husband investigated, convinced he was stealing her money. A woman born into a wealthy family, she had founded a company that became very successful.

She met a man, fell in love, and married him. She gave him a position in her company after an opening became available. All was good for a time, but then she started getting the sick feeling that her husband was skimming money from the business account. That was where Carolyn came in.

She discreetly interviewed the husband's assistant by running into her at a bar. Loading her with drinks, Carolyn asked leading questions to get the young woman to talk. She adored her boss, so charming, etc. The assistant insisted he would never steal from the company. She also found it inconceivable that he would cheat on his wife. He just wouldn't. The revelations surprised Carolyn since, by the time she received a call, the client was usually right.

Then Carolyn started following the man. Not only was he stealing from the company. He was also stealing from the wife's personal accounts. The money was going into a joint account under his name and that of his girlfriend. Even assistants get it wrong.

"The report says that you heard Stanley Webber and Sonia Jensen arguing with one another," Carolyn said. "What were they fighting about?"

"It wasn't really a fight," Fiona corrected. "Neither one was the type to fight about anything. It was more a disagreement."

Carolyn had to resist the urge to roll her eyes. "Then what was the disagreement about?"

"I'm sorry," Fiona said. "I don't know."

"You just told me you knew everything," Carolyn reminded her.

"Well, not that," Fiona admitted.

"If you don't know what it was about," Carolyn asked, "how do you know they were arguing?"

"They got kind of loud," she explained.

"But you couldn't hear what they were saying?"

"They were in his office," Fiona said. "I was at my desk. It was all muffled."

"And how can you be sure they weren't fighting?"

"Because when they came out everything was normal." Fiona readjusted herself. "They were speaking to one another. Whispering, but not like they were angry."

"And you didn't hear anything?" Carolyn asked.

"No," Fiona said. "Not really."

"Not really?" Carolyn frowned. "What does that mean?"

"When they came out of the office," Fiona said. "Sonia was talking about something being evident."

"Evident?"

"Yes." Fiona nodded. "But Stan didn't think it was."

"What did he say?" Carolyn pressed. "Exactly."

"Something like, it wasn't enough." Fiona tried to think back. "Or maybe, they needed more. I assumed they were talking about returns."

"Fiona, is it possible?" Carolyn said. "That the word Sonia used wasn't 'evident'? Could she have said 'evidence'?"

"I suppose," the assistant conceded.

"Thanks for your time." Carolyn turned away abruptly and fast-walked back to her car.

79

The department seemed louder than normal, forcing Detective Morris to press a finger to his ear while struggling to hear the person on the other end of his phone call. After being on hold for nearly an hour, he did not want to miss out on the information being given.

"Okay. Thanks." Detective Morris hung up and sat back in his chair.

"Forensics came back on the bowling alley." Patricia started speaking before Theo had the chance. "Turns out there were two weapons used to kill the four men. One was shot with both."

"Two shooters?"

"Looks like," Patricia said. "Maybe Jensen and Winters. Or Andrews. There were far more casings from the weapons the victims carried."

"Well, I was looking into Brian Andrews," Theo explained. "Too many results to track down. So, I ran the plates of the SUV he jumped into."

"Good thinking," Patricia said.

"Turns out the SUV is not registered to a Brian Andrews," Theo said.

"Stolen?"

"No," Theo said. "Rented. It's owned by a rental company out by the airport."

"You think Brian Andrews isn't local?" Patricia asked.

"Looks like it," Theo said. "But the SUV wasn't rented to a Brian Andrews either."

"One of the goons, maybe?"

"A company," Theo said. "Black Wolf Protection Agency rented the SUV two days ago."

"Carolyn Winters owns a protection agency," Patricia said.

"She does," Theo confirmed.

"That would explain why the two of them were together," Patricia said.

"But it doesn't explain why," Theo said, "when he got into the SUV, Carolyn didn't."

"That does seem odd if you're supposed to be protecting him."

"That's what I thought," Theo said. "Which is why I looked into the ownership of Black Wolf Protection Agency."

"Brian Andrews?"

"No." Theo grinned. "And no Carolyn Winters either."

"Neither of them?"

"No," Theo said. "But the website for Black Wolf has a 'Meet the Owners' page. Complete with photos."

The detective turned the screen of his computer for his partner to see. Black Wolf Protection Agency only had one owner. There were several paragraphs outlining his history and that of the company. On the left side of the screen was a portrait. The face staring back at them was that of Brian Andrews. Only that wasn't the name above the bio. In bold print, it said, Colonel Jackson Porter.

"He's a colonel?"

"That's what it says," Theo said. "Retired."

"Not Brian Andrews."

"Nope."

"Do you think Carolyn Winters works for him?" Patricia asked.

"It would seem likely." Theo studied the colonel's face.

"It could be they were the ones at the bowling alley," she suggested.

"It was Richard Jensen's car," Theo reminded her.

"If they were protecting Jensen," Patricia said. "Maybe he was there too."

"I feel like Richard is keeping things from us," Theo scowled. "You want to go for a ride?"

"You want to question Jensen again?"

"Yes," Theo nodded. "But first I want to talk to the colonel."

"You know where he is?"

"I made some calls," Theo said. "Found out Black Wolf paid for a suite at The Royal Jewel Inn."

"Pricey," Patricia commented.

"Let's go ask him why he's here."

80

Richard tipped his second server as well as he had the first when he finally gathered his papers and relinquished the booth. The young woman gave him a cheerful thank you when he passed her on the way to the exit and suggested he return soon, even though he held the table hostage for a couple of hours.

Richard spent that time reviewing every spreadsheet and every notation in Sonia's files. In checking names and dates to find a connection that would suggest who was behind what could only be described as fraud, he discovered two more incidents of inaccurate reporting. But without further information, he could not identify the person behind it all.

He reached the exit just as a couple was coming in. He stepped to the side and held the door until they passed. They did not acknowledge him in any way, prompting him to want to comment. He decided instead to move on. People like that were self-centered, and yelling at them would only justify why they didn't speak to begin with.

The parking lot for the restaurant was small, though it did flow into the lot for the large building set farther back from the street. The empty shell had once been a popular department store that had long since vanished from the retail landscape. Businesses rarely wanted that type of square footage anymore, so most likely a few more years down the road, the owner would demolish the structure and replace it with smaller options.

Approaching his car, Richard felt a sense of unease. He stopped mid-stride and looked around to see if anyone lurked in the shadows, watching him. He scanned the other cars in the lot, the windows of nearby businesses and anywhere else that might serve as a vantage point. Richard identified several places that would make decent perches. He focused on each one but saw no movement. Deciding his paranoia was getting the better of him, he continued forward to the car. As he neared, he pressed the button on the key fob to unlock the door. Reaching for the handle, a reflection in the rear window caught his eye. A man rushed toward him. Richard pulled the pistol from his shoulder holster and spun.

The man was only a few feet away when Richard confronted him with the gun. He skidded to a stop, his hands raised to chest level, showing he was unarmed and uninterested in dying.

Richard did a quick check to be sure the man was alone, and no one was coming up behind him. When he was sure, he focused on the man before him. "Who sent you?"

"Listen." The man appeared to be talking to the weapon. "How about I slip away and promise you'll never see me again?"

"You didn't answer my question."

"You know I can't tell you that." He shrugged apologetically. "Besides, even if I did. You know he didn't use his real name."

"What did he look like?" Richard asked.

The man shook his head. "I never met with him. Just text messages."

Richard looked the man over. "You aren't armed. How did you think this was going to go?"

"Well." The man gave him a half grin. "Obviously, I wasn't expecting you to be packing."

"So, what was the plan, exactly?" Richard checked the area again.

"I was supposed to rough you up a bit," the man explained. "Tell you to stop looking into whatever it is you're looking into."

"Who told you to do this?" Richard asked again.

The man remained silent.

"We've already established he probably used a fake name," Richard reminded him. "Give me the fake name. What harm could it do?"

"And you won't tell him I told you?" The man looked around, his nerves getting to him.

A couple leaving the diner forced Richard to lower his weapon out of sight. He held it between his body and the man he was interrogating. "The name."

"Yeah," the man nodded. "He called himself Bart Barnes."

"Bart Barnes?"

"I told you." The man shrugged. "Sounds fake, doesn't it?"

Richard was hoping the name would be familiar to him, or at the very least be a clue to the identity of the man behind everything.

"You said all of your communication was done through email," Richard said. "How did he find you to begin with?"

"I lost my job a while back," the man answered. "I've been on those sites where you can get odd jobs."

"You answered his ad?"

"No." The man shook his head. "You can make a profile with your skills and availability. He found me that way."

"So, you were looking for work," Richard summarized. "And you get a text. And you decide you're willing to commit assault for a few bucks?"

"He offered me five hundred dollars," the man defended his decision. "Which I won't get now, since, well, you know."

"Am I supposed to feel bad for not letting you beat me up?"

"No," the man grimaced. "It's just…I have a family to feed. I needed the money."

He looked down at his feet in shame and kicked at a small pebble on the pavement. Richard sighed, put his weapon away, and pulled out his wallet. He took out two fifties and held them out. "Here. Go buy some groceries."

The man looked at the money and then up to Richard's face. "Are you serious?"

"Take it."

He took the bills from Richard's hand and folded them before shoving them into his pocket. "Thanks."

Richard's phone rang. He had to shift the files from one arm to the other in order to answer, distracting him for a moment. He put the phone to his ear just in time to watch his would-be attacker jogging away. "Bulldog?"

"Not Bulldog."

"Carolyn?" Richard started for his car again. "Did you learn something?"

The question was difficult for him to ask. Carolyn had set out to prove or disprove a possible affair between Stan and Sonia. An answer this soon suggested she found proof of one, since it would take much longer to prove that nothing happened. He wasn't sure he wanted to hear what she had to say.

"I learned that Valarie Webber is not someone to be messed with," Carolyn reported. On a whim, she circled Valarie's house looking for clues or unexplained footprints. "She tried to hire me to kill the person who took her husband. Assuming we find them, of course."

"You're kidding?" Richard met Mrs. Webber only a few times, but she did not strike him as the vengeful type. "What did you say?"

"I told her she couldn't afford me," Carolyn chuckled.

"You didn't."

"Of course not." On the back side of the house, Carolyn had to be careful passing sliding glass doors, French doors, and plate-glass windows. It wouldn't do to be seen. "I told her we didn't offer that kind of service. What did you think I would say?"

"Do you think she might try to hire someone else?" Richard unlocked the car door and fell into the driver's seat. He deposited Sonia's papers onto the passenger seat and shut the door.

"I doubt it," Carolyn said. "She doesn't run in those circles. I think I was there, so she asked."

Richard considered talking to Valerie to assure she didn't ruin her life further.

"I think Stan and Sonia were doing something together," Carolyn announced.

"Of course they were," Richard confirmed. "Boss and employee. They were working together."

"I know," Carolyn said. "But there was something more."

"You found proof of an affair?"

"Not yet," Carolyn admitted. "Which leads to why I'm calling."

"What?"

"Did Sonia have any close friends?" Carolyn asked. "Someone she talked to more than others?"

"That would be Helen Gray," Richard said without hesitation. "They did almost everything together."

"Do you know where she lives?"

"Across the street and one house down from us," Richard said. "You can't miss it. There's an enormous magnolia tree in her front yard."

"I remember seeing it." Carolyn had reached the front of the house once more. "I'll go talk to her."

Richard disconnected the call, and his phone rang again. He looked at the screen this time and saw Bulldog's name.

"What've you got?" Richard answered.

"Hello to you, too." Bulldog's deep voice filled Richard's ear.

"Hello, Bulldog," Richard relented. "What've you got?"

"You never change, Money," Bulldog said. After a brief pause, he continued. "So, that company is a mess."

"What kind of mess?"

"Seems the false reporting has been going on for a while," Bulldog explained. "They're bleeding money. Thing is, according to the financial reports I reviewed, it seems they are making the money the customer reports suggested. However, the actual accounts show losses."

"Someone's skimming," Richard concluded.

"It seems like it," Bulldog agreed. "They're making differences appear to be typos, two numbers out of order. I guess to suggest human error if they get caught. But whoever is entering the data is purposely switching the two digits on the customer accounts and transferring the difference."

"The data would be entered by the account manager," Richard muttered. "Sonia."

"But it isn't just Sonia's accounts," Bulldog announced. "It's across the board. Every account has been skimmed from. Someone is socking away millions."

"Every account?" Richard perked up. "Who would have access to every account? Halstead? Stanley Webber?"

"Or someone has gained access to their coworkers' accounts," Bulldog suggested. "I'll get the employee list and investigate their personal finances. We'll figure it out."

"What if it's a hacker?" Richard asked. "I mean you got in. Could be someone else outside the company."

"It's possible, but unlikely," Bulldog said. "Besides, if Sonia found out what was going on and it was a hacker, she wouldn't be able to expose them.

The hacker would just close shop and move on. There wouldn't be any reason to silence her or Stanley Webber. It must be someone she knew, someone she posed a genuine threat to. I'll find them."

"Thanks Bulldog," Richard said. "I appreciate your help on this."

"Don't get mushy on me, Money," Bulldog said. "I'll call when I have something."

"Thanks," Richard said. "Oh, and if you can, would you look into the name Bart Barnes. It'll probably be nothing. But someone using that name hired someone to work me over."

"You okay?"

"Nothing I couldn't handle," Richard assured him.

"Well, watch your back." Bulldog disconnected.

Richard pulled away from the diner, watching his rearview mirror for signs of being followed. A single car pulled out just after him, confirming his suspicions. He kept his eyes on the mirror as he gained speed. At the first intersection, the trailing car turned off the road, suggesting his suspicions were unfounded. Even with his possible stalker gone, his unease lingered.

81

Colonel Jackson Porter stood in the center of the suite he had rented for his stay. His bag was packed and ready at his feet. In contradiction of the stereotype, Dutch emerged from her room carrying one small bag with a backpack over her shoulder. She joined her boss where the two could wait for Clay, their driver.

After butchering her real name, Trijntje Graafland, Jackson anointed her with the nickname of the language her name originated from. Though she had never been to the Netherlands, the home of her ancestors, she had taken to the nickname with pride.

Clay finally stumbled out of his room, dragging two large cases. One was his personal gear, while the other was for the equipment Jackson required to be with them. With a slight shake of the head to express his disappointment in having to wait, Jackson led the way out of the room. In the hall, he handed his bag to Dutch.

"You two load the car," he ordered. "Then meet me in the dining room. I don't want to eat on the plane."

"Yes, sir." They responded in unison.

The two grunts walked to the elevator while their boss passed on by in favor of the stairs. He wasn't claustrophobic but hated elevators, and did not relish the idea of repeating the same crowded conditions he had suffered on their arrival when a family of five joined them on the ride up. Besides, his doctor had told him to get more exercise. Two flights of stairs should make him good for the rest of the week.

The hotel's restaurant was an award-winning establishment, far better than the heat and serve meals stocked on the plane. Jackson could still remember the rations he had in the military. During those years, he considered anything not in a can or pouch a luxury.

He stopped by the bar for a gin and tonic before choosing a table in the back corner where he could see anyone entering. In this setting, the greatest threat he was likely to encounter was a wealthy couple with grating voices and awful taste in clothing. But some habits were hard to break.

Jackson scanned the menu and placed his order, asking the server to fire his order right away but to be prepared to take orders from his two guests when they arrived. With a nod and a smile, she laid two menus on the opposite side of the table before walking away. He lifted his drink only to be interrupted by the ringing of his phone, drawing dissatisfied looks from neighboring tables.

He gave them a stern look before lowering the glass and digging out the phone. On the screen the words Hacker Nerd identified the caller as Brady. He answered.

"Brady?" Jackson did not hide his surprise. "That was fast."

"You get what you pay for," Brady quipped, reminding the colonel how expensive his services were.

"What did you learn?"

"I learned not to piss you off," Brady declared. "I mean those missions were dark. It's no wonder they were buried behind nearly hack proof firewalls."

"I don't pay for commentary." Jackson grumbled and drank. "What about the families?"

"Not much left of them," Brady reported. "Your team was pretty thorough. There were some survivors, but they don't have the power and resources they had before. The only one to come to the states in the past year was killed in a hate crime. I mean the police said it was a mugging gone bad, but it seemed obvious to me. How's that for sad?"

The grunts arrived and settled into the seats across from him. They began reading the menu while Jackson continued his call.

"The only person connected to any of those families that came to the states is dead?"

"That's right," Brady said. "I went back two years to be sure. I can go back farther if you like."

"No," Jackson said. "That's good. Thanks. Issue an invoice. I'll sign off on it."

"Always a pleasure, colonel." Brady hung up before Jackson could respond.

Jackson gulped down the rest of his drink and waved the empty glass at his server across the room. The young woman gave a slight nod and retreated to the bar. She reappeared a short time later with his cocktail and his dinner balanced on a serving tray. She placed everything in front of him and turned her attention to those who had joined him. Jackson started carving bite-sized chunks of his steak, using his fork to deliver the meat to his mouth. Only after the server had taken his minions' orders and left did he set his utensils down. He picked up his phone again and dialed.

He sat listening to the ringtone for what felt like an eternity before someone answered.

"Jackson?" Carolyn took steady deep breaths as she fast-walked from Valarie Webber's home to her car. "What do you want?"

He held his tongue to prevent saying something out of anger. He took a breath before speaking. "There are no family members looking to avenge any of our targets."

"How could you know that already?"

"My guy is good." Jackson took his fork and stabbed a pile of green beans. "Not to mention the team did their jobs well. Weren't a lot left to track down."

"Yeah, okay." Carolyn dug out her keys and clicked on the remote to unlock the door. "But none of them traveled to the states?"

"Only one." Jackson shoved the beans into his mouth and chewed.

"And they aren't a threat?"

"No."

"How can you be sure?" Carolyn settled into her car and started the engine. She buckled in and backed out of the driveway. "Do you know where they are?"

"Dead." He held his fork like a weapon. "Now if you don't mind, I need to finish eating. I have a flight to catch."

"You own the plane, Jackson," Carolyn challenged.

"I didn't say I was in danger of missing it," Jackson said. "Now, tell your boyfriend that revenge is not the motive."

"He's not my boyfriend," Carolyn snapped.

"Whatever," Jackson said. "I've got to go."

He disconnected the call, set down his phone and returned to his meal.

82

The evening was giving way to darkness when Carolyn parked in Helen Gray's driveway. The magnolia tree covered most of the front of the house, as promised. She wondered what it looked like in full bloom.

Giving a quick glance toward Richard's house before walking up to the front door, Carolyn leaned in to ring the bell. The woman who answered reminded Carolyn of a friend of her mother from twenty years ago. Something in the way she carried herself said she was superior to those around her, though she would make no one feel inferior on purpose. Her eyes gave Carolyn the once-over, sizing her up and evaluating. Her eyes came to rest, locked on her unexpected guest's.

"Helen Gray?"

Her brow knotted slightly. "And you are?"

"My name is Anita Brown." Carolyn gave her the same alias she gave Stan's assistant. "I'm investigating the disappearance of Sonia Jensen. Richard tells me you and she were close."

"You've spoken to Richard?"

"I have."

"How is he doing?" The features on Helen's face softened.

"Improving," Carolyn said. "Devastated about his wife."

"We all are." Helen's eyes watered. "She's a lovely person, a wonderful friend. After so long, it's difficult to be positive. But I hope she's found safe and sound."

"That's still the goal." Carolyn gave her a sympathetic smile. "If you don't mind, I would like to ask you some questions."

"Yes, of course." Helen opened the door wider. "Come in. I hope you don't mind sitting in the kitchen. I'm doing a little baking. Would you like some wine?"

"That would be nice." Carolyn followed the woman to the back of the house, thinking how trusting some people could be. A dozen years ago, she had entered a house in Eastern Europe under a similar premise; a friend of a friend. Three people died in that house, two human traffickers and one of their unsuspecting mothers. Carolyn always felt bad about an innocent being killed. A bullet intended for Carolyn struck the woman when she had the misfortune of stepping into the line of fire. So, if she were honest, she felt more grateful than bad.

"White or red?" Helen asked as they reached their destination.

"Pardon?" Carolyn snapped back to the present.

"Wine," the woman clarified. "White or red?"

The friend of Carolyn's mother returned to her thoughts. She would come to the house almost every evening with a bottle of wine in tow. The two women would sit on the back porch drinking and laughing for hours. As far as Carolyn remembered, they did nothing else together. After her father died in action, the drinking continued, but the laughing stopped. Not long after, the friend's visits stopped as well. Eventually, Carolyn and her mother moved away. The last time she saw her mother, she still drank a bottle a day.

"Red," Carolyn answered. "Thank you."

Helen grinned as she poured two glasses, sliding one across the island. She checked the timer and nodded. "We have about ten minutes before this batch is ready."

The aroma of fresh-baked cookies filled the air, reminding Carolyn she had not eaten yet. The two of them moved to the kitchen table where Helen placed a small plate of snickerdoodles between them. Wine and cookies. This woman was winning Carolyn over.

"How close were you and Sonia?" Carolyn asked.

"The day she and Richard moved in, I walked over to introduce myself." Helen lifted the plate. "With cookies, of course. I took an instant liking to her. She was so sweet and smart. We talked for hours that first day, becoming fast friends. She had just moved here and didn't know anyone. I had only been here about a year and never really met anyone outside work. So, we bonded."

"Did she talk to you about her personal life?" Carolyn asked.

"You mean Richard?" Helen smiled. "She wouldn't not talk about him. She adored the man. I mean, you've met him. You understand."

Carolyn did not respond. "What about work? Did she talk about that?"

"At times." Helen drank some wine. "Usually, when she was upset. I would prod her into telling me what the problem was. And most of the time it was something about her job."

"Was she unhappy at work?"

"Isn't everyone at some point?" Helen shrugged. "I mean, overall, she loved her work. But there's always something that upsets you."

"Upset enough to think about moving on?"

"Oh, no," Helen shook her head. "Not that she told me at least."

"Did she ever tell you what she was upset about?" Carolyn prodded. "At work. Did she ever give details about what was going on? Especially in the weeks leading up to her disappearance?"

"Maybe," Helen admitted. "You have to understand. I consider myself to be a smart woman. But Sonia, she was on a whole other level. She would talk about things, and I didn't understand half of it. That's why we seldom talked about work. Family, Fashion and Food. Those were our topics."

"She didn't mention being nervous or afraid of something?" Carolyn asked.

"No," she responded. "Never. Do you think someone at work took her?"

"We're looking into every possibility," Carolyn said. "But I need to ask you something a bit more sensitive."

The timer sounded and Helen jumped to her feet. She rounded the island, opened the oven and pulled out a sheet of cookies. Sliding them onto a cooling rack, she sniffed and smiled. "Perfect."

Carolyn held up the half of a cookie in her hand. "They really are."

"Thank you," Helen smiled again. "What were you going to ask?"

When the woman returned to her seat. Carolyn's expression became somber. "Did Sonia ever talk to you about an affair?"

"You're kidding," Helen laughed. "Richard would never."

Carolyn grinned. "What about Sonia?"

Helen choked on the wine she had just sipped. "Are you serious? Sonia? There's no way."

"You're sure?"

"Absolutely."

"Okay," Carolyn said. "I had to ask."

"Just wouldn't happen," Helen repeated.

"Okay." Carolyn downed the rest of her wine. "Thank you for your time."

"Hope I helped."

As she stood, Carolyn's phone started ringing. She looked at the screen. "I've got to go."

83

Detectives Morris and Stevens parked near the entrance of The Royal Jewel Inn. The space was clearly marked 'loading zone' but they paid it no mind. A young man dressed in the hotel uniform asked if he could take their bags, and Theo waved his shield in front of the porter's face.

"Is he serious?" Patricia muttered.

"What's your problem?" Theo regretted asking as soon as the words left his mouth.

"He thought you and I were getting a room?" She hooked her thumb toward the porter. "Like I couldn't do better than . . . uh, sorry. I don't mean that you're . . ."

"Just stop talking." Theo pushed his way through the front door and steered himself toward the check-in counter.

The woman behind the desk displayed a huge smile that resembled a used car dealer who sold Theo a crap car a couple of decades ago. In a twist of fate, two years later, Theo was the detective called in to investigate the salesman's murder. Turned out not all unhappy customers reacted the same to being cheated.

"Good evening," the woman greeted. "Are you and your wife checking in?"

Theo suppressed a smile, though he knew without looking that Patricia was not suppressing her thoughts at all. He produced his shield again. "We need to speak with one of your guests."

"Oh, uh," the woman stammered. She turned to the computer. "Room number?"

"If we had the room number," Theo sighed. "We would already be there."

"Right," she grimaced. "Name then?"

"Brian Andrews." Theo gave the alias the man had given him.

The woman typed, paused, and typed some more. "Uh, no. No Brian Andrews."

"Try Jackson Porter." Patricia kept her voice flat. Only Theo picked up the angry undertone from the wife comment.

"No," Theo interrupted. "Black Wolf Protection Agency."

"Oh, them," the woman perked up.

"You know them?"

"Oh, yes."

"Three of them," Theo said. "Correct?"

"Yes, sir."

"Room number?" Theo asked.

The woman turned to her computer and typed. Her brow furrowed, and her lips pursed. She typed some more and shook her head.

"Listen." Theo lowered his voice. "These people are suspects in two kidnappings. We need to stop them. Do you understand?"

"Yes, um," the woman started typing again. She stopped and looked Theo in the eye.

"Are you giving me the room number or not?"

"Yes," she said. "Or, um, no."

"Which is it?" Patricia asked. "Yes or no?"

"They had a suite," the woman grinned, though her eyes expressed a wariness.

"Had?" Theo repeated the single word. "Past tense? As in they're no longer here?"

"That's right," the woman said. "You just missed them. It says they checked out about fifteen minutes ago."

Theo closed his eyes and considered how much time they had spent at the desk talking to her, calculating in his mind how much farther away Jackson Porter had gotten in that time.

"Any idea where they may have gone?" Patricia asked.

"No idea, ma'am," the woman said. "I'm sorry."

"I know where they're going." Theo spun on his heels and walked toward the exit.

Patricia turned to follow, turning back to the woman behind the counter. "You really thought he was my husband?"

The woman did not respond, prompting Patricia to huff before jogging off in pursuit of her partner.

84

When Jackson's plate and glass were empty, he left the table to settle the bill while his associates finished their meals. That done, he moved on to the front desk, where an older man checked him out. It took longer than Jackson thought was necessary for the man to process him out and print the invoice, and longer still to pay the bill. By the time he finished, his grunts had joined him in the lobby.

The three of them walked through the hotel to a side exit near where they had parked their SUV. Jackson climbed into the back and waited for the others to get situated. He sat back, thinking about the events that had brought him to the town he was now preparing to leave. He hadn't seen Richard in years and had given little thought to the man. But knowing that someone was pulling strings to orchestrate a reunion, left him concerned for his former employee's wellbeing. He hated leaving, but if the plan was to have them together, it would be best to put distance between them. At least, that's what Jackson told himself.

They pulled out of their space and maneuvered through the parking lot to the exit. As they passed by the front of the hotel, Jackson saw the two detectives that had been at Richard's house getting out go their car. They were undoubtedly looking for him, and for a brief second he considered stopping to see what they wanted. Thinking better of it, he told Clay to hurry along.

On the highway, Jackson stared out the window at the trees passing by, watching the sun set behind them. He was not fond of this place and was glad to be leaving. He no longer had a client in the town and made a mental note not to accept any more jobs in the area. His plan was to move on and forget ever having been there, which is what he was doing.

With the loss of sunlight came the inevitable darkening of the sky. Dusk, when the world turned gray, was one of Jackson's favorite times. He had spent many an evening sitting on his deck at home, watching the sun go down. With his job, he had done the same thing in more countries than he could remember.

"Louie says the plane is fueled and ready, sir." Dutch glanced back at her boss as she spoke, putting away the phone he hadn't even realized she was on.

"Good." Jackson replied. His eyes shifted to her. "How long before we arrive?"

"Shouldn't be long," Dutch reported. "Give me a second and I can tell you exactly."

"That's okay," Jackson said. "Not important."

He was just about to turn back toward the trees when the SUV shimmied and dipped. Clay swore under his breath and clutched the steering wheel, directing the vehicle to the side of the road.

"What was that?" Jackson asked.

"It appears we've blown a tire, sir." Clay stopped and shifted to park. He grabbed his phone. "Front passenger side. I'll call the rental company to send another car."

"Just change the tire," Jackson said.

"Change it, sir?"

"Yes," Jackson frowned. "Unless you didn't get the spare tire replaced after they knifed it earlier."

"We didn't change it then," Clay explained. "We just called for another car."

"Oh, for God's sake," Jackson looked from one grunt to the other. "Have neither of you changed a tire before?"

Their silence confirmed his suspicions.

"Okay, Clay, get in the back and look for the jack," Jackson ordered. "Dutch and I will assess the situation."

Clay jumped out and dashed back to the storage space. A compartment next to the wheel well indicated the jack could be found inside. He moved the luggage to make room.

Clay opened the plastic door and retrieved tool, rounding the vehicle just as Jackson knelt by the tire. Dutch leaned against the front fender watching him.

"Here you go, sir." Clay stood over his boss holding out the jack.

Jackson froze. His hand moved to the sidewall of the tire, and his finger felt the hole there. He looked up at Dutch, yelling, "Driver's side! Now!"

Dutch spun and ran, circling the vehicle as fast as she could. Clay hesitated. The shot rang out and sent the young man sprawling forward into the side of the SUV. His right leg struck Jackson, causing him to topple onto his boss. The weight of the younger man pushed Jackson to the ground. Another shot rang out, and the impact pressed Clay harder into the older man.

Jackson heard the panicked heavy breathing of his driver slow and stop. Nothing could help him now. Jackson lay on the pavement and looked under the vehicle at Dutch's feet. She was on one knee directly across from him.

"Dutch!" Jackson yelled. "Lay down!"

Dutch lowered herself to the ground and looked under the vehicle at her boss. He gave her a reassuring smile. He pulled his phone out of his pocket as a third shot rang out. This one passed clean through Jackson's calf. He closed his eyes and clenched his teeth. He had been shot before, but many years ago, when he was a younger man.

Opening his eyes, he slid the phone across the pavement under the car to Dutch. It came to a stop just out of her reach. She slid under the vehicle and grabbed it before backing out again.

"Code three, three, seven, four," he said. "Find a number for Bulldog. Say nine, one, one and give him our location."

"Three, three, seven, four." She repeated the numbers as she entered them. Opening the phone app, she scrolled to Bulldog's name and hit call. It rang only once.

"Hey, old man," Bulldog's deep voice filled Dutch's ear.

"Nine, one, one," she said.

"Who is this?" Bulldog asked.

A shot rang out, and Dutch watched as Jackson's body jerked. He winced but kept his eyes locked on hers. Another shot slammed into his leg. His eyes closed and then opened again. The next shot struck his shoulder.

"Oh, my God," Dutch gasped.

"Where are you!?" Bulldog demanded.

85

Richard sat on the hood of the Mercedes, waiting for Carolyn to arrive. He chose the parking lot of an abandoned factory situated halfway between the two of them for a meeting place. The location also offered a decent amount of privacy. When she turned in, she came to a stop next to him and jumped out to join him.

"How did you get here so fast?" She slid onto the hood beside him.

"Didn't hit a single red," he said. "How did it go? Did you learn anything?"

"Well." She let the word linger for a minute before continuing. "If Sonia was having an affair with Stanley Webber, no one knew about it. They all pretty much agreed the idea was insane."

"Told you." Richard grinned, but he allowed himself a silent sigh of relief.

"Jackson called me," Carolyn announced.

"Okay?"

"Not sure how he found out so fast," she said. "But he says there was only one person attached to our targets that traveled to the states in the past couple of years."

"What do we know about them?"

"He was killed in a mugging gone wrong," Carolyn said. "So, not our guy."

"Are we sure he was killed?" Richard asked. "Maybe he faked his death to have time to …"

"You were the one that didn't think our old targets were what this was about," Carolyn accused.

"I don't know," Richard admitted. "It's a stretch. But something needs to pan out, so I know where to look for Sonia."

"I hear you." She patted his leg. "You miss her, don't you?"

"Yes." He looked down at a crack in the pavement. It looked like his heart felt without Sonia. "I do."

"We're going to find her," she assured him.

The lack of confidence in her voice resonated in Richard's ears.

"What about you?" she asked. "Did you find anything useful?"

"Someone at Halstead Enterprises has been skimming profits," Richard said. "Millions. It's possible Stan and Sonia found out. Someone stealing that much money would have a lot to lose if they went to the authorities."

"Stan's secretary says they argued that morning," Carolyn pointed out. "Maybe she found out it was him."

"And he couldn't let her turn him in." Richard closed his eyes and let out a long sigh.

"Any way to find out, for sure, who was skimming?"

"Bulldog's looking into it for me," Richard said. "No guarantee he'll get a name, but if anyone can find out who it is, it's him."

"What do you want to do while Bulldog does his thing?" Carolyn asked.

"I don't know," Richard said. "Listen. Did you notice anyone following you today?"

"No." She crossed her arms. "Were you being followed?"

"Some wanna be thug," Richard acknowledged. "Brought his fists to a gunfight."

"You didn't?" Carolyn demanded.

"What? No," Richard defended. "Almost. He tried to rush me from behind."

"How did that go for him?"

"Let's just say, he's unlikely to try that again," Richard said. "He said someone hired him to rough me up. And to tell me to stop looking into things."

"So, we're pushing someone's buttons." Carolyn perked up. "That's good."

"Maybe." Richard was less optimistic. "It would help to know which button we pushed."

The problem with approaching an investigation from three different sides was not having the means to track the ripples from the waves created. They once planned a mission to do something similar. In that case, they seemed to get multiple results. They couldn't determine the source of the data that came back. The information seemed to come from everywhere, which is what happened. All the targets interconnected. The resulting plan called for three simultaneous strikes.

Richard's phone rang. "Speaking of Bulldog. This is him."

"He really is good."

Richard held the phone out and answered. "Hey, Bulldog, you're on speaker with me and Carolyn."

"You have a name for us?" she asked.

Bulldog's deep voice filled the air. "Jackson's under attack."

86

Theo buckled in and sat with the engine running by the time Patricia climbed into the car. He gave her just enough time to get strapped in before he backed out of the space and sped toward the nearest exit.

"Where do you think he's going?" Patricia grabbed the armrest with a white-knuckle grip.

"I think he's trying to get out of town without talking to us." Theo steered through traffic as if he were late for his own wedding. "I'm guessing airport."

"Makes sense."

Though considered an airport hotel, the Royal Jewel Inn was far enough away that its clientele did not have to deal with planes flying overhead all night long. If the colonel had left minutes before the detectives' arrival, he would still be on the highway.

Theo merged into traffic at high speed, swerving in and out of lanes, passing cars on both sides in his effort to catch their subject before he could fly out of town. Each lane change evoked an under the breath curse from his partner. He would have found it humorous were he not so focused on the road ahead.

Theo approached a curve that would put them on a straight stretch leading to the airport. A car crossed in front of them, forcing him to slow before spinning the wheel. The reduced speed turned out to be fortunate. Once on the straightaway, Theo had to slam on the brakes, sliding to a stop just shy of hitting the rear bumper of the car in front of them. Traffic was at a standstill.

Theo approached a curve that would put them on a straight stretch leading to the airport. A car crossed in front of them, forcing him to slow before spinning the wheel. The reduced speed turned out to be fortunate. Once on the straightaway, Theo had to slam on the brakes, sliding to a stop just shy of hitting the rear bumper of the car in front of them. Traffic was at a standstill.

"What in the world?" Theo muttered.

"Must be an accident," Patricia offered.

Even as she said the words, sirens blared as emergency vehicles passed by on the shoulder. Police led the way, followed by a firetruck, an EMT, and an ambulance. Two troopers brought up the rear.

Detective Morris pulled the wheel tight and pulled onto the side of the road behind them. Once there, he flipped on their emergency lights and accelerated. Passing stranded drivers, he wondered how many of them were about to miss their flights.

About a mile down the road, they came upon the issue. The flashing blue and red lights of emergency vehicles that had come from the opposite direction mixed with the new arrivals in the dark sky. Though the sun was almost gone, the area was lit up like the Vegas Strip. Theo rolled to a stop a couple of car lengths away from the trooper they had followed.

The detectives saw the black SUV dipping forward on the front right side. A sheet lay over what they assumed to be a body on the passenger side.

"Isn't that …"

"Looks like it," Theo confirmed. "Let's find out what happened."

They stepped out onto the street and approached the scene. A highway patrolman intercepted them but said nothing after they flashed their shields at him. Theo noted the woman sitting in the backseat of an open trooper's car before turning toward the passenger side of the SUV where the victim lay. He and Patricia held their shields at the ready.

"Who's in charge here?" Theo asked.

Three faces turned in unison to the oncoming detectives. Two of them abruptly turned. The trooper who did not, moved to block them. "That would be me. What can I do for you …?"

"Detective Theo Morris." He put his shield in his jacket pocket. "My partner, Detective Patricia Stevens."

"What brings you to my crime scene, detectives?"

"We're looking for a person of interest." Theo pointed at the blood-stained sheet on the ground. "We want to make sure this isn't him."

The trooper lowered his eyes to the ground. "Take a look. If you can identify either one it would help."

"Wait?" Patricia said. "There's two?"

"What happened?" Theo walked to the edge of the sheet and squatted.

"They were getting ready to change the tire when these two were shot," the trooper reported. "The third one managed to get out of the line of fire."

Theo knew the woman he had seen in the back of the trooper's car would be the third. He reached down and lifted the corner of the sheet to expose the two men beneath. Closer to the SUV, Colonel Porter was lying flat against the ground, his head turned as if looking under the vehicle's carriage. He had multiple gunshot wounds, each accompanied by a pool of blood. The man had bled out.

Between him and the detective was a younger man on his side. Though shot more than a dozen times, the blood pooling was minimal. His heart had stopped beating with an early hit. The shooter had continued to shoot to get to Jackson. The scene was horrific.

"And the shooter?" Theo looked up.

"No one ever saw the shooter," the trooper answered. "Our guess is he used a sniper rifle. Is one of them your person of interest?"

Theo lowered the sheet and shifted his gaze to the tire. He pulled out a small flashlight and shone it on the tire. "The older one. Has anyone examined this tire? It looks like a bullet hole."

"That's what we thought." The trooper stepped up next to the detective. "Looks like your guy was targeted. Who was he?"

"Colonel Jackson Porter."

"A colonel?"

"Ex military," Theo added. "He owned a protection company. We were hoping to ask him who he was protecting. Maybe the other guy."

The detective put his hands on his legs and listened to the cracking of his knees as he rose to his full height.

"You said there was a third?" Patricia said. "Is that the woman?"

"It is," the trooper nodded. "Hasn't said much. Muttered about trying to change the tire. But that's about it. You're welcome to give it a try."

A quick thank you and the detectives circled the SUV to the car where the woman sat in the back seat. A trooper stood next to the open door, rigid and watchful. The woman's feet were planted on the lower frame of the opening, her elbows anchored on her knees, her face buried in her hands. She did not look up at the oncoming detectives. Though she felt their approach, she was not sure they were coming to her until she saw their shoes in front of her.

"Miss?" Patricia said. "Can we get your name?"

Dutch looked up to the woman and then to the man. They were the detectives she had seen at Richard Jensen's house. "Trijntje Graafland."

"Did you say Graafland?"

In her native tongue, Dutch started a narrative of what happened to Jackson and Clay. She left out no detail, even though she knew the two detectives did not understand a word she said. Her audience gave one another confused glances as she spoke. When she finished, she lowered her face back to her hands.

"What language was that?" Patricia asked.

"I don't know," Theo answered. He visually examined the woman. She wore a suit. Her nails were painted but cut short. "Are you the woman Colonel Porter was protecting?"

Dutch's head snapped up at the sound of Jackson's name. In clear English, she said, "Are you the ones who shot him?"

87

Richard chose to leave the Mercedes and rode shotgun in Carolyn's rental as she followed the directions Bulldog gave them. Racing up the on-ramp to the highway, she maneuvered traffic with ease. Reaching the last exit before the airport, she cut across two lanes to take it. Horns blared at the offensive move. Carolyn had no time to concern herself with the other drivers, reaching the top of the off-ramp at a speed that forced her to slam on the brakes. The car slid down the ramp, coming to a stop just short of colliding with the truck waiting at the light.

Without hesitation, Carolyn stomped on the accelerator and steered around the truck into cross traffic. She adjusted speed and direction to find a gap to place her in the flow headed toward the airport. Carolyn weaved in and out of lanes, using the median and roadside when needed to continue advancing. Sitting in the passenger seat, Richard wondered why they hadn't used her to drive on more missions all those years ago.

About two miles from the airport, traffic stopped altogether. Carolyn guided the car to the median, where she sped past the vehicles waiting in the driving lanes. One driver lunged toward the median, causing Carolyn to spin the wheel to the left and back to the right again, sliding around the man, the driver's side tires throwing up a cloud of dirt and vegetation. Richard could see the driver's face in the headlights of the cars behind him. A mix of terror and anger consumed expression.

Carolyn cruised another half mile, slowing when they neared the emergency lights in the darkness. She coasted to a stop a hundred yards from the scene.

"Can you reach my bag?" Carolyn asked. "On the back seat."

Richard unbuckled and twisted between the seats to drag the bag back with him. With the bag between them, he unzipped the top. "What are you looking for?"

"There should be a pair of eyes in the side pocket," she said.

Richard adjusted the bag and opened the indicated pocket, finding a pair of binoculars inside. He pulled them out and slid the bag to the floorboard. He opened his door and stepped out as Carolyn did on the other side.

A car rolled to a stop behind them and flashed its brights. Richard turned to the driver, spread his arms, and shrugged. He spun again and moved to the front of the car, where Carolyn waited. Without missing a step, Richard stepped from the ground to the bumper, to the hood. Facing the emergency lights, he raised the binoculars to his eyes. He scanned the area where the emergency vehicles were, climbed down from the car, and handed the binoculars to Carolyn.

"You're lucky this is a rental." Carolyn put the strap over her shoulder. "Just give me the highlights."

"It's Jackson's SUV." Richard raised his hands defensively. "Before you ask how I could possibly know, I saw the girl. The one that was following us."

"What's she doing?"

"Sitting in a squad car, looking bored or sad."

"What about Jackson?" Carolyn looked through the binoculars, but the cars on the highway blocked her view. "They're starting to let traffic go. Should we snatch her? She could tell us what happened."

"You just want to grab her from police custody?" Richard frowned.

Carolyn raised an eyebrow and tilted her head. "Uh, yes."

Richard stared at her for a moment before moving back to the passenger side of the car. "Fine. You drive. When we get close, I'll jump out, get her and we'll catch up to you. And if I see Jackson, I'll get him too."

Carolyn returned to the driver's seat, smiling. "That's the spirit."

"Just drive," Richard said.

Carolyn moved with the rest of the traffic as it advanced on the scene at a snail's pace. A trooper stood between them and what appeared to be an accident, twirling his arm to direct cars to the median, where they could skirt around and carry on with their lives. About twenty-five yards away, Richard opened his door and stepped out. Carolyn continued in the slow-moving line while he jogged ahead in a crouch, to avoid being spotted.

Knowing where he was going, Richard made his way through slow-moving cars, attempting to merge into the progressing lane. He received some confused looks from drivers but, surprisingly, no gestures or honks. Reaching the edge of the accident zone, where a trooper concentrated on keeping traffic flowing, Richard paused. The rest of the emergency personnel were examining the SUV or talking amongst themselves.

Richard stood and walked as if he were supposed to be there, straight toward the car where Jackson's employee sat. He was trying to come up with a response to the question the trooper standing next to her was bound to ask. Just before he reached the car, two suits stepped in front of him, walking in the same direction. Richard lowered his head, following close behind. When the man spoke, Richard knew the voice belonged to Detective Morris. He raised his head and realized the other suit was Detective Stevens.

While they threw questions at Jackson's employee, Richard calculated his way out of the area. Before he could formulate a plan, a string of sentences in a foreign language stopped him. His eyes locked on the woman as Theo asked if Jackson was protecting her.

"Are you the ones who shot him?" She was staring straight at him.

The detectives turned.

"Mister Jensen?" Theo looked around the area. "Where did you come from? For that matter, why are you here?"

"I, uh," Richard glanced at the woman. "I got a call from …" His mind raced trying to remember the alias Jackson had given the detective.

"Can you not remember his name?" Theo asked. "Or just the one he gave us?"

Richard pursed his lips and inhaled deeply through his nose, holding it for a minute before exhaling. "Where is he?"

Theo noticed a change in the man. The detective stood to his full height, far less intimidating than the trooper standing next to him. "You still haven't told me why you're here."

"Checking on a friend." Richard decided to go the honest route. He moved his eyes to the woman. "I received a call that he might be in trouble."

Dutch grimaced and nodded. Her sad eyes lowered to the ground.

"So, I'll ask again," Richard said. "Where is he?"

"Behind the SUV." Theo gestured with his head. "Where's your cane?"

"In the car." So much for the honest route. "Is he okay?"

Theo stared Richard in the eyes wondering what the man's reaction would be. "He's dead."

"Dead?" Richard's head snapped to the SUV. "What happened?"

"Good question." Theo's gaze lowered to where Dutch sat. "Our only witness hasn't said anything."

Richard kept his eyes on the SUV. He noted the pitch of the vehicle, the angle it was parked in. The tree line in the distance was just visible in the darkness. "You're going to find a tracker on the car. There will be a bullet hole in the tire." He turned back to the detective. "I assume he was shot."

Theo faced the man and narrowed his eyes. The two of them were staring at one another when Patricia appeared.

"What's going on here?" Detective Stevens stepped up to the two men. "Richard Jensen?"

"It seems our friend knows more about what happened here than we do." Theo gritted his teeth.

"Were you here?" Patricia gestured to the SUV. "Did you do this?"

Richard's expression softened. "Of course not. Jackson was a friend."

"Wouldn't be the first time someone was killed by a friend," Theo said. "So, Jackson was his real name then?"

"Yes."

"What about the other one?" Patricia asked. "What's his name?"

"Other one?" Richard furrowed his brow. "Wait. A younger guy?"

"That's the one."

"I didn't know his name." Richard looked down at Dutch. She was looking up at him.

"Clay." Her voice was barely audible. "His name was Clay."

"Clay what?" Patricia asked.

"I don't know." Dutch's eyes watered. "I only knew him as Clay."

Theo shifted his attention from Richard to the woman. "Now that you're talking, you want to tell us what happened here? Starting with your name."

"My name is Trijntje Graafland." She glanced toward the SUV. "Jackson just called me Dutch."

"Okay, Dutch," Theo said. "Talk me though it."

"It was like he said." Dutch pointed to Richard. "Our tire was shot out, though we didn't know it at the time. We thought it was just a blowout. So, we got out to change it."

"All of you?" Theo asked.

A nervous chuckle escaped her. "When Jackson found out Clay and I had never changed a tire before, he took it upon himself to teach us."

"The three of you got out and gathered near the tire," Theo prompted.

"Jackson was giving us pointers," Dutch said. "That's when he found the hole."

"The bullet hole?" Theo clarified.

"He just told me to run." She closed her eyes, remembering. "When he said that, I knew."

"What did you do?" Theo asked.

"I ran." A single tear rolled down her cheek. "I thought they would be right behind me."

"You hid behind the SUV?"

"That's right," she nodded. "When I realized they weren't behind me, I got low and looked under the vehicle. That's when I saw Clay. A single shot to the head."

"You were lucky," Patricia said.

"The strange thing was that with Clay, it was like they were an expert marksman," Dutch said. "But with Jackson, it was like they couldn't hit their target."

"What does that mean?" Richard intervened.

"They couldn't seem to hit what they were aiming at," she said. "They would shoot but could only hit his arms and legs. They just couldn't get a kill shot."

Richard looked at the detectives. Theo responded. "She's right. They hit him several times. But there was no kill shot. We're pretty sure he bled out."

"In other words," Richard grumbled. "They didn't just kill him. They tortured him."

88

Deciding it neither the time nor the place for proper interrogations, Detectives Morris and Stevens allowed Richard and Dutch to leave the scene with the understanding they remain available for questioning.

The two of them walked the short distance to where Carolyn waited. She expected Dutch to climb into the back. Jackson not following caught her by surprise. Richard kept his explanation of what happened brief, and Carolyn only took a moment to let the news absorb before she threw the car into gear, cut through the line of cars circumventing the scene, and drove through the median to the opposite lanes of traffic taking them back to town.

They stopped by the hotel to find it fully booked for the evening, leaving Dutch with nowhere to go. After discussing options, Richard agreed to let her use the spare room in his house. The three of them ended up sitting in a semicircle in his sitting room. Richard poured drinks for everyone, and they made toasts to their fallen friend and to Chad.

"I can't believe he's gone." Carolyn watched the ice spin in her drink.

"I want to know why." Richard sat back and set his drink on the arm of the short sofa. "If we're right and someone set us up…"

"Set you up?" Dutch perked up for the first time. "What do you mean, set you up?"

"We think someone drew Jackson and me to this town," Carolyn explained. "To get the three of us in one place."

"And if that's true," Richard continued. "And he's been toying with us. Why the sudden change? Why kill Jackson?"

"Maybe because we were leaving?" Dutch offered.

Richard thought back to the days when working in the field. A common tactic when you knew where the target was and where they were going was to set up an ambush somewhere en route. For the mission to be successful, however, certain details had to be known.

"How would they have known you were leaving?" Carolyn asked. "And when?"

Dutch's head bobbed in acknowledgement.

"That wasn't rhetorical." Carolyn leaned forward and pointed a finger at the younger woman. "Who knew you were leaving?"

"Carolyn." Richard's voice was calming. "Let's be civil."

"I'll be civil after she answers the question."

Dutch focused on Carolyn's finger. "Well, we checked out. So, the hotel staff knew. We called the pilot to ready the plane and file a flight plan. So, the airport staff knew. If our phones were being monitored, I suppose whoever was keeping tabs on us knew as well."

Carolyn relaxed and sat back, letting her accusing hand lower to her lap.

"Did you really think she had something to do with this?" Richard asked.

"She was the only survivor," Carolyn said. "We would be remiss to not consider the possibility."

"What reason would she have?" Richard defended.

"I don't know, Richard," Carolyn snipped. "And I won't know until we question her."

"I didn't," Dutch said.

"What?" Carolyn snapped at her.

"I had nothing to do with this," Dutch insisted. "Jackson was a good boss. And Clay was a friend. I want to find who did this just as much as you do."

"I'm sorry," Carolyn said. "But I don't know you from Adam. I can't just take your word for it."

Watching the two women facing off reminded Richard of his teen years. Nancy was often at odds with their mother, usually over her choice of clothing or where she had been. It got so bad for a few months that Nancy took to countering anything their parents said, even when they were right. What Richard remembered most was that while they were fighting, no one was paying attention to his transgressions. He got away with a lot that summer. The battle ensued for about three months with an almost daily dose of raised voices, slammed doors, and hurt feelings. Then, one morning, Richard woke to find his mother and sister sitting in the kitchen talking and laughing like nothing had ever happened. He always wondered what had changed, but never had the guts to ask, fearing he might reignite sparks between them.

"Can we all agree that Stanley Webber can be taken off our suspect list?" Richard interjected.

"Who is Stanley Webber?" Dutch asked.

"You don't know who Stan is?" Richard countered.

"No," she answered. "Should I?"

"Probably not," Carolyn answered. To Richard she added, "You're right. If this were about Stan, Jackson and I would have never been called. This is about the three of us. Which means whatever financial issues Sonia may have turned up at Halstead is likely to be a coincidence."

"You had to use the 'c' word, didn't you?" Richard moaned.

"You don't believe in coincidences?" Dutch asked.

"Jackson never told you about coincidences?" Carolyn asked.

"No." Dutch's eyes moved from one to the other. "What about them?"

"He said they didn't exist," Richard explained. "And when you thought there was one, just remember that the first four letters spell coin. And therefore …"

"You should follow the money," Carolyn finished. "Which leads back to Halstead."

"But no one at Halstead would know who Jackson was," Richard said. "Let alone want him dead."

"Charles Halstead and Jackson are about the same age," Carolyn pointed out. "Maybe they served together."

"First of all," Richard countered. "If Charles served in the military, it would have been a short stint, decades ago. Why wait until now for revenge? And second, how would that tie in to you being here? And don't say coincidence."

The three of them fell into silence, each waiting for the others to come up with the winning theory that would move them forward. Richard was becoming agitated. He didn't know who was skimming money at Halstead Enterprises. He didn't know who had killed Jackson. And he was no closer to finding Sonia than he was the day he woke up in the hospital.

When he was young, whenever he became frustrated, his father told him to attack the problem until he beat it. His mother advised him to take the time to think it through, and a solution would come. Nancy would do what sisters do, assaulting him with relentless teasing until he was too angry to think straight. Ironically, the cooling-off period most benefited Richard. He could clear his head and solve his problem. He had evolved from that time in his life but longed for something to push him in the right direction.

Richard's phone rang, bringing him out of the semi-trance he had slipped into. He looked at the device and saw Bulldog's name. He answered without hesitation. "Hey, Bulldog. How's it going?"

"Still can't get over what happened to Jackson." The man's deep voice carried the weight of his sadness. "You safe?"

"I'm safe," Richard assured the man. "I'm here with Carolyn and Dutch."

"Aces!" Bulldog shouted into the phone, causing Richard to pull it away from his ear. In doing so, Carolyn heard her nickname.

"Hey, Bulldog," she said toward the phone. "Love ya, man."

"You guys going to get the man who did this?"

"That's the plan." Richard returned the phone to his ear. "Just trying to figure out where to start."

"You said Dutch was with you?"

"She is," Richard confirmed. "They won't let her leave town, so she's going to stay in our spare room."

"That's good," Bulldog said. "She's good people."

"You know her?"

"Naw," the man's southern accent exposed itself. "But Jackson spoke highly of her."

Richard focused on Dutch. She was staring down at the drink resting on her knee.

"So, yeah," Bulldog said. "I'm actually calling for a reason."

"What's up?"

"You asked me to look into Bart Barnes for you," the man said. "I found two in your area. One is ninety-three, living in a home for dementia patients. The other is six. I doubt he's hiring hitmen, even if he's mature for his age. That doesn't mean the guy isn't from somewhere else. And before you ask, yes, I checked and no one by that name flew in during the past two months."

"I figured whoever it was, didn't live around here," Richard said. "If that's even his name."

"Can't help you with that." Bulldog paused for a moment. "I checked into the finances of Halstead employees like you asked. They have seventy-two employees by the way."

"I owe you," Richard said.

"Big time," Bulldog agreed. "Anyway, I was looking for anything that might tell us who your embezzler is. I figured I would start at the top of the food-chain, so it took a minute."

"You found someone?"

"I did," Bulldog confirmed. "One employee making consistent deposits a little too high for his salary. So, I did a background check. This guy's credit history only started six years ago. And the kicker is, he's been dead for two decades."

89

Detective Morris sipped from his lukewarm coffee. When he was younger, he would have thrown the dark liquid out and grumbled about needing another cup. As the years passed, he became less and less particular as long as he was getting caffeine.

He checked his watch and saw that midnight was fast approaching. Just the suggestion of the hour caused him to yawn. He regretted agreeing to take the first five-hour shift watching Richard Jensen's house while his partner was home getting much needed sleep.

Movement caught his eye and Theo leaned forward in time to see a red fox dart across the street before vanishing into a neighbor's bushes. The detective rolled his eyes and returned his attention to the house. Several windows were still aglow, but he had not seen signs of movement for some time, leaving him to wonder if the occupants had sneaked out the back.

Theo knew Richard as the grieving husband who couldn't walk without the help of his ever-present cane, not the man who appeared out of nowhere earlier in the evening. The new Richard had complete mobility, wore a Kevlar vest and packed a holstered pistol under his jacket. Theo considered the missing years in the man's background and wondered if the new Richard might actually an older version of the man. Even the man's demeanor changed. The detective found it difficult to ignore the feeling of being played.

It wouldn't be the first time someone played him. With the number of years he had been on the force, it was bound to happen. The worst case was a young woman who called 9-1-1 to report an intruder in her home. The man attacked her, and in the process of defending herself, had killed the man. Theo had been assigned the case with the second partner of his career. They took the woman's statement, and the details of her story matched with every bit of forensic evidence. Everything pointed to an obvious case of self-defense. Until someone came forward offering contradicting testimony. The man claimed the woman had invited him to her home with the lure of drinks and sex. She poured him a drink, which he realized too late included a tranquilizer. Instead of the promised sex, she tried to stab him with a kitchen knife. He managed to escape because the dose she gave him was not strong enough. He never reported the incident but warned everyone he knew to stay away from her.

Theo ordered a tox screen, and sure enough, the man was so loaded with drugs he couldn't have stood up, let alone attacked anyone. Turns out the innocent acting young woman just wanted to know what it felt like to kill someone and get away with it.

Theo's revelation that Richard may have been lying to him from the moment they first met in the hospital was why the detective was sitting in his car in the middle of the night rather than being bundled up in bed. Theo spent the time recounting the conversations between himself and the now suspect, trying to remember if he missed any obvious red flags. He needed to know if Richard, the man devastated by his wife's disappearance, could be responsible for her vanishing.

Theo lowered his window, removed the lid from his cup, and poured the cooled liquid onto the ground below. Even he had his limits. As the glass raised back into place, the sound of a car engine starting greeted his ears. He shoved the cup into the holder on the center console and searched the darkness, up and down the street. Theo saw no signs of movement, no glowing taillights. But he knew he had heard something.

He looked up at Richard Jensen's home. From his vantage point, Theo could see a large portion of the house, including windows on both levels. What he couldn't see through the foliage were the front door and the driveway. The only place he found where he could see them would have meant blocking the driveway to a neighboring house. He considered taking the risk of rolling forward to get a better look. Before he could decide, a car backed down the driveway, into the street, and drove toward Theo's parked car. As the vehicle sped past, the detective glimpsed three individuals inside, impossible to identify in the darkness, though he had an idea who they were.

The detective started his car and reached for his cellphone. Executing a U-turn with ease while scrolling through his contact list, Theo tapped on his partner's name, followed by the call button and the speaker. The ringing continued for longer than Theo expected. It stopped, but a few seconds passed before he heard a voice.

"Hello?" Patricia was groggy.

"Get dressed," Theo barked. "They're on the move. Call me when you're on the road."

"What time is it?" She muttered and yawned.

"Just after midnight," Theo answered. "Hurry."

"Are they running?"

"Don't know," Theo said. "I could use some help."

"Patty?" The man's voice was barely audible, but Theo did not miss it. "Who are you talking to?"

"It's work. Go back to sleep," Patricia said. "I'll call you in five, Theo."

The line went dead, and Theo increased his speed to get closer to his target, but not so close they would notice he was following. Adjusting his speed and changing lanes from time to time, he followed them through a series of turns until they were on a straight stretch out of town.

Patricia called him back, and he passed on their location and direction.

"I'll be there in ten," Patricia promised. "Don't do anything stupid."

"I'm just tracking them," Theo assured her. A moment of silence passed before he said, "Oh, crap."

"Theo?" Patricia called out. "Theo?"

He did not respond. Patricia stepped down hard on the accelerator.

90

W e're being followed." Carolyn watched in the rearview mirror. After joining Jackson's team over a decade ago, she always kept a lookout for tails. More than once, the habit saved her life. Her current profession was no different. Being followed could be dangerous, or informative. Even when not working, she kept her eyes on her surroundings. Which is why she easily spotted the car making a U-turn as they left Richard's home, and why she knew that it still followed them.

"Do you think it's him?" Dutch tried to get a look out the window.

"No idea," Carolyn answered. "But we need to assume it is. Make sure your weapons are ready."

Bulldog gave them the name and address of the man he believed was skimming profits from Halstead Enterprises. Knowing the who, made it easy to conclude that Sonia and Stan uncovered the truth, resulting in the events that followed to ensure their silence. Whether they were being held somewhere or died weeks ago was yet to be seen. What wasn't clear was how it all connected to Jackson, Carolyn and Richard.

The three passengers in the car made a unanimous decision not to wait. Richard wanted to find Sonia and put his family back together. Carolyn needed to save her reputation by bringing Stan home. And Dutch wanted to find the person responsible for Jackson's death. Different agendas with a singular goal.

"We're not going to open fire on a car that may just be an innocent that happens to be going the same direction we are," Richard insisted.

"You don't really believe that," Carolyn countered. "They were in front of your house."

"I understand chances are they are after us," Richard agreed. "But if there is even a one percent chance they aren't, we have to be cautious."

"You haven't changed," Carolyn sneered. "Didn't you learn anything when Lance died?"

Richard's mind flashed back to Operation Mexico City. The team gathered in the last room, completing the last task to finish the mission before moving out. Richard saw the muzzle of the machine gun first, raising his weapon to neutralize the threat. Then he saw the boy, his face still round with youth. Richard hesitated; years of training rendered useless by an image that did not compute in his mind. A fragment of his mind believed the kid wouldn't open fire, wanted to believe. Enough to make Richard freeze long enough to be proven wrong. All hell broke loose, and his friend lost his life.

"That was different and you know it," Richard argued. "We were in enemy territory. The boy was armed. I should have fired. But we don't know if the people in that car are the enemy. We don't know they're armed. You want to risk killing an innocent family?"

Carolyn stewed a moment before exhaling a loud burst of air. "Fine, but we need to find out and if they take a shot, or I even see the hint of a weapon, I will not hesitate."

"Agreed." Richard looked back at Dutch. "Are you ready?"

She gave him a thumbs-up.

They came to a curve in the road, and Carolyn accelerated into it. She hit the brakes hard, spun the wheel and killed the lights in a smooth, trained maneuver. They came to a stop, blocking both lanes of the road. Piling out of the car on the side away from the following car, they readied their weapons and waited.

Headlights illuminating the pavement showed the car still followed. Richard moved off the roadway and into the deep grass of the ditch. Carolyn, following his lead, took the opposite side.

Unlike Carolyn, the driver of their tail slowed for the corner. The front of the car appeared around the tree line, and the headlights swung from right to left. Carolyn was lit up for a moment as they passed over her, before landing on the car blocking the road. The driver braked hard and came to a skidding stop.

Richard and Carolyn rushed forward from both sides. The two of them had performed the maneuver dozens of times in the past. Though it had been years, they moved as a unit, their training still as fresh as it had been then. They shouted commands, as effort to intimidate and prevent the occupants from doing anything that would lead to gunfire. Richard reached the vehicle seconds before Carolyn and yanked the driver's door open, his gun raised. Seeing the man sitting behind the wheel, he lowered his weapon to his side.

"Stop!" He raised his empty hand toward Carolyn. "Weapon down!"

Carolyn slowed to a stop, looking over the car at Richard and then down to the passenger glass. The interior lights were not on, even with the door open. She could not see through the darkness, a situation she did not want to be in.

With deliberate hesitation, she lowered her gun as well. "What? A family?"

"No," Richard slid his pistol into its holster. "Detective Morris."

91

Theo kept his eyes locked on Carolyn. She had not put her weapon away since the four of them had gathered in the street, preventing Theo from doing the same. Richard stepped between them, preventing them from shooting one another without shooting him first.

"Why don't we move the cars off the road before someone hits us?" Richard suggested.

Theo gave a cautious nod to acknowledge his agreement. Slipping behind the wheel of his car, he steered it off the road and turned the motor off before exiting again. Carolyn finally put her weapon away and did the same, parking her car across from the detective's. The four of them gathered in the headlights of Theo's car.

"Can I assume you all have licenses to carry those weapons?" Theo started.

"We do," Carolyn answered.

Richard didn't contradict her, although his concealed carry permit expired years earlier.

"Your leg seems better." Theo pointed at the limb.

"It is." Richard patted his thigh. "Gets a little better every day."

Headlights alerted them to another car coming. They all turned to watch the vehicle pass by. Instead, it pulled off the road and came to a stop behind Theo's sedan. To no one's surprise, Detective Stevens joined them.

Richard's thoughts drifted to a gathering from years earlier. He, Jackson and Lance sat on one side of a table, across from three members of a Mexican cartel. The reason for the meeting was to negotiate the release of a man the cartel had kidnapped. Richard did not know the man, only that his family was paying them to bring him home. Like the detectives, the cartel was trying to determine who Jackson and his team were. They also decided their captive must be more important and more valuable than they originally thought and demanded more money. Negotiations broke down, tempers flared. Two of the cartel members died at the table. The third gave up the location of the kidnap victim after a bit of coercion. A few hours later, they were flying him home to his wife and kids.

"What's going on here, exactly?" Patricia asked.

Theo had been talking to his partner when the subjects of his surveillance had turned the tables, catching him off guard. His phone had flown out of his hand, and being worried about the immediate threat, he forgot to call her back.

For Patricia, she had worked herself into an adrenaline rush, preparing to come in hot and heavy to protect her partner. Finding them all standing on the side of the road, talking, was almost a letdown. She still took measured breaths, attempting to calm her nerves.

"It appears I am not as good at surveillance as I thought," Theo said.

"You know." Carolyn grumbled. "Our friend was just murdered, so maybe following us around in the dark wasn't your best idea."

"I can see where that might have made you nervous," Theo conceded. "Now you're saying the gardener was a friend?"

"Yes," Richard answered. "Not a gardener, but a friend."

"Why did you deny it earlier?" Patricia asked.

"Jackson likes to …," Richard caught himself, "… liked to keep private."

"You understand how it looks?" Theo asked.

Richard nodded. "Like we were hiding something."

"Right," Theo confirmed. "So, I have to ask. Were you hiding something? Something you were mixed up in that got your wife kidnapped? Or maybe something you've done to her and Stanley Webber?"

"No!" Carolyn's voice was a little too loud. "We," she waved her arm to include the others, "didn't do anything to anyone."

"But you know who did." Not a question. Theo was sure they knew more than they were saying. "Why else would you be armed to the teeth? Not a good idea, by the way."

"We don't know anything for sure." Richard crossed his arms. "But we have a theory. The problem is it doesn't explain certain details."

"Like what?" Theo's eyes moved from face to face.

"Like who killed Clay and Jackson." Dutch had remained silent up to that point.

"But you have a theory," Theo said. "Based on what?"

Richard glanced at Carolyn, who rolled her eyes before giving her approval.

"Based on," Richard said, "we think we know who was embezzling from Halstead Enterprises."

"Embezzling?" Patricia questioned.

"This is the first we're hearing of anyone embezzling," Theo frowned.

92

The five of them stood in a circle on the side of the road illuminated by Theo's headlights. Tensions rose between them as the detectives demanded the name of the man they suspected of embezzling from Halstead Enterprises. Theo argued an investigation needed to be conducted into what they had found, evidence gathered, allowing for a proper arrest.

Richard and Carolyn countered his argument with their own, insisting the man might be responsible for taking Stan and Sonia. They needed to act now to bring them home. Dutch remained stoic, not wanting to add fuel to the volatile situation.

They went back and forth, but the detectives realized they would not get a name. They got one piece of information when Richard let it slip they were on their way to confront the man. A fact that renewed the detectives' arguments and protests, it became the breaking point.

In a huff, Carolyn stormed across the street and climbed into her rental car. She started the car and demanded the others follow. Dutch hesitated only a moment before jogging over and getting into the back. Richard alone faced the detectives and their continued insistence to remain where they were. Hands moved to weapons, but Richard turned away and moved to the passenger side of the car.

"We have to do this," he called back to the detectives. He sat next to Carolyn, and she slammed her foot down on the accelerator, spinning the vehicle into a U-turn before speeding away.

The detectives were already on the move, racing to their individual cars and racing to pursue the trio. They stayed close, refusing to lose them and to remind them that they would not be allowed to go in guns blazing.

The small convoy traveled the outskirts of the city and into a middle-class residential area, where they slowed. The streets were all but abandoned because of the late hour, but they did not want to run down some random kid out past curfew. The decision gave the detectives an opportunity to catch up to them.

Reaching their destination, they parked in a line in front of an unassuming house in an average-looking neighborhood. Stepping out of the car, Richard was left wondering what the man had done with the money he had supposedly embezzled.

The five of them reached the front of the home together, no more than a cramped alcove. Jockeying for position found Theo shoulder to shoulder with Carolyn in the front. She pressed the doorbell, and they listened to the chime inside while waiting for someone to answer. The door opened and there was a collective inhale.

"Jeremy Griffin." Theo let his mind replay his interviews with the man.

"Detectives. Always a pleasure." Jeremy remained calm. He looked past the others to the man in the back. "Richard. What a surprise to see you here."

"Do I know you?" Richard's confusion was clear.

"We met at the Halstead party, albeit briefly" Jeremy said. "But in truth, I've known you for years."

"Lucas Brody." Dutch's voice was barely above a whisper.

"Richard, meet Lance's brother." Carolyn turned to Dutch. "You two know each other?"

"Jackson hired me a couple of months before firing him," Dutch confirmed.

"Oh, Trijntje." Jeremy used her proper name. "I'm flattered you remember me."

"It's hard to forget the man who used every mission as his personal shooting gallery," Dutch said.

Jeremy grinned but narrowed his eyes. "Please, everyone, come in. Let me get you some drinks."

Leaving the door open, Jeremy walked away. The others followed him, their hands resting on their weapons. He led them to the sparsely furnished living room, waving a hand to the three mismatched chairs as he continued to the kitchen.

"I hope beer is okay," he called to them. "It's all I have."

He reappeared with three bottles of beer in each hand setting them down on a card table that served as his dining room. Keeping one for himself, he twisted the cap off and took a drink. None of the others made a move to take one.

"No? Well, suit yourself." Jeremy took another drink.

The others stood about the room watching their host and counting doors.

"Detective Morris, I assume you are here because you have more questions about Sonia." Jeremy pointed the beer bottle at him. He stared at Richard with disdain and said, "I'm not sure why the rest of you might be here."

It was Carolyn who spoke first. "What are you doing here, Lucas? And who is Jeremy Griffin?"

Theo and Patricia slipped their weapons out of their holsters and held them down at their sides. Richard was less stealthy as he raised his pistol and trained it on Jeremy's chest. Dutch took a step back and toward a hallway behind her. Jeremy noted each move, with a smile.

"Jeremy Griffin," he said. "Who is Jeremy? Now, that is a good question. You see, Jeremy is a friend of mine. Or he was when we were ten years old. We were good friends, he and I. Used to meet up at this wooded area and play for hours. Cops and Robbers, Cowboys and Indians, you get the idea."

"We don't need to hear this," Carolyn interrupted.

"You!" Lucas yelled, an extreme break from his calm demeanor. He took a second to compose himself. "You asked who Jeremy Griffin was and I am telling you."

"Where is Sonia?" Richard asked.

Lucas looked Richard in the eyes. "We took turns. I'd be the cop, him the robber. He'd be the cop, me the robber. Me cowboy, him Indian. Me Indian, him cowboy. You get it. Fun was had by all."

"We get it," Carolyn said. "Where is this going?"

"Patience, Carolyn. Patience." Lucas took a deep breath. "One day, we had been playing for a couple of hours, and I was having a bad day. He kept winning. Over and over again, he won. No big deal. We were having fun. But Jeremy decided to have even more fun. He started mocking me. Calling me a loser. Bragging about how much better he was. So, I suggested a new game."

Lucas fell silent with a slight grin on his face.

"What new game?" Carolyn felt a sinister turn in the story coming.

"So glad you asked, Carolyn," he smiled. "I suggested we play Assassin. And I would go first. All he had to do was go into the woods and hide. I, being the assassin, would find him. Game over."

"Sounds like fun," Richard scoffed. "Where is my wife?"

"Jeremy ran into the woods to hide." He did not take his eyes off Richard. "But let's face it. He was bad at hide-and-seek. I tracked him down in a matter of minutes. It was too easy. Don't you think? I thought so. So, I changed the rules. I walked up behind him, pulled out my pocketknife, and stabbed him in the neck."

"Oh, my god," Carolyn said.

Behind her, Dutch gasped. The detectives raised their weapons.

"Yes," Lucas smiled. "You asked me who Jeremy was. He was my first. And years later, after Jackson fired me, I tracked down his birth certificate and became him. Fresh start with a new identity."

"Why are you telling us this?" Carolyn asked. "You just admitted to murder in front of two cops. Are you ready to tell us everything?"

"Carolyn, you silly girl," Jeremy shook his head. "I was ten years old. I spent two years in juvie for manslaughter. My records were sealed. I've already paid for the crime."

"Lance never told me ..."

"What?" Lucas laughed. "Lance never said, 'oh, by the way, my kid brother killed another kid'? When does that come up in conversation?"

"Enough!" Richard took three quick steps forward, shoving his pistol into the man's face. "Where is she?"

Lucas stopped smiling and dropped his beer. The bottle shattered on the floor.

"Richard!" Theo yelled. "Stand down."

"Not until he tells me where Sonia is." Richard raised his gun higher and pressed the barrel to Lucas's forehead. "Where is she?"

"What makes you think I know?" Lucas remained calm.

93

"Tell me where she is!" Richard pushed the gun hard against Lucas's head.

"I don't know what you're talking about." He was almost convincing but ended with a slight curl of his lip.

"I suppose you don't know about the money you embezzled from Halstead Enterprises either?" Carolyn took a step forward.

"Oh, that," Lucas smiled again. "Do you have actual proof? Or just a theory?"

"Actual proof," Richard said.

"What proof?" Theo asked.

"We have a guy who traced the money from Halstead Enterprises through a number of transfers until they landed in an offshore account in his name," Richard said.

"Bulldog is the best," Lucas said. "Had it not been for your wife sticking her nose into my business, no one would have been the wiser. It was the perfect plan really."

"What plan, Lucas?" Dutch asked. "What was the goal here? Money?"

Lucas shifted his eyes to her. "You always were a pain, you know. Sorry I missed you."

"Missed me?"

"How was Jackson in the end?" Lucas asked. "Was he whimpering like a scared kid?"

"Are you admitting to killing Colonel Jackson Porter?" Patricia asked.

"Why would I admit to something like that?" Lucas feigned surprise. "That would be crazy."

"If the shoe fits."

Lucas bore his eyes into Dutch. She held his gaze briefly before looking away.

"You know," Lucas turned back to Richard. "Jackson firing me wasn't a bad thing. I became Jeremy Griffon. Got a degree in finance, then a job. Started doing well for myself. Then I ran into Emily Halstead in a chance meeting. I was smitten. She was the one. After she convinced Charles to give me a job I was happy."

"Until you cheated on her," Richard added.

"I screwed that one," Lucas nodded. He chuckled. "Or rather I screwed

Trisha."

No one else saw the humor.

"Even then," Lucas said, "after destroying my future at Halstead, I was fine. I was making good money. I didn't need anything more. Things were good. Until, one day, I was talking to Sonia, and she mentions her husband. You. Of all the companies I could have ended up at, I wound up working with the wife of Richard Jensen."

"Where is she?" Richard demanded.

Lucas shifted his eyes toward Dutch who stood at the opening to the hallway. Richard turned slightly to see what he was looking at, an amateur mistake.

Lucas swung his arm up and batted Richard's weapon away, pulling his own pistol from his waistband at his back. As he dove for the cover of the closest doorway, he fired a shot, striking Theo in the chest. The detective fell back as Richard, Carolyn and Patricia fired a succession of shots into the cabinets and walls of the kitchen.

Patricia knelt to check on her partner. Theo gasped for air, ripping his shirt open, revealing the bulletproof vest he wore beneath. He lay on the floor breathing heavy, labored breaths.

"I'm fine," he insisted.

Dutch raced down the hall while the others jockeyed for position, dragging the few pieces of furniture in the room to provide minimal cover. Lucas's arm appeared long enough to fire a random shot that struck the wall well above their heads. Richard and Carolyn returned fire in concentrated bursts.

The sounds of doors opening and closing reverberated from the hallway. A moment later Dutch reappeared. "She's not in the bedrooms."

Richard grimaced.

"Jeremy? Or Lucas?" Patricia called out. "What was the significance of knowing Sonia's husband was Richard Jensen?"

"You don't know?" Lucas' disembodied voice replied.

"No," Patricia responded. "Why don't you enlighten me?"

"Richard Jensen killed my brother, detective," Lucas answered.

"He didn't kill Lance," Carolyn defended.

"He may as well have," Lucas sneered. "He didn't kill the kid with the gun. He didn't protect his team. And my brother died because of it."

"And I live with that every day." Richard called out. "And I'm sorry."

"You're sorry," Lucas laughed. "You didn't know sorrow. You went on to live a happy productive life. What sorrow?"

"This was revenge?" Carolyn asked.

"Why didn't you just kill me?" Richard demanded.

"Kill you?" Lucas said. "How would killing you make you suffer? No, I didn't want you dead. I wanted you destroyed. I wanted you to feel what it is to lose."

"How?" Theo asked. "By stealing from Halstead Enterprises? How did that hurt Richard?"

"Oh, detective," Lucas acted concerned. "I thought I put you down. I do hope you're okay."

"I'm fine," Theo responded. "Now, how was stealing from Charles Halstead going to hurt Richard?"

"You lack imagination, detective," Lucas said. "I was embezzling. But the evidence all pointed to Sonia. When I got what I wanted, I was going to blow the whistle on her. She'd go to prison. Richard would be devastated. I would have the money. Win. Win."

"But she noticed what you were up to," Richard concluded.

"Cleaver girl, our Sonia," Lucas confirmed. "She didn't know it was me, but she knew what was going on. I overheard her talking to Stan about it. They wanted to do some deeper research and then go to Charles. At that point, I knew my days were numbered. So, I switched to plan 'B'."

"And what was plan 'B'?" Carolyn asked.

"You were plan 'B', Carolyn," Lucas chuckled. "You and Jackson. I started a threat campaign against Stan. Then, the week of the Halstead party, I hired you to come protect him. And I hired Jackson's company to follow Sonia."

"But why?" Dutch asked. "Wouldn't that make things harder for you?"

"It got everyone responsible for my brother's death in one place," Lucas explained. "I figured you would all collaborate at some point, and I could take you all out together. But Jackson didn't even come. And it was like Richard and Carolyn didn't even know each other."

"I hadn't seen her in over a decade," Richard said.

"And I hadn't seen Jackson in six years," Carolyn added. "We didn't keep in touch."

"Which meant I needed to give you a nudge," Lucas rolled his eyes. "Honestly, I was just getting bored. So, I decided to go ahead and kill Sonia, bankrupt Richard's company, and make him suffer."

"You're the one who drained our bank accounts," Richard said. "And my accident."

"But you managed to screw that up for me, too."

"How did I ...?"

"I don't know." Lucas whined. "Because you're you. I had calculated just when and how hard to hit you to put the passenger seat directly into that tree with enough force to kill her. Yet, you were able to do just enough to keep that from happening."

"What can I say?" Richard said. "Some of us are good."

"When I went down to make sure she was dead, she was already crawling out of the wreckage," Lucas recounted. "I should have finished her there, but there was a car coming. So, I put her into my car and took off."

"That was us," Dutch said. "We were following her."

"Where is Sonia, Lucas?" Richard shouted. "What did you do with her?"

"Richard. Richard. Richard," Lucas said. "If I told you that, how would you suffer?"

"So, she's alive?"

"Maybe." Lucas suddenly appeared in the doorway, firing a shot that hit Richard in the shoulder. The man spun and fell. Lucas adjusted his aim at Carolyn, but before he could pull the trigger, a volley of rounds from Carolyn and the detectives struck him. Thrown back through the doorway and into the kitchen, he fell to the floor and did not move.

"No!" Richard shouted. He rose to his feet, clutching his shoulder.

Carolyn was at his side in seconds, tearing at the sleeve of Richard's shirt to expose the wound. She gave it a quick look. "It's a through and through." She made eye contact with Dutch. "Bring me a sheet."

Dutch turned back down the hall, and they could hear a door open and close again. She returned with a folded white sheet.

"This can wait," Richard insisted.

The detectives had moved to the kitchen to check on Lucas.

"He's alive," Patricia called out. "Barely. Call an ambulance."

Theo pulled out his phone and dialed as his partner did what she could to stop the bleeding.

"You're no good to anyone if you lose much more blood." Carolyn pushed Richard down into a chair and took the sheet from Dutch. Pulling out a knife and cutting a strip from it, she wrapped it around Richard's shoulder and pulled it tight, causing him to wince from pain. She cinched it down tighter and tied it in a knot. "That should hold until we get you to a hospital."

"I'm not going to the hospital until I know where Sonia is." Richard stood, wobbled and then headed for the kitchen. He pushed his way past Theo who gave details to the 9-1-1 operator.

Lucas lay on the floor in front of the stove. Patricia leaned over him applying pressure to the worst of his wounds. She glanced up with concern. Richard ignored her and stooped to slap at Lucas's face. He did not stir. A heavy sigh escaped Richard's lips. He stood straight, noticing three doors in the room. He yanked open the closest door and saw that it led to the garage. Parked inside was an SUV with an impact bar like the one that hit Richard's car the morning of the accident. He wondered why Lucas hadn't tried to escape.

The second door he opened exposed an empty pantry. Richard moved to the last door, swinging it open, revealing a staircase leading down.

"Basement!" he called out.

"Jensen!" Theo yelled. "Wait!"

94

Richard stood at the top of the dark stairway, looking down into an even deeper darkness. Ignoring Theo's protests, he slapped at the light switch, but nothing happened. He retreated to the main room and looked at his companions.

"Flashlight," he said.

Dutch moved her hand to her belt and in one smooth motion tossed the requested item to him. He nodded to her and turned it on.

"Richard." Theo stepped up to the man. "You don't want to go down there. You don't know what you'll find."

Richard was already moving away before Theo's words faded. The detective looked at his partner before following him. Richard was halfway to the floor when Theo started down, his own flashlight lighting his way.

Richard slowed as he neared the basement floor, pulling his weapon free even though he didn't expect a threat to be waiting in the dark. Multiple cracks covered the bare concrete surface, suggesting a bad foundation. The walls were bare sheets of plywood all the way around.

Theo came up on Richard's shoulder and swept his light across the space, chasing away the darkness for a short time before it reclaimed the room. He swung the light back to where the beam joined Richard's, focused on a chest freezer in the otherwise vacant room.

Carolyn reached the bottom of the stairs as Richard stepped up to the freezer. "Money. You don't want to do that."

"I need a crowbar." He studied the padlock that kept the lid fastened down. "Or the key."

"Richard," Theo came up beside him. "Let one of us do this. You don't have to."

"He's right," Carolyn stepped to his other side and placed a firm hand on his shoulder.

Richard turned and Carolyn saw a fear in his eyes she had never seen in all the years they worked together. She put an arm around his shoulder and led him away.

"We need a crowbar!" Carolyn shouted up to the open door at the top of the stairs.

Moments later, Dutch appeared with the requested tool in hand. She climbed down the stairs with cautious steps. "Found this in the garage."

She handed it to Carolyn who passed it on to Theo. The detective positioned the flat edge of the crowbar against the latch, shoved it underneath as far as he could, then pressed down on the opposite end. He strained until the latch gave. Theo flipped it out of the way and pulled up on the lid. He dropped the crowbar, picked up his flashlight and shone it inside.

Carolyn left Richard where he stood and moved to Theo's side, gazing into the fog of the freezer. "Oh, Stan."

"Stanley Webber?" Theo asked.

"That's him." Carolyn turned to Richard. "It's only him."

A wave of relief overcame Richard, followed by the agonizing realization that he still didn't know Sonia's whereabouts, and that the only person who knew lay on the floor upstairs, barely clinging to life.

"What was that?" Carolyn jerked her arm to shine her flashlight on the wall to their left.

"What?" Richard asked. "The wall?"

"I saw the glint of something like metal." Carolyn walked toward the wall.

"Where?" Richard followed. "I don't see anything."

"It was a thin line," she said, moving her light back and forth.

Theo was on his phone calling for a forensic team, watching the ray of light move like a pendulum. "There."

They followed his finger to the seam between two sheets of plywood.

Carolyn ran her hand along the wood and directed her light between the boards. Closing one eye, she focused on what she was seeing. "There's a hinge."

95

Theo reached the top of the stairs just as paramedics were arriving. The team moved Patricia out of their way and assessed their patient's injuries. The detective stood holding her blood-covered hands out to her sides. She watched on as the pair worked to save the wounded man's life.

"Use the sink to wash up," Theo pointed. "We'll notify forensics when they arrive."

She hesitated before moving to the double well sink and turned on the water with two fingers. Once the water was warm, she began rubbing her hands together under the stream to clean the blood off.

"Stanley Webber is in a freezer downstairs," Theo announced.

Patricia added soap to her routine and repeated the rubbing motion. "That's too bad. Any sign of Sonia Jensen?"

A loud thud came from the basement.

"What was that?" Patricia's head snapped to the stairway.

"We found hinges hidden in the wall," Theo said. "I came up to find a power saw. It sounds like Richard isn't waiting."

"Shouldn't one of us be down there?" Patricia asked. Theo smiled. She sighed. "I'll search the garage for a saw."

Patricia retreated to the garage while Theo descended the steps two at a time, surprising himself that he had it in him. Reaching the bottom, he found Richard swinging the crowbar at the plywood. Unable to locate a handle or a release mechanism, he didn't know what else to do. Blood ran down his arm while Carolyn stood nearby, pleading for him to stop.

"We don't even know which side is the door," she reasoned with him.

A valid argument, Richard let his arm drop to his side, still clutching the crowbar. He stared at the wall, his anger boiling just below the surface. With a rush of energy he didn't think he had; the crowbar swung in a large arc until it struck the wood about head high. The tip of the tool splintered the plywood and wedged into the hole it created. Richard yanked and yanked to free it, to no avail.

Two firefighters appeared, their boots sounding like thunder on the wooden steps. Lamps on their helmets lit the basement like daylight. One carried an axe, the other a power saw. Carolyn slapped the wall.

"Three hinges," she relayed. "Here. Here. And here."

The power tool came to life, and sawdust flew as the firefighter started at the bottom and worked his way up. At each hinge, sparks sprayed the room. When he finished, the firefighter lifted his visor and surveyed his handiwork. Aside from the gap between the board being wider and the black marks where the sparks from the hinges had scorched the wood, nothing had changed.

"Was something supposed to happen?" he asked.

"There should be an opening on one side or the other," Richard said.

The second firefighter stepped forward. "Stand clear."

He gripped his axe and swung it at the wall. Wood splintered as the blade penetrated the board. He swung a second time, and a section of the plywood fell away, revealing cinderblock behind it. The firefighter shifted to the other side of the hinges and repeated the process. Through the second hole, they saw a dark substance.

"What is that?" Theo asked, stepping up and reaching through. His hand came away with a dense foam material. "Sound proofing."

"Step back, sir." The firefighter with the axe positioned himself, waited for the detective to follow his request, then took a powerful swing. The axe penetrated the wood and the soundproofing material beyond, embedding itself deep inside. When he pulled to free the blade, it didn't budge. The firefighter took a firm grip on the handle and yanked. The axe did not give, but the plywood separated from the sheet next to it before snapping back into position.

"Again." Theo joined the firefighter on the opposite side of the axe. Each taking hold of the handle. "One. Two. Three."

Giving it all they had, they pulled. The plywood bent with their effort, creating a gap between the two pieces of wood. As they heaved, the second firefighter stepped up and grabbed the edge of the board to assist them. Richard pushed past Carolyn, sliding the crowbar into the opening just below the firefighter's hands. Using it for leverage, he put his weight into the effort, and the entire wall scraped in protest as it dragged along the floor.

Everyone in the room repositioned so that everyone was pulling or pushing to make the opening wider. They strained from the effort, and the wall slid two or three feet in a surge. Everyone stopped and redirected lights into the space beyond.

Cowering in the corner of the closet-sized room was a woman, shielding her eyes from the light.

"Sonia!" Richard rushed forward and threw his arms around his crying wife.

96

Richard cradled Sonia in his arms as he climbed the stairs, carrying her from her makeshift cell to a waiting ambulance. The paramedics helped secure her on a gurney, loading it into the back for transport. Richard climbed in next to her, clutching her hand and not letting go. Her frail appearance made his eyes well with tears, which he fought, not wanting Sonia to know how concerned he was. He forced a smile, which she tried to reciprocate, but lacked the strength.

At the hospital, Richard followed as the staff ushered Sonia into a room. The paramedics relayed her vital statistics before transferring her to the bed and returning to the ambulance. Richard leaned against the wall while a doctor did a quick examination, ordering fluids, which the nurse set up. While the medical professionals continued to discuss Sonia's condition, she lay back with her head tilted in her husband's direction, her eyes locked on his. Richard zoned out and focused his full attention on her.

Promising to return, the doctor and then the nurse left them alone. Richard dragged a chair to the bedside where he could sit and hold her hand. When a tear ran down her cheek, he lost all control and began sobbing, laying his head on the bed next to her. She reached across with her free hand and stroked his hair until exhaustion took over and he drifted to sleep.

Déjà vu struck Richard as he woke. The hospital room sent him back to where it all began. He bolted upright when he realized he was alone in the bed. He searched the room until he saw Carolyn leaning against the wall next to the doorway.

"Don't look so disappointed," she grinned.

"What happened?" he asked.

"You passed out from blood loss," Carolyn informed him. "They had to stitch you up. They moved you into here so you wouldn't disturb Sonia."

"How is she doing?"

"She hasn't said anything," Carolyn answered. "The doctor's running tests. But I'm sure she'll be fine. She strikes me as a fighter."

"She is," Richard agreed. "Can you take me to see her?"

"Sure."

Carolyn moved to his side as he swung his legs off the bed. He slid to the floor and draped his good arm over her shoulders. She guided him out of the room and across the hall to where Sonia slept. Carlyn walked him to his wife's bed and helped him sit next to her.

"Well, I only have a few minutes to say good-bye." Carolyn pushed off the wall.

"You're leaving?" Richard frowned.

"I was being paid to protect Stanley Webber," Carolyn said. "Which I obviously failed to do. Without him, I don't really have a reason to stick around."

"Aren't you a witness or something?"

"Lucas confessed if you recall," she said. "I gave a statement. If he pulls through and they need me to testify, I'll be glad to come back. Meanwhile, I need to get back to work. Dutch and I have a plane to catch."

"Dutch?"

"I'm taking her with me," she said. "Figure I can train her. Be her mentor."

"She can learn a lot from you." Richard said. He stared at his old friend for a long moment. "Thank you."

"For what?"

"Helping me find her." He gestured toward Sonia.

"That was mostly you," Carolyn deflected.

"Accept my gratitude," Richard chided. "If for no other reason, for not letting me open the freezer."

"For that," Carolyn smiled. "You're welcome."

She moved forward, hugged him, and turned away. Richard watched her leave the room only to be replaced by Detective Morris, who stepped in. Over his shoulder, Richard could see Detective Stevens following.

"Detectives."

"Mr. Jensen." Theo nodded.

"How is she?" Patricia looked to the sleeping woman.

Richard shifted his gaze to his wife. "She was locked in a dark room for a month. So, not good."

"Actually," Patricia said. "Evidence suggests the room was assembled more recently than that."

Richard gave her a look that caused the detective to divert her eyes to the floor. "Why are you here?"

"We were hoping to ask your wife some questions." The tone of Theo's voice suggested regret.

"Hasn't she been through enough?" Richard demanded. "Lucas confessed."

"It's alright, Richard." Sonia's voice was just a whisper as she squeezed his hand. Her eyes opened and focused on her husband before moving to Theo, a motion that took some effort on her part. "Ask your questions, Detective."

"Detective Theo Morris, ma'am," he introduced. "This is my partner, Detective Patricia Stevens. First, we want to offer our sincere regrets for everything you've been through."

Theo stepped closer, pulled out a small tape recorder, turned it on, and set it on the food tray table next to the bed. "Mrs. Jensen, can you describe for me, the events that led up to and following your abduction?"

Sonia laid her head back, closed her eyes and took deliberate breaths, releasing the last one slowly. Her eyelids fluttered, and she refocused on the detective.

"We were on our way to the lake house," Sonia recounted, squeezing Richard's hand in a firm grip. "It was raining, really hard. And something hit us, causing us to crash. Richard was unconscious, and I, I knew I had to get out of the car to look for help. I guess the window shattered when we crashed, because I was getting drenched. So, I tried to climb out through the opening. That's when he showed up."

"Who showed up?" Theo asked.

"Jeremy," Sonia said. "I remember I was surprised to see him, standing there in the rain. He seemed surprised to see me too. But I was glad because he helped get me out. Then he walked me up the hill to his truck, saying he would go back for Richard. Only he didn't."

Her eyes became glassy, then tears streamed down her face. She pulled her knees to her chest and hugged them.

"That's enough." Richard rose to his feet and sat on the bed next to her, placing himself between them.

"One more question," Theo promised. "Then we'll leave her alone."

"What is it?"

"What happened to Stanley Webber, Mrs. Jensen?" Theo asked. "What happened to Stan?"

"Stan?" She looked up at the detective, confused. "What about Stan?"

"We found him in the freezer in the basement with you," Theo informed her.

"Oh, my God," her face scrunched up in despair. "Stan."

"Sorry for your loss," Patricia said. "I understand the two of you were close."

"He was a good boss," she said. "And friend. Did you catch him? Jeremy? Do you know why he did this?"

"Apparently you caught on to him embezzling from the company," Theo informed her. "He wanted to keep you quiet. And yes, we caught him, with the help of your husband."

"He didn't make it," Patricia added. "He succumbed to his wounds in the operating room."

Richard nodded his acknowledgment. The detectives turned to leave, and Richard watched them go.

He leaned over and kissed Sonia on the forehead before sliding off the bed. He dragged a chair as close to her as he could, then settled in next to his wife, where he remained until the doctor discharged her.

97

Richard!" Sonia called out. "We're going to be late."

Her husband appeared in the doorway, fully dressed. "Are you sure you want to do this?"

She crossed the room, wearing an off-the-shoulder floral dress that flowed as she moved. Richard couldn't help but smile. When she reached him, Sonia wrapped her arms around his chest and pulled him close. He did the same.

"It's been six months," she informed him. "I need to get out of this house. Besides, it's not like it's a dangerous mission we're going on."

"I don't know." Richard kissed the top of her head. "Dinner with Nancy and my parents sounds pretty dangerous to me."

"We have to tell them sometime." She looked up at him with a grin.

They kissed and held their lips together for a long time before separating.

"Would you get my coat?" She asked. "The red one."

"Of course." Richard went into the closet to retrieve the garment.

"Do you tell them?" Sonia asked. "Or do I?"

"Why don't we just throw the picture of the sonogram on the table and see what happens?" Richard laughed, holding the coat out for her.

"You are incorrigible, Mr. Jensen." Sonia slipped her arms into the sleeves and pulled it on.

"And you are wonderful, Mrs. Jensen." He wrapped his arms around her again.

"We really are going to be late," she whispered.

"They'll wait," he assured her. Then he pulled her closer for a long kiss.

THE END

Thank you for reading!

Dear Reader,

I hope you enjoyed reading *A Collision of Secrets* as much as I enjoyed writing it. At this time, I would like to request, if you're so inclined, please consider leaving a review of *A Collision of Secrets*. I would love to hear your feedback.

Website: **https://www.williamcoleman.net**

Facebook: **https://www.facebook.com/williamcolemanauthor/**

Many Thanks,

William Coleman

More by William Coleman

Jack Mallory Mysteries series:

MURDER REVISITED
DOG WALKERS
FATAL ACCOUNTING
DEATH BEFORE DAWN

S. Hawke Investigations series:

THE CONTRACT
THREE DAYS GONE

Stand Alone Novels:

THE WIDOW'S HUSBAND
PAYBACK
NICK OF TIME
FIRST FRIDAYS

www.ingramcontent.com/pod-product-compliance
Lightning Source LLC
Chambersburg PA
CBHW031335020726
47499CB00005B/1281